Serendipity

CATHARINA MAURA

This is for all my readers that took the time to contact me to let me know how much they loved The Tie That Binds. Many of you told me that you would love to hear Daniel's side of the story, so this one is for you.

PS. There's an exclusive extra scene linked after the last chapter that I think you'll really love

Author's Note

Serendipity largely follows the same storyline as The Tie That Binds.

It starts years before The Tie That Binds does, so the first part of Serendipity is all new content, but this book was mostly written to give you insight into Daniel's point of view throughout The Tie That Binds.

I do not recommend reading this without reading The Tie That Binds first.

Alyssa & Daniel's Songs

You can find Daniel & Alyssa Playlist on my Spotify account

Daniel's song for Alyssa, in particular, is *Speechless* by *Dan + Shay*

Contents

One

I smile as I walk into DM Consultancy, the company my father and Charles Moriani built together. It's their legacy, and one day it'll be mine. Mine and Alyssa's. I rejected half a dozen offers from other consultancy firms to return to London, and I don't regret it for a second. I doubt I ever will. I'm excited as I walk into Charles's office. Too excited, clearly, because I walk right into someone.

"Ouch," she says, rubbing her nose.

I laugh and place my hands on her shoulders to keep her steady. "Still so clumsy, Alyssa," I say. She looks up at me in surprise and smiles from ear to ear before throwing herself in my arms for a quick hug. She's grown up a lot in the time I was gone. She was sixteen when I left for my MBA, so she must be eighteen now.

"You're back," she replies. I hug her back tightly and grin. Being back here feels like coming home.

Charles walks up to us and claps me on the shoulder. "You're back, son," he says. I nod and Alyssa takes a step back to stand next to her father. The two couldn't look more different. Charles looks perpetually grumpy, while Alyssa looks perpetually cheerful.

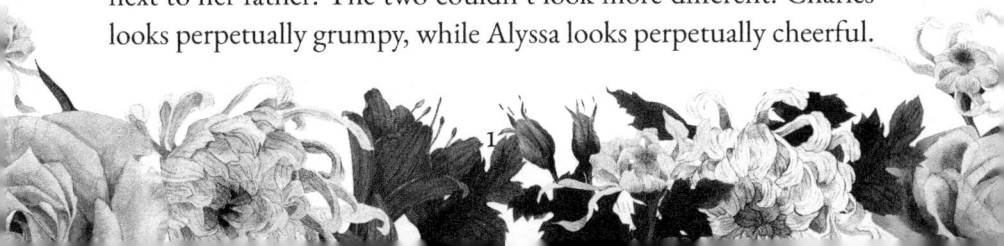

She has her mother's looks and her father's eyes. It's the eyes that give away the relation.

"What are you doing here?" I ask Alyssa. I expected to see her around the house now that I'm back, but I didn't expect to see her at the office.

Charles smiles proudly and throws his arm around her. "My baby is all grown up now, Dan. She's going to intern while studying at Imperial. Before I know it, she'll be taking my job."

Alyssa blushes and my heart oddly enough skips a beat. Alyssa has always been beautiful, but I've never seen her as more than a kid — as my younger brother's best friend. She's ten years younger than me, so why do I suddenly find her so stunning?

"Interning, huh? I definitely wasn't doing that at eighteen," I murmur. I can barely even remember my first year at uni. I definitely can't remember Fresher's week. Alyssa has always been very responsible, but interning so young? I wonder if Charles might be pushing her a bit too hard. He's been pushing her to become CEO of DM consultancy since she was five. She should be having fun instead of interning here. Alyssa smiles back at her dad and my heart does it again. It skips a beat. I look away and stare down at my shoes, suddenly feeling awkward.

"That reminds me," Charles says, his face lighting up. He walks back to his desk and retrieves a rectangular gift-wrapped package. Alyssa's eyes light up and I look at it suspiciously. Charles hands it to me and I shake it to assess what might be in it. "Go on, open it," he urges. I frown and carefully unwrap the clumsily packaged gift. My heart races as I take out the new name plaque. It says Daniel Devereaux, CEO.

"I'm thinking that we can probably share this office, the way your dad and I did in the early days."

I look up at Charles in disbelief, and he smiles at me proudly. "You didn't need the MBA, son. You were ready to become my co-CEO long before you decided you had to have one. Now that you're back, you can finally start easing my workload. I'm old, son. I want to go to fewer meetings and play more golf."

I laugh and shake my head. Charles Moriani is a devout workaholic. He enjoys what he does far more than he'd ever enjoy a round of golf. He's taught me everything I know. When my father died three years ago, Charles took me under his wing. He continued training me like my father used to and groomed me to take over my father's vacant seat as his co-CEO. He pushed me as hard as I'm sure he's going to push Alyssa. It's thanks to him I can assume my new role with confidence.

"I think it might be good if you train Alyssa the way I trained you. I'll still supervise, but she's been complaining that I'm too harsh on her. I think it might benefit you both if you're the one to train her. After all, you'll be working together in the future, anyway."

I nod and look at Alyssa. She's looking at me with such hope and excitement that I can't help but smile. It probably is better if I'm the one that trains her. If she's only just started, she hasn't experienced the true horror that is her father's training regime. To say that he's a tough love kinda guy is an understatement. If I can keep Alyssa from going through that, I'll gladly do it.

"You'll need to hire an assistant," Charles says. I nod and stare at my new name plaque. I knew it was coming. I just didn't expect to be appointed on my very first day back.

"I've got someone in mind for that," I reply. I immediately think of Kate, my friend Carter's sister. She's talented, but she's had a rough couple of years. She did her MBA with me to make up for lost time, and a position as executive secretary might just give her the break she needs.

Charles frowns and looks worried for a second before nodding. "Good. You sort that out then, lad."

I nod and tip my head towards Alyssa. "Wanna come with me to a department meeting?" I ask, checking my watch. Alyssa nods, her eyes brimming with excitement, and I can't help but chuckle. To be this excited for a department meeting... Oh, the good old days.

I walk out of Charles's office and Alyssa follows me, her heels clicking against the stone floor. I glance down and frown.

"Since when did you start wearing those?" I ask.

Alyssa was a tomboy growing up, but it looks like she's outgrown that phase. She merely shrugs. "They're pretty," she tells me. I can't help but silently agree. She's wearing red bottomed heels that look surprisingly hot. I don't have a thing for shoes in the slightest, but these are different somehow.

"All you need to do for the next couple of days is shadow me and takes notes of absolutely everything, okay? I'll grill you on details every once in a while. I need you to understand everything that's going on to the best of your ability. Don't just repeat things verbatim, okay?"

Alyssa nods seriously, as though she already knows the drill. She probably does. I wouldn't put it past her to have interned here her entire summer. And I definitely wouldn't put it past Charles to let her.

Two

I walk into the office to find Charles shouting at someone. I sigh inwardly and shake my head. I pity the fool that managed to get in his way. Charles has endless patience when it comes to explaining concepts, but he has a zero-tolerance policy for mistakes. Errors have gotten more than one person fired and I'm pretty sure I'll be signing a severance cheque later.

"How the hell could you miss such a monumental mistake? You put an extra fucking zero on that slide. At a *client meeting*. What kind of rookie error is that? Who the hell allowed you to work on client deliverables, anyway?"

I sigh and check my meeting schedule for the day. It's only ten and I'm already tired. I'm pretty sure I'm going to have to do some damage control with the client now, and I really can't be bothered with that.

"I'm sorry. I'm so sorry."

I freeze. I know that voice. I look up to find Alyssa standing in front of her father. She's trembling as he chews her out and my heart fucking drops. She looks devastated. What the hell even happened? I didn't ask her to work on a client presentation, so why the fuck is she being blamed for this? She hasn't made a single mistake in the three months she's been working with me. How could this have happened?

I glance around the room to find Christian hiding behind his screen. He's the one that was meant to make the presentation, and it's obvious he pawned off his work on Alyssa. I walk up to her and put my hand on her shoulder in a show of support.

"What exactly is going on?"

Charles looks at me and grits his teeth. "Is this how you train her?" he shouts. His face is red and he glares at me. Just a couple of years ago I'd have been shaking in my boots, much like Alyssa is now. I tighten my grip on her shoulder and she leans into me subconsciously.

"I didn't ask Alyssa to work on the client proposal. Either way, as an intern, she cannot be held accountable for this. If you want to blame anyone, blame me. You do not, however, get to speak to my trainee this way. Going forward, I expect you to take it up with me directly if she makes a mistake. I am, after all, the person training her. Am I not?"

Charles looks at me through narrowed eyes and then looks at Alyssa. She takes another step closer to me and I wrap my arm around her shoulder fully.

"You're lucky Daniel is standing up for you, Alyssa. If it were up to me, you'd be out the door by now."

I know he doesn't mean that. He's said similar words to me a thousand times, so I know he doesn't mean a word. Alyssa doesn't know that though. The way her body trembles makes my heart ache. Charles walks away and Alyssa stares at his closed office door, frozen. Eventually she snaps out of it and steps away from me. She rushes towards the bathroom and I inhale deeply.

I follow her and lean against the wall while she disappears into the ladies' room. I have no doubt that she's crying her heart out and indeed; she emerges ten minutes later with red eyes.

She looks startled to find me standing here and looks up at me with wide eyes. I sigh and hand her my bathroom card.

"This gives you access to the executive bathroom," I tell her.

She takes the card from me with trembling hands and stares at it. "I know this is probably hard to believe, but he's always acted the same way with me too. I know you probably can't see it now, but his craziness does work. Clients do actually behave in the same irrational, angry way far more often than you might think. You'll get used to it soon enough, but feeling like you've let him down never gets easier, Alyssa."

She looks at me wordlessly and closes her hand around the card I gave her. She's clutching it so tightly than I'm worried she'll hurt her fingers.

"I may or may not have had to hide in the bathroom on numerous occasions after receiving a verbal lashing from your dad. At least the executive bathroom is private. No other stalls. No one witnessing your mini breakdown. And there will be many. Even I might upset you sometimes. I hope I won't, but I can't be sure. Things do get a little tense around here every once in a while."

Alyssa laughs, and my unease settles just a little. "Did you really?" she asks. "Did you really hide out in the bathrooms too?"

I smile down at my shoes in embarrassment and nod. "Yeah. I respect the hell out of your dad, but he's a fucking psycho."

Alyssa bursts out laughing and puts the card away. "Thank you, Daniel," she says. I smile and fall into step with her as we walk back to the office. I can see Charles pacing nervously and he pauses when he catches sight of Alyssa smiling. His relief is palpable and I bite down on my lip to hide my smile. If he's going to feel this bad about it, then why shout at her in the first place?

"Why don't you write up this morning's meeting minutes?" I ask Alyssa. She looks up at me and nods, her usual eagerness back on her face. I walk past her and pause at Christian's cubicle. He looks up at me with dread.

"Conference room. Now."

I walk away, and he follows me reluctantly. He seems nervous and starts trembling as he sits down. I take the seat opposite him and cross my arms. I don't even have to ask him what happened. He starts rambling nervously.

"I'm sorry, Mr. Devereaux. She was so eager to help, so I let her. I didn't know the quality of her work would be so poor. She seemed quite bright. Guess I was wrong."

Wrong fucking words, buddy. "So you asked an intern to do your job for you and then didn't even check for errors? *You* seemed quite bright. Guess I was wrong."

He looks up at me with wide eyes and shakes his head. "No, Mr. Devereaux. She said she double checked, so I assumed everything was fine. Like I said, she seemed so eager to help. I thought I was doing her a favour. It was bad judgement on my part."

I just about keep from rolling my eyes. "You thought you were doing her a favour by asking her to do a job I specifically assigned to you?"

He looks panicked and is no doubt coming up with yet more excuses. I sigh and check my watch. I have exactly seven more minutes before I need to be in my next meeting.

"You know the deal, right? You're fired, buddy. We have a zero tolerance policy for basic errors at DM. Especially in the executive office. Since the task was assigned to you, the end responsibility lies with you."

He jumps out of his seat, and I rise too. I walk out before he can start begging to keep his job. If he'd just *done* his job, we wouldn't be in this situation. If he'd done his job, Alyssa wouldn't have cried her heart out the way she did.

Three

I press my hand to the biometric scanner at Charles's house and the front door swings open. The house smells amazing and my stomach grumbles immediately. When was the last time I ate? Did I even have lunch? I've been so busy all day that I genuinely can't recall.

"Hey, you're here," Alyssa says, sticking her head out into the hallway. She's got her long hair wrapped in a messy bun and she's in comfy house clothes. Looks like she's wearing nothing but a loose tee and some sleep shorts. My eyes automatically drop to her breasts. I can see a hint of her nipples through the fabric and my heart starts to race. I blink and look away. What the hell is wrong with me? I've known Alyssa all my life. Why am I suddenly attracted to her?

"Hungry?" she asks. My stomach grumbles again and she laughs. "That's a yes, then. Come in."

She disappears back into the kitchen and emerges minutes later with a large serving dish. I glance at the pasta she made longingly and she chuckles as I take a seat next to Charles.

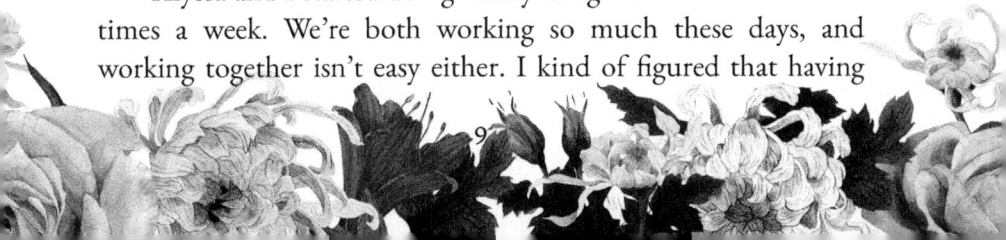

"Alyssa and I started doing daddy-daughter dinner dates three times a week. We're both working so much these days, and working together isn't easy either. I kind of figured that having dinner a few times a week might help her not hate me. I'm not the easiest boss to have, and she has to live with me too. She's already threatened to move out twice."

I'm hit with an intense sense of longing but smile nonetheless. I'd give the world to work with my dad and to have dinner with him one more time. Charles has done his best to treat me as his son, but it isn't the same. It doesn't make me miss my dad any less. If anything, it makes me miss him more.

Alyssa grabs a large serving spoon and proceeds to fill her father's plate with pasta and salad, before moving her attention to me. I'm so startled that I don't even have time to protest or to insist that I can do it myself.

I've gotten so used to the serving staff at home that Alyssa serving me instead makes me feel flustered. How long has it been since I've had a meal that truly feels like a homemade one? One that isn't made by a chef and served by staff.

"Thank you," I say. She smiles at me and my stupid heart skips another beat.

"So you're buying an apartment, huh?" Charles says. I nod at him as I take a bite of my food and try my best to hide my expression. The food looks amazing, but it doesn't taste quite right. Charles bites back a smile and shakes his head as I force myself to swallow down the pasta.

"Yeah," I say. "I found one I really like, overlooking Hyde park."

Charles nods thoughtfully. "Close to the office then. What area is it, Knightsbridge?"

I nod and he smiles approvingly. "Sounds great, son. I had a look at that Aston Martin you've been wanting to buy as well. Not sure about the options you picked."

Alyssa rolls her eyes and takes a bite of her food. Her eyes widen and she grimaces as she swallows the food down, and I can't help but smile. She grabs a large amount of parmesan and throws it all over her own food and ours, though I doubt that'll save the dish.

"God, stop it already. All this talk about buying apartments and cars. Next you two will make a cost-benefit analysis."

Charles and I look at each other and nod at the same time. "Excellent idea," I murmur, causing Alyssa to roll her eyes.

Dinner passes peacefully and I can't remember the last time I had such a homely meal. I love my mother to bits, but she's always worked so hard that we've never really done many family dinners. We've done even less of them since my father died.

I follow Charles to his office and the two of us finish our paperwork while he advises me on client issues I've had. I've missed this. The MBA I did doesn't hold a candle to one-on-one mentoring sessions with Charles.

He seems fidgety and nervous as he reads through the proposal I crafted, and I lean back in amusement. I know there's nothing wrong with the proposal — it was a piece of cake. Instead, he's gearing up to ask me something. Something about Alyssa, no doubt.

"So, how is my little girl doing?" he asks, eventually. The edges of my lips tip up and I try my best not to smile. Charles Moriani is the most fearless and ruthless businessman I know, but he's a softie when it comes to his daughter.

"She's doing great, Charles. She's eighteen, and she's already handling the workload of a graduate staffer. Even more than that, actually, considering she's working in the Executive Office. I'm worried it's too much, though. I'm worried her school work and working at DM on top of that is a lot."

Charles shakes his head. "No, not for Alyssa. This is a walk in the park for her. She's amazing."

I sigh and bite down on my lip. Nothing I say will convince him that the only reason she's working so hard is because of all the pressure he puts on her. Alyssa has always been scared of letting her father down.

"Don't you think you're a bit tough on her, though? That incident last month with the small error on the client proposal, that was a bit much."

Charles hesitates and looks away. "That's how I taught you, Daniel. Look how great you turned out. I want Alyssa to learn in the same way — in the way I know works."

I finish my cup of tea and nod respectfully. I don't agree with him, but it's not my place to argue either. All I can do is shield Alyssa from his tough love training as best I can.

I rise and grab my teacup. "Want a refill?" I ask. Charles nods and hands me his cup, seemingly lost in thought. I know he's worried about pushing his daughter away, and he should be.

I'm surprised to find Alyssa at the kitchen table with her laptop and notepad. She's sipping a cup of tea of her own and looks up when I enter. I glance at my watch and frown.

"It's eleven, Alyssa. Shouldn't you be heading to bed sometime soon? You have classes tomorrow, don't you?"

She nods and yawns. "I know, but I have an essay due soon and I don't have enough time to finish it."

I walk towards the kettle and refill it. "You know you don't have to come in every single day, right? If you're busy with classes, then just reduce your working hours."

She sighs and shakes her head, her long brown hair falling over her chest. "No, I couldn't," she murmurs.

I sit down next to her. She pushes her laptop towards me and looks up at me with her stunning hazel eyes. "What do you think?" she asks, hopeful. She's totally giving me puppy eyes and I'm totally falling for it.

I read through her essay and highlight a few sections where she needs more references, and another few that aren't quite clear enough. "Work on this," I tell her, running her through my notes step by step.

She looks up at me with wide eyes, and I've never seen her look at me that way before. I've never seen her look so mesmerised. Or, well, I guess I've never seen her look that way *at me*. My cheeks heat up slightly while my heart rate increases, and I push away from her.

"Thank you, Daniel," she says.

I smile at her and shake my head. "It's nothing, Alyssa. I'm always here if you need help. I'm serious about work too. If you want to work less hours, let me know. I'll talk to your dad for you."

She considers it for a second and then shakes her head. I sigh and bite back a smile. I already know that I've got another workaholic on my hands.

Four

Alyssa fidgets with the straps of her bag as we walk into the client's building.

"Executive summary," I bark. Alyssa freezes for a second and then nods, her expression hardening as though she's getting her game face on.

"Star Enterprises. A fast-growing media company that's looking to hire us to streamline their finance department. Based on my assessment, it seems they aren't equipped to deal with how fast they're growing."

I nod at her, pleased with her progress. It's been almost eight months of us working together, and she never ceases to amaze me. She keeps up, no matter what her father or I throw at her, and she excels while she's at it. I definitely wasn't anywhere near that professional when I was her age.

We walk into the meeting room and I place my hand on Alyssa's lower back. "You do the presentation," I murmur.

She looks up at me with wide, panicked eyes and shakes her head. I smile at her and nod. "Yes," I whisper, just as she whispers, "no."

This is exactly how Charles pushed me into my first client

presentation. Alyssa and I are both aware she knows the material better than I do — she *made* the presentation. She's as ready as she'll ever be, but she can't be given a chance to overthink things.

I sit down and leave her to it, and I'm not even remotely surprised when she completes the presentation successfully. The only giveaway of her nerves is her slightly trembling hands, but I doubt anyone noticed.

My eyes roam over the meeting participants and linger on one of them. A guy in his early twenties that's looking at Alyssa with far more than professional interest. I grit my teeth and look down. I've never been in a situation like this before — how am I supposed to protect her from sleaze bags like that?

He walks up to her as soon as she's done, no doubt with a list of bullshit questions. I approach her with her coat in my hands and take the folder with files from her.

The guy that was obviously chatting her up freezes and looks at me warily. I hold my hand out for him and he shakes it. "Daniel Devereaux," I say, shaking his hand a bit tighter than necessary.

"Grayson Smith," he murmurs, his confidence shot. He flexes his hand once I let go of him and grabs the business card I give him.

"You're welcome to email me directly with any questions you might have about the presentation. Alyssa here is merely one of our interns, she won't be able to assist you."

His eyes roam over Alyssa's body with regret, and I clench my jaw in annoyance. What a dick.

Alyssa is quiet as we get back in the car, and the way she folds her arms tells me she's mad.

"What's wrong?" I ask her, my voice soft. She turns to glare at me and I bite down on my lip. Alyssa doesn't get mad at me very often, and I hate it when she does. It makes me want to do whatever it takes to placate her.

"It's nothing," she snaps, before looking out the window. I sigh and drive to the office in silence.

"It's obviously not nothing. You're mad."

Alyssa grits her teeth and continues to ignore me. I inhale deeply and sigh, my own annoyance rising.

"Lyss, if you don't tell me what's wrong, then I can't make it right. Why are you so mad? If you're going to be mad at me, at least tell me why."

She glares at me heatedly and then looks down. "You said I was merely an intern. I shouldn't even be mad because it's true, but I work so hard, Daniel. I can't believe you still see me as just an intern."

I exhale in relief. That's what she's mad about? The edges of my lips turn up into the smallest smile and I look away.

"Alyssa, I let you take lead on a client presentation and had full faith that you'd do well. How could you possibly think I see you as yet another intern?"

She looks away petulantly and I grin to myself. She's so cute when she actually acts her age.

"You did great, Alyssa. I only asked Grayson to email me with his questions because he was obviously just flirting with you."

She looks at me with wide eyes, and I chuckle as I park the car. The two of us stay seated as I turn off the engine of my precious Aston Martin.

"He *wasn't*," she says.

"Was too."

"Was *not*."

We both burst out laughing, and the way her eyes light up in amusement does funny things to my heart.

"Was he really?" she asks, seemingly fascinated. My heart drops. Surely she wasn't actually interested in Grayson? The idea of her with him doesn't sit well with me at all.

"Yeah," I murmur. "We have a policy against improper client relationships though," I say. I have no idea if we actually do have a policy against it, but suddenly it seems like something that definitely needs to be implemented.

Alyssa rolls her eyes. "He's *so* old, I'd never go there. I was just surprised that someone might actually be into me."

I frown at her words. Grayson isn't exactly old. He might very well be younger than I am, but I guess to Alyssa I'm old as fuck. Twenty-eight probably seems ancient when you're only eighteen.

"What do you mean you're surprised? Surely guys hit on you all the time?"

Alyssa looks away, a sad and insecure expression on her face. What could've possibly put that look in her eyes? She's one of the most beautiful women I know. How could she not see that?

I clear my throat awkwardly. Part of me wants to tell her I find her beautiful beyond compare, but as her boss I could never say something like that. Even outside of work, it wouldn't feel appropriate. The last thing I want is to make her even remotely uncomfortable around me.

"Anyway, I'm really proud of you, Alyssa. You've done so well and you've learned so much in such a short amount of time. Your dad told me you're doing really well at uni too. I couldn't be more proud. Let's celebrate, okay? How about we go watch The Nutcracker?"

She looks at me in amazement. "The ballet?" she whispers, as though she's scared to say it out loud lest I change my mind. I grin at her and nod.

"Oh my god, yes!" She squeals, and I chuckle.

"Okay, let's go this Saturday."

Alyssa's expression drops slightly and she shakes her head. "I can't," she says, her voice tinged with regret. "Dominic and I have plans."

The way she smiles when she says my little brother's name makes me uncomfortable and I tug on my tie, suddenly irritated.

"No problem," I tell her. "We can go anytime, to be fair. No rush."

Why am I so disappointed? I don't even like the ballet. The only reason I offered to take her is because I know how much she loves it. She's been trying to get her dad and Dominic to accompany her, but both have been refusing.

"Okay, let's do next week," she tells me, her eyes sparkling with excitement. I nod at her, suddenly really excited too. Who would've known I'd one day be excited to go to the fucking ballet, of all things?

Five

"We should do a housewarming," Dominic says, and I shake my head immediately. My new apartment should be done in a few weeks, and the last thing I want is to invite anyone. That place is going to be my own little sanctuary. I'll be damned if I so much as let anyone come over for dinner.

"Hell no," I snap.

Dominic shoots me a pleading look, but I shake my head and lean back on the sofa.

"Think of all the parties we could have," he says, and I roll my eyes. I outgrew partying years ago. The mere idea of a party at my new apartment sounds like my version of Hell. No thanks.

Dominic and I both look up in surprise when Alyssa walks into the living room. Her eyes light up when she sees Dominic, and the way she looks at him makes me feel invisible.

"There you are," she says as she drops onto the sofa next to him. His arm finds its way around her shoulder and the two of them settle into a relaxed and far too intimate hug. Dominic presses a kiss to the top of her head that sends a brief flash of rage coursing through my body. I look away, dismayed. Why the fuck does my heart feel so funny?

"Thought we were gonna check out that new bar in Covent Garden?" Alyssa says, sounding whiney and cute. She's never like that with me. I can't really expect her to since we're usually together in professional environments, but I'm oddly jealous of Dominic and Alyssa's closeness. Dominic pulls her a little closer and smiles down at her.

"Sorry, I lost track of time, Lyss. I was just chatting with Dan about his new apartment. Don't you think we should throw a big ass house party?"

Her face scrunches up in disgust, her feelings mirroring mine exactly, and I smile to myself.

"Ugh, no. Can you imagine going through all that effort to decorate your house and then when it's finally done you have a bunch of people over that might just mess it all up? No, thank you."

I laugh and nod at her, and she looks at me in surprise. It's like she only just realised I'm here. She smiles at me tightly and pushes away from Dominic a little. I breathe a little easier as soon as she does.

It seems like Alyssa and Dominic have gotten even closer in the time I was in the States for my MBA. They've been best friends all their lives, much like our dads were. I guess it was inevitable with them being the same age and being pushed together by our dads all the time. I always thought their friendship was cute, but now... now I find myself wishing they weren't quite this close. Did their friendship turn into something more while I was away? The way Alyssa looks at Dominic makes me wonder if she might have feelings for him.

"When will your apartment be ready?" she asks.

"Soon. Two more weeks or so."

I hired an interior designer to help me decorate it while my Mum has taken charge of the kitchen. She's got some state-of-the-art design in mind or something. I'm not too fussed about it, to be honest. If it makes her happy, she can do whatever the hell she wants.

Dominic gets up and returns with a bottle of wine and three glasses. It's still weird for me to see Alyssa and Dominic drink, even though I know they're eighteen now. I take a sip of wine absentmindedly while Alyssa and Dominic settle back into their cuddled-up position.

"How about we watch a movie instead?" he asks, his voice soft. My little brother is so gentle with Alyssa I barely recognise him. He's been giving Mum grief with the way he's been drinking, partying and pissing away money. When he's with Alyssa. I don't see the troublemaker we usually have to deal with at all.

She nods at him and smiles, her eyes twinkling. Dominic shifts slightly to get her closer and I tense, my attention wavering as they pick a movie.

What's going on? Why am I so affected by their closeness? I don't think I have feelings for Alyssa per se, but I'm honest enough to admit I'm attracted to her. It's not just her beauty, it's her mind too. She's so fucking clever and hardworking. Her family is almost as rich as mine, yet she never lost that kindness and humility that I love about her. She's everything I could ever want in a woman, but until I got back from my MBA, I didn't even *see* her as a woman.

I know I won't ever stand a chance with her, though. If she thought Grayson at Star Enterprises was old, then I must be ancient to her. Besides, I could never date an employee. Add to that that she's my little brother's best friend and the odds are stacked against me even more. I thought I'd be okay with that and that my attraction would wane, but it hasn't. In the months that she and I have worked together, it's only gotten stronger. I'm now at a point where I can't stomach the idea of her harbouring feelings for my little brother. I'm a fucking mess. How did I ever let it get this far?

"Come on," she murmurs, her voice soft. "Please."

Dominic sighs exaggeratedly and puts on the chick flick she asked for. I feel like a total third wheel. It's like they're on a cute little date or something, and it pisses me off. It annoys me that

Dominic gets to see a version of Alyssa that she won't ever show me.

I grab my phone and scroll through my texts, pausing on one from Giselle, a model I've slept with a few times. Maybe all I need is to get laid. Maybe I'm obsessing over Alyssa the way I am because I haven't been with a woman in so long. Giselle is always down for a no-strings-attached night.

I glance at Alyssa and Daniel, all cuddled up and clench my jaw. I need to nip whatever this is in the bud.

I sigh and text Giselle. This has gotta be the first time I'm not actually looking forward to spending a night with her. It's a good thing she knows the score and never has any expectations beyond sex. I definitely can't be bothered with any of that.

Giselle texts back almost immediately and I glance at Alyssa again. She smiles up at Dominic, and my mind is made up. This can't go any further.

Six

I walk into the office to find Linda snickering at her computer screen. She's usually quiet and serious, so that should've already clued me in. Alyssa smiles at me brightly as I walk past her desk and her eyes roam over my body in a way they never have before. Her eyes meet mine and she struggles to hide her curiosity and amusement.

I don't know what's going on, but I'm clearly not in on the joke. I frown and walk to the office that Charles and I now share, only to freeze right in front of it. I stare at the photo on the door in disbelief. Someone stuck a photo of Giselle and me on the door. She's giggling, with her head tipped back, while my lips are pressed against her neck. It's an obviously intimate and embarrassing photo. How the hell did this make it into the tabloids so quickly? And more importantly, why the fuck is this stuck on my office door? I rip it off angrily, only to be met with more snickers.

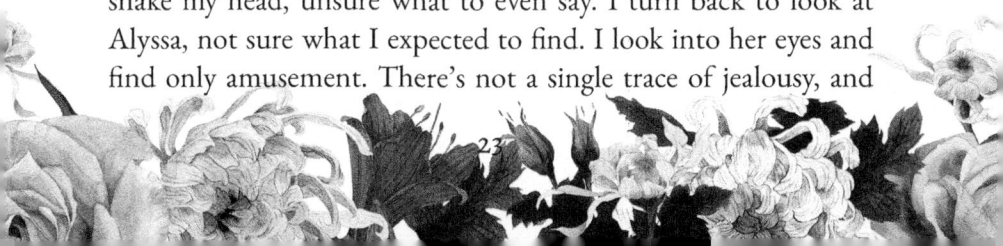

Charles walks up to me and claps me on the shoulder. "Wild night, huh, son?" he says, grinning from ear to ear. I'm so fucking embarrassed that even my ears feel hot. I close my eyes briefly and shake my head, unsure what to even say. I turn back to look at Alyssa, not sure what I expected to find. I look into her eyes and find only amusement. There's not a single trace of jealousy, and

I'm not sure why I was even hoping for it. I already knew she didn't care for me that way.

I grit my teeth and walk into the office, almost slamming the door in Charles's face in anger. He follows me in, still smiling for ear to ear.

"So, who is she? Can I expect to meet her soon?"

I groan and turn my computer on silently, intent on ignoring him.

"Well?" he says.

I sigh and look up at him. "You won't meet her.".

Charles laughs and wiggles his brows annoyingly. "Just a fling, huh? Looks like she's a model? A famous one?"

I drop my head to my desk and inhale deeply. Charles *loves* gossip. He's even worse than my mum.

"She's just a girl, Charles. It's nothing serious."

He chuckles and hovers around my desk like an annoying mosquito. "So a one-night-stand then?"

I nod and try my best to get to work. I'm hoping he'll eventually get the message if I just ignore him. I'm so fucking embarrassed.

Alyssa knocks on the door and walks in, her amused expression still in place. I hate she doesn't look even remotely envious or annoyed. I'd be pretty fucking pissed if I saw a photo like that of her and some guy.

"Looks like you had an interesting night last Friday," she says as she hands her dad a stack of papers.

I grit my teeth and nod. "You and Dominic seemed to be having a pretty interesting night too," I snap.

She blinks up at me in surprise, her cheeks reddening. For a few seconds she seems lost in thought, as though she's recalling Friday's events. My heart fucking sinks. She looks so happy and dreamy as she thinks of Dominic.

It takes her a few seconds to snap out of it, and she blushes shyly. "Oh well, we just watched movies," she murmurs. I can't help but wonder if that's all they did. Dominic and Alyssa have always been friends, but when they were younger, everyone teased them about getting together, myself included. It's not so funny anymore.

I'm absentminded as I try to get to work. I thought a night with Giselle would make me forget about this silly crush I have on Alyssa, but it didn't. Not even slightly. I thought my mood would improve once I got laid, but I'm just pissed off all day.

I walk out of my office to find all my staff giggling to themselves, and I look back to find a new copy of the photo on my door. I stare at it in disbelief for a few seconds and then rip it off the door.

"Whoever put that on is getting fired," I yell. Alyssa looks at me with wide eyes and tries her best to keep from smiling. Her lack of shock or fear tells me instantly who it was. Fucking Charles.

I turn towards Kate, who is barely keeping from laughing, and I look at her through narrowed eyes. Kate's brother and I go way back and I've known Kate for years. I was the primary investor in Carter's Fintech company, and the guy has single-handedly made me even richer. He's become a very good friend too. Considering my history with her brother, I expected a bit more solidarity from Kate. She tries to look apologetic but totally fails.

"Who was it?" I ask her, my voice dangerously low. Kate purses her lips and looks away. She doesn't fear me in the slightest. She knows I'm barely half as efficient without her excellent organisational skills, and she never hesitates to remind me.

Eventually she grins at me. "The first time it was Linda, then it was Charles. We made a roster of who's putting it up next." She glances at her computer screen and chuckles. "Next up is Alyssa. Good luck firing us all."

I sigh and walk back into my office, slamming the door loudly. What a fucking shit show.

Seven

I'm oddly nervous as I walk to Charles's house to pick up Alyssa. I know tonight is just meant to be a reward for Alyssa's hard work, but I can't help but be excited to spend some time with her outside of work.

I press the bell to announce my arrival and then place my palm against the biometric scanner. I know Charles always says I'm as welcome here and that there's no need for me to ring the bell at all, but it still seems polite to do so.

Alyssa enters the hallway as I walk in and my heart stops. She's wearing a skintight black dress that hugs every curve, and I freeze. My eyes roam over the cleavage she has on display and I struggle to drag my eyes away. She looks so fucking hot.

"Hey," she says, grinning. Her eyes are shimmering with excitement and I smile at her.

"Hey," I murmur. "You look amazing tonight, Alyssa."

She blushes and looks away, a sweet smile on her lips. "Oh, I forgot my purse!"

She turns around and gives me the most amazing view of her ass. Fucking hell. That dress with those heels... she looks fucking irresistible.

Charles clears his throat and I tense. I didn't even realise he was standing here. He looks at me and smiles knowingly.

"So you're taking Alyssa out on a date?"

My heart is hammering in my chest as I face him. "No, it's just a reward for her recent performance at work and at uni."

Charles barks out a laugh that only makes me feel even more anxious. "You're taking her to the *ballet* as a work reward? That's one hell of a reward, isn't it? Kate has been doing great work too; are you taking her to the ballet as well? What about Linda and the new guy, Luke?"

I fidget with the hem of my sleeve and look at him nervously. "Uh, I should, shouldn't I? Yeah?"

Charles grins at me and shakes his head. "Are you asking me or telling me?"

I gulp, and he claps me on the back. I'm relieved when Alyssa walks towards us, saving me from this chat. I've not felt this awkward speaking to Charles in years.

She walks past us and grabs my hand, yanking me along. "Come on, we're gonna be late," she says excitedly. Her hand feels tiny in mine and I entwine our fingers, letting her drag me to my car.

I walk up to the passenger door and open it for her. The way she smiles up at me makes my heart feel funny. Why can't I shake this thing I've got for her?

I try to clear my mind as I walk around the car. I drive us to the London Coliseum while Alyssa tells me all about the piece we're about to see. I can't believe I'm voluntarily going to the ballet. The mere idea of it has always creeped me out. It's the feet — it just isn't natural.

"You're quiet," Alyssa says as we take our seats in the theatre. "Aren't you excited?"

I don't have the heart to tell her I absolutely hate the ballet, so instead I nod and smile at her. "Of course I'm excited," I murmur, leaning in. She turns her head to look at me, her face so close to mine that I could lean in and brush my lips against hers. I can't help but wonder what Alyssa might taste like. I'm fighting these feelings so hard, yet every day I lose a bit more of myself to her. I don't understand how I let this happen. She and I can never be together, and I'm far too old to be having crushes. I'm twenty-eight, for god's sake.

Alyssa grabs my hand as the dancers step into a hot air balloon and I stroke my thumb over her hand soothingly. She's enthralled by the piece, and I'm mesmerised by her. Following the array of emotions on her face is fascinating. Her face morphs from surprise, to agony, to excitement and at times, to longing — all within a couple of minutes. Watching her is far more interesting than the ballet could ever be.

I'm surprised when the curtains close, because it doesn't seem like we've been here that long. Did I actually manage to stare at her the entire time? I'm such a creep. I really need to knock this off.

Alyssa grabs my arm and gushes about the play. "Oh my god, it was so exciting, wasn't it?" she says. I nod and she frowns. Alyssa turns around to face me and grabs my upper arms. I'm tempted to hold her by her waist and pull her closer.

"How could you be so lacklustre? God, that's gotta be the most exciting thing I've ever seen," she says, her eyes sparkling with happiness. I smile at her and brush her hair out of her face gently.

"I'm glad you enjoyed it, Lyss," I murmur. She smiles up at me and tilts her head to the side.

"You never call me Lyss anymore, you know. It's always Alyssa. I guess that makes sense since we're usually working."

I nod. When did I start calling her Alyssa instead of Lyss? "You call me Daniel instead of Dan," I reply. She looks startled, as though she didn't realise, and then nods.

"Come on, let's grab a drink before I take you home," I tell her, offering her my arm. She beams up at me and hooks her arm through mine.

"It's weird that you're old enough to have a drink with me

now," I say. Alyssa tips her head back and laughs, and my heart skips a beat. She looks so fucking stunning when she laughs like that.

"I'm not a child anymore, you know."

"I know." I know all too well that she isn't a child anymore, though I wish I could still see her as one.

We walk into one of the nearby pubs and Alyssa orders a glass of wine while I get a beer. She holds her glass up and I clink my bottle against it.

"Thank you for taking me to the ballet, Daniel. I really enjoyed it. It was amazing."

I shake my head. "You're welcome, Alyssa. You've worked so hard, you really deserved it. How has it been? I know you're doing really well at school and you're definitely doing well at work, but how are you finding it?"

She inhales deeply and looks away, her long brown hair falling over her shoulder. It only makes her look even more alluring.

"It's all good, I guess. I don't really know. I grew up always knowing what I'd do, just like you. I always knew I'd end up at DM, and I always knew that taking over my father's role as CEO was the goal. But some of my classmates... they don't even know what they want, you know? It's like the entire world is open to them, and they have so many choices that I don't have."

I grab a strand of her hair and push it behind her ear gently. "Alyssa, if DM isn't what you want, then all you need to do is tell me. I'll buy you and your dad out, no questions asked. I want you to be happy and pursue your dreams."

She smiles up at me with such tenderness that my heart fills to the brim. "You really would, wouldn't you?" I nod, and she sighs again. "That's the issue, though. I do want this, and I do love everything about both my degree and my job. But I guess I wish it was more of a choice. That doesn't make sense, does it? I'm being selfish and ungrateful."

She looks so remorseful for merely uttering her thoughts, and

I can't help but chuckle. I drop my arm to the back of her chair and scoot closer.

"You're not being selfish or ungrateful at all. I felt the same way when I was your age. I always knew I'd end up on the board of Devereaux Inc, and I always wanted to be CEO of DM Consultancy, like my dad was before me. Neither of those things were a choice per se, and I did wonder what I might want to do if I *had* a choice... but truthfully, I'd be doing the exact same thing. I guess I feel the same way you do."

She looks at me with wide eyes. "Shit, I forgot you're on the board for Devereaux Inc too. How do you get everything done?"

I grimace and shrug. "I work a lot of hours," I tell her honestly. "I work at Devereaux Inc most mornings, and then I work at DM most afternoons. Whatever I can't get done during the day, I end up doing before bed. It's hard work, but I love it, so it doesn't always feel like work to me."

Alyssa looks up at me adoringly. "You're amazing, Daniel. God, I hope I can be like you one day."

I look away. What she means as a compliment just makes me feel so fucking old. I have ten whole years on her. I'm only twenty-eight — most days I don't even remotely feel like I have my own life figured out, but to her I must seem like an old responsible adult. I fucking hate that that's how she sees me, but it's something I need to learn to accept. She's way too fucking young for me to even be thinking about the way I have been.

Eight

I'm swamped with work. My bed is literally filled with paperwork. I don't think I've ever been this stressed out. I was so convinced that my MBA would prepare me for the role I knew Charles was getting ready to bestow on me — but it hasn't. Not even remotely. Most days it feels like I'm drowning. I feel like I'm stuck between my mother and Charles, both of them wanting me to commit more to Devereaux Inc and DM, respectively. I feel like I'm spread thin already, and it's only been a little over a year. Both my mother and Charles keep giving me more and more responsibility, both of them obviously gearing up for retirement, yet I'm not sure I can handle the workload. I wish I could rely on Dominic to take on some work, but he's refusing to even intern at Devereaux Inc. I wish he were a little more like Alyssa. If he was open to being trained for an eventual management position down the line, then that would set me at ease. Knowing I wouldn't have to do everything by myself would take so much weight off my shoulders. But not my brother... no, all he cares about is partying and getting drunk instead of attending his lectures. He can't even be trusted to keep up his attendance at uni, so I guess it's not surprising he's refusing to intern.

I'm startled when I hear a noise in the hallway and check my watch. It's two in the morning. Guess my little brother just got home. I tense when I hear a girl giggling and roll my eyes. Mum hates it when Dominic brings girls home and he knows it. I can't believe he's doing this to her after the way she pleaded with him last weekend.

I sigh and get up to give him an earful, only to freeze in surprise. Alyssa is in his arms, the two of them barely keeping each other up, both of them drunk off their faces. She giggles at something he says and he bursts out laughing. Neither of them notices me leaning back against my door in the dark hallway.

Dominic's arm wraps around Alyssa's waist in the way I've always wanted to hold her, and he pulls her closer. She goes willingly and puts her hand on his chest.

"That was so much fun," Dominic says. "You should come out with me more often. The best parties are on weekdays, you know. That's when all the students are out. The vibe is so different, Lyss. You'd really love it."

Alyssa smiles up at him and nods. "I should, shouldn't I? God, I wish I didn't have to work weekdays. Who do you think would fire me quicker if I showed up to work drunk or hungover, Daniel or my dad?"

Dominic laughs and shakes his head, the two of them slowly making their way across the hallway. "Dickhead Daniel, for sure. God, he takes himself so seriously. But then your dad is fucking terrifying, so I don't know."

Alyssa giggles and nods. "It's a tie," she says, laughing. My heart twists uncomfortably. I don't want her to see me as just her boss or an authority figure. I genuinely thought we got a little closer after we went to the ballet last week, but I guess not.

"I love you, Lyss. Fuck, this was so much fun. I still always have the most fun with you."

They reach Dominic's bedroom and Alyssa freezes. She has her own bedroom here, so he'd better not be taking her into his.

"I love you too," she says. Dominic smiles at her, but she

shakes her head and pushes against his chest until she's got him against the wall.

"I'm serious, Dominic. I love you," she whispers. Something in the way she says it makes my stomach drop. Dominic and Alyssa have said they love one another all their lives, and I've never thought twice about it. But tonight... tonight Alyssa sounds different. Desperate, almost.

"I love you too," Dominic repeats and Alyssa pushes against his chest angrily.

"No," she says. "You don't love me." She sounds distressed as fuck, and she's clearly drunk. I'm not sure if I should intervene and make sure she just gets into bed okay.

"I do, Lyss. You're my best friend in the whole world. You always have been, you know that."

Alyssa sniffs as though she's holding back her tears, and she shakes her head frantically. "Not like that, Dominic. Don't tell me you don't realise. I know *you know.* You know I'm in love with you. I've been in love with you for as long as I can remember. How long are we going to pretend like I'm not?"

My heart fucking shatters. I guess part of me suspected it, but I've been telling myself it couldn't be true. I've been ignoring the way she looks at him when I know she hasn't once looked at me that way. I knew I never stood a chance with her, but I was hoping I'd at least never have to see her with someone I know. For it to be my brother... I don't know if I can deal with that. The idea of her kissing Dominic or the two of them dating, I can't cope with that shit. Him touching her in the way I've been imagining I want to... *Fuck*. If he feels the same way and they start dating, Alyssa will end up being my fucking sister-in-law. Even if their relationship doesn't last, that's what she'll always be to me and my family. Fucking hell. I knew I'd never be with her, but for her to be in love with *my brother.* What the actual fuck? This has gotta be some sort of fucking joke. My pain morphs into rage, and I clench my jaw.

"You're not. You can't be," Dominic says. "You and I are just friends, Lyss. We can't — we couldn't. Fuck, I'm a fucking mess and you know it. I could never be the person you deserve. You can't love me, Lyss. You're just drunk. Fuck."

She bursts into tears, and he takes her into his arms, hugging her tightly. "Lyss, I fucking love you to the moon and back, as my best friend. Nothing more. You're just drunk, Lyss."

Dominic lifts her into his arms and carries her to her bedroom. He walks and looks up at me, surprised to find me standing here so quietly. His eyes meet mine and I'm surprised at what I find in them. He looks fucking heartbroken. He might say he doesn't have feelings for her, but it's obvious he feels *something*. I'm a fucking asshole for being so happy that he won't act on his feelings when I know nothing would make Alyssa happier.

Nine

Alyssa has been out of it for days now. She's absentminded and makes small mistakes that she usually never would. It's getting harder for me to keep her little errors from Charles. I hate seeing her so heartbroken and so... sad. Alyssa usually gets over things easily, yet this week she's been inconsolable.

"Budget analysis?" I ask, my voice soft. Alyssa looks up at me with blank eyes and then blinks before jumping into action. She shuffles the documents around and frowns when she can't find the right one. Usually she can give Kate a run for her money with her organisational skills.

My eyes meet Charles's and he looks at me with raised brows. I'm surprised he hasn't snapped at her yet. The fact he hasn't said a thing means even he knows something is seriously wrong with her.

"Here, it's here," she says, handing me the document. I scan through it and spot a handful of formatting errors that she would never usually miss. Her work is always impeccable and presentable.

"Can you write up the meeting minutes and get them to me in the next twenty minutes or so?"

She nods and gets to work, but her usual enthusiasm is lacking severely. Charles tilts his head towards the office and I follow him reluctantly.

"What's wrong with her?" he asks as soon as the door closes behind us.

"I'm not sure," I lie. Charles looks at me through narrowed eyes and all of a sudden I feel like a child all over again, eager to confess. I look away and Charles sighs.

"She's been like that all week. It's unlike her. Something happened."

I nod and walk to my desk. Charles and I reorganised the office so we both have half the space, our desks facing each other. I was hoping he'd just get to work, but no such luck. He follows me to my desk and hovers in front of it.

"Do you know what happened?"

I sigh and lean back in my seat. "How could I possibly know?" I murmur. Charles frowns and crosses his arms.

"The two of you work closely together. I know you've gotten closer recently. It's not completely inconceivable that she'd confide in you."

I inhale deeply and shake my head, unsure what to even say to that. I wish we'd gotten closer, but we haven't. Not at all. I'm not sure if I should be happy with that, in hindsight. I'm not sure how I would've coped if she told me about her feelings for Dominic. Would I have been able to smile and encourage her?

"Maybe you can take her out for dinner. Don't you think that might be nice?"

I freeze and look up at Charles nervously. "Are you joking? She only just turned nineteen. What are you talking about?"

Charles shrugs and looks at me with shrewd eyes. I can't help but wonder if he might be aware of the feelings I've started to develop. Surely he should be warning me away from her?

"It might cheer her up," he says.

I nod and try my best to focus on my work. A dinner date with Alyssa? I'd love to, but she'd just sit there with me wishing she was with Dominic instead. I can't believe I failed to see how she felt about him. They've always been close, and I should've suspected that they might be more than they let on. Just the way they're always cuddled up together should have clued me in, but I chose to ignore it. How long has she been in love with Dominic? I can't believe my luck. I'm falling for a girl that's in love with my younger brother.

I'm still toying with the idea of asking her out by the time the day is over, but it doesn't seem like a good idea. It doesn't feel right.

I sigh and drop by her cubicle. I lean against her desk, but she barely notices me. She's staring at her screen blankly, lost in thought. I hate seeing her like this.

I clear my throat and she looks up at me, startled. I inhale deeply and tip my head towards the meeting rooms behind us. "I need a word," I murmur.

Alyssa gets up, flustered, and follows me to the meeting room. She's silent as she takes a seat at the conference table, her expression crestfallen. It's obvious she knows she's been fucking up, and I hate to be the one to confront her with it.

I sit down in the seat next to her and turn towards her, my knee brushing against hers. I run a hand through my hair in frustration. Had this been anyone else, I'd have fired her long ago.

"What's been going on with you?" I ask, my voice gentle. I don't want her to feel reprimanded. I hate having to be the person to have this talk with her. I hate being her boss. "Your performance hasn't been the same. You've been making small careless errors that would've gotten anyone but you fired, and you haven't been paying attention. This can't go on like this, Alyssa."

She bites down on her lip and nods at me. "I know," she whispers. "I'm sorry."

She looks down at her hands and visibly shrinks. I know I'm supposed to tell her off, but I don't have the heart to do it.

"What's going on?" I ask again, half fearing she might actually tell me about her feelings for Dominic. It's stupid, but I'd rather ignore all of that.

Alyssa looks up at me and smiles tightly. "It's nothing, Daniel. I apologise. I guess things have been a bit much for me lately. I'll work harder. I know I fucked up, and I know you've been covering for me. I'm sorry," she says, her expression so sorrowful that I immediately want to reassure her, but I can't. Not as her boss.

"I'm glad you realise it. Your behaviour has been subpar, Alyssa. I can't condone this any longer. If you can't get your shit together, then you'll leave me no choice. I'll have to fire you. One week — that's all I can give you. If your performance isn't back to what I'm used to, then you better be handing me a resignation letter instead."

She gulps and nods vigorously, a semblance of a spark back in her eyes. I hope this is enough to make her snap out of the funk she's been in. I can only hope so, because if it isn't, I'll actually have to fire her.

Ten

I wake up feeling disoriented. It takes me a good few seconds to realise what woke me up. I glance at my phone in annoyance, only to freeze when I realise Alyssa is calling me. Why the hell would she be calling at four in the morning on a Saturday?

"Hello?" I murmur, my voice still gravely and sleepy.

"Daniel," she murmurs. I'm alert instantly. She doesn't sound right. "Daniel, I — he... I can't... please," she rambles, clearly drunk.

I get out of bed and walk into my wardrobe with my phone in hand. "Where are you?"

I hear shuffling and then giggling. For a second I'm worried she just dropped her phone, but then she speaks again. "Inferno," she says.

I close my eyes and inhale deeply. "Stay there, sweetheart. I'll come get you, okay? Don't move."

Alyssa slurs something unintelligible and I clutch my phone tighter. "Stay on the phone, Lyss," I plead with her as I grab my car keys and my wireless earphones. Within minutes I'm in the car, belatedly realising that I might've thrown on a tee and some joggers, but I walked out wearing my house slippers. For fuck's sake.

Alyssa murmurs random nonsense, clearly fucking wasted, and I speed up more than I really should. I want to call my buddy Vaughn, the owner of the worldwide Inferno chain, but it means I'd have to hang up on Alyssa, and I don't want to risk her walking off. Besides, he's in the States, so I'm not sure if there's anything he can do at such short notice.

It's been months since I had to have a talk with her about her work performance. It took her a week or so, but she managed to pull herself together. I thought she got over the whole thing with Dominic, but she clearly hasn't if she's getting this drunk. As far as I know, she doesn't even like going clubbing.

When I finally pull up at Inferno, she's sitting on the curb, a bouncer standing next to her. The bouncer eyes my car and then me, before recognition hits him. His eyes widen and he glances at Alyssa, a hint of worry in his eyes.

"Hey, sweetheart," I murmur, bending down to help her up. Alyssa looks up at me and blinks before grinning.

"Daniel," she says, slurring slightly. Alyssa refuses to stand up, so I lean in and lift her into my arms.

"Mr. Devereaux," the bouncer says. I glance at him in irritation and he hurries to explain himself. "She was so drunk we had to ask her to leave. I didn't realise..."

I frown at him while Alyssa plays with the collar of my t-shirt, her head resting against my shoulder.

"What? You didn't realise she's *mine*?" I snap.

The bouncer looks down at his feet and shakes his head. I want to chew him out, but I can't fault the man for doing his job.

"Get the door," I tell him, tipping my head towards my car. He jumps up and eagerly walks to my Aston. I roll my eyes as I walk around the car to put Alyssa in the passenger seat. She's so drunk she's barely responsive. I'm not even sure if I should take her home or to a hospital. I've never seen her in this kind of state. What the hell was she thinking?

She keeps shifting uncomfortably in her seat as I drive to her house and I shake my head. She's going to feel like hell tomorrow.

I murmur her name as I park my car in front of her house and she hums in response, but she won't budge. Her eyes flutter open and she looks at me, her lips slowly spreading into a smile. "Daniel," she whispers, almost in awe.

I look at her, properly, for the first time tonight. I've been so worried about her I didn't even notice the skintight dress she's wearing. She looks stunning. I'm glad she called me. I worry about what kind of situation she might have gotten herself into tonight, looking as beautiful as she does and being this defenceless.

"We're at your house," I say. Alyssa blinks at me and lifts her arms, wordlessly asking me to carry her. I chuckle and shake my head as I get out of the car, walking around to get her.

I lift her into my arms, and she wraps her arms around my neck eagerly. "Thank you," she whispers. I tighten my grip on her and hoist her up higher to press my palm to the scanner at her front door.

"Shh," she hisses loudly. "Daddy's sleeping."

I can't help but chuckle as I carry her to her bedroom. "Just how much did you drink, huh?"

Alyssa shrugs and snuggles closer, her lips brushing against my neck. "Not enough," she says. "Not enough to forget."

I bite down on my lip as I put her on her bed. She drank this much in an effort to drown her feelings? I turn to grab her a glass of water, but she grabs my hand and looks up at me, panicked.

"Bathroom," she whispers, and I jump into action. I lift her into my arms and get her into her bathroom right before she throws up. One second later and she'd have missed the toilet. I groan and pull her hair out of her face as she pukes out the insane amount of liquor she must've drank. All she's puking out is pure liquid — I can literally smell the Jägermeister she had tonight.

Alyssa leans against the toilet and suddenly bursts into tears. I panic and rub her shoulders, trying my best to console her. "What's wrong, Lyss?" I whisper.

She closes her eyes as a sob tears through her throat, and my own heart breaks alongside hers.

"I want it to stop, Dan. I want my heart to stop hurting."

She turns towards me and wraps her arms around my neck. I hold her tightly as she sobs in my arms. "Why am I not enough?" she whispers. "Why can't it be me?"

I tighten my grip on her and inhale deeply. "You *are* enough, Alyssa. It isn't you, I swear. You're perfect. It's his loss."

She cries even harder and I lift her into my arms. I carry her back to bed and sit down with her still in my lap.

"I love him. I love him so much it hurts. I don't remember a time I didn't love him."

My heart fucking breaks. What the fuck is wrong with Dominic? How the hell can he reject a woman like Alyssa? He should be counting his lucky stars — I know I would if she felt this way about me.

I hold Alyssa in my arms until her sobs die down and her breathing slowly but surely evens out. I continue to stroke her back until her eyes flutter closed and she's fast asleep.

I can't even remember the last time I got as drunk as she is tonight. I have no doubt she drank enough to almost black out.

I put her into her bed carefully and cover her with her blankets. Her lashes flutter slightly and then she's fast asleep again. I look back at her one more time before I walk out of her room, my heart heavy.

I'm so absentminded that I don't notice Charles standing in the hallway until he clears his throat. I freeze and look up at him, startled. He glances from me to Alyssa's bedroom and frowns.

"How is she?"

"I — she's okay. Just drunk. Why are you still awake?"

Charles sighs and stares at Alyssa's door. "I can't ever sleep if she's not home. I don't want her to know, because she'd never go out if."

I nod in understanding and Charles glances at me, his eyes roaming over my outfit, pausing on my slippers. "Thank you," he says. "For being there when she needs you. I don't think she even realises you're the one she reaches out to when she needs someone. She does it when she has an issue at work, and she does it with her school assignments too. She doesn't realise it, but she reaches out to you when it matters most."

I shake my head. "It's nothing like that," I reply. I wish it were, but it isn't like that at all. I guess it's more that I'm a mentor of sorts to her. It isn't because she needs me, it's because I'm just there.

I *want* it to be more, though. Is that wrong?

Eleven

I've been worried about Alyssa all morning. I wonder if I should text her and ask how she's feeling. I'm willing to bet she's got the worst hangover she's ever had.

My mother knocks on my bedroom door and walks in, her eyes roaming over the countless documents on my bed. She looks at me in disapproval and I know exactly what she's thinking.

She purses her lips but doesn't give me the usual speech about quitting my job at DM to work full-time at Devereaux Inc, so she must have something more important on her mind.

She hesitates and looks at me with so much worry in her eyes that I don't even have to guess who this conversation is going to be about.

"What did he do?" I ask, sighing. She only ever looks that way when my little brother has done something to upset her.

Mum sighs and looks away. "I think you should talk to him. Nothing I say is getting through to him. He's going out and coming home drunk every single day. I'm sick and tired of it. Every time I bring it up, he threatens to move out. Can you imagine the security implications if he does?"

I sigh and close my eyes. I really don't want to deal with this, but I can't say no to her either. I nod at my Mum and try my best to smile reassuringly.

"I'll talk to him, Mum. Don't you worry about it, all right?"

She exhales in relief and smiles. She glances at the papers on my bed again and shakes her head. "You really should quit that job at DM. I need you at Devereaux Inc."

I nod at her, knowing that nothing I can say will get her to change her mind about that. No matter what I say, she doesn't understand the importance of DM to me. It's the company my father started and cherished. I want to be a part of it — I want to be part of his legacy. I owe Charles the world too. I wouldn't know half the shit I know now if not for him. The expertise my mother values so much was all bestowed to me by Charles. The least I can do is repay his kindness by working with him for at least a while longer. Just until Alyssa can take my place.

My mum stares at me expectantly and I sigh. She really expects me to go talk to him right now? I shake my head and walk to Dominic's bedroom. I'm not even surprised that he's still asleep at three in the afternoon. He obviously went out last night, but it doesn't seem like he was with Alyssa. She'd never have called me if they were together.

I sit down at the edge of his bed and push against his shoulder impatiently. "Get up," I snap. "It's bloody three in the afternoon. How the hell are you still asleep?"

Dominic groans and turns around. He throws his arm over his face and I shove him again. Dominic opens his eyes and glares at me.

"What the fuck do you want?"

I look him over in disgust. "You fucking stink. I can literally smell your fucking drinks. What the hell, Dominic?"

He rolls over in annoyance and pulls his sheets over his head. "Fuck off," he murmurs.

I cross my arms and stare at him. How the hell is he my brother? I went overboard in my first year at uni too, but Alyssa and he are almost at the end of their second year now. She's working her ass off, and he's still fucking around.

"You won't even get an upper second class at this rate, and you know nothing less than a first class degree is acceptable. You're a Devereaux, for fuck's sake."

Dominic shrugs, his sheets bunching up. "Fuck it. I'll just donate a couple of million to the uni and they'll give me a first. I don't give a fuck."

His attitude drives me insane. "Like hell you will," I snap. Mum retains full control over his trust fund until he turns twenty-five, so he knows he won't be able to do that. Not that I'd let him anyway.

"You can't buy a degree, Dominic. You need to earn it. You can't solve every issue with money. Life doesn't work that way."

He turns to look at me and laughs. "It does when you're a Devereaux."

I grit my teeth and inhale deeply. What the fuck happened to my cute little brother? How the hell did he grow up to be such a bellend?

"Look, Mum's worried about you, okay? She's already got it tough with work, and you know she never recovered from losing Dad. Don't make her worry about you."

Dominic looks away and I wonder what I could say to get through to him. Mum has been asking me to talk to him every few weeks since I got back. At first I tried my best to be patient and to reason with him, but I know better now. Nothing I do or say makes a difference.

I run a hand through my hair and rise to my feet. I've got too much work to do to waste my time here. I glance back at him in disappointment before walking out. Maybe he'll grow out of this phase he's going through. God, I can only hope so. What the hell does Alyssa see in him?

I sigh and grab my phone. I hesitate for a second and then decide to call her anyway. She picks up almost immediately.

"Hey," she says, her voice soft. I hear rustling in the background and bite down on my lip.

"Hey," I murmur. "You still in bed?"

Alyssa sighs, and I can just imagine her turning around in bed, trying to get comfortable. "Yeah, I have the worst headache ever. I'm dying. The world won't stop spinning. It's the worst."

I chuckle and sit down on my bed. "I kind of figured. You seemed really wasted last night."

"Dad told me you picked me up? Truthfully, I don't remember much. I remember going out, but half the night is just blank. I can't remember anything from the second part of my night. I don't even remember calling you, but I saw your number in my call history. Honestly, I can't thank you enough. I'm so sorry. I can't imagine how inconvenient that must've been for you."

I shake my head even though she can't see me. "It's fine, Alyssa. I'm glad you called me. But honestly, you shouldn't be drinking that much. I'm worried about you."

Alyssa chuckles and I lie back on my bed, my eyes falling closed. I don't remember the last time we called just for the hell of it. We only really talk when there's some sort of need for it. Usually it's about work or her dad.

"You don't need to worry, I promise. This was a one-off. I just needed this, I guess. One night to just let loose. Last night... did I say anything?"

I know what she's asking, and I'm not sure how to respond. Technically, she didn't tell me about Dominic, since she never said his name.

"Not much. I could tell you were hurt over something, but you were mostly chatting shit."

She laughs and breathes a sigh of relief. "Okay, that's good," she says. I can hear the smile in her voice, and I smile in return.

"I wonder why it was me you called," I say, thinking out loud.

Alyssa is silent for a couple of seconds before she answers. "I don't know either," she replies. "I guess subconsciously I knew you're one of the few people that'd be there for me."

I can't help but wonder if she tried calling Dominic first. I wouldn't be surprised if she did, but there's no way he would've been in a state to help her last night. I doubt he'd even have picked up.

"I'm glad. I'll always be there if you need me, Alyssa. Don't ever hesitate to call me if you need me."

"Thank you, Daniel. Same, you know? You've done so much for me in the two years. I've learned so much working with you, and you've just generally been amazing. If there's any way I can repay you, please let me know."

I shake my head and sigh. "It's all good, Alyssa. You get some rest, okay? Drink plenty of water and you'll be fine."

"I will," she says. "See you tomorrow."

I don't want to hang up, but I don't have an excuse to keep her on the phone either. I wish I did.

Twelve

I glance at the bottle of Macallan Lalique in my hands. It's a 62-year-old Single Malt Scotch bottle of whiskey that Charles is going to love. Took me ages to get my hands on it, but it'll be worth it.

I'm grinning from ear to ear as I walk up to his house. I can't wait to see his reaction. I press my palm to the biometric lock and the front door swings open. I walk in to find him working at his desk in his home office.

I knock on the open door and lean against the doorframe. "Aren't you well on your way to retirement? What the hell are you doing working on your birthday?"

He glances up and smiles at me. "Daniel, son. Is it that late already? I haven't gotten ready for dinner yet. Alyssa will kill me."

I shake my head and walk up to him. I place my birthday gift right in the middle of his desk. He glances at the bottle and then back at me. "You pulling me leg, son? Is this really what I think it is?"

I grin at him and nod. "Happy birthday, Charles."

He grabs the bottle and looks back at me in disbelief before staring at it yet again, and I can't help but chuckle.

"You got me a fifty thousand quid bottle of whiskey?"

I shrug, only mildly surprised he knows the price of the bottle at a glance. "You deserve it," I tell him honestly. Charles stares at the bottle in his hands, completely awestruck, and I smile to myself. It was hard to find something I thought would genuinely make him happy, but it seems like I nailed this.

"Would you like to be left alone with your bottle? Should I give you two some privacy?"

Charles glares at me for half a second before his attention is drawn back to his whiskey. He doesn't snap out of it until Alyssa walks in.

I look up at her and freeze. She's wearing a stunning figure hugging red dress and I can't for the life of me tear my eyes away from her. She smiles at me and my hearts fucking stops. "You look stunning," I murmur without thinking. Alyssa looks startled and then smiles even wider. Her eyes roam over my body and for a second, I see appreciation in them.

"You look great tonight too," she says politely, before turning to her father. "But *you* — you look like you're still wearing the same clothes you were wearing an hour ago, Dad. Didn't you tell me you were gonna get changed right away?"

Charles smiles sheepishly and glances at me. I know that look. He's about to throw me under the bus. "I was about to go and put on my suit when Daniel came in. I told him I needed to get changed, but he insisted on giving me my birthday present." He shows her the bottle of whiskey proudly, but Alyssa merely frowns, clearly not understanding how rare the bottle is.

"So you spent an hour talking about a bottle of liquor?"

She turns to glare at me, and I throw Charles a dirty look. I only got here ten minutes ago; why the hell is he blaming me? He smiles smugly and walks away, leaving me to deal with Alyssa's annoyance.

She grins at me as soon as the door closes behind Charles. "He lied, didn't he?" she says.

I nod and grin back at her. "Totally. I literally got here ten minutes ago."

Alyssa shakes her head and grabs my arm. "I *knew* it," she says, her voice filled with fervour. She drags me along to the front door, and I kinda want to grab her hand. How would her hand feel in mine?

"How have you been? How's uni?" I ask her. I've been so busy recently I've barely seen her. We've been working together for well over two years now, and I more than trust her to handle her own workload. She doesn't need as much mentoring as she did when she first got started. Unfortunately, that means I don't see her every day anymore, and when I do see her, we really only talk about work.

"Good," she says, smiling up at me. How the hell does she get more and more beautiful every year? I thought I'd get over my silly crush on her, but it's just kept growing into something I don't even dare name.

"Can you believe I'm almost done? In just a few months, I'll be working at DM full-time. How exciting will that be?"

I smile at her indulgently. "It'll be amazing. A little birdie told me a promotion to senior consultant is coming up."

Alyssa looks at me, wide-eyed. "Seriously?"

I wink at her just as Charles comes rushing towards us. "Shh," I whisper, and Alyssa giggles excitedly. Her eyes sparkle and the way she smiles up at me makes my heart do somersaults.

Charles glances at the two of us and smiles happily. I wanted to throw him a big birthday party, but he wouldn't let me. All he wanted for tonight was a nice little dinner, so that's what he'll get.

Charles is beaming by the time we reach the restaurant, and I'm relieved he's having a good night. I booked us a secluded table at one of the hotels my family owns, and he looks around wide-eyed as we're led to our table.

"You worked on this?" he asks me. I glance around and nod, smiling to myself. I was involved in every part of opening this hotel.

"It's the first large project I handled on my own. I'm pretty proud of it."

Charles grins and glances at Alyssa. “What do you think?” he asks her.

Alyssa looks around in wonder and then smiles at me. “You’re a man of many talents, aren’t you? I love it. The interior and the vibe are spot on.”

I smile at her and can’t quite make myself tear my eyes away from her. She looks amazing tonight. Her long brown hair is straightened perfectly and the dress she’s wearing has enough cleavage to satisfy my curiosity, yet leaves me wanting more. I can’t get enough of her.

Charles chuckles and I snap at out it, certain he caught me ogling his daughter, but thankfully it’s his phone he’s laughing at.

“Put it away, Daddy,” Alyssa scolds, before turning her attention to me. She glances at my phone on the table and grabs it. “I’m confiscating this until dinner is over,” she tells me, and I look at her in amusement.

I want more of this. I want more of these family dinners with Charles and Alyssa. I want to spend more time with Alyssa treating me as a man, and not just her boss.

I want too much, and I know it. But I can’t help myself. The more time passes, the more of her I crave.

Thirteen

I walk into my house and immediately consider walking back out, but I promised my mum I'd stay the night. She's been unhappy ever since I moved out, and I ended up compromising, promising her I'd stay over every once in a while.

I can't believe I have to deal with my little brother's girlfriend *again*, though, A few weeks ago Dominic suddenly introduced us to Lucy, his girlfriend. Prior to that day, neither Mum nor I had ever heard of her. I'm not even sure why he's dating her — or why he's dating at all. It isn't like him. I'm pretty sure she's the first girlfriend he's ever brought home, and he doesn't even seem to like her much.

"Oh, hey!" Lucy yells as soon as she sees me walk in. I sigh to myself. "Hello, Daniel! How are you? Did you have a good day?" she asks excitedly. She irritates the hell out of me. The girl has too much damn energy, and I don't like the way she looks at me. Lucy's eyes roam over my body, and I can't tell if she's appraising the worth of my suit, or if she's fucking checking me out. Either way, something isn't right with her.

"Lucy," I say, nodding at her politely. She's here more often than she's not, and I fail to understand how Dominic tolerates her. She must be a good lay or something, because she certainly has no redeeming features that I'm aware of. Lucy beams up at me and tugs on my coat jacket. I want to shake her off, but I can't be rude to her.

Mum glances at me in amusement and I raise my brow, but I should've known she wouldn't intervene. She finds great enjoyment in seeing me suffer under Lucy's irritating clinginess.

"You must be tired," Lucy says as she runs her hand over my arm. Dominic barely looks up from his phone. It surprises me he overlooks her fascination with me so easily. If it were me, I'd never be okay with my girl flirting with my damn brother.

Part of me wonders if he started dating her to keep Alyssa away. Things between them haven't been the same in months now. It seems like they're just pretending the whole confession thing didn't happen, but things changed nonetheless. They don't hang out as much as they used to, and I'm low key relieved about it. I've always hated seeing the two of them together. I know I'll never be with her, but it still hurts to see her be so intimate with my brother.

I tug on my tie and ignore Lucy's endless chatter. I wanted to have a quiet night in and hang out with my mother and brother. Instead, I'm stuck with this nut job.

I sit down on the sofa and glance over at my brother, only to find him staring at a photo of Alyssa. He's so focused on her latest selfie on Instagram that he doesn't even notice me sitting right next to him. His expression irritates me. He looks so fucking awestruck. If that's how he feels about her, why would he reject her? Does he even know how much he hurt her?

Lucy sits down next to me, her thigh grazing mine. I grit my teeth in annoyance and rise from my seat, opting for an early night instead.

I can't even fucking sleep once I get to bed, my mind filled with countless things I still need to do. My to-do lists are endless these days. I'm spread thin between DM and Devereaux Inc. I'm not sure how long I can even keep this up. It'll still be a few more years before Alyssa will be ready to take over my job.

I can't resist temptation and end up grabbing my phone. I hesitate slightly and then open up my Instagram app. I don't ever use it, but tonight I find myself looking for Alyssa's profile. I can see why Dominic was so obsessed with the last photo she posted. She's beyond stunning. It looks like she's naked in bed in the photo, her shoulders exposed and her hair a beautiful mess. She's smiling right at the camera, and I can just imagine her lying next to me like that. Fucking hell... I don't ever dare think of her that way, but my body has no such reservations. I sigh and put my phone away, feeling just the slightest bit guilty for imagining her naked in my bed. I toss and turn until I finally fall asleep, and I fall right into a dream.

Alyssa gets into bed with me and chuckles before she runs her fingers over my chest, down and down until she's brushing the tip of her fingers over the waistband of my boxer shorts. She doesn't hesitate to slip her hand underneath the fabric and wraps her fingers around my dick, palming it gently. I moan and push my hips up against her hand, wanting more. She obliges and grips me tightly, her movements experienced and so fucking delicious. She gets me to the edge in no time at all, and I groan.

"Alyssa," I whisper, and she stops. I turn in bed, missing her touch already. Before I know it her fingers are replaced by wet hungry lips, and she sucks me off like her life depends on it.

"Alyssa, baby," I whisper.

I reach for her hair, wanting to wrap it in my fist... and I startle awake, slowly realising what's going on. I grab the hair I've got in my hand and yank on it.

Lucy yelps as I pull her up and I push her away, shocked. I glance down and sort my boxer shorts out before getting out of bed. I grab her arm and pull her along. "What the fuck do you think you're doing, huh?"

She looks up at me, only the smallest amount of fear in her eyes. "Don't act like you didn't want it. I had you ready to come for me."

I shudder in disgust. The only reason I was even remotely

turned on was because I was dreaming about Alyssa. "Don't overestimate yourself."

I open Dominic's bedroom door with so much force that it slams against the wall loudly. He's seated on his bed, his phone in hand. He looks up in surprise when I push Lucy into his room. She stumbles and falls to the floor, but I genuinely couldn't care less.

"Found your girlfriend in my bed, her lips wrapped around my dick while I was fast asleep. I don't care how good of a fuck she is, you need to ditch her."

Dominic stares at me in disbelief and then glances at Lucy. I walk out, not wanting to get involved in the psychotic mess this is about to turn into. I hear her make excuses as the door closes behind me, but I can't imagine her talking herself out of this. I knew the way she's been looking at me wasn't right, but I never expected her to act on it. Fucking hell.

Dominic could have had Alyssa, yet he chose this fucking hussy over her? What the actual fuck. If I were ever so lucky to have a shot at being with Alyssa, I wouldn't dare *look* at another woman. He's a fucking moron, but unfortunately for me, he's the moron that owns Alyssa's heart.

Fourteen

I glance at the documents on my bed and inhale deeply. It's freaking eleven at night and I'm still not done working. I've barely been sleeping lately. I've easily worked anywhere between eighty and a hundred hours a week, working through weekends just to get everything done.

Alyssa started working for me full-time after finishing her degree and that has helped tremendously, but she still isn't confident enough to take on my workload without supervision.

I run a hand through my hair and look around my bedroom, a small smile on my face. It took far longer than expected, but I'm beyond pleased with how my apartment turned out. I'll have to invite Alyssa and Charles over for dinner sometime soon. I wonder what she'll think of it.

My phone buzzes and I glance at it in irritation. These days my phone only ever rings when someone wants something from me. I frown when I realise that it's Alyssa.

"Hey," I murmur.

She's silent, but I can hear her breathing, or gasping, rather. "Alyssa?" I say, worried.

"Daniel... I — I can't... I don't know. Dad, he just... please, can you come to the hospital?"

I jump out of bed and search for clothes as Alyssa tells me where to go. She's barely coherent as I run to my car. "Stay on the phone with me, Lyss. Tell me, what happened? What did the doctors say?"

It's rare for her to be so flustered. I've thrown things at her that would've intimidated some of my most senior consultants, but Alyssa has always handled everything with grace and a smile. Something must be incredibly wrong for her to have lost her composure so badly.

"He just collapsed. He was rubbing his hand over his heart during dinner, but he said he was fine. I'd already gone to bed when all of a sudden I just kind of felt wrong. I don't even know how to explain, but I just knew. I went downstairs to grab some water, thinking it was all in my head, but there he was, on the floor. I called an ambulance and they took him away. I have no idea what's happening, Daniel. I think... I think he might have had a heart attack."

I park my car in front of the hospital and rush to the waiting room Alyssa is in. "I'm here," I tell her over the phone. She turns around as I walk up to her, her phone still to her ear. The second she sees me, her expression crumbles. She walks up to me and throws her arms around my waist, hugging me tightly. She clearly jumped into the ambulance in whatever she was wearing, because she's in a fluffy robe with her house slippers on. I hug her back tightly and she starts to tremble.

"Daniel," she says, her voice breaking. She sniffs and I tighten my grip on her.

"I've got you, sweetheart," I tell her. Alyssa bursts into tears and I stroke her back soothingly, my heart breaking.

"It's been an hour," she says, her voice muffled. "I don't know what happened and no one will tell me."

I inhale deeply, trying my best not to worry. It doesn't sound good, but I can't lose it too. Not when Alyssa is already this distressed. She takes a step away from me and wipes her eyes. I trace her cheek with my thumb, catching a few stray tears, and she looks up at me. The look in her eyes fucking guts me. I've never seen her look so lost before — not even that night she got so drunk she blacked out.

"Where's Dominic?" I ask, looking around the room. Alyssa looks up at me in surprise and then blinks. "You haven't called him?"

She looks away and shakes her head. "I... I was just so panicked. I didn't know what to do. I should've called him, of course."

I smile at her and brush her hair out of her face. "That's not what I meant," I murmur. "I just assumed you had, I'm not saying you should."

I'm a little surprised she called me, but not him. Does she realise it's me she reaches out to when she needs help?

Alyssa and I sit down in the waiting room, her hand in mine. I stroke the back of her hand with my thumb, barely able to keep my own worries at bay. We sit together like that for another hour until a doctor finally walks into the waiting room. We both jump up, Alyssa's hand still in mine.

The doctor looks at us and my heart drops. "Are you Charles Moriani's family?" he asks, and I nod. Alyssa tightens her grip on my hand, but it doesn't stop her from trembling.

The doctor looks down and exhales. "I'm sorry," he says, and Alyssa bursts into tears. I take her into my arms and bury my hand in her hair as the doctor continues to explain to us that Charles had a heart attack, and they were unable to save him.

The two of us stand there like that — for how long, I'm not sure. I can't believe he's actually gone. The nurses let us see him, but to me it merely looks like he's sleeping. I can't convince myself that he's truly gone, even though I'm fully aware I'm in denial. The nurses won't let us stay in the room for long, and eventually they tell us they'll have to move Charles. It hits me then, and I tremble just as badly as Alyssa does as we're led out of the room. The two of us stand in the hallway, speechless. Neither one of us has spoken a word in hours now.

Alyssa is a wreck, and I'm not in any state to drive either of us home. I grab her hand and end up leading her to a taxi. I'm in a strange type of shock. When my father died, I cried my heart out, but this is different. I'm barely even thinking straight. How could he be gone?

Mum looks up at us as we walk into the house. I didn't even realise I gave the taxi driver her address instead of mine. I only just about manage to tell her what happened. I repeat the evening's events as though I'm talking about a work meeting, feeling completely detached and shocked. Part of me still feels like I might wake up soon, and this will all be a bad dream. Like tomorrow, I'll go to work and find Charles smiling at me from his office.

Dominic walks up to Alyssa and lifts her into his arms. She throws her arms around his neck and buries her face against his chest. She hasn't cried since the hospital, and I'm worried about her. I hope Dominic will be able to console her. Things are about to get even harder. Neither she nor I can do without Charles. I don't want to have to get used to a world that he isn't a part of. I don't want to go to work if he won't be there. I can't even imagine how Alyssa must feel.

Fifteen

I stare into the mirror, my eyes tracing over the bags underneath my eyes and the black suit I'm wearing. The last couple of weeks have been tough, to say the least. Alyssa was in no state to arrange the funeral, so I ended up having to do most of it. Thankfully, my mother helped a lot .

"You ready?" my mum asks. I turn around to look at her and shake my head. I don't think I'll ever be ready. She smiles tightly at me, her own eyes filled with heartbreak. Charles was a good friend of hers, and this can't be easy for her either.

"Alyssa needs us," she tells me, and I look down at my feet. I've barely even seen her in the last couple of weeks. She's been holed up in her house, refusing to leave. I've seen even less of her since her grandmother arrived. I'm worried about her, and I feel guilty for not checking up on her more. I've been ridiculously busy, running DM without either Charles or Alyssa — and trying to stay on top of my workload at Devereaux Inc. too. If I'm truly honest with myself, I've mostly been throwing myself into work to try to cope. I don't know how else to deal with the emptiness I feel.

I'm absentminded as I walk to my car. I stare at my Aston Martin and think back to the day I went to buy it. Charles drove me to the car dealer so I could drive the Aston back home myself. We spent months deciding which exact model I'd buy and with which specs. It was our thing. He was the first person to go on a drive with me, and the only one I've ever allowed behind the wheel. I drop my head to my steering wheel and inhale deeply. To think he won't ever sit beside me anymore guts me. I won't go over to his house and work from his home office. No more crashing dinner at his and pretending Alyssa's food is edible. No more reassurance when I'm filled with uncertainty and no more guidance or mentorship.

I try my best to pull myself together as I drive to the cemetery. I'm in the same type of shock I was in on the day Charles died. It's all so surreal — it's like I'm not actively experiencing this day. Like my brain has shut off, because it doesn't want to deal with reality.

I walk up to Alyssa and stand beside her, while Dominic stands on her other side. She's staring at the rectangular hole in the ground so intensely that she doesn't even notice us. A priest approaches and I grit my teeth. Charles wasn't even remotely a religious man, so it seems ridiculous to have a priest at his funeral. I know he wouldn't have wanted this, and I know Alyssa knows that. I can only assume she ended up giving into her grandmother's endless demands. The woman is trouble, that's for sure. I always found it hard to believe that Charles, who's always treated me as his own son, would cut off his mother. It's starting to make sense now. Even the way she looks at Alyssa is calculative. We're burying her only child today, yet all she does is look around the cemetery in excitement. She keeps eying the various politicians and celebrities that came to pay their respects, and it irritates me. This should've been a small private funeral, but she turned it into a spectacle. I hope Alyssa doesn't come to regret giving her grandmother so much control of today's events.

Alyssa and I both tense as the priest gives us some speech about heaven and Charles's soul being at peace now. I bet Charles would laugh if he could see this. He'd glance at me mockingly, and I'd smile back at him knowingly.

The priest hands Alyssa a single red rose, but she's unresponsive. Dominic takes the rose from the priest and holds Alyssa's hand gently. I'm glad he's at least somewhat stepped up to be there for her. He's still with Lucy, and she still keeps ensuring that he keeps Alyssa at a distance, but thankfully he's tried his best to be there for her nonetheless. Dominic opens her fingers carefully and places the rose in her palm, before closing her fingers around it. She stares at the rose in disbelief, and I see a flash of panic in her eyes. I guess it's finally sinking in for her now.

I wrap my arm around her shoulder and grab the hand she's holding the rose with. She looks up at me with so much sorrow in her eyes that I almost burst into tears myself. A tear drops down her cheek as I raise both our hands, and the rose falls on top of her father's casket. My heart shatters alongside Alyssa's and I tighten my grip on her hand, needing her more than she needs me. The sound of mournful sobs surrounds us as soon as the priest drops a handful of soil onto the casket, and Alyssa closes her eyes.

Dominic wraps his arm around her waist, and I nod at him. She won't last much longer here. It's time to take her home.

I watch the two of them walk away, their arms wrapped around each other. Today especially, I want her in my own arms. I want to be the one that's there for her, and I want to seek solace in her arms myself. I follow behind Dominic and Alyssa, my heart numb. Much to my surprise, it's my car he leads her to. He glances up at me as I reach them and looks back down at his feet.

"Will you take her?" he asks.

Alyssa freezes and looks up at him in disbelief, but his eyes are already on Lucy. She's standing beside his car, waiting for him.

"Pathetic," I murmur as he walks towards Lucy. "Must be some magic pussy for him to abandon his best friend on a day like this."

The edges of Alyssa's lips turn up slightly and I grin at her as I open the door. It's not quite a smile, but at least she isn't crying. I haven't actually seen her cry since that day in the hospital.

I walk around the car and take my seat, glancing at the cemetery one more time before I pull away. It feels strange to leave Charles behind. To return to his house, knowing he won't be there. Knowing he won't ever step foot in there again.

"When are we going to discuss everything?" Alyssa asks. I tighten my grip on the wheel and shake my head. My lawyer told me Charles's last will and testament is quite unconventional. One last laugh from beyond the grave, I'm willing to bet. I'm not even surprised.

"Not today," I murmur. "Today is for mourning and honouring the man we all loved. To say our goodbyes and make peace with a devastating loss. The company isn't going anywhere."

Sixteen

I'm exhausted by the time I walk into Charles's home office. Neither Alyssa nor I wanted to do the reading of the will today, but her fucking grandmother managed to incite so much gossip that we have no choice but to deal with it head-on.

I walk up to the little bar in the corner of the office and grab the bottle of whiskey I got Charles for his last birthday. He didn't even get to drink it. I open it without thinking and pour myself two fingers, before pouring Alyssa half of that. I hand her the glass and empty my own, not even bothering to savour the taste. Fuck it.

Alyssa follows my lead and scrunches up her face in such a cute way that I can't help but chuckle. I bet that whiskey is burning down her throat. I should've poured her something else instead.

She rolls her eyes at me and sits down on the sofa. She looks up at me expectantly and I sit down beside her, my thigh grazing hers. She looks like she hasn't slept in days, yet despite that, she looks beautiful.

"All right. Let's get this over with," Vincent, my lawyer, says, sounding tired. He's worked with Charles for most of his career, so this can't be easy on him. He glances at Alyssa's grandmother and I follow his gaze. She looks expectant and almost… excited. I can't stand her.

"Mr. Moriani is leaving the cottage in France to his mother. Everything else goes to his only daughter, Alyssa Moriani."

She jumps up in disbelief, rage marring her face. "That can't be all he left me. That little cottage? What about money? Who is going to pay me my monthly stipend? I assume he expects Alyssa to be responsible for that now?"

Alyssa's expression crumbles. Until this moment, she must've held out hope that her grandmother isn't as bad as she is. I guess she's been clinging to what appears to be her last remaining family member. I just wish she'd realise that my family and I will be there for her. That *we're* her family.

Vincent stares at the will for a few seconds before responding. "The only thing he left you is the cottage. There is no request for Alyssa to pay for your maintenance."

She stares at Alyssa in such a disturbingly calculative way that my hackles are raised. I have half a mind to assign Alyssa her own security team. I don't trust this woman as far as I can throw her.

"Very well," she murmurs. She glances at Alyssa one more time and then walks out of the room, slamming the door shut behind her.

Vincent tenses and glances at me before looking down at the papers in his hands. "There's a clause in the will, Alyssa. It's about your father's shares in the company."

I freeze just as she does. What the fuck? There's no way Charles would mess with the company. It's his legacy.

"The clause states your shares are to be given to your grandmother unless you marry the man of your father's choosing within a month from now."

My heart drops. What the fuck? How the fuck could he request that of her? My heart twists painfully at the mere idea of her getting married. I'll buy her grandmother out before I let her walk down the aisle. There's no way that's happening.

Alyssa shakes her head in disbelief. "That can't be," she whispers. "I'm only twenty-two. I just graduated from university. I can't get married. My dad always discouraged getting married too young. There's no way he'd ask it of me now. No way he'd put his company on the line to make it happen."

She stares at Vincent as though she hopes he's joking, and I stare him down too — far more threateningly than Alyssa is. He avoids my gaze and looks down before speaking again.

"Your father's wish is for you to marry Daniel. There isn't anyone he trusts more with his company and his daughter."

I blink in disbelief and stare at Vincent in shock. Charles wanted *me* to marry Alyssa? Why? Did he always know about my feelings for her? I doubt it... I've been quite sly about it.

"Did you know about this?" Alyssa asks, her voice dangerously soft.

I shake my head. "Lately your father had been making some strange remarks. He kept pushing me to take you out for dinner and mentioned that he thought we'd make a good couple. I never expected this though."

I think back to the last conversations we had, but nothing indicated he knew how I felt about her. He'd often joke and tell me to take her out for dinner, but I thought he meant as a friend or as a mentor, the way he'd often take me out for dinner. He's jokingly told me we'd make a good couple a handful of times, but I was certain he was saying it in jest. It appears I was wrong, and he was quite serious about it all.

"I can't believe this," Alyssa murmurs. "You're ten years older than me. And he knows. He knows I..."

I finished her sentence wordlessly. He knew how she feels about Dominic. She's been in love with him her whole life, and I doubt she's ever once even looked at me as a man. I'm reminded of one of the first client meetings I took her to, when it became painfully clear that she thinks I'm ancient. Of course, she'd never even consider being with me — even if she *wasn't* in love with my brother. I stare at Alyssa as she rips the will out of Vincent's hands, her expression falling when she realises he isn't lying to her.

I walk up to Charles's drinks cabinet and refill my glass before emptying it in one go. If Charles saw me disrespect his whiskey like this, I'd be getting an earful.

I glance at Alyssa, my eyes roaming over her body. Alyssa as my wife... my heart skips a beat at the mere thought of it. I force myself to look away and clear my throat.

"We can't lose those shares," Alyssa says. "If they fall into her hands, the company will never recover. It'll never be the same."

Alyssa stares at her feet, looking lost as hell. I know I need to tell her it doesn't matter. That she can give the shares to her grandmother, and I'll buy them back for her for twice the price. It'll cost me millions, but it'd be worth it.

I stay silent though. My mind stuck on the idea of Alyssa as my wife.

"He always wanted you as his son. I guess he's getting his wish granted in death," Alyssa says bitterly.

I don't think that's what it is. I think he genuinely wanted me to be with her. He was subtle about it, but in hindsight it's all clear to me. Asking me to coach her, teasing me about taking her to the ballet, telling me to take her for dinner all the time and inviting me over for dinner at his. He was subtly pushing us together, but neither she nor I realised it.

I speak without thinking. "We can do a paper marriage, Alyssa," I say. "We can both keep our lives. Nothing needs to change. You won't have anything to worry about. We'll have an iron-clad prenup, so you'll be protected. Whatever you own, you'll keep, including your shares. I won't take advantage of you in any way. We'll divorce in a year and you'll have your estate and anything you might have earned during our marriage."

Logically, it's the easiest solution, and it won't cost me millions either. Even just having her as my wife on paper... it'd be amazing. We'd be honouring Charles's wishes, and we'd be protecting the company. It's a win-win for both of us.

Vincent clears his throat and looks at us with a cautious expression. "There's more," he says. I close my eyes and inhale deeply. Of course there is. This is Charles we're talking about. If his goal is to get me and Alyssa together, then he'll make it happen.

"The two of you will have to live together and stay married until Alyssa either becomes CEO or turns twenty-five. If you two separate or divorce before then, the shares are still to be given away. We could potentially contest the will, but I'll tell you now that I won't be the one to take that case on. I won't disrespect Charles's last wishes like that."

Alyssa and I both stare into space, neither of us even aware of when Vincent left the room. I can't believe Charles wanted us together so badly that he'd put his company on the line.

"I can't believe he'd do this to us," Alyssa whispers yet again, and I look up at her. Is the idea of marrying me so horrible to her? I bet she wouldn't be responding this way if it were Dominic she was asked to marry. Her reaction fucking hurts.

"I know you're stuck between a rock and a hard place, Alyssa," I say. "You either marry me and lose a part of your personal life and a chance to make that unrequited love of yours work. Or you lose the company that's rightfully yours. It's a tough situation, but it's no walk in the park for me either. The last thing I need is to be saddled with a teenybopper for the next few years. However, I will marry you if you're willing. Even if it's just to honour your father's last wish. He's never asked anything of me before today and I won't let him down now."

Alyssa glares at me and crosses her arms over each other. "Teenybopper, really? Okay, boomer. Don't forget that you're getting something out of this too. If you don't marry me, the company is doomed and so is most of your fortune."

I look at her in amusement. I honestly don't even know if DM even pays me a salary. It certainly doesn't add much to my fortune, but Alyssa doesn't need to know that.

"Yes. I won't deny that there are benefits for me too. The last thing I want is to lose the absolute control your father and I had over the company. We had a vision that I intend to realise, but I can't do it without major interference. And yes, if your grandmother were to interfere with the way the company is run, the share price would likely drop, which would indeed affect me financially."

It wouldn't affect me much, but I guess it would a little. Alyssa frowns at me and I can't help but want to take that frown away.

"I guess we'll have to get married," she murmurs, and my heart skips a beat. I look away and nod. I've never dared dream of marrying Alyssa. Hell, I never thought she'd even date me. But this is still incredibly anticlimactic. I stare out the window and sigh, wishing things were different. Wishing she'd give me an honest chance. I wish Charles had told me how he felt about the two of us. Maybe then I'd have dared to pursue her the way I've been wanting to.

"I guess there's only one thing left to do," I say. I walk up to Alyssa and drop down in front of her. She's so startled that she freezes, and I can't help but smile up at her. I grab her hand and look into her eyes, my heart racing.

"Alyssa Moriani, will you do me the honour of becoming my wife?" I ask, my voice soft but clear.

Alyssa inhales deeply and nods. I can barely believe this is even happening. Alyssa Moriani as my wife... it's my dream come true. I wish it were hers too.

Seventeen

"Are you sure you want to go through with this?" Mum asks me yet again. I glance at her and then at the empty church we're standing in, a frown on my face.

"Bit late, isn't it?"

Mum sighs and shakes her head. "It's never too late. You're a Devereaux, Daniel. You don't need to marry Alyssa if you don't want to. We'll find a way. We have a whole army of lawyers."

I shake my head and straighten my bow tie. I saw Dominic walk into the bridal room just a few minutes ago. Since he found out I'd be marrying Alyssa, he's been a bit weird. I guess it's finally sunk in that he's losing her, and I'm scared he's going to act on the feelings I know he has. He's good at deceiving himself, but he can't fool me. I see the way he looks at her when she isn't looking. He's managed to distract himself with Lucy, but that won't last. I can't figure out why he stays away from Alyssa, but I'm relieved as hell that he does. I'm worried he's about to stop doing that, though. Something about the look on his face when he walked into that room doesn't sit well with me. I sigh and glance at my mother.

"I want to do this, Mum," I tell her. "I *want* to marry Alyssa. I want to honour Charles's last wish."

She glances at me, her eyes filled with regret. She inhales deeply and nods. "Very well," she says. "I'd better go get your bride, then."

I watch her disappear into the bridal room, my heart racing. I can't believe I'm actually marrying Alyssa. I'm nervous as I wait for her, and I can't help but wonder what this church would look like if our marriage was a conventional one — if it were filled with friends and family. Even though our marriage isn't a real one, Mum insisted we got married in our family's church. I'm glad she asked this of us. I fear our wedding day would've felt too clinical if all we did was sign the papers.

The doors open and my heart skips a beat. Alyssa looks stunning. She isn't wearing a wedding dress like I'd hoped she would, but she *is* wearing a white dress. I smile at her, my heart racing, but it isn't me she's looking at.

Alyssa stares at Dominic, her broken heart reflected in her expression. She looks at him with so much hope that I can pretty much guess what she's thinking. She's hoping he'll stop her.

Dominic's eyes meet mine, and the hatred and helplessness in them startle me. I'm not sure what might have happened between them just now, but something certainly did.

Dominic and Alyssa pause right in front of me, and he hesitates, as though he can't bear to put her hand in mine. I take Alyssa's hand and Dominic stares at our joint hands with gritted teeth before turning and walking straight out of the church. Alyssa stares after him with so much anguish on her face that I know she'd go running after him if her father's shares weren't tying her to me. What the hell am I even doing? It's not me she wants... I should be finding a way for her to pursue her happiness instead of standing in the way of it.

Alyssa turns to look at me and I smile at her mockingly, my heart aching. I lean in, my lips brushing against her ear. "I guess that love wasn't as unrequited as I thought," I whisper.

Alyssa pulls her hand out of mine and glares up at me. She might as well have stabbed me in the heart. I had no illusions about my marriage with her, but fucking hell. I expected to at least have her attention on our wedding day. She stares somewhere over my shoulder the entire time, and when it's time to say *I do,* I have to nudge her. She seems startled and repeats after the priest in a completely monotone voice. It all feels so impersonal. I don't even get to hold her hand during our wedding ceremony, and I can't help but be filled with regret. I can't believe I did this to her, when I should've helped her find a solution to the challenge her father threw at us.

Her hands shake as she signs the marriage certificate, and for a second I wonder if she might actually burst into tears. I sign my own name next to hers, and it's done. Alyssa has officially become Mrs. Devereaux... just not quite the way I think she imagined it.

She's quiet on the drive home. There's distance between us that didn't used to be there, and I hate it. I park in front of her house, unsure what to say. I walk up to her front door and press my hand to the biometric scanner. The door swings open and Alyssa follows me in.

We both freeze when we hear chatter and laughter coming from her living room. We follow the sounds to find Alyssa's grandmother surrounded by some of the most influential women in London. I have no idea how she managed to get her claws into them, but I'll be damned if I let her use Alyssa's or DM's influence.

"Grandma," Alyssa says, sounding tired. She trembles slightly, and I know the expression in her eyes all too well. She looks so fucking helpless and defeated.

I grab my phone and text my security team, instructing them to book Alyssa's grandma a hotel and guard the house to prevent her from re-entering. This lady needs to go.

"You two look stunning. Did you attend some event today?" she asks, sounding peeved. I have no doubt she thinks she missed out on some sort of influential occasion she could've networked at. I place my hand on Alyssa's shoulder and smile at her — if you can even call it that.

"Mrs. Moriani, you're still here," I say. "I've booked you a room at the Shangri-La and a flight back to France in two days. My driver is waiting for you outside and will help you with your luggage."

She looks at me with wide eyes and then laughs. "Oh, there's no need. I'll be staying here for the foreseeable future. After all, Alyssa shouldn't be alone now. She'll need me."

The ladies surrounding her nod in agreement, and so do I. Alyssa, on the other hand, physically shudders. "Indeed. That's why she's coming home with me. As you're well aware, my younger brother is her best friend and my mother is as much of a mother figure to her as your son was a father figure to me. She indeed needs to be surrounded by people who know and love her. People she's used to."

Alyssa inches closer to me and looks up at me as though I'm her hero. I smile down at her while her grandmother rises from her seat. I speak before she gets a chance to talk her way into staying in Alyssa's house.

"As such, Alyssa won't be able to host you. Of course, if you wished, you could extend your stay here by finding a place to live or by extending your stay at the Shangri-La. I've already pre-paid your two nights there, but I'm sure you'll be able to extend that if you wished."

I then turn towards the ladies present and bow my head. "All of you lovely ladies, please accept my sincerest apologies for cutting your tea time short. Please allow me to make it up to you. If you give my secretary your contact details, I'll be sure to set up an afternoon tea appointment for next week, should your schedules permit it."

They all smile, none of them even remotely angry. If anything, they look excited about having tea with me. I fucking dread it, but it's a small price to pay for Alyssa's peace of mind.

I lean back against the wall as they all leave, one by one, until only Alyssa and I are left.

Eighteen

"Thank you, but I could've handled that myself, you know," Alyssa says.

I smile at her and stroke her hair, messing up her hairdo just a little. She pulls away from me in annoyance and tries her best to fix it. "Yes," I say. "But you don't have to."

Alyssa looks up at me gratefully and races up the stairs to collect whatever her grandmother might have left behind. She shows me all the stuff in her hands and shakes her head. "I knew she'd do this. I knew she'd find a way to get back into the house."

I grin at her as she hands the stuff over to her security staff. I walk over to her sofa and grab my phone to instruct my security team to deliver her grandma's stuff.

"Come and sit for a minute," I say. Alyssa nods and sits down so far away from me that another person easily could've sat between us. Is she that wary of me? I sigh and tug my bowtie off. Why the hell am I even wearing a tux anyway? It's not like this is a real marriage.

"I know I told your grandmother you'd be staying with us, but that was just to get her out of your house. If you'd like to stay here, then I can move in here."

I place a stack of documents that my security team just

handed me on the coffee table in front of us. It's every clause related to our marriage, and I know she recognises the papers at a glance.

Alyssa looks around the room, haunted by the memories of her dad.

"Would it be okay if we stay somewhere else for a little while?" she asks, and I nod. I know I said I'd stay here if she'd want me to, but I'm not sure I'd be okay either.

"Would you like us to stay with my mother or in my apartment?"

I'm hoping she'll choose to stay in my apartment, but I know she'd never do that. Not when being at my mother's house means being with Dominic.

"I'd like to stay with your mother."

A flash of disappointment strikes me and I inhale deeply. I know full well where I stand with her, so why do I do this to myself?

"Very well," I murmur. "We need to discuss the specifics of our marriage, though."

Alyssa nods uncomfortably.

"I'm happy to do this verbally, on a trust basis, but we can draw up a contract if you feel more comfortable with that."

Alyssa shakes her head. "I doubt that'll be necessary. We have an iron-clad prenup that protects both our assets. What more could we need?"

I nod in agreement, but before I get to respond, Alyssa interrupts. "I want our marriage to remain between us," she says. "I don't want it publicly announced and I don't want anyone to find out about it."

I stare at her in surprise. Somehow I didn't see that coming. She's legally my wife now, and while I didn't expect our marriage to be a traditional one, I did expect it to be public knowledge that's she mine.

"Very well. Nonetheless, there are some things I expect of you, and some things we must abide by per your father's requirements," I say, unable to deny her.

Alyssa nods for me to continue, and for just a second I lose myself in her beauty. My stunning wife doesn't want anyone knowing that she's married to me. Me, the guy that's been proclaimed the most eligible bachelor in London three years in a row. Oh, the irony.

"I'm happy to keep our marriage a secret, but this doesn't mean I'll condone cheating. As long as we're legally tied to each other, I expect you to be faithful to me, as I will be to you."

Alyssa frowns. "What? That's ridiculous. Do you seriously think you'll be able to keep it in your pants for three years? You're photographed with a different model every weekend."

My eyes roam over her body hungrily. Three years... she's right that I won't last for three years, but I have no intention of becoming celibate. I'm fully planning on seducing my wife. I tear my eyes away from her body with difficulty.

"Hmm. Nonetheless, I won't condone cheating, Alyssa."

I see the challenge in her eyes, and I just know she's about to say something ridiculous.

"How about we both do our own thing discreetly? After all, you need this marriage as much as I do."

She wants to fuck around on me? I don't need to guess to know who she intends to do that with. I'll be damned if I let her get away with cheating on me. I chuckle humourlessly and pin her down with a stare.

"That's where you're wrong, sweetheart. I'm a Devereaux. I never worked for DM Consultancy because I needed the money or the shares. That's not why I married you, either. I did it because I loved your father like he was my own. We Devereaux's have more than enough money to fund the next couple of generations comfortably."

Alyssa gulps uncomfortably, as though she's only just reminded of *who* I am. I cross my arms over each other and stare her down.

"Rule number one," I say. "We'll be faithful to each other. Defy that rule and I'll divorce you, shares be damned."

Alyssa nods reluctantly and indicates for me to continue.

"Rule number two. You'll keep an appropriate distance from Dominic. I don't want to hear any rumours about you two, or about any other men for that matter."

Alyssa laughs. "You're crazy if you think you can keep me away from my own best friend. I know you're ancient, but this isn't the Middle Ages. These days you don't get a say in your wife's life."

I grin at her. "Try me."

"You're an asshole, Daniel," she whispers.

I grin to hide that her words hurt and look away. "I said *an appropriate distance,* Alyssa. Be as close to him as you want to be, so long as you keep things appropriate."

"Very well," Alyssa says. "Rule number three is that we keep our marriage a secret. I don't want anyone to know beyond the people closest to us. If anyone needs to be told, I'd prefer that we discuss it beforehand. In three years we'll divorce, and I don't want to be known as your ex-wife for the rest of my life."

I nod. "The rest of the rules... we can make up as we go."

Nineteen

I sit down on my bed in my mother's house and look around in annoyance. I want to be in my own apartment. I want some peace and quiet… but this is where Alyssa wants to be, so this is where we'll stay for the time being. I glance at my closed bedroom door and sigh. To think I got married and won't even be sleeping in the same room as my *wife*.

I inhale deeply and reach for the letter on my nightstand. Vincent handed me two letters, one for me, and one for Alyssa. I recognised the handwriting on the envelope at a glance — it's Charles's. I put Alyssa's letter on her nightstand before dinner, and I imagine she's probably reading hers right about now. My hands tremble as I open the envelope addressed to me.

Hi Son,

I hope you won't ever have to read this letter, but if you do, then that means two things:

1. I'm no longer here, and I've had to leave Alyssa behind all by herself.

2. Congratulations are in order, because you honoured my wishes and married my daughter.

. . .

I bet Alyssa looked beautiful walking down that aisle. I wish I could've been there with her — with both of you. I know you'll take great care of her in my stead, Daniel. I know you'll make her happy.

I always knew how you felt about her, and I've always wished for you two to be together. Thank you for granting that wish. I know I acted selfishly, and I know I've put the two of you in a difficult situation. I've already asked so much of the both of you, yet I'd still like to ask you one more thing: please give your marriage with Alyssa an honest chance. Pursue her. Turn what you think of as a business arrangement into a real marriage.

I promise you, you won't regret trying. My baby girl might not realise it, but you're the one she reaches out to when life gets tough.

I doubt you've ever noticed it, and I doubt she has either, but the way she looks at you, Daniel... that's the way my beloved wife used to look at me; with unwavering faith and admiration. With time, you'll end up seeing love in those eyes too.

Please, Daniel. Please give your marriage a chance to succeed. I know no one will make my daughter happier than you will, and if you give her a chance, she'll make you just as happy.

Charles

I close my eyes as a wave of pure grief rolls over me. He knew about my feelings for her? I can't imagine what he was thinking, pushing us together like this. I'm not sure what he saw, but I'm certain Alyssa doesn't even find me attractive.

I fall back on my bed and stare up at the ceiling. I can't help but be a little hopeful. What if Charles is right? What if, with time, Alyssa might fall for me? I'm not sure I even dare hope for it.

I sigh and let my eyes flutter closed. The peace and quiet around me lasts only for a few moments. Even through my closed door, I can hear muffled moans. I can't believe Dominic is having sex on my wedding night when I'm not.

I grit my teeth and sit up. I can't believe my fucking brother. Is he seriously banging Lucy when he knows full well that Alyssa can hear them? She must've just read her father's letter. The last thing she needs is this bullshit on top of it. I can't even imagine how devastated she must feel. I fucking hate that she has feelings for Dominic, but I hate the idea of her hurting even more.

I walk up to her bedroom and drop my forehead to her door. I hesitate for only a couple of seconds before walking into her room. Alyssa sits up in bed and wipes the tears off her cheeks.

"I knew you'd be crying," I murmur.

I walk up to her and get into her bed wordlessly. I open up my arms for her, and she hugs me. I shift so her head is resting on my chest and Alyssa sniffs. It isn't until I feel her hair tickling my chest that I realise I probably should've put more clothes on before walking in here. I'm wearing nothing but my sleeping bottoms, but Alyssa doesn't seem to notice. I sigh and wipe away her tears. My eyes fall to the opened letter on her nightstand, and my heart twists painfully. I wonder what her letter said. Would Charles have asked her to give me a chance? And if so, will she?

"I'm sorry," I whisper.

She shifts in my arms and looks up at me. She's so close... I could so easily lean in and kiss my wife.

"It's not your fault," she says.

I look away in guilt. "I was the one who put the letter there. Vincent asked me to give it to you after the wedding, but maybe I should've... I don't know. Maybe I should've told him to do it himself. Maybe I should've given it to you personally. Maybe I should've just thrown that girl out so you wouldn't have to listen to this shit."

Alyssa snuggles into me and shakes her head. "It's not your fault, Daniel," she repeats.

She repositions herself so she's more comfortable, and I start counting back from two thousand. Her body is flush against mine, and her breasts feel amazing against my chest. She rests her hand on my chest as she listens to my heartbeat, and I wonder if she'll realise that she's making my heart race.

I gulp and shift away a little — just enough so she won't notice how fucking hard I am. I feel like such an asshole for getting turned on when all she wants from me is a hug, but I can't help it. I've done really well at resisting her or even thinking of her sexually. But fucking hell, when she's wrapped around me like this... I can't help but want her.

"Thank you," she whispers, and my guilt intensifies. I thread my hand through her hair and hold her tighter.

"Anytime, sweetheart," I whisper back.

I hug my wife to sleep like that. This isn't exactly how I'd imagine my wedding night to be, but at least we're in the same bed. At least we're falling asleep together. I'll take that for now.

Twenty

I stir, naturally waking up early in the morning. Alyssa is still fast asleep in my arms, her breathing deep and even. I tighten my grip on her, wanting to cherish this moment with her a little longer.

Alyssa stirs when I shift away from her, her eyes fluttering. For a second I worry I woke her up, but then she sighs and falls back asleep. I slip out of her bed carefully and make my way to my own room to freshen up and grab my tablet.

The entire house is dead silent; I love little moments like these. I walk to the kitchen to make myself a cup of coffee and decide to make breakfast while I'm at it. It's a Sunday, so the staff all have the day off. Usually Mum would make us breakfast, but since I'm up I might as well do it.

I work absentmindedly, not even realising when Lucy walks up to me, dressed in a skimpy nightgown. She really ought to cover up. I just about keep from rolling my eyes.

I've tried my best to avoid being alone with her since I found her in my bed. She somehow managed to convince Dominic that she was too drunk to realise I wasn't him. It sounds like bullshit to me, and it only further proves that Dominic doesn't really care that much about her. She's just a distraction, and she probably knows it.

"Hey," she murmurs.

I ignore her and start frying eggs. The rest of the house will wake up and join for breakfast soon enough. I wonder what this morning would be like if Alyssa and I had been at my apartment. Would it have felt a bit more intimate? I loved waking up with her, but it isn't enough. I want more of her. I want her to myself.

"I didn't know you could cook, Daniel. You're a man of many talents, huh?" Lucy says.

I sigh and flip the eggs in one fell swoop. I don't get why Lucy is even here. I can feel her eyes on my skin and I fucking hate it. What kind of girl checks out her boyfriend's *brother*?

I feel a hand on my lower back and turn around, infuriated. I can't believe she's trying to touch me again. How fucking shameless. I'm ready to lose my shit when I come face to face with Alyssa. She looks startled to see the anger on my face and takes a step away. I see the shock in her eyes and rush to reassure her.

"Oh, Alyssa," I murmur. "Sorry. I didn't realise it was you."

I brush her hair out of her face gently and smile at her. Unlike Lucy, she's wrapped up in a fluffy and appropriate robe, but I can't help but remember what she's wearing underneath. Her nightgown isn't much less revealing than Lucy's, and I didn't appreciate it enough last night.

Alyssa nods at me and hands me a bright pink apron. "Wear this. The oil might splash on you," she says, her eyes flashing with an emotion I can't quite place. She glances at Lucy, and I follow her gaze. Alyssa looks... possessive. I grin to myself and take the apron from her.

Her eyes roam over my body, pausing on my chest and my abs. She's never once looked at me this way. I've never seen lust in her eyes before. If she keeps looking at me that way, I'll end up giving her more of a view than she bargained for.

I put the apron on, and Alyssa sighs. I wonder if she realises how transparent she is. I fucking love this. Looks like I'm never wearing a tee around the house again.

"How come you're cooking today?" she asks.

"Sundays are family days, remember? Most of the staff have the day off. Usually my mum would've cooked, but I was up earlier so I thought I might as well."

Alyssa nods and helps me set the table as Mum and Dominic come walking in. The two of us ignore Lucy, and I can feel her gaze burning on my skin. Lucy does not cope well with being ignored, and it won't sit well with her that I treat Alyssa so differently. Lucy isn't my problem, though.

I notice Alyssa staring at Dominic, and I follow her gaze. Dominic is only wearing sleeping bottoms, just like me. Alyssa stares at his body, and I grit my teeth. The idea of her wanting him fucking guts me.

I take my apron off and throw it on the kitchen counter with more force than required, and Alyssa looks up at me. She bites down on her lip as her eyes drop to my abs and takes her seat, unable to tear her eyes away. It's dumb, but I'm instantly filled with relief. I want her eyes on me, and no one else.

I grin to myself and hide my smile in my coffee cup. The way she's looking at me right now... that isn't how she was looking at Dominic. When she looked at him, she seemed to be comparing him to me. My little brother works hard, but he isn't as ripped as I am. Looks like my wife is quite the fan of my muscles.

I glance at Dominic, but he's staring at Alyssa, when he should be stopping his girlfriend from eye fucking me. He clears his throat, and both Lucy and Alyssa look up at him, startled.

"I said have you settled in okay?" he snaps.

Alyssa's eyes widen and she nods. "Yes, thanks for asking," she says, flustered.

I cross my arms over each other and glance at her. "You might want to change rooms, though," I say. "There are plenty of other guest rooms, so just pick whichever one you want."

Alyssa's expression drops, and I see a brief flash of pain in her eyes, and I hate knowing I'm responsible for it. I shouldn't have reminded her of it at all.

"What? Why would you pick a new room? The room you're in has been yours since we were kids," Dominic says, confused.

I raise my brow and level him with a pointed stare. "You and your girlfriend kept us up most of the night with your little show."

Dominic blanches and looks at Alyssa, distraught. "You heard us?" he asks, looking down guiltily.

Alyssa looks away and takes a sip of her tea, clearly unsure how to reply. Dominic looks at me and frowns.

"But how did you... did you two... were you together?"

He looks jealous and possessive, and I want to wipe that look off his face. He had his shot with Alyssa, but he chose to be with a tramp like Lucy. The least he can do is be a good friend to Alyssa, but he can't even manage that.

"Alyssa lost her father and just moved into a new place. Her best friend, the one person she should've been able to count on, was too busy screwing his girlfriend to realise she shouldn't be left alone. Of course I was there to console her. The question is, why weren't you?"

Alyssa looks up at me in surprise, and I can pretty much guess what she's thinking. I know I told her to keep her distance from Dominic, but that doesn't mean I don't want them to be *friends*. It doesn't mean she doesn't deserve Dominic's loyalty.

"Did you know she read a letter last night that her father left her? You're so preoccupied with yourself that you haven't even taken the time to ask her if she's okay."

Dominic looks down in shame. "I'm sorry, Alyssa. He's right. I've been a terrible friend. Let me make it up to you."

Alyssa shakes her head, but I see the disappointment in her eyes. "It's fine, Nic," she says. "You had other things on your mind. I understand."

She looks heartbroken as she says it, and I can't understand why Dominic has been behaving this way. She looks up at him and tries her best to smile, but it comes out all wrong. I hate seeing her like this. I hate seeing her pine after my brother, and I hate seeing him hurt her.

One way or another, I'm going to make my wife mine.

Twenty-One

I walk out of my room to find Alyssa walking out of hers at the same time. I pause, surprised. She looks stunning. She's wearing a form-fitting dress that hugs her every curve, paired with heels that make her legs look sexy as hell.

"Where are you going?" I ask. Why is she so dressed up? She even straightened her hair, which she rarely does.

Alyssa looks away guiltily, and I already know I'm not going to like her answer. "Oh, Dominic and I are going out for ice cream," she says.

Ice cream? She's going on a fucking date with Dominic? I walk up to her and she automatically takes a step back, her back hitting her closed bedroom door. I put my forearm against the door and lean into her, almost caging her in with my body.

"You're going for ice cream dressed like *that*?"

Just one step closer, and I'll have her body pressed up against mine.

"Dressed like *what*?"

I chuckle and push her hair behind her ear with my free hand, truly caging her in. "Are you sure this is appropriate?" I whisper.

Alyssa bites down on her lip and looks up at me nervously. "Of course."

I scowl at her, unable to help myself. There's no way she doesn't realise that this is a goddamn date. There's no way that she doesn't know dressing up like that for another man is inappropriate.

"Daniel? Alyssa?"

Alyssa jumps at the sound of Lucy's voice and I pull away from her, both of us turning to Lucy, who's staring at us in shock. Her eyes flash with disbelief and irritation as she glances at Alyssa.

"Are you also joining us for ice cream, Daniel?" she asks.

I see Alyssa's expression crumble, and my initial annoyance melts away. It's obvious that she assumed it'd be just the two of them. She drops her head back against the door and closes her eyes, inhaling deeply. She looks so hurt that I'm willing to do anything to take her pain away, even though she's hurting over another man.

"No, I'm not," I tell Lucy. "Change of plans. I'm taking Alyssa out for dinner. Please let Dominic know she won't be joining you."

Lucy smiles and nods. "Oh, dinner sounds great! We'll come with you. We can always do dessert afterwards."

I chuckle and shake my head. "Yeah, no."

Alyssa bites back a smile, and I exhale in relief.

"What?" Lucy says, a confused look on her face. It's like she isn't used to people refusing her anything, and her expression amuses me.

I grab Alyssa's hand and pull her past Lucy. We walk past Dominic in the hallway, and I entwine my hand with Alyssa's. I wave at him with my free hand and grin. "Enjoy your date," I tell him. I pull Alyssa out the door before he has a chance to reply.

I'm oddly irritated. I knew how Alyssa feels about my brother when I married her, so why does it still hurt so much? Why do I suddenly feel so wronged? I know our marriage isn't a traditional one. Alyssa owes me nothing.

I'm quiet as I drive us to one of the hotels my family owns. It's got a beautiful rooftop restaurant that I think Alyssa will love. I wish I could take her here on a proper date. I wish she'd dress up for *me*.

Alyssa follows behind me quietly as we walk into the lobby. "Are you okay?" she asks as the lift doors close behind us. I glance up at her in surprise and nod.

"Yeah, fine. Just lost in thought, sorry."

The hostess smiles at us politely and asks us if we have a reservation. Alyssa shakes her head and seems disappointed. The restaurant is clearly fully booked, and it seems my wife forgot we own this entire hotel.

I hand the girl my black Devereaux Inc. card, and she stares at it blankly, clearly never having seen one before. She swipes it through the system, and her eyes widen. She looks up at me in shock and clears her throat.

"I didn't recognise you, Mr. Devereaux. Please forgive me," she says. She leads us to a small secluded table in the corner of the terrace.

I hand Alyssa my card as we sit down. She stares at it curiously and turns it over. There's nothing on it to indicate what exactly it is — it just looks like a regular credit card, with the Devereaux family crest on it in gold.

"What is this?" Alyssa asks.

"Put it away and keep it on you. It'll give you access to any facility owned by the Devereaux family. We always have at least one table for VVIPS at every one of our restaurants and at least one room in our hotels. It'll also give you discount at all the shopping centres and other stores owned by us. Every Devereaux has one of these cards. This one is currently registered to me, but I'll transfer it to you tonight."

Alyssa stares at it with wide eyes. "I had no idea something like this even existed. Dominic never told me about it. I've never seen him use it either."

I sigh. Her mind always returns to Dominic. "Hmm, yeah. I developed it a few months ago. *He* doesn't have one because I don't trust him with it. Probably didn't tell you because he's bitter as fuck about it. Last thing I need is that little asshole racking up bills everywhere and demanding superior treatment. He can have one when he finally grows the fuck up."

I can't contain my temper. I can't understand why he owns Alyssa's heart when he can't even sort his own life out. His grades are shit, he's always drinking or clubbing, and he refuses to learn anything about the family business. What does she even see in him? What does my little brother have that I don't?

Alyssa doesn't reply to my outburst and stares out the window instead. "Thank you. You didn't have to take me for dinner, you know," she says.

I smile at her and shake my head. "And let you sit through a night of Lucy and Dominic's PDA? I wouldn't wish that on anyone."

Alyssa laughs as I fill both of our champagne glasses. I raise my glass to hers and look into her eyes. "Here's to us," I say simply. We haven't even celebrated us getting married. I guess to Alyssa it probably isn't something worth celebrating at all.

"To us," she says as she clinks her glass against mine. I smile at her, my heart racing. Sitting here with her, I can almost make myself believe that this is a real date.

A waitress comes over to take our order and tells us about tonight's specials. Alyssa glares at her when she realises the waitress is checking me out. I can't help but grin to myself. My wife is getting possessive, and I love it.

I glance out the window, my mind drifting back to the way she looked when she realised Dominic was letting her down again tonight. I turn to look at her, and I can't help but ask.

"How long has it been?"

Alyssa frowns and tilts her head in question. "How long has what been?"

I look away and sigh. "How long have you been in love with Dominic?"

Twenty-Two

Alyssa freezes and stares at me in shock, as though she didn't expect me to ask the question.

"I — why do you ask?"

I shrug. "Just curious," I say, keeping all emotion out of my voice. It's becoming clear to me what she feels for him is more than a crush. I initially thought she might just think she's in love with him because they've been best friends all their lives, but it doesn't seem to be that. It looks like she's well and truly in love with my little brother.

"I don't even know, to be honest. I think I've always loved him. It was a very gradual thing."

I smile bitterly, my heart aching. I never stood a chance with her. I wonder what Charles was thinking. Alyssa would be so much happier if he'd asked her to marry Dominic instead. It's not me she wants, and he must have known that.

"What about you?" she asks. "Is there anyone you love?"

I pause and take a big sip of my champagne before nodding, deciding to be as honest as I can, given the circumstances. "Yeah, there's a girl. I'm not sure I'm in love with her, per se. But there's someone that I can't seem to get off my mind."

Alyssa smiles at me, but there's something in her eyes that gives me hope. There's just the tiniest bit of jealousy.

"How? I've seen the tabloids and the photos that get stuck on your office door. You make it in there almost every week, photographed with one model or the other, and that's been ongoing for as long as I can remember."

I laugh. I always knew that damn tradition would come back to bite me in the ass someday. I should've nipped it in the bud the first time around.

"It's complicated. That girl wasn't available. I couldn't pursue her," I say somewhat cryptically. I'm not even sure Alyssa is available now. She's married to me, but it doesn't seem like her heart is even remotely available.

"*Wasn't*?" she repeats, an edge to her tone that wasn't there before.

I nod and smile at her, my heart fluttering a little. It seems like she doesn't like the idea of me with someone else. I hope I'm not reading too much into this. "Yeah. I think I might have a shot now, but like I said, it's complicated."

Alyssa tenses and glares at me. "Yes. And you're *married*."

I grin to myself and look away. I wasn't wrong. She's being possessive. I look up as the waitress brings over our meal. She sets it down in front of us. Alyssa waits until she leaves before probing further.

"How long has that been a thing?" she asks, sounding annoyed.

I take a bite of my fish, not wanting to go too much into this. It's *her* I'm talking about, after all. This is getting out of hand, fast.

Alyssa stares me down as I chew my food, and I know she isn't going to let this go. "A couple of years. Since around the time I did my MBA, I guess."

Alyssa's expression crumbles, and I look at her in surprise.

"That was four years ago. Quite some time to hold a torch for someone," she says, her tone sharp. The way she looks at me makes my heart soar. I'm a fucking loser, but fuck it. I want all she'll give me, even if it's merely possessiveness.

"Who is she?"

I can see the gears in her mind working, and I know I need to cut this conversation short. I know what Alyssa is like. She's going to try to figure out who it is, which will only complicate matters more. I smile tightly, hoping she'll just drop the topic.

"Well, if you want to pursue her, I won't stand in your way. If you've waited four years for her, then I won't make you wait another three years until we divorce."

Hmm, will she now? She looks jealous and possessive, yet she still claims she's fine with me being with someone else.

"Is that so?"

I see a flash of panic in her eyes and try my best not to smile. This girl. She thought I wouldn't take her up on the offer. I doubt she even realised she *isn't* okay with it until now.

"I... Well... Yeah. If that's what you want, it's fine by me," she says, but her expression says the exact opposite. She grabs her glass and empties it, clearly angry.

"Hmm. There's no need. If she's the one for me, then she'll still be there in three years," I tell her, unable to help myself.

Alyssa laughs. "You believe in fate?" she asks, shocked. It isn't fate per se, but our marriage is going to last for three years. If things work out between us, we won't be getting divorced, and she won't be going anywhere. I merely shrug at her.

Alyssa shakes her head. "You're crazy. Life waits for no one."

I lean in and smile at her. "I'll make you a bet. If I propose within the next four years and she says yes, then you'll owe me a new Aston Martin. It'll have to be whichever model has just come out. If you win, I'll buy you an apartment the equivalent of the Aston."

If I'm lucky, we'll be laughing about this bet three years from now. Alyssa grins and shakes my hand. "That's a deal, Daniel. I'll start looking at apartments," she says confidently.

I shake my head and smile at her, my heart racing. She's just so bloody stunning, sitting here, looking at me with those beautiful twinkling eyes.

"You should come back to work soon, Lyss."

Alyssa looks down and nods. She hasn't been in the office since her father passed away, but it's been over a month now. She can't stay on leave forever. I know it's hard on her, but she can't keep avoiding the office. It'll be good for her to get back to work, and I've missed her at work. Not just because she's so good at what she does — I've just genuinely missed seeing her there. It's the one place that's just ours. It's the one place she shares only with me, and not with Dominic.

Twenty-Three

I stare at Jake in annoyance. Luckily for him and unfortunately for me, I owe his father a favour. There's no way he'd have gotten into DM otherwise.

"I'm excited about this opportunity," he tells me, smiling so wide that I've gotta wonder if he's hurting his cheeks. I nod at him and let Kate take over. No way in hell I'm gonna onboard a rookie myself.

I glance at my watch impatiently. Today is meant to be Alyssa's first day back. I wanted to drive her to work, but I had a much earlier start than she did. I walk out of my office impatiently, relieved when I find her in her cubicle.

Jake and Kate follow behind me, and Alyssa's eyes flash with recognition. Something about the way she looks at Jake isn't quite right.

"Alyssa," I say. "Meet Jake, your new colleague."

She stiffens and stares at him in disbelief. The way she looks at him has my hackles raised. I turn to Jake and hand him a stack of documents. "Alyssa will be your senior and mentor from now on. She'll help you get started and she'll be the one you can reach out to if you have any questions."

Jake and Alyssa stare at each other, and I suddenly feel uncomfortable.

"Alyssa," Jake says eventually. "I didn't know you worked here. The executive programme, as well. You've done surprisingly well for yourself."

I frown at him. What a goddamn idiot. He clearly doesn't know her as well as I feared if he doesn't realise she's the company's largest shareholder. I glance at her and raise my brow.

"You two know each other?"

She sighs and nods, looking embarrassed. Jake answers my question before Alyssa has a chance.

"Yes, we attended the same university. We dated for a while," he says.

I look at Alyssa coldly and grit my teeth. "Hmm, really now?" I say, my voice low. Trust me to hire my wife's ex. Fucking hell. My luck is so bloody rotten. I hire my own goddamn competition. I stare at Jake and shake my head. He's tall, but he's thin. His physique is just slightly shittier than Dominic's. Is that her type?

Alyssa nods at me and smiles. "We broke up because he said I'd never be good enough for his rich family," she tells me, a mischievous grin on her face. I look at her in disbelief and burst out laughing. Jake's entire family doesn't have shit on Alyssa's personal net worth.

"Must not have been that serious then," I murmur, pleased. I tip my head towards my office and indicate for her to follow me. "Join me in my office for a minute, Alyssa."

She follows me in but pauses at the threshold, her eyes glued to her father's empty desk. I haven't had the heart to move anything, but I should've known seeing it would be tough on her. She visibly tries to pull herself together and pastes a smile on her face. I want to ask her if she's okay, but I have a feeling what she needs right now is for me to ignore her moment of grief.

I walk to my desk and shake my head. "That guy?" I murmur. "Really?"

Alyssa rolls her eyes and stands beside my desk. "Don't judge. I've seen some of the girls you've been with."

I lean back in my chair and shake my head. "No, Lyss," I say. "You've seen some of the girls I've been *photographed* with."

She blinks in surprise, and I push a folder her way before she can overthink it. "Luxe. One of our oldest clients. Out of everyone, they are the one client I thought would stick with us, no matter what. But now they're threatening to terminate our contract after we deliver the new packaging designs and our proposed marketing strategy, unless we give them twenty-five percent discount. They're saying they don't have faith in us without your father here."

Alyssa shakes her head. "Impossible. We need them to let us implement the marketing strategy. We can't afford to give them more discount because we're barely making any money on them as it is. If we give them more discount, that'll set a precedent I'm not comfortable with."

I nod at her, pleased with her quick thinking. "Exactly. Can you handle this?"

She looks unsure, but I know she's got this. My eyes drop to Charles's desk, and I run a hand through my hair. Luxe never would've considered leaving us had Charles still been here. He *was* DM, and I'm not sure I can fill his shoes.

"Are you doing okay?" Alyssa asks, sounding worried. She turns to look at her father's desk and sighs. "We can remove the desk, you know. You shouldn't leave this all here. I can pack it all up. Looking at it all day will just be hard for both of us."

I shake my head. There's no way I could do it without falling apart, so Alyssa definitely won't be able to do it either. "Hmm... I'll get someone to do it this weekend. I don't think it's something you or I are ready to do so soon, but it needs to be done."

"Okay, all right," she whispers. She takes a step closer to me and combs through my hair with her fingers, carefully straightening out the mess I made of it. I look up at her in shock. This has gotta be the first time she's reached out to touch me spontaneously. She catches me staring and her eyes widen. She pulls her hand away and cradles it.

"Oh, I'm so sorry, Daniel. I didn't mean to..."

She looks mortified, and I don't even know how to reassure her. I shake my head and smile at her. "It's fine. I don't mind. Thanks for fixing my hair."

She looks at me, her cheeks tinged pink, and steps away. She clears her throat awkwardly and turns to leave. "I'd better get back to work," she murmurs, all but running out of my office.

I grin to myself as she walks out. In the last couple of days, we've gotten slightly more intimate. Every once in a while I'll throw my arm around her shoulder at home, or I'll play with her hair when we're sitting on the sofa. They seem like small changes, but it's like day and night for us — we only ever used to interact with each other in a polite and distant way.

I'd hoped to spend more time with Alyssa while at work, but we're both too busy to have a second together. Having to do Charles's job all of a sudden has been tough as fuck.

The sun has already set by the time Alyssa walks back into my office. I check my watch and indicate for her to take a seat while I finish up my client call, but she walks to my window instead.

"I think they're bluffing," she tells me. "I've gone over the data and calculations over and over again. None of our competitors can afford to give Luxe the rates we do. I'm eighty percent sure they're bluffing."

I turn to face her and nod. "I agree."

She fidgets with the hem of her dress as she works up the courage to ask me something. It's cute, but I kinda wish she were more comfortable with me, and more confident in herself. She's not a regular employee, and she never will be. I want her to act like she's on equal footing to me, because in my eyes she is. I guess it'll take her a bit longer to get there, though.

"Would it be okay if I request a meeting with them?" she asks, her voice soft.

I tilt my head in question and look into her eyes, curious what she has in mind.

"I want to talk to them in person. Remind them of the relationship they had with my dad and how much of a betrayal it is for them to do this to us right now. I'm a Moriani, after all."

I smile at her and nod. She's not just a Moriani. She's a Devereaux, too. My wife is a fucking powerhouse. "That might just do the trick. Have your asshole ex sign an NDA and bring him with you."

She hesitates. "Are you sure?"

I nod. Alyssa has always used her mother's maiden name at school and at work in an effort to fit in better. I have no doubt the little shit has no idea who she is — there's no way he'd have told my girl that she isn't good enough for his family, otherwise. It's about time he finds out who Alyssa really is.

Twenty-Four

Kate stares into space, and I wave my hand in front of her face. "You okay?" I ask, my voice soft. She's been out of it all day, and I can't quite figure out what's wrong with her. Kate looks up at me and smiles, but her eyes betray her.

"I'm fine," she says, her voice shaky. I sigh and lean against her desk, brows raised. Kate runs a hand through her hair and shakes her head.

"My best friend's dad... he's sick. I guess it's unfair to even say that she's my best friend. I haven't spoken to her in ten years. She's one of the reasons I came here, you know? She's one of the reasons I accepted the job here in London. She lives here. She moved here ten years ago, and it was all because of me. It's complicated, I guess."

I smile down at her and nod. "Emilia," I murmur. "Emilia Parker, right?"

Kate looks up at me in surprise, and I smile to myself. How could I not know about the girl Carter talks about every single time he gets drunk? I didn't realise it'd been ten years. He speaks of her as if their break-up was a recent thing.

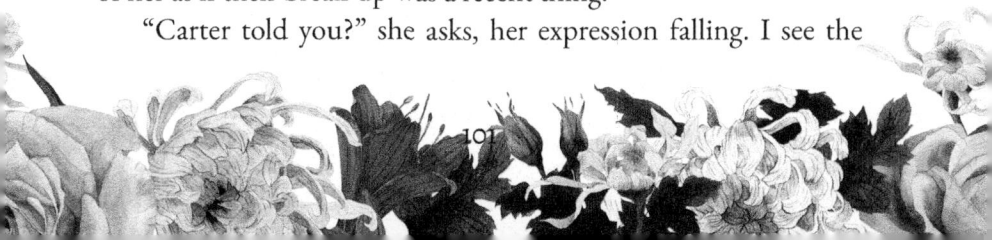

"Carter told you?" she asks, her expression falling. I see the worry and humiliation in her eyes and shake my head. I know there's a story there, but it's not my place to pry.

"He hasn't told me much. He just talks about her whenever he's drunk. I kind of got the gist of it."

Kate inhales deeply and nods. "I came here thinking I'd be able to right my wrongs, but I did none of that. I didn't even have the guts to apologise to her. In the end, all I did was run away yet again. Even worse, I managed to get married and divorced, when I was supposed to come here to try and make up for everything I've done. Instead of doing that, I ended up fucking up my life even more, and I just disappointed everyone else around me yet again. I guess today is one of those days; my lawyer just called me to tell me my divorce has officially gone through."

I don't know much about Kate's marriage, but from what I gathered, she was indeed running away from her past. It seems like she thought getting married might give her the new start she needed.

"Kate, change doesn't happen overnight. I'm not a hundred percent sure what happened, but I can tell you you're doing great. You make running this office a breeze, and I couldn't function without you. You've done very well for yourself. Hell, you've got an MBA. Your past is what it is, but your future is unwritten. You're not who you used to be. The Kate I know is incredibly hardworking and clever, and definitely someone to be proud of. If you have regrets, you need to just push aside your fears and do what needs to be done. Either that, or live with your regrets."

She nods thoughtfully and looks down. "I want to be there for her and repay her for everything she's done for me and my family, but I don't know how."

I smile at her. "Your heart is in the right place, so I'm sure you'll find a way. I'll be here for you if you ever need help."

She grins at me and shakes her head. "I'm sorry. I'm fine, really. Honestly, tonight I just want to celebrate officially getting divorced. I think that's already a step in the right direction."

I nod and glance at my phone. "There's a bonfire tonight. I attend every year. Would you like to come with me?"

Her eyes widen. "Shut up," she says. "*The* bonfire?"

I chuckle and nod at her. The bonfire is famous, and it isn't actually just a bonfire. It started as one, but it slowly turned into an event with live music, food stalls and plenty of games to play. The location is kept secret, and invitations are scarce. I've been looking forward to attending with Alyssa.

I text Kate the details and rush home to change. Alyssa and I haven't hung out in a while. I'm really looking forward to tonight.

By the time I'm done changing, Alyssa still isn't home. I know she's got her meeting today with Luxe, and it looks like it's taking longer than expected. I sit down on the sofa, opposite Lucy and Dominic. I'd usually never voluntarily spend time with the two of them — particularly Lucy, but the bonfire is special. I wouldn't miss it for the world.

"God, why is she so late?" Lucy asks, annoyed. "Can't we just go and ask her to meet us there?"

I don't even look up at her. Every single thing that comes out of her mouth irritates me. I exhale in relief when Alyssa walks in. I'm not sure how much more of Lucy's bullshit I can handle.

Dominic looks up at her, and I don't appreciate the way his eyes roam over her body. "Alyssa, you're home," he says, waving her over.

She walks over to us and sits down next to me, her thigh grazing mine. She leans into me and I wrap my arm around her shoulder. "How was work?"

I smile on her face tells me she managed to accomplish what I couldn't, just like I knew she would.

"It was fine. They'll pay full price, but we need to move the timeline up and deliver sooner. Liam said they'll sign the implementation contract this week."

I look at her in disbelief. "You're kidding me."

Alyssa shakes her head, her eyes sparkling with pride.

"Liam *Evans*?" Dominic asks, sitting up. He pulls away from

Lucy and looks at Alyssa through narrowed eyes. She nods and Dominic rolls his eyes. "That guy has had a hard-on for you for years. If you told him you wanted to *raise* the price, he probably would've agreed. Let me guess. He asked you on a date in return?"

I tense, my grip on her shoulder tightening. Liam is a nice guy, good-looking too. And my wife... she's breathtaking. I can't even blame the guy for wanting to make a move. No, my issue is with Alyssa. She promised me fidelity.

"Did he ask you out?" I ask, my voice harsh. Alyssa freezes, and I have my answer.

"Yeah. We should probably discuss that later," she whispers. She glances at Lucy, who's staring at us with interest, and then looks away.

"Holy shit," Lucy whispers. "Liam Evans is wicked hot. I hope you said yes to that."

I know she said yes. If she hadn't, she would've just told me so immediately. Dominic glares at Lucy and she looks at him sheepishly. Alyssa rises as though she wants to escape to her bedroom, but Lucy stops her.

"Wear a cute dress," Lucy says. Alyssa stares at her blankly. "Tonight is the annual bonfire, remember?"

Alyssa sighs and nods, clearly only just remembering. I can't believe I've been looking forward to spending time with her tonight, and she completely forgot we were even going to the bonfire together. On top of that, she agreed to go on a date with fucking Liam Evans. I'm sick and tired of this shit. I'm sick and tired of the way I feel about her. She's dated fucking Jake, she's in love with Dominic, and she's agreed to a date with Liam. It's just me who doesn't stand a fucking chance with her.

Twenty-Five

My entire mood is ruined. I need to knock it off with this bullshit. Alyssa and I have been married for almost three months now, and we still aren't any closer. I'm still pining after someone that has no interest in me. It's stupid.

Alyssa sits next to me in the car, but it's Dominic she's focused on. It's him she's chatting and laughing with. I'm such a fucking fool. How long am I going to kid myself?

I grab my phone and text Kate to make sure she's en route. Once we get there, the cell reception is going to be rubbish. If I don't find her before we go in, I won't find her at all.

Alyssa glances over at me curiously, but she doesn't say anything. She looks amazing tonight, but this time it just pisses me off. I'm mad at myself for feeling the way I do, when she clearly doesn't even remotely feel the same way.

I jump out the car and walk to the beach without waiting for the rest of our group. It's not like they'll miss me anyway. I need some space. I need distance from Alyssa.

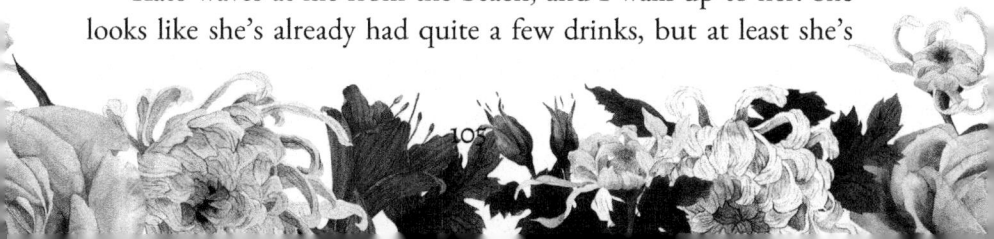

Kate waves at me from the beach, and I walk up to her. She looks like she's already had quite a few drinks, but at least she's smiling. She looked so crestfallen this afternoon that I was tempted to call Carter and let him know.

"Daniel!" she yells. I smile at her, and she hugs me when I reach her. "Ugh, it's even better than I expected. This is so cool."

I smile at her indulgently, just as Alyssa's voice sounds behind me. "Kate?" she says, sounding shocked.

Kate turns around and smiles at Alyssa. "Hey, Alyssa! I didn't know you'd be here too."

She walks over to Alyssa and hugs her. "Did the boss invite you too?" she asks.

Alyssa looks at me, and I can't quite decipher her expression. "No, I've attended for years. I was invited."

Kate looks around in amazement, her eyes twinkling. "It's even better than I imagined. I haven't been out in forever. Now that my divorce has finally come through, I'm so ready to just celebrate and let loose."

"Divorce?" Alyssa repeats. "I didn't know. Congrats, I guess?"

Kate laughs. "Congrats indeed, thank you."

Kate grabs my arm and looks up at me with excitement. "They have cotton candy, should we get some?"

She looks so much more upbeat than she did earlier this afternoon. I nod at her indulgently and let her drag me off. Much to my surprise, Alyssa follows. I don't even notice her standing behind us until I've handed over a cotton candy stick to Kate. I thought for sure that she'd cling to Dominic instead. I can't figure out why she's with me, instead. Did she lose him or something? Alyssa keeps giving me mixed signals. Sometimes she'll act possessive and she'll make me think she might want me. But then other times she'll try to go on an ice cream date with Dominic or she'll agree to go on a date with Liam, even though she promised me fidelity. I'm tired of being jerked around. I can't even be mad about it, though. She owes me nothing. I don't want to ever knowingly stand in the way of her happiness, and I'm starting to feel like that's exactly what I've been doing.

"God, this reminds me of that time we went to the carnival in

San Fran. Except they had that pretty blue and pink cotton candy, remember?" Kate says.

I smile at the memory. That's the first time I saw Carter wasted, and it's the first time I heard all about Emilia Parker. I tear off a piece of cotton candy and grin to myself.

"When did you go to San Francisco together?" Alyssa asks, her tone sharp. I can't figure her out. It's like she doesn't want me, but she doesn't want me to be with anyone else either.

"Ah, we did our MBA together at Stanford. That's how we met. Didn't you know? Daniel offered me a job as his executive assistant when we finished. We keep things professional at work but we usually manage to hang out every couple of weeks at least."

Alyssa looks shocked and takes a step back. My first instinct is to reassure her; to prevent her from overthinking anything. But I resist. I need to stop offering her things she hasn't asked for. She doesn't need my explanations. Hell, she probably doesn't even need or want my loyalty and fidelity.

Alyssa looks at me, her eyes flashing with anger. "Guess I'll be buying you that Aston Martin, after all," she snaps.

I look at her with wide eyes, and it all clicks. Alyssa grits her teeth and storms off. I run a hand through my hair and inhale deeply. That fucking bet. I guess she's taking it serious. I can't believe she still remembers what I told her.

"Okay, what just happened?" Kate asks, confused. I groan and stare up at the starry sky.

"My wife thinks I'm in love with you, or some shit."

Kate looks at me, shell-shocked. "Wait, what? Your *what*?"

I shake my head. "Alyssa is misunderstanding something, and honestly, I don't know if explaining things to her is even worth it. I'm not sure if she actually cares, or if she's just being territorial."

Kate just blinks at me. "You're married... to *Alyssa*?"

I nod. "It's complicated, to say the least. We're keeping it a secret, and our marriage is... not traditional. I shouldn't have said anything. Honestly, just act like you don't know."

I inhale deeply and pull my fingers through my hair. "Look,

Kate. I'm sorry, but I really want to go home. Do you think you'll be okay? I can find my younger brother for you, if you want?"

She shakes her head and waves me off. "I'm fine! Go on ahead. I have Dominic's number if I need anything. Don't worry. Thank you for inviting me. But seriously, you should go after Alyssa. She seemed pretty mad."

I glance down at my feet and shake my head. "It's not me she wants," I tell Kate honestly. I hate seeing the pity in her eyes as I walk away. I need to stop doing this to myself. There are plenty of women, why did it have to be Alyssa I fell for?

I hop into a taxi and give the driver my apartment's address instead of my mum's. I need some actual space. I want to be in my own home for a little while. Away from Alyssa. For just a little while, I want to put myself first. I'll go crazy if I keep going the way I am now.

Twenty-Six

I've been on edge all day. Alyssa has been behaving erratically and her mood has been terrible, but no one at the office has any idea why.

I glance at Kate and frown. "You know what's going on?"

Kate shakes her head. "No idea. She was already pissed off when she walked in. I guess something must've happened last weekend? Did you do something?"

I purse my lips and shake my head. I'm willing to bet it's because she was stuck with Dominic and Lucy all weekend. Their PDA is over the top, and I'm sure it would've made her uncomfortable. I guess it might've hurt her too. Usually I'm there to distract her from all that, but this time I stayed away. I spent all weekend at my apartment, going back to my mother's house only to sleep.

I sigh and try my best to focus on work. I can't keep worrying about Alyssa. I can't keep giving her so much of my attention when she won't give me any of hers. I shuffle through my documents and frown before walking out of my office again.

"Alyssa, I asked you for the info on Takuya. Why is not on my desk yet?" I ask, my annoyance rising.

She lifts her head and twists her desk chair towards me. "You asked for it *fifteen minutes* ago, Daniel. Do I look like a robot to you?"

I can't help but glare at her. She's been on edge all morning, when none of us have done anything to deserve her wrath. "I didn't ask for sass. I asked you to do your damn job. I should've had it on my desk five minutes ago."

I walk back to my office and slam the door closed. This fucking girl. She gets under my skin so easily. She drives me fucking insane.

Twenty minutes later Jake walks into my office, the report in his hands. Why the fuck isn't Alyssa bringing this to me herself? Is she avoiding me now? I grit my teeth and cross my arms over each other.

"Executive summary," I bark out. Jake stands there and blinks at me blankly, before glancing down to read the report.

"Just get out," I tell him. "If you can't even give me a summary of a report you just helped write, then why the fuck are you standing in my office?"

I run a hand through my hair, messing it up entirely, and walk out behind him. "Alyssa!" I shout before walking back in.

She follows me in and closes the door behind her. "You called for me?" she says, her voice monotone.

I lean back beside the window, barely able to control my temper. I'm so done with everything. I'm done with her shitty attitude, and I'm done with my feelings for her. I was stupid to believe Charles might have been right.

"Explain to me why Takuya is threatening not to sign with us after all the effort we went through."

She looks at me in annoyance and clears her throat. "Their R&D is through the roof and they have nothing to show for it. Their profitability has been decreasing every quarter since Mr. Takuya's son took over. Looks like they'll run into liquidity issues soon. They need us to save their company. They definitely won't be able to do it themselves. We just need to convince them they need us. I suggest going in person. The issue will be more that Mr. Takuya's son won't want to admit to his failings, and he probably knows hiring us will result in that."

She walks up to my desk, and I follow her. She turns just as I reach her and takes a step back, her hips banging against my desk. I lean in against the desk and cage her in, my arms on either side of her.

She looks startled and the expression in her eyes changes. "What are you doing?" she whispers.

"Tell me why you've been so mean to me all morning," I reply.

She places her hands against my chest and I expected her to push me away, but instead she slides her palms up to my shoulders. "I'm not being mean."

We stand together like that, our bodies so close that just a single step would have her body pressed against mine. "You are. What's got you so worked up?"

Alyssa shakes her head and grabs my tie, straightening it out. She looks at me, and then her eyes drop to my lips. My heart starts to race, and for just a second, I wonder what she might do if I lean in and kiss her.

"It's nothing. I'm sorry. I didn't realise I wasn't behaving professionally, but then neither are you," she says.

I raise my brows and look at her, genuinely confused. What the hell have *I* done?

"You keep smiling at Kate and she keeps giggling at you. Do you think flirting at the office is appropriate?" she says, her tone harsh.

My eyes widen and I just about keep myself from smiling. She's jealous? I guess she's still got that damn bet on her mind. I know she feels possessive every once in a while, but this seems like it might be more.

"I've been treating her the same way I always have," I murmur. I take a step closer to her, closing the remaining distance between us. Her body feels amazing against mine. I love the way her breasts feel pressed up against me, and I wish I could just kiss her.

"So you've always been flirting with her and I only just noticed? No wonder you said you didn't need to amend our rules to win the bet."

I thread a hand through her hair and shake my head. What if I tilt her head and lower my lips to hers?

"I'm not flirting with her, Alyssa. It's just friendly banter." She laughs humourlessly and tries to pull her hair away, but I won't let her. "Speaking of our rules. Sounds like you had a great time with Liam Evans."

Alyssa glares at me. "It was for work. It wasn't even just the two of us. Jake was there too."

I smile at her humourlessly, wanting to call her on her bullshit. "Yeah, but you agreed to go out with him again, didn't you? How are you going to accomplish that while still abiding by our rules?"

Alyssa pushes me away and walks to the window and I join her. "The same way you seem to be getting away with it. Asking Kate to the bonfire. Letting her put her arm around yours and sharing cotton candy? All the while making it obvious that your own *wife* is the third wheel. If you can do that, then why can't I? Seems like your definition of not cheating is just not having sex with someone else. I'm pretty sure I can manage that."

I can't help but be a little amused at her jealousy. Every time I'm ready to give up on her, she does something like this. Every time I'm ready to let her go, she goes and gives me *hope*.

"Come to think of it. Where the hell have you been all weekend?" she snaps.

I bite down on my lip to hide my smile and slip my hand in my pocket to take out my wallet.

"I've been at home, sweetheart. In my own home. My apartment. Being at my mum's is overwhelming at times. I needed a bit of rest and some time to clear my mind. I came back to sleep at my mum's so we don't breach the terms of the will. We can only stay away from each other a total of fifteen nights a year, so it's best if we keep those for emergencies."

I hand her a keycard to my apartment. "You can keep this. It's the access card for the building. The entrance to the apartment itself is through biometrics. Security is the same firm as your house and the Devereaux mansion, so I asked them to transfer your existing biometrics to my apartment as well."

Alyssa looks at me through narrowed eyes. "Were you alone?" she asks, sounding angry. The idea of me being with someone else pisses her off, huh?

I nod and brush a strand of her hair behind her ear before cupping her face gently. "Yep. You can check the guest log if you don't believe me. There are cameras by the entrance as well. I registered your name to my residence so you're formally a co-habitant of my apartment. You have access to all the same security feeds that I have access to."

The relief in her eyes is clear as day. She relaxes and leans into my hand, and I move closer to her. I slide my hand over her skin until I'm holding the back of her neck.

"I didn't realise living at your mother's house would be tough on you. I guess it makes sense. You haven't called it home in so long. Maybe we should stay at your apartment during weekdays at least? It's closer to the office, anyway. We could stay at your mum's on the weekends."

I look at her gratefully and nod. "I'd really appreciate that, Alyssa. Let's give that a try, and if you're not comfortable there, we'll move back."

She nods and clears her throat, hesitating before she speaks. "I think we should add some more details to the rules. Cheating from now on includes anything ranging from flirting to sleeping with someone else."

I grin and look away. My jealous little wife is cute as hell. I thought she couldn't care less about me, but if she gets this jealous about me inviting a co-worker to a huge event that we were attending as a group, then she must care at least a little. Maybe even more than a little.

"Very well. If you say so, Wifey. Those rules apply to you too, though."

Alyssa blushes at the endearment I use, and I love the way she's looking at me. "I evaded Liam's request by saying he couldn't ask me out while he's got a contract over my head, but it's been signed now and he asked me to go celebrate with him. I thought of saying I'm seeing someone... but if in a few months I'm clearly not dating, then he'll just think I was lying all along."

I take a step closer to her and press my body flush against hers. I look into her eyes and tilt my head, my lips hovering over hers. "So just date me, wife," I whisper.

Alyssa bites down on her lip and looks away. She takes a step back and gulps. "I — I guess we can think about our options when the time comes," she stammers.

"Hmm, yeah. Think about that, Alyssa."

Twenty-Seven

I'm surprisingly nervous as Alyssa and I step into the lift in my building. I'm worried she won't like it, or she won't feel comfortable. I'm worried she'll want to move back, and I really don't want that. I think I might actually have a shot with her, especially if we're living together, just the two of us.

The lift doors open right into my foyer, and we step out. Half our luggage has already been sent up by my security team and is stacked neatly against the wall.

"I love it. No wonder you missed this place so much," Alyssa says, genuinely looking impressed.

I show her the living room and she sighs in delight. It's probably one of my favourite places too. There's so much natural light coming in that the space looks even bigger than it is. An entire corner of the room is made of glass, overlooking a magnificent skyline, and the kitchen is open plan.

Alyssa walks around curiously, touching this and that, and I can't help but smile. I was worried for nothing. She seems to like my home just fine.

"There is one guest room that my mother usually uses, but you can have that one now. Unless you prefer the master bedroom?"

I show her my guest room, and she peeks into it. The room was done up by my Mum, and it's entirely her style. It doesn't at all fit in with the rest of my house either. The wooden bed frame and the daisies on the bedsheets don't match the modern décor, but it's so her.

I walk past the guest room, and Alyssa follows me. "This is my bedroom. I think you might be more comfortable in here, so you're welcome to have it."

I walk into my bedroom and sit down on my bed while Alyssa takes in my room. Her eyes are sparkling as she stares at the skyline. One of my bedroom walls is made entirely out of glass, and she seems to love it as much as I do.

"God, I can see why you'd miss this place. It's wonderful. I wouldn't dare take your room though. I'm happy with the guest room, but I may have to sneak into your jacuzzi one night."

I immediately think of her all wet and naked in my jacuzzi, her body covered with bubbles. I'd give the fucking world to see that.

"I — I mean... when you're not there, I mean."

I smile and shake my head. "You're welcome to use anything here, my bathroom included. We're married, Alyssa. This place is yours as much as it is mine."

"How many of the staff have access to this place?" she asks.

"Not many. Two designated security officers, one housekeeper and a cook. The housekeeper comes once a day, and the cook comes whenever I ask her to. It's up to you when you want them to come. Would you prefer for us to do our own cooking?"

Alyssa nods, and her expression softens. I know she's thinking about the dinners she used to cook with her dad. Charles never missed dinner with her, even if it meant he had to work overtime in his home office. I'd often crash their dinners, and I miss it as much as she does.

"Maybe we can just cook ourselves a few times a week? If you don't want to, then I can do the cooking?"

I smile and walk up to her. I cup her cheek gently and nod. "Of course. I'd be happy to do that. Though you have to promise you'll make it home for dinner every day like you did with your dad. I'll do the same. If we have to work overtime, then I have a big enough home office to facilitate us both. I'll get you a desk chair so we can share my desk."

She looks at me, her expression so grateful that I almost can't resist. I really want to kiss her.

"Yes, of course. I promise."

She looks away and takes a step back. "I — I'll go unpack," she says, flustered. She rushes out of my room and I chuckle. So she's affected by me, huh?

She stays hidden in her room for hours. By the time she finally walks out again, she's in a thick fluffy robe. She walks towards the sofa and smiles at me.

"You changed."

She looks down at her outfit and nods before looking at me. I showered and changed into pyjama bottoms and a tee, and her eyes linger on my arms.

"Ah yeah, so did you," she says, flustered. Alyssa sits down next to me, her cheeks pink, and I struggle to keep the smile off my face. She's attracted to me. When did that happen?

"I — I like the glasses," she says, and I blink. I forgot I was even wearing them. I push the black-rimmed glasses up and smile at her.

She shakes her head and clears her throat, and I try my best not to stare at her. I love seeing her so affected. I shuffle closer to her and throw my arm over her shoulder, pulling her into me. She glances at me in surprise, but I keep my eyes on my documents, trying to play it cool. She gets comfortable next to me and puts her feet up next to mine.

"What's this?" she asks, looking at the documents over my shoulder. I turn to look at her, finding her face far closer to mine than I expected. I pause, my eyes dropping to her lips for a second, before turning back to the papers.

"It's for Devereaux Inc. My mother can hold her own as CEO, but every once in a while I actually have to put some work in as the CFO. This year I want to focus on tightening our internal controls, but it isn't easy. I'm thinking of hiring a team from DM Consultancy to implement the strategy I have in mind."

She looks at me in awe, before that very awe makes way for guilt. "How can I help?" she asks, undoubtedly realising why my workload is so much higher now. I hook my arm around her neck and pull her closer to kiss the top of her head.

"You can help me by training as hard as you can. Within one or two years you'll be able to take over as my co-CEO. Who knows, you might even want to be the sole CEO."

She frowns at me, and I wonder if it's because she realises that her being CEO means the terms of her father's will would be fulfilled. Does she realise that our marriage will be over when that happens?

Twenty-Eight

Alyssa stands next to me as I cook dinner. The two of us have been in our own little bubble for the last couple of weeks, and I wish we'd moved to my apartment months ago. I knew we'd get closer if we lived together — just the two of us in our own space. It's actually starting to feel like we're married now, and I'm loving every second of it.

Alyssa stares at me suspiciously as I chop up the vegetables, totally showing off my knife skills. "You know, I've never eaten dinner you've made. Yet, you've had dinner made by me so many times, both at my house and here."

I grin up at her. It's taken me weeks to convince her to let me cook, because she's been convinced I can't cook at all. Thankfully, her food is much better now than it was years ago. "Guess I've got some making up to do, huh?"

Alyssa nods seriously. "I think you should tackle dinner this week and I'll do breakfast. Deal?"

I pretend to think that over and nod. We've gotten so much more playful with each other, and I fucking love it. Alyssa watches movies on the sofa while I work, my documents spread all over the living room. Every day she gets more comfortable with me. These days she's always touching me one way or another, and

I wonder if she even realises it. Last night she cuddled up with me while she watched her movie, and I ended up spooning her. They're all little things, but they've made me pretty damn happy.

"Are you going to hover over me or are you actually going to be helpful?" I ask.

Alyssa giggles and shrugs. "Hover."

I love the way she laughs. Seeing her so happy makes my damn heart skip a beat.

"I liked the pink apron better on you."

I glance down at my neat black apron and think back to the very first day after we got married, when Alyssa caught Lucy ogling me in the kitchen. I wonder if she gave me the apron to hide my body from Lucy. Was she already feeling just a little bit possessive then?

I smile to myself and throw the peppers in the pan. "Buy me one and I'll wear it, but you'd better get yourself a matching one too."

Alyssa laughs, and my heart flutters. I love these small moments with her. All of these everyday things. "Joke's on you," she says. "I like pink."

I laugh too and shake my head. I turn to look at her, losing myself in those twinkling eyes of hers. "No you don't. You *hate* pink, thoroughly dislike purple, and you love maroon."

Alyssa stares at me in surprise, and I look away. These are things she never told me, but that I learned about her nonetheless.

"Is it weird that I kinda hope the food won't taste good? It's just unfair if you're an amazing cook too."

I frown and turn to look at her. "What do you mean?"

Alyssa looks flustered and shakes her head. "Never mind. Doesn't matter."

I grin at her and tip my head towards the pan. "Come here," I murmur. She moves closer and I hook my arm around her waist to pull her against me.

"Stir this for me while I crack the eggs," I say. Alyssa melts into me and nods. I smile down at her and almost don't even want to move. Alyssa takes the spoon from me and purses her lips in disappointment when I let go of her to grab the eggs. I can't help but smile to myself. I love that she enjoys these little touches as much as I do.

I walk back to her with the eggs in hand and stand behind her. She looks startled when I reach around her to break the eggs. I've pretty much got her wrapped in my arms. Just one step closer and our bodies will be flush against each other. I wrap my hand around hers and stir leisurely.

Alyssa turns around all of a sudden, and I let go of the spoon. She places her hands on my chest, palms flat. The way she's looking at me drives me crazy. I wonder if it's still too soon to kiss her. Things have been so perfect between us — I don't want to fuck everything up by moving too quick. I tear my eyes away and take a step back.

"Dinner's done," I say. Alyssa blinks and nods, before disappearing to set the table. She walks away so quickly that I worry the intimacy freaked her out a little. I give her a minute before I join her at the table.

"I wonder if it'll be as good as it looks. Where did you even learn your mad knife skills? Food channel?"

I burst out laughing and shake my head. "No, I took some cooking classes when I moved out of my mother's house. It was that or eat macaroni cheese every day."

Alyssa takes a bite and moans, the sound going straight to my dick. "Holy shit. This is amazing," she says.

I bite down on my lip and look away. If that's how she sounds when tasting my food, then I'll need to take over cooking duties permanently.

"Really, it's awesome," she says, and I grin up at her.

"Hmm. You know, I could probably get away with not working tonight. We could watch a movie, and I promise I won't fall asleep this time."

She smiles at me knowingly, as though she's certain I *will* fall asleep, and she's probably right. "Okay, but I get to pick the movie," she says.

I shake my head indulgently. She always picks the movie and I'm always happy to let her.

"How about Star Wars?" I ask, knowing that it's one of her favourites.

She looks at me in surprise and frowns. "That's a trick question. Which episode? Original trilogy or the prequel? Or any of the newer ones?"

I grin at her, knowing I've got her now. "How about The Empire Strikes Back?"

She looks at me with wide eyes, and the look of adoration she throws my way makes me laugh.

"Hmm, well, I guess we can," she murmurs, trying to hide her excitement.

She's almost jumping with joy by the time I put the movie on after dinner. I can barely cope with how incredibly cute she's acting. Lately she's been showing me a side of herself that used to be reserved for Dominic.

Alyssa jumps on the sofa like an excited child, and she shrieks when the intro starts to play. I shake my head and hook my arm around her neck, pulling her into me. I was trying to score brownie points by suggesting her favourite movie, but it looks like she's going to be more interested in the movie than me.

I pull her closer and shift so I'm spooning her, keeping a bit of space between us to hide how ridiculously hard she gets me. I've got my arm wrapped around her, my thumb only an inch away from the underside of her breast. I could easily move closer and touch her where I want to.

I shift just a little closer so my lips are almost touching her neck, teasing and testing just a little. I lower my nose to her neck, and Alyssa's eyes fall closed, her breathing deep. I was worried I was imagining things, but I wasn't... she wants me too. I gently trace a line from behind her ear to the middle of her neck. She tilts her head ever so slightly, subtly trying to get closer, and I smile against her skin. I press my lips against her neck, giving her the softest kiss. She's so focused on the way I'm touching her, she doesn't notice her phone lighting up.

"Baby, your phone has been ringing non-stop. Maybe you should check who it is," I whisper reluctantly, the endearment slipping out.

Alyssa blinks in confusion and sits up. She grabs her phone in annoyance and I glance over her shoulder to find that Dominic called her nine times. My mood sours instantly when it rings again, and I cross my arms as she picks up.

"Hey, what's up?" she says.

Her phone volume is loud enough for me to just about hear what Dominic is saying. He asks her where she is, and Alyssa drops her head to my shoulder, setting me at ease a little.

"I'm home. Where else would I be on a Sunday night?"

I look down at her, and she smiles at me.

"Yeah, I'm at the downtown apartment, I mean. Not my dad's place. Anyway, what's up?"

She's quiet as she listens to him, and I start to get worried. Every time Alyssa and I get close, something gets between us. I'm worried this'll be the same.

"Yeah, of course. I'll be there in twenty minutes or so, okay?" she says, and I sigh. How could I forget who she actually loves?

"I — Dominic called..."

I laugh humourlessly. She has no idea how fucking hard I've had to work to have an entire evening off with her. Even if she did know, would it matter? Would she ever choose me over him?

"Let me guess. My little brother called and you're going running?"

She frowns at me and sighs. "It isn't like that. He seems distressed about something. I'm just going to check up on him."

I nod and turn back to the TV as she rises to go to her bedroom to change. Every fucking time. Every time we get even a little close, I'm reminded that she won't ever be mine. What's the fucking point in trying?

Twenty-Nine

I stare at the pancakes I'm making and sigh. Alyssa came home late last night, and I can't help but wonder what happened. What did she do with him? She didn't even text to let me know what was going on. I guess I shouldn't have expected it of her either.

I hear her footsteps behind me and turn around. She's in a skimpy nightgown that highlights her amazing body, and I fucking want her. She's gotten comfortable enough with me to ditch the fluffy robes she usually wears, and I can't tell if this change is better or worse. It's getting harder to hide how much she turns me on.

Alyssa glances at my bare chest with interest, and I realise I forgot to throw on a tee before leaving my room. Since we've been living together, I've been trying my best not to make her uncomfortable, but considering the heated way she's looking at me… I don't think me being half naked is uncomfortable for her at all.

I smile and hand her a cup of coffee. She takes it from me and takes a big sip before lifting herself onto the counter, her nightgown riding up. She swings her feet around and stares at me as I finish cooking.

"Pancakes?" she asks, glancing over at the batter.

I nod and work quietly, feeling a little out of it. Even though she did nothing wrong, I can't help but feel disappointed with her. I hate that she went to see Dominic last night. That she doesn't feel the need to tell me what happened or where she went.

"Can you show me how this coffee machine works later?" she asks. I chuckle at her expression and nod. She's always thought my coffee machine is way over the top, and she has yet to figure out how it works.

"It's quite simple once you get the hang of it."

Alyssa looks at me through narrowed eyes and shakes her head. "Making coffee isn't something that should come with a learning curve."

I laugh at the contempt in her eyes as she glares at the coffee machine. She's so fucking cute.

"You know, you never laugh at work. You rarely even smile. It's a good thing, too. The girls would be all over you even more."

She likes my smile? "Hmm, maybe I should start smiling more."

Alyssa bites down on her lip and looks away. "Well, come to think of it, you have no problem smiling at Kate. It's just the rest of us you can't be bothered with."

I turn the stove off and walk up to her. Alyssa grips the kitchen counter tightly and I put my hands on her legs, spreading them as I pull her flush against me, her thighs around my waist. Her skin feels amazing against mine.

Alyssa puts her hands on the counter and leans back, inadvertently pushing her chest out for me. My hands wrap around her waist and my eyes drop to her breasts. I can see the outline of her hard nipples and I force myself to look up.

"This again, Alyssa?"

She's breathing as hard as I am, and I can't help but wonder what she's thinking.

"I told you I'm treating her the same way I always have, but if you think the way I treat her is inappropriate, then I'll be sure to address that. You're my wife, Lyss. You're the only woman in my life. Why is it you insist there's something between me and her when there isn't?"

She narrows her eyes and glares at me. "Nothing there? How would you feel if I ignore your existence and invite someone else to an event we'll both be at? If I let him hold my hand in your presence? Besides, she's the woman you met during your MBA, isn't she? The one that was unavailable. She's divorced now, so I'm not surprised you started flirting with her. Sharing cotton candy with her was quite cute, I gotta admit."

Sharing cotton candy? I literally had one bite and she acts like this. Yet she'll share everything with Dominic and expects me to turn a blind eye.

"Lyss, I'm sorry. You're right. It was a shit thing to do, but isn't it the same thing you've always done to me when Dominic's around?"

She looks away in guilt. She can't even deny it.

"Dressing up to go for dessert with him when you've never once dressed up for me. Laughing with him and making inside jokes that you know I won't get. Making me feel like an outsider even though I'm your husband. It doesn't feel nice, does it? How would you feel if I go running as soon as some other woman calls me, even though you cleared your busy schedule to spend some time with me?"

She looks up at me in regret, but it's what I want. I don't want to guilt trip her into spending time with me. I want her to choose me.

"I didn't know, Dan. I'm sorry. I don't know what you expect me to do. He's still my friend. He seemed so upset last night on the phone..."

My heart twists painfully. I don't even know what to think. I don't want to feel the way I do. I'm tired of coming second to Dominic when I've always put Alyssa first. I pull away from her and walk out of the kitchen; the half-baked pancakes still on the stove.

My day just gets worse when I walk into work, and Kate

inform me that Liam called to reschedule his meeting with Alyssa. I'm so fucking done with everything. I wonder who Alyssa would be with if she weren't chained to me. Would she go out with Liam or would she pursue Dominic? I have no idea, but what I do know is that she'd never choose me. The only reason she's attracted to me now is because she's forced to constantly spend time with me at home. I've been fucking deluding myself, and hell... I've probably been standing in the way of her happiness too.

I ignore Alyssa as best as I can when she gets to the office, calling for Linda each time instead. It only lasts a few hours before she decides she's done with being ignored.

She walks in and my heart twists painfully. She looks fucking beautiful, and it's obvious she went all out today. All of this for Liam, huh? I'm a fucking idiot.

"Did I tell you to come in?" I snap.

"No," she says simply.

"Why are *you* here? I asked for Linda." Alyssa ignores the question and just stares at me. "I asked you why you're here," I say.

She walks up to my desk, hesitating only slightly before walking around it. "The document you requested," she says.

She looks so beautiful today, and all it does is make me irrationally jealous. Has she ever dressed up for *me*? Even once? Has she ever wanted to impress *me*?

"Noted. Dismissed," I snap, unable to anger.

Alyssa sighs and leans back against my desk, unfazed. "Can we talk?" she asks, her voice soft.

I look away and focus on my screen, wishing she'd just go. All she ever does is play with my fucking feelings, and she doesn't even know she's doing it. I need to stop giving her so much power over me.

Alyssa suddenly lifts herself onto my desk, her feet dangling. I look up at her in surprise. She's never once acted inappropriately at work.

"What the hell do you think you're doing, Ms. Moriani? Get

the fuck off my desk or I'll be making a call to HR," I say, losing my temper.

She looks down at her legs, and then at me, her eyes flashing with fury. "*Enough*," she says, her voice barely above a whisper.

She hooks her leg through my armrest and pulls my chair closer until I'm sitting right in front of her. I move to get up, but she pushes her red bottomed shoe against my chest, forcing me back into my seat. I sit back, shocked. She spreads her legs and places her feet on either side of my thighs, caging me in. My eyes drop to her exposed red lace panties and I stare at them open-mouthed.

Alyssa grabs my tie and I tear my eyes away from the enticing red fabric. She grabs my desk phone and hands it to me. "Go ahead. Call HR. I'd love to see how that goes. Go ahead and tell them *Mrs. Devereaux*, your *wife*, is harassing you."

My eyes drop back to her panties and I lick my lips. I want to spread her fucking legs and pull her even closer.

"Hmm? Not calling?"

I look back up at her and shake my head. My wife can be pretty intimidating, huh?

She places the phone back in its holder and tightens her hold on my tie. "Come here," she tells me.

I stand up between her thighs and she hooks her legs around my hips, pulling me in closer. I put my hands on the desk on either side of her hips, preventing her from pulling me flush against her. If she does that, she'll have one really hard dick pressed up against her. I have a feeling that'll just fuel her anger further.

"Now tell me what's going on, Daniel. What happened? One second, we were having breakfast together and the next you storm out. We had a great weekend, so I don't get where this is coming from. If you don't talk to me, then how am I supposed to know what's on your mind? If you don't tell me where I went wrong, how can I learn from my mistakes?"

I look away, unsure how to even explain. She hasn't done

anything wrong, and that's just the issue. I expect things of her that she doesn't owe me.

"I'm sorry, Daniel. I'm sorry I haven't been putting you first. That'll change now, if you'll give me a chance."

I shake my head and sigh. I've forced her into a position she never wanted to be in by making up those rules at the start of our marriage, when she made it quite clear she didn't see me that way.

"No. Why would it? Why would you do that? When we got married, we said things would stay the same between us. Our marriage is nothing but a piece of paper. We have no obligations to each other. I've been too narrow-minded. My view of marriage has always been traditional, but this *isn't* a real marriage. Fidelity and loyalty... they aren't things I expect of you. Hell, they aren't even things I *want* from you."

I don't want forced loyalty. I don't want to stand in the way of her happiness. I want her to choose me, and I need to be okay with it if she doesn't.

"I'd really prefer it if you and I could remain the way we were before we got married. Let's forget about the rules too. I'd like us to start seeing other people," I say, barely able to get the words out.

"You — you want to start seeing other people?" she repeats, confused. I clench my jaw and nod.

"No," she says, and I chuckle humourlessly. She doesn't like the idea of me being with anyone else, huh? She doesn't want me, but she doesn't want me to be with anyone else either. No more of that.

"You don't have a say in this, Alyssa. Divorce me, for all I care. I love DM, but it's just a company. It isn't the same without your father here, anyway. I have plenty on my plate with Devereaux Inc."

She lets go of me and crosses her legs over each other, looking shocked. "What, you just can't wait to get back to fucking a different model every weekend? Not having sex for a few months was too much for you?"

I hesitate, wanting to tell her I'm not even remotely tempted to do that. But I don't want to guilt trip her into remaining faithful to me. Our marriage isn't real. She should be able to do whatever the hell she wants.

"Very well, Daniel. If that's what you wish... if that's what'll make you happy, then that's what we'll do. It's not like I can keep you from doing what you want."

I sigh and run a hand through my hair. If she feels even remotely the same, then this shouldn't make a difference. She'll still choose to be with me. I cling to that tiny amount of irrational hope and nod.

"Yes," I say. "That's what I want."

Thirty

I glance at my watch and sigh. I can't help but wonder what Alyssa is up to. I've barely seen her since our argument last week — if you can even call it that. Part of me foolishly hoped that she'd miss me now that I've been working late at Devereaux Inc. instead of at home. I thought she'd reach out and text me, at least.

I glance at my phone and smile wryly. What was I thinking? The reason I told her we should start seeing other people is because I'm tired of forcibly chaining her to me, so why am I now surprised that she's enjoying her newfound freedom? I wonder if she took Liam up on that date he asked her out on. The idea of her with anyone else fucking tears me apart, but it's high time I face reality.

My phone buzzes, and I jump up, my heart racing. I grab it, only for my mood to sour when I realise it isn't Alyssa.

"Hello," I snap.

"What got up your butt today?" a familiar voice says. I smile automatically. Giselle and I dated for a couple of months a year or two ago, and our break-up was the most amicable out of all of them. We still talk every once in a while, and I'm always happy to hear from her.

"Sorry, Giselle. Having a bad day, what's up?"

"I figured as much. I was wondering if you'd like to join my cousin and me for dinner at Regale? I have a favour to ask."

I love that she never beats around the bush. She never tries to charm me or any of that bullshit. She's always been straight to the point, and I've always appreciated that about her.

I glance at my watch and nod. I've mostly been having takeout at the office in an effort to create some distance between Alyssa and me. If I don't physically stay away, I won't be able to let her be.

"Sure," I murmur, grabbing my suit jacket. I pack up whatever I'll need to finish later tonight and walk to my car, willing myself to stop thinking about Alyssa. She'd love Regale, and I'd love to take her someday.

Giselle and her cousin are already seated when I walk in, and both rise to greet me. Giselle hugs me and introduces me to her cousin, Sarah.

"You look like a train wreck," Giselle says, and I glare at her.

"You look wonderful, as usual," I tell her honestly. She's glowing today, and she looks happier than I've seen her look in a while.

Giselle grins at me and places her palm on her stomach. "I'm pregnant," she says. "I'm trying my best to keep it out of the tabloids for another couple of months, but I'm getting married next week too."

Sarah smiles. "Her fiancé is amazing. He's so kind and the way he pursued her... it makes me swoon. Is swooning still a thing?"

I smile at her and try my best to hide my surprise. I had no idea she was even dating. She sees through me easily and shakes her head. "It was an accident," she tells me honestly. "Neither he nor I even wanted to get into a relationship, but I guess fate intervened."

I nod and take a sip of the whiskey I ordered just as the waiters fill every inch of the table with dishes. Looks like Giselle already ordered, and it looks like she went way overboard.

"Guess it's only right to share some secretive news of my own," I murmur.

Giselle looks up at me with wide eyes, always one to get overly excited about gossip. I shake my head at her admonishingly and try my best to hide my smile.

"I got married."

Giselle and Sarah both stare at me open-mouthed, and Giselle grabs my hand, disappointed when she finds me not wearing a wedding ring.

"What the hell? Seriously? I thought for sure you'd be the ultimate bachelor. Who's the lucky girl?"

I grin as I think about Alyssa. I fucking miss her. "Her name is Alyssa Moriani."

I see recognition flash through Giselle's eyes and frown at her in confusion. I don't think Giselle and Alyssa have ever met before.

"She's the reason I broke up with you, you know." She tells me. My confusion must be apparent because she smiles and shakes her head. "When we were dating, you once got really drunk," she says, glancing at her cousin. "And you, well… you called out her name."

I stare at her wide-eyed, hearing the unspoken words. I called out for Alyssa while in bed with Giselle? What the fuck?

"I didn't know who she was, but I knew you had real feelings for her. That was years ago, so I'm glad you two ended up getting together."

I shake my head and look away. "It's complicated… we're married, but I'm not sure we're actually even together. Our marriage isn't a traditional one. It's all fucked up."

She nods in understanding, and I can't help but wonder if her upcoming marriage is going to be similar to mine.

We finish up our food and I sit back, satisfied and stuffed. "So what did you think of the food?" Giselle asks.

I nod, and both Giselle and Sarah smile. "Sarah works in the kitchen here at Regale. She cooked all of this shortly before you got here. She's been trying to get promoted to sous-chef, and your current chef here told us she'd get the promotion if she could gain your personal approval."

Ah, so that's the favour. I bet my chef assumed Sarah would never be able to gain access to me. What an asshole.

Giselle looks up at me pleadingly and I wink at her before asking one of the waiters to get me the chef.

He appears before me just a minute later, looking flustered. His expression turns stormy when he sees Sarah sitting at the table, and he shifts uncomfortably.

"I understand Sarah was offered a promotion provided that she could impress me with her cooking," I tell him. He grits his teeth and nods. I can't tell what his deal is. Is he worried she's a better cook, or is it because she's young and a woman? Either way, whatever excuse he's got won't be enough.

"Consider me thoroughly impressed. Congrats on your new sous chef."

He nods politely, unable to refute me, and walks away. Probably to rage in privacy. I couldn't care less. The food was amazing and the presentation was top-notch. Sarah deserves the promotion.

Both Sarah and Giselle exhale in relief, and Sarah grabs my hand tightly. "Thank you so much," she says. She jumps out of her seat and starts to clear the table, flustered and excited.

Giselle laughs and takes a sip of her orange juice. "She's been so tense all evening. I'm surprised she even managed to utter a single word. Just the idea of you intimidated the hell out of her."

I roll my eyes, never able to understand why people act that way around me. It's not like I'm some sort of monster.

"Come on, let me take you home," I tell her. "I assume Sarah is going to stay back to talk to her boss?"

Giselle nods and I lead her to my car. She shivers as we step outside and I take off my suit jacket, wrapping it over her shoulders instead. "You're pregnant, Giselle. You really need to take better care of yourself."

She smiles up at me gratefully and nods. “I know, I know,” she murmurs as I help her into my car.

My mind can’t help but go straight to Alyssa. I can definitely see her being the mother of my children one day… I wonder if ever she’ll want that too.

Thirty-One

I walk into the office only to be met with giggles. I frown as I walk to my door, and stop right in front of it, my stomach dropping. Someone stuck a photo of me and Giselle on it. It's obviously a paparazzi photo, and it looks suggestive as hell. They captured the exact moment I draped my suit jacket over her shoulders, my car in the background.

I rip it off the door in anger and turn around to face my employees. "The next person who sticks a photo on my door is fired. I'll personally review the security camera feed if need be. Don't fucking try me."

They all look at me with wide eyes, surprised at my anger. I've let their antics be for years, but that was before I was married. I glance around, relieved to find that Alyssa isn't at her desk. With a bit of luck, no one will tell her about the photo, but my odds are slim to none. But then again, will she even care?

I grab my phone and call Vincent to get a lawsuit in place. I need this bullshit rectified as soon as possible. It's not just me that this affects, it's Giselle too. She's getting married next week, for god's sake.

Alyssa walks into my office just as I hang up and pauses in front of my desk. She slides a document my way and smiles stiffly.

"This is the proposed timeline. I contacted the Singapore office and they agreed to assist with the presentation. The itinerary has been approved by Sasuki, Mr. Takuya's son."

I'm tense as hell. I can't tell if she's mad or not.

"Daniel?"

I stare at her, unable to decipher her expression. "You — are you all right?" I ask, my voice soft.

"Why wouldn't I be?"

I guess she either hasn't seen it, or she just doesn't care. I inhale deeply and glance at the document she handed me.

"Come with me to Singapore. You know this project better than anyone else. You can take the lead."

She smiles politely, and something just seems off. "That's a wonderful opportunity, boss. I won't let you down," she says.

I rise to my feet and frown at her. "Boss? You haven't called me boss in months. What's going on?"

Alyssa shakes her head and keeps her polite smile on her face. I'd rather she snap at me or question me about Giselle, but instead there's just nothing.

"Nothing," she says. "Would you prefer it if I call you Daniel at all times?"

I look at her warily and then look away. "You saw the photo."

Alyssa inhales deeply and nods. Yes, of course. Me and everyone else at the office, and probably a couple hundred thousand other people. She's pretty."

What the fuck? "She's *pretty*?" I repeat numbly.

Alyssa purses her lips and looks away, seemingly unaffected. "If that's all, Daniel, I'll get back to work."

She turns to walk out of my office, but I grab her wrist before she reaches my door. She turns back to look at me with raised brows.

"That's all you've got to say?" I snap.

Alyssa clenches her jaw and looks away. "She's just your type, isn't she? Tall, blonde and with no curves to speak off. No wonder you wanted to start seeing other people. All the girls you've been with are the opposite of me. Like I said, she's pretty. What else am I supposed to say? Well done?"

All the girls I've dated in the last couple of years have been the opposite of her for a very good reason. I've been trying to get over her for as long as I can remember, and I've been falling deeper for her the entire time.

"You asked for things to go back to how they were before we got married, and I guess you made it happen. I hear you now. I get it. I'm sorry I kept clinging to you all of last week. I kept pestering you to watch movies with me and to eat with me. I won't do it again. I apologise. You were quite clear when you told me you wanted to see other people... that you wanted us to be the way we were before we got married. I'll work to make that happen. I won't overstep again."

Fuck. I fucked up. I grab her wrist and pull her closer. She stumbles in her heels and only just manages to balance herself.

"Alyssa, no. That's not..."

I don't even know what to say. Should I even explain myself? I pushed her away for a reason, yet now that she's actually distancing herself, I find I can't stand it. "Look, nothing happened between me and her. It was just a business meeting. That's all."

Alyssa laughs humourlessly, obviously not believing me for a second. "I don't remember ever attending a meeting and holding a business partner's arm while his jacket is wrapped around my shoulder. But sure."

She yanks her wrist out of my grip and walks to my door. "I didn't cheat on you, Alyssa. *I swear.* She's just an old friend that had a proposal for me. That's all."

She turns back and smiles at me. "You don't need to make excuses, Daniel. Our marriage isn't the type where that is required. Like you said... You'll do what you want, and there's nothing I can do about it if I want to inherit my father's shares. Point taken. You needn't worry. You've made it clear that I don't have any rights to you. I'll stop now. I'll stop seeing things that clearly aren't there."

She walks out, and I'm left thinking about what she just said. She'll stop seeing things that clearly aren't there? What does that even mean?

Alyssa avoids me for the rest of the day, and I don't really know what to say to her either. In the end I leave work early, intent on making things up to her somehow. I end up cooking her dinner and setting the table. I'm in the middle of lighting the candles when she walks in. She pauses when she sees me, her eyes roaming over the room. I can't quite decipher her expression. She almost looks hurt, but that makes no sense.

"Hey, you're home."

Alyssa looks at me and nods numbly. "Do you have plans?" she asks. "If so, I can just leave."

I freeze and stare at her in disbelief. Does she seriously think I'd ever have another woman over? In the house I share with her? What the fuck?

"No. Of course not. I just thought we could have dinner together."

Alyssa shakes her head and takes a step back. "I'm not really hungry. Thanks, though."

She turns to walk to her room, but I run up to her and hold her shoulders from behind.

"But it's tradition, isn't it? Weren't we going to have dinner together a couple of times a week? How about we do twice a week? You'll cook once and I'll cook once."

She pulls away from me and turns around. "I didn't think that was still a thing considering you didn't show up for dinner once last week. It's not a tradition if you only keep to it when it suits you. Besides, it isn't something we used to do before we got married. You wanted things to be like what they were before we got married, right? You don't need to humour me with this," she says, waving her hand towards the table.

She moves to walk away, but I grab her hand and entwine it with mine before pressing them to my chest.

"I take it back. I take it all back, Alyssa. I don't even know why I said that. I don't want things to go back to how they were before we got married. I wasn't thinking clearly. I didn't mean it at all. I just didn't want you to... I didn't want either of us to feel forced in this relationship. I didn't want you to feel like you're just with me because you have no other choice. I wanted us to be able to do whatever we want, yet hopefully still *choose* to spend time together."

She pulls her hand out of mine and looks at me through narrowed eyes. "So I can cheat on you tomorrow and then tell you I want to take it back? That I wasn't thinking clearly when I *clearly* told you I wanted to see someone else? Also, how fickle are you? Didn't you tell me you had someone you wanted to pursue? Didn't you bet you'd marry her? So who is this girl you're seeing now?"

I run a hand through my hair and groan. Why the hell won't she believe me? I already told her I didn't cheat on her. "Fuck, Alyssa. I'm telling you. I didn't cheat on you. Do you want to ask Giselle? I can call her right now."

Alyssa blinks and grits her teeth. "Giselle? The girl you were with last Saturday is your ex? The one that miraculously lasted more than three months?"

Fucking hell... how does she even know about Giselle? I never introduced her to my family or to Charles, and we really only lasted a few months.

"Just have dinner with me, Alyssa. Please. I understand that you're angry, but I swear it's not what you think at all. If you can't give me anything else, then at least give me a chance to have dinner with you twice a week. Let's be friends? We'll live together for at least the next couple of years. Won't it be so much more comfortable if we're friends?"

She's clearly mad at me, even if she can't quite figure out why herself. Alyssa hesitates and then nods. I'm nervous as I pull her seat out for her and serve her dinner. I don't want to agitate her again by bringing up Giselle, but it seems like saying that I didn't cheat on her wasn't enough either. I can't figure out where I stand with her.

"So how about we spend some extra days in Singapore to do some sightseeing?" I ask. A couple of years ago, Charles told me she really wanted to go to Singapore. As far as I recall, she hasn't been yet. "We can stay in the Sands for a couple of days?" I add. That finally catches her attention and she looks up at me, a small smile on her face.

"The hotel with the infinity pool?" she asks. I nod and grin at her. I've got her now. If I can manage it, I'd love to be away with her for two weeks. Maybe all we need is to be away for a while.

"Sure, but you're paying for it."

I laugh and shrug. "You got it, babe."

Alyssa mostly stares at her plate while I try my best to keep the conversation going, but she isn't giving me much. "We can also go see the Gardens by the Bay, and one of my friends recommended a beach club in Sentosa. I think you'll really like that."

She gets up as soon as she's done eating, and I panic.

"Thanks for dinner," she tells me. "Let me know when you're done, and I'll come tidy it all up."

I shake my head. "No, that's fine. I'll do it. But I was thinking of watching the rest of The Empire Strikes Back. We didn't get to finish it last time, remember?"

She usually can't resist her favourite movie, but this time she shakes her head. "I think I'll head to bed," she says.

I'm dejected and lost as fuck as I clear the table. I need to do something... *anything*. I walk to my own bedroom and take a quick shower, hoping that'll clear my mind. As I walk out, I think back to the way she's been looking at me recently, and rather than putting on pyjamas, I walk out of my bedroom wearing nothing more than my boxer shorts. I might just be able to tempt my wife into forgiving me for upsetting her.

I turn the TV on and set the volume so loud that Alyssa will be able to hear it from her bedroom. Sure enough, just a couple of minutes later she walks out of her room.

"Oh, hey," I murmur. "Come watch with me."

I turn back to the TV, trying my best to act like I don't care if she joins me or not. I have a feeling she'll walk away if she realises how badly I want her here — just to spite me.

Alyssa sits down further away than she usually would and leans back. It only takes a couple of minutes for her to become so invested in the movie that she doesn't even realise I've slowly but surely inched closer to her. I put my arm on the back of the sofa and extend my legs, my entire body on display for her.

Alyssa glances at me subtly, but not subtly enough. She takes in my chest and abs before pausing on my dick. If she keeps looking at me that way, we're gonna have a problem. I grab the blanket that we usually keep on the sofa and cover my rapidly hardening dick, obscuring her view.

I smile at her and tilt my head. "Wanna join?" I ask, lifting part of the blanket. Alyssa looks at me alluringly and nods, scooting closer.

I extend my arm and she cuddles into me, her back against my side, and her head resting on my arm. I place my hand on her waist and sigh in relief. I knew she wouldn't be able to resist her favourite movie.

Thirty-Two

Things still aren't the same between me and Alyssa, but at least she doesn't seem upset with me anymore. She's still cold towards me, though.

My office door opens and I look up with a smile, expecting Alyssa. She's usually the only one that walks in without knocking, but instead I find Giselle.

"Hey, what are you doing here?" I ask, confused.

She holds up a bag of takeaway from Regale and smiles at me. "I come bearing gifts. Sarah cooked you lunch as thanks. She says she's really happy with her new position and she's learning a lot."

She places the bag on my coffee table and sits down, unpacking the food. "This might actually be a good opportunity," I murmur. "Seems like my wife is mad about that photo of us in the tabloids."

Giselle grins up at me. "My fiancé wasn't too pleased about that one either."

I run a hand through my hair and rise to my feet. "I already sued the paper. I suggest you do the same."

I lean out of my office and glance over at Alyssa. "Lyss, can you come to my office?"

She looks at me and then back at her screen, her eyes flashing with anger. She's mad about Giselle's presence, huh? "No. I'm busy."

"Please, Lyss," I murmur, grinning. I was a fool to suggest we see other people. It's obvious she feels something for me too. I've gotten so used to her dismissing me, that I overlooked how much things have changed between us.

She glares at me and rises to her feet, walking my way painfully slowly. I place my hand on her shoulder and close the door behind us as soon as she's in my office.

"What is it?" she snaps.

"Come have some food with us, Lyss. Giselle brought some Tapioca pudding. That's your favourite, isn't it?"

"Have you lost your mind? That's what you called me in for? Stop wasting my damn time, Daniel," she says, fuming.

Giselle glances up at the two of us, amused. "Liz? Is that short for Elizabeth? It's nice to meet you. I'm Giselle," she says.

Alyssa nods at her politely. "It's short for Alyssa, actually."

She turns to walk back out, but I grab her hand and hold on tightly, just as Giselle jumps up excitedly.

"Oh my god, Daniel. This is Alyssa? *Your* Alyssa? You work together?"

I smile at Giselle and nod. "Yep. This is my wife, Alyssa."

Giselle shakes her hand, and the surprise on Alyssa's face is priceless. "Oh my god, I've been hearing about you for years. To think Daniel and you finally ended up together. I'm so happy for you," she gushes, and I blanch. Alyssa has no idea how I feel about her, let alone *how long* I've been feeling this way.

"I need to go now, but thank you so much for hiring my cousin as Regale's sous-chef. I promise she won't let you down. She made these dishes for you as a thank you, and I told her you'd fire her if she makes the smallest mistake. She reassured me she's got this, though."

Giselle walks to the door and turns back. "Oh yeah, before I forget. I already instructed my PR team to deny all allegations about me and you, Daniel. I apologise, Alyssa."

Giselle winks at me and walks out, and I breathe a sigh of relief. That should clear things up sufficiently.

I pick up the tub of pudding and take a bite before offering Alyssa a spoonful. She reluctantly opens her mouth and lets me feed her. I try my best to keep from smiling. It's so obvious that she's relieved that nothing was going on with Giselle.

I sit down on the sofa and pull her over. She stumbles and ends up in my lap. Before she has a chance to move away, I wrap my arm around her waist and reposition her so she's sitting more on my knee.

"Told you I didn't cheat on you, Lyss. It really was just a business meeting. Her cousin was there too, but she stayed back to talk with the chef. When I said I wanted to take back everything I said to you, I meant it. I take it back. Let's reinstate the no cheating rule."

She's silent as she thinks it through, and I'm nervous as hell. "I don't know, Dan. It might be better if we do see other people. Considering your track record, it'd be a surprise if you can actually last three whole years without getting laid."

I chuckle and tighten my hold on her. I brush my lips against her ear, eliciting a shiver from her. "Who says I'm planning on going without sex for three years?" I whisper. I'm done second guessing myself. I know she feels something for me. Even if it's just lust, I can work with that.

I press a soft kiss against the back of her neck and she inhales sharply, her thighs clenched. She probably won't admit it, but she wants me.

"Surely you don't think I'd actually sleep with you," she says, her voice husky.

I chuckle and lean in, my lips brushing against her neck. "Do you want to bet on whether or not I can make you beg for it?"

Alyssa shifts in my lap and clenches her thighs together, and I grin to myself. She wants me. She's flustered and moves to get off my lap, but I wrap my arms around her and hold her captive. "Tell me you'll be faithful to me, Alyssa. I'm not asking you to sleep with me. I'm just asking you not to sleep with anyone else."

I press another kiss to her neck, and a small sigh escapes her lips. "Tell me you'll be mine for as long as we're married, Alyssa. Promise me you'll be mine like I am yours."

She leans back against me, her eyes shuttering closed. "*Are* you mine, Daniel?"

I graze her neck with my teeth before biting down softly. "Yes, sweetheart. I'm yours," I say. "I promise."

She arches her back and grinds her hips against my leg. I've never seen Alyssa turned on like this, and I fucking love it. My hands wander up until I'm holding her right below her chest. I draw circles on the underside of her breasts with my thumb.

"Daniel..." she whispers. She turns to face me just as my office door opens. Alyssa jumps up and straightens out her clothes as Kate walks in.

"Your 11am meeting is commencing soon. I escorted Mr. Davis to conference room A."

I glare at her, but she merely looks at me in amusement. She smiles knowingly before walking out again, leaving Alyssa and me standing here alone.

"I need you to promise me, Alyssa."

She crosses her arms over her chest and looks away. "And what if I won't? I'm not the one who decided to create or abolish the rule in the first place. You do whatever the hell you want and expect me to agree. What if tomorrow you change your mind again?"

I close the distance between us and bury my hand in her hair to tip her head up. "I won't change my mind. We can get it down on paper. I'm happy to sign a contract. I'll give you my DM shares if I ever cheat on you."

She looks at me wide-eyed. "You're really serious about this, huh? Why did you say you wanted to start seeing other people only to change your mind again two weeks later?"

I drop my forehead to hers. How do I even explain what I was thinking? How do I explain I wanted her to be with me by choice, and not by force? “It’s complicated, Lyss. Just know that I didn’t and won’t ever cheat on you. Can you say the same?”

She looks into my eyes and nods. “Yes. Okay. I promise you fidelity, Daniel. But this time we’re signing a contract.”

I grin at her and kiss her forehead gently. “I’ll get Vincent to draft it.”

Thirty-Three

I'm exhausted. It's been four days since Alyssa and I promised each other fidelity — truly, this time. We signed a contract and defined cheating as having sexual intimacy with someone else; the fine being our respective shares in DM Consultancy.

I expected us to get closer, but life got in the way. I've been working late at Devereaux Inc. most evenings, while Alyssa has been extremely busy with DM. By the time we get home we both collapse. I've managed to take most of my work home tonight, so at least I'll be able to see her, but I'll still have to work.

I look up at Alyssa when she walks into the house and smile. She walks up to me and throws her arms around me, startling me. Usually our touches are far more subtle than this. "I missed you," she whispers.

My heart skips a beat, and I tighten my hold on her. "I've missed you too, baby."

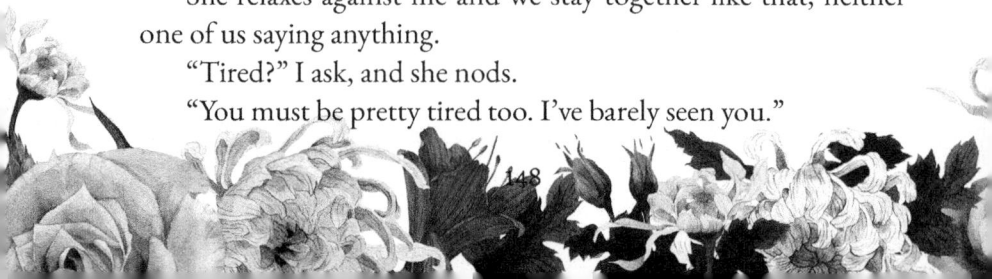

She relaxes against me and we stay together like that, neither one of us saying anything.

"Tired?" I ask, and she nods.

"You must be pretty tired too. I've barely seen you."

I nod, my stubble brushing against her hair. "Exhausted," I whisper.

She pulls back and sits down next to me. "Are you going to work all weekend again?" she asks, pouting. She's so fucking cute.

"I won't. I'll keep Sunday free, okay?"

Alyssa nods and gets up to cook, but I grab her hand to stop her. "Let's just get some takeout. Why don't we open a bottle of wine?"

She nods and walks to the wine fridge. "How about red?" she asks. I nod at her and lean back to watch her as she grabs a bottle and two glasses.

She sits down on the small patch of the sofa that isn't littered with documents and puts the wine bottle on the table, handing me a glass. I clink my glass against hers and take a sip.

"Pretty damn good," Alyssa mutters.

I wink at her. "We only have the best in our house, babe."

She smiles up at me with so much adoration that my heart starts to race. We might not have seen much of each other lately, but things are certainly better between us now.

"Go on. Go take a shower and get into comfy clothes. I'll order some Italian. It'll be here by the time you get out."

Alyssa nods. I place our order while she's in the shower, and I rush to take a quick shower myself. The food gets here a few minutes before she walks back out of her room, wrapped in a fluffy robe. My eyes roam over her body, and I can't help but wonder what's she's wearing underneath.

Alyssa looks at my bare chest with interest, and I bite back a smile. I purposely only put on my pyjama bottoms and no top.

She tears her eyes away from me and takes a bite of her pasta. "Delicious," she murmurs, smearing pasta sauce all over her mouth.

I chuckle and wipe my thumb across her lips, before lifting it to my tongue and licking it. Alyssa stares at me speechlessly, her cheeks crimson. She grabs her wine glass to hide how flustered she feels, but she isn't fooling me.

"Should we watch a movie later?" she asks. "We can put something on while you work, maybe."

I nod and hand her the remote. She browses through the movies while I continue to read through my documents, occasionally taking a bite of my food.

I see Alyssa acting suspiciously from my peripheral vision and frown when she raises her phone. I turn to look at her and she's in such a rush to hide her phone that she nearly drops it. I take it from her, but she's managed to lock it just in time.

"What are you doing?" I ask, eying her flushed cheeks.

She shakes her head and smiles innocently. "Nothing," she says, far too quickly.

I point her phone at her and unlock it using the facial recognition. The first thing on the screen is a photo of me. Alyssa took a sneaky photo of me? That's so fucking cute.

She jumps up and tackles me in an effort to grab her phone back. I grin at her and turn us over so I'm on top of her, all my documents crinkling and flying off the sofa.

"Taking unauthorised photos of me, Wifey?"

I hold myself up on my forearms and push her legs apart with my knee, settling in-between them.

"I — No. I would *never*. Why would I?" she denies fiercely.

My face is hovering over hers. Just a bit lower and my lips would be on hers. I wonder what she'll taste like.

She places her trembling hands on my chest and slowly slides her palms up to my shoulder and then around me. My eyes drop to her lips and I bite down on my own.

I feel myself hardening against her thigh and pull away in embarrassment, her arms slipping away. I'm like a teenager when I'm near her.

I sit up and run a hand through my hair as I try to sort out some random documents in an attempt to calm myself.

"Daniel," she whispers. She rises to her knees and looks at me.

"Hmm?" I murmur, not daring to look at her. I'm hoping she didn't notice I was getting a boner from being near her. The last thing I want to do is freak her out when things are finally back to normal.

Alyssa tugs the tie on her robe loose and lets it fall open. She cups my cheek gently and turns my face towards hers. I look at her, confused.

Her eyes drop to my lips, and she licks her own. My heart starts to race when she slowly lowers her face to mine. She kisses the edge of my mouth before pressing her lips against mine, once, twice, before gently sucking down on my lower lip.

I'm frozen in shock. I can't believe she kissed me. Alyssa pulls away and stares at me, her expression vulnerable.

"I — I'm sorry," she says. She rises to her feet and walks away, but she only takes three steps before I grab her arm and pull her back to me. She stumbles and places her hands on my chest to stabilise herself. I tangle my hand in her hair while I put the other around her waist.

I tip her head up and my lips crash against hers hungrily. I moan when Alyssa rises to her tiptoes to deepen the kiss.

My hands roam over her body eagerly, and I tug on her robe. It falls off her shoulders and pools at her feet. I lift Alyssa up in my arms and she wraps her legs around my waist as I push her against the wall. I drop my forehead against hers, both of us panting.

"Alyssa," I murmur. She tilts her head and captures my lips again, as desperate as I am. I kiss her roughly and push my hips against hers. I'm rock hard and the way she moves her body against mine drives me crazy.

"Daniel," she moans against my lips. I pull back a little to look at her, my eyes drifting to the nightgown that barely even covers her.

"Fuck, Alyssa." I press another lingering kiss to her lips and sigh. "You have no idea how long I've wanted to do this," I whisper.

Alyssa smiles at me and nips at my lips. "You have no idea how long I've been waiting for you to kiss me.".

I look into her eyes and my heart skips a fucking beat. "I — I thought... I didn't know—"

She cuts me off by kissing me again. I smile against her lips and kiss her back, gently and deeply this time. She runs her hands over my shoulders and down my arms, caressing me.

The sound of an alarm goes off all of a sudden, and I pull away, startled. I carefully drop her down to the floor and walk up to the lift.

"What is that?" Alyssa asks.

"Means security has tried to contact us on our phones and they couldn't get through. They checked whether we're home, so they've now sounded the alarm to let us know one of them is coming up to speak to us. They usually only do this if it's urgent, though."

I stare at the camera feed next to the lift and groan. "Go grab your robe, babe."

She nods, confused, and walks back to pick it up. She's just about got it tied around her waist when the lift door opens to reveal Bennet, my security guard, holding up a clearly drunk Dominic.

"Good evening, Mr. Devereaux. Your brother showed up here thirty minutes ago and refuses to leave. He isn't on your approved list, so we couldn't grant him access, and we were unable to reach you or Mrs. Devereaux."

I sigh and mentally curse my fate. "It's fine, Bennet. You did the right thing."

Bennet lets go of Dominic, who glares at him. He straightens out his clothes and walks into the apartment. He walks straight past me and throws his arms around Alyssa, hugging her tightly.

"I broke up with her, Lyss."

Thirty-Four

Dominic hugs Alyssa tightly and buries his face in her hair. I expected her to step away from him, but instead she sighs and hugs him back.

Why I expect anything from her at all, I don't know. Year after year and time after time, she's proven it's him she loves. She might want my body, but I doubt she'll ever want more than that.

I sigh and turn to walk away, but Alyssa grabs my hand. "Why don't you make Nic a cup of tea?" she murmurs.

I hesitate and then nod at her. Alyssa leads Dominic to the sofa, and he clings to her the entire way. He sinks down into the pillows and pulls her down with him. She doesn't even remotely resist. Instead, she smiles when he hugs her tightly and puts his head on her shoulder.

I walk away to go make my brother some tea, feeling fucking out of it. How many times are we going to do this? How many times am I going to let her hurt me like this? Every single time we get close, something happens to remind me it isn't me she wants. I guess it's life's way of reminding me that I'm coveting someone whose heart already belongs to someone else. Fucking hell… I still remember how she cried over Dominic when she got drunk two years ago. Why do I keep hoping I might stand a chance?

I put two tea cups down in front of them with more force than I intended. I'm tense, and I want to walk away from them, but Alyssa tilts her head, indicating for me to sit down next to her. I hesitate before doing so.

She grabs the teacup and hands it to Dominic. "Have some. You'll feel better," she says, her tone worried and caring. I wonder if she's ever spoken to me that way. I think I'd remember if she did.

Daniel takes the cup from her and glares at me in between sips. "Why the fuck are you walking around half naked, anyway? You did it at our house too, when Lucy and Alyssa were around. Don't you think it's inappropriate?"

I sigh and glance at Alyssa helplessly.

"I'm asking you a question, asshole."

Dominic sits up, his tea sloshing over the edge. Alyssa takes it from him and glares at him. "Watch it," she snaps. "I'll kick you if you spill on my sofa."

Dominic looks at her in surprise. "*Your* sofa?"

"Fine. Daniel's sofa. *The* sofa."

Dominic kicks his shoes off and folds his feet underneath him. "We broke up because of you, Alyssa. She's convinced I'm in love with you."

My heart fucking drops. I know she still has feelings for him. If he feels the same way, then I'm done for. My chances with Alyssa will be over.

"That's bullshit. I know she's insecure, but that's taking it too far," Alyssa says angrily.

Dominic looks up at her and I close my eyes, bracing myself for what I know is about to come. "Is it, though, Lyss?" he says. "I started dating her shortly after you told me you're in love with me. I was terrified of what being in a relationship would mean for us and what might happen to our friendship if we dated and ended up breaking up. I felt like the only way to get over wanting you was by dating someone else. I guess she could always tell I wasn't a hundred percent committed to her."

I inhale deeply and rise to my feet. I don't need to hear this. I can't stand here and watch him win over my wife. I can't stand here and be happy for her.

I walk into my bedroom feeling completely devastated. One single kiss. That's all I ended up sharing with her.

I get into bed numbly, my heart breaking. I bet she's happy he returns her feelings after being in love with him for so many years. She and I have only really had a thing for the last couple of months, and it's never been more than lust. I'm willing to bet she'll ask me to forget about the kiss.

I sit up and stare out the window at the endless London skyline, a million memories passing through my mind. I can't even remember a time when she wasn't in love with him. I don't know how long I sit there like that, but it feels like hours.

Eventually the sound of fabric hitting the floor catches my attention, and I turn to look at my door. Alyssa is leaning against it, her robe pooled at her feet.

She walks up to me slowly until she's standing right next to me. "I put Dominic in my bed," she tells me quietly.

What is she doing here? I didn't think she'd leave Dominic alone after such a heartfelt confession. "Hmm," I reply, unsure what else to say.

Alyssa fidgets with the hem of her nightgown and hesitates before slipping into my bed, surprising me. I was certain she came here to talk to me about Dominic. I figured she might even want to convince me to break the fidelity contract — so why is she getting into my bed?

"What are you doing?" I ask, crossing my arms over each other.

She sits up and leans back against my headboard. "I told you. I put Dominic in my bed."

I stare at her, trying to read her and failing. "That doesn't explain why you're in *my* bed, Alyssa."

I want her to tell me not to worry about Dominic's confession. That she couldn't care less about his words and that it's me she wants. Even after all this, part of me still hopes she'll choose me.

"I — well... I mean... if it's okay with you, could I sleep here tonight? If you're uncomfortable, I'll move to the sofa, it's not an issue. Actually, maybe that might be better."

She's here because she needs a place to sleep? That's all? Alyssa lifts the sheets to get up, but I place my hand over hers. "It's fine. You can stay."

I lie down and close my eyes, willing myself to hide my broken heart. It's good that she doesn't know how I feel about her. This way I probably won't lose her entirely when she eventually walks out of my life.

I struggle to sleep with her so close to me, and it seems like she isn't doing much better. She slowly inches closer to me until there's barely any distance between us. I'm hyperaware of her. She places her hand on my shoulder and lets it glide down until she's covering my hand with hers.

She closes the remaining distance between us and presses her body flush against mine, her breasts crushing against my back. Even after all of this, I fucking want her.

She rests her forehead against my back and slips her hand underneath my arm to caress my abs. What the hell is she doing? She slowly slides her fingers down my stomach, until she reaches the waistband of my pyjama bottoms. I grip her wrist tightly and keep it in place.

"You're playing with fire, Alyssa," I whisper.

She presses a kiss to my back and wriggles her fingers, trying to reach deeper. "I thought I was playing with my husband. I mean, you're hot... but likening yourself to fire is a bit over the top, isn't it?"

What the hell is she thinking? She kisses the back and side of my neck, and I shiver when she hits the right spot.

"Go to bed, Alyssa," I whisper. I doubt she's thinking clearly after that confession. She's never acted this provocatively with me, so something is definitely up.

She grazes my neck with her teeth before sucking on it softly, ignoring my demand. I groan and turn around so I'm on top of her. I grab her wrists and push them above her head, pinning her down with my weight as I settle my erection right between her legs.

"Stop," I snap, showing her exactly what she's doing to me. She might be using the lust between us as a distraction, but to me it's more than that. I don't want her to use me just to get her mind off Dominic's words. "Go to sleep. Don't try me, Alyssa, or so help me God, I will throw you out."

She nods slowly and looks away. "I'm sorry, Daniel," she whispers. "I... I'm sorry. I shouldn't have touched you without your consent. I wasn't thinking."

She looks up at me, so distraught and hurt that I immediately regret my words. Fucking hell, even if she did want to use me, I'd gladly let her. I shouldn't have snapped at her.

"Hey, look at me," I whisper. She stubbornly looks out the window and ignores me, so I lower myself on top of her a little and hold myself up on one arm so I can cup her cheek. I gently turn her head towards mine just as a tear escapes her eyes. My heart fucking shatters. She's looking up at me with so much insecurity in her eyes that I wish I could take it all back.

"It's not you who should be sorry, baby. I'm sorry for snapping at you. You always have my consent to touch me. Whenever, wherever. I told you I'm yours, right?"

I lean in and kiss away the tear that dropped down her cheek. Alyssa sniffs and shakes her head. "You say that, but then you'll change your mind and go eat your stupid cotton candy with Kate, or you'll tell me you want to see other people and ignore me for a week straight. You say one thing and do another. I'm tired of guessing, Daniel. I'm tired of wondering whether you want me too. I'm done."

My heart skips a beat, and I look at her in disbelief. Did she just say she wants me? She pushes against my chest in an attempt to throw me off, but I lower my upper body against hers and press a gentle kiss to her forehead. I pull back slightly to look into her eyes.

"Alyssa... you do the exact same thing. You agree to go on a date with Liam Evans, then you go running when my brother calls, and even now you disregard me as soon as he's here. I bet you're happy he returns your feelings after all. You've loved him for as long as you can remember, right? Must be nice to have him love you back. You don't need to come in here and pretend it changes nothing when it changes everything. I bet you really regret signing that fidelity contract now, huh? How long do you think you'll last before it's his bedroom you'll be sneaking into?"

"Hmm... well, I see your point," she says. "By that reasoning, and since you're threatening to throw me out of your bed if I so much as touch you... I guess I'll just return to my own bed. To the person you say actually loves me back."

She might as well have stabbed me in the heart. Is she seriously saying she'll go to Dominic? Fucking hell... that really fucking hurts.

I move away from her and turn on my back, throwing my arm over my face to hide my anguished expression. "Very well," I murmur. "I'll have the share transfer agreement ready for you tomorrow morning," I threaten. I know I said I wouldn't tie her to me forcibly, but when it comes down to it, I can't let her go to my brother either.

Alyssa pulls the sheets out of the way and straddles me, startling me. I pull my arm away from my face and look at her, dazed and confused.

"What are you doing?" I ask, tensing.

"You did just say that you're mine, right? That I always have your consent? That I can always touch you? Didn't you say something along the lines of whenever and wherever?"

What the hell is she saying? "Alyssa, I'm not in the mood to play games with you," I murmur. I'm tired, and I'm so fucking devastated. I'm in no mood to keep running around in circles with her.

Alyssa leans forward and kisses my chest. I stare at her in confusion as she makes her way down my abs, and I push myself up on my elbows to look down at her. She doesn't stop until she reaches the waistband of my pyjamas.

"I promise I'm not playing with your feelings, Daniel. But I can't promise I won't play with your body."

She kisses my erection through the fabric and I stare at her, frozen. I'm almost scared to find out what she'll do next. This entire evening has been all kinds of confusing.

Alyssa grabs the edge of my pyjamas and slowly pulls them down. I swallow hard and grab her hands, pausing her movements. She looks up at me, disappointed, and I shake my head. I sit up and grab her by her waist. In one fluid motion I've got her underneath me, our positions reversed.

I kiss her cheek gently and hover my lips over hers, hesitating. I'm terrified she isn't thinking clearly. I'm terrified she'll wake up tomorrow and she'll still tell me it's Dominic she wants.

Alyssa threads her hands through my hair and pulls me down to her. I relax on top of her when our lips finally meet. I kiss her gently at first, but within seconds the kiss turns scorching hot. It doesn't take long for me to have her moaning underneath me. She wraps her legs around me and rolls her hips, silently asking for more.

I kiss her neck, nipping at her the way she did to me. I move down slowly and pause at the top of her breasts. I look up at her for permission and she nods. I hesitate before my lips brush over her nipples through the fabric.

"Daniel... more," she pleads.

I grin and drag her nightgown down with my teeth, inhaling sharply when her breasts finally come into view. I grab one and lower my lips to the other.

"So fucking perfect," I whisper.

Alyssa groans in disappointment when I move back up, and I shut her up by kissing her. When I pull away, we're both panting.

"We need to get some rest, my love," I whisper. I'm so

tempted to take things further, but this is Alyssa. She's the love of my life, and I want to do this right.

I kiss her again, gently this time, and turn onto my back. I pull her into me, hugging her tightly. I wonder if the way she feels about me will change when day breaks. I wonder if Dominic will be able to convince her of his feelings. Hell... I don't know. What I do know is that for tonight she's still mine.

Thirty-Five

I wake up with Alyssa in my arms and tighten my grip on her. She sighs happily and presses a soft kiss to my neck. I want this every day. I want to wake up with her like this every day.

Alyssa stirs and rises, smiling at me as she gets up. I sit up in bed, the sheets falling to my hips, and watch her.

She walks into my bathroom and rummages through my drawers to find a spare toothbrush. She glances back and notices me looking at her from the bed, and she blushes as she kicks the door shut.

I thought she might sneak into her own bedroom to use her en-suite bathroom, but I'm glad she isn't. I'm glad she's using mine instead. I rise to my feet and walk out of the room, walking into Alyssa's instead. Dominic is still fast asleep, the entire room reeking of liquor. Just how much did he drink?

I grab Alyssa a change of clothes and sigh, Dominic's confession still fresh in my mind. I'm pretty sure she thinks it was drunken chatter, but I don't think it is. I'm worried about what might happen if he decides to pursue her for real.

I place Alyssa's clothes on my bed and walk back out, not wanting her to feel awkward. I'm absentminded as I make us breakfast. This isn't what I imagined today would be like. After she kissed me last night... hell.

I nearly burn the pancakes and jump when Alyssa takes the spoon from me. "You okay?" she asks, a sweet smile on her face. I nod at her and glance at the eggs, cringing just slightly. "Go and shower," she tells me. I hesitate, not sure what to say to her, and end up walking away. I want to talk to her, but I have no idea whether to bring up Dominic's confession. Maybe it's best if we pretend it didn't happen.

Alyssa has the table set and breakfast laid out by the time I walk into the dining room. She's quiet as we eat, and for the first time in forever, things are awkward between us. I had hoped we were fine after the way she got into my bed last night, but now I'm not so sure.

"About last night," I murmur.

She looks up at me and blushes before looking away. "I don't know what I was thinking," she whispers. "Let's not talk about it. I'm so embarrassed."

I grin at her and shake my head. "Don't be. I thoroughly enjoyed it."

She looks at me through narrowed eyes as she takes our plates to the kitchen, and I follow her in. I wrap my arm around her waist, feeling a bit more relieved. Alyssa grins up at me and then walks to the sofa. She seems... odd. I can't quite put my finger on it, but she's being distant somehow.

I sigh and join her on the sofa, grabbing my laptop just as she picks up the remote control. I know I have a lot of work to do, but all I want to do is talk to her.

"You're being awkward," I tell her as my laptop starts up. She glances at me and then looks away, ignoring me. I sigh and get to work. I guess she was a bit impulsive last night, and maybe she's feeling shy. Or maybe she regrets it. I can't figure her out. I don't know why I even try.

Dominic walks into the living room looking dishevelled, and Alyssa smiles up at him. He groans and sits down next to Alyssa, dropping his head on her shoulder. I tense automatically, the proximity making me uncomfortable. I'm too fucking old to still be getting jealous like this. I clench my jaw and look back at my laptop.

"Feed me, Lyss," Dominic says. He repositions himself so he's resting his head on Alyssa's lap and I look up at her, frowning — her attention isn't on me, though. She doesn't even notice my discomfort.

"I'm dying," Dominic says, and Alyssa chuckles.

"It's your own fault, you know. I told you to stop drinking, but you wouldn't listen. You barely even drank the water I gave you either. Daniel made some pancakes earlier. I think we might have some left. Do you want some?"

Dominic shakes his head. "I want your scrambled eggs," he says.

She gently lifts his head and gets up, and I can't tell if I'm relieved or angry. What the fuck? I can't believe she's actually going to make him scrambled eggs when we still have leftover pancakes.

"You're the best! Love you," Dominic shouts as she walks to the kitchen.

"Yeah, yeah. Love you too," Alyssa says, and my heart twists painfully. They say it so casually, and I really should be used to it by now, but I'm really not.

"You want some coffee too?" she asks him. I glance at my empty mug, but she never even bothers to ask me if *I* want a refill.

Alyssa puts a plate and a glass of orange juice on the coffee table and helps him sit up before putting the plate in his lap. "You're so useless," she murmurs.

I stare at the food she prepared for him and can't help but wonder if she's ever spoiled me like that. I can't remember a single time that she did. We've been married for almost a year now, and she's never once treated me the way she's treating Dominic.

He smiles at her and kisses her cheek. "Thanks for breakfast, Lyss."

The intimacy between them is painful to watch. The ease he touches her with makes me uncomfortable.

Alyssa glances at me and smiles. "How do you feel about a rom com?"

I'm surprised she's even speaking to me. When Dominic is in the room, it's like she forgets I even exist. I shrug at her and look back at my laptop, feeling ridiculous.

"Ugh, no, can't we watch something interesting?" Dominic says.

Alyssa sighs. "Adding random explosions doesn't make a movie more interesting."

Dominic sits up to look at her. "You jump every time a planet explodes and stare at the screen open-mouthed when the Death Star explodes, even though you've seen it happen a million times."

They know each other so well. It's strange to know he'll probably always know her better than I do. It's no surprise he's the one that's got her heart. A history like that... you can't compete.

Alyssa puts on Two Weeks Notice and Dominic groans. "We've seen this like a hundred times. We both know you just want to watch Hugh Grant."

I glance at the screen. I didn't even know she liked Hugh Grant.

"I don't even see the appeal. He isn't that hot," Dominic adds.

Usually Alyssa would be cuddled up against me if she's watching a movie, regardless of whether I'm trying to work. But now that Dominic is here, she's sitting as far away from me as she possibly could be. I'm not sure what to make of her behaviour.

Dominic looks at her and smiles. "I might have been drunk, but I meant every word, you know."

I tense and look at Alyssa, panicked. She smiles at me and then turns to look at Dominic. "How're you feeling this morning, anyway? Feel sick?" she asks, ignoring his words. My heart is pounding loudly. I've always known how she feels about Dominic, but I foolishly hoped he'd never feel the same way.

Dominic pulls a hand through his hair and looks at her, exasperated. "Is this payback for ignoring your confession last year?" he asks.

Alyssa shakes her head. "Nothing like that. I just don't think right now is a good time to discuss it."

What does that even mean? Why can't she just reject him outright? Dominic sighs and leans back on the sofa.

"When you moved out you said you'd be back on the weekends, but you haven't been back at all in a month now," he says, accepting the change of topic. "Mum misses you, you know? You should come back tonight. She's been making your and Daniel's favourite dishes every weekend because she keeps expecting you to turn up, but you never do."

"I didn't know," she whispers. She looks up at me pleadingly, and while I feel just as bad as she does, the last thing I want to do is go back home where there's so much distance between us. Not now that we're finally getting somewhere. We finally kissed after dancing around our attraction for months. I thought I had a shot, but then my brother showed up and ruined everything. If we go home now, I'm scared I'll lose her all over again.

"Dan? Maybe we should go back soon," Alyssa murmurs.

Dominic nods. "Let's all go back together today," he says excitedly.

I guess the odds are stacked against me. "Why don't you go shower, Nic? We can go home together once you're done. I'll take my work with me."

Dominic yawns and nods. "Borrow some of your clothes?"

I nod. "I'll put some in Alyssa's room for you."

Dominic looks up at Alyssa and grins. "That reminds me. Did you sleep okay? You weren't there when I woke up. I hope I didn't trash in my sleep."

I freeze and stare at her in confusion.

"I slept fine," she replies. "But you did seem out like a log."

Dominic chuckles as he walks to the bathroom, and I put my laptop away.

"He thinks you slept with him last night?"

Alyssa fidgets with the hem of her skirt and nods. "Seems that way," she murmurs.

"Why would he think that?" I snap. I fucking hope she'll deny it. Fucking hell. Please don't say she got into bed with him.

"Did you get into bed with him before you sneaked into my room?"

"I — why do you have to say it like that? It wasn't like that at all. I just put him to bed and waited till he fell asleep. That's all."

"Did you get *into* bed with him or did you just put him *to* bed?"

She hesitates, and I've got my answer. What the fuck? He confessed to her and she fucking cuddled him to sleep? No matter who it was, I'd never do that to Alyssa.

"It's a simple question, Alyssa."

"I — I... It's not like that. I did lie down next to him for a bit, but that's all."

My heart twists painfully. Will it always be like this? Will the lines between them always be this blurred? When she kissed me I was so sure that it was me she wanted, so what the fuck?

"God," she whispers. "What is going through your mind? He's my *friend*, Daniel. We grew up together. You tucked us into the same bed countless times. Don't you remember?"

I laugh humourlessly. "Don't pretend it's the same as when you two were five. You got into bed with him after he told you he loved you."

She knows as well as I do that she's making excuses. How the hell could she have done that knowing how he feels about her?

"Just because he uttered a drunk confession doesn't mean he suddenly ceased to be my best friend."

I run a hand through my hair, frustrated as hell. "You can't act like it doesn't change anything, because it does. Besides, he told you he meant every word. He's not drunk now, is he?"

I rise to my feet and shake my head. What was I even thinking? I always knew it'd end up like this.

Thirty-Six

I lean back against the kitchen door, just watching Alyssa with my mum. She fits in so well… it'd be perfect if she and I could actually work out. I can't ever go back from here. I won't ever be able to accept her being with my brother. I have no idea what to do, though. I can't force her to be with me. I can't force her to choose me.

"Has Daniel been good to you? Are you comfortable at his apartment?" Mum asks.

"Of course. He's always good to me, you know that. The apartment is amazing. The views are stunning and I'm so in love with the kitchen."

Mum grins at Alyssa and nods. "Yeah, me too. Back when Daniel first bought that apartment, I'd go over all the time just to play around with all the fancy equipment he put in there. Such a dream kitchen."

Alyssa smiles and helps Mum cut up the apple pie she just baked. "I did wonder how he accumulated so many utensils that he never seems to use."

I watch as they chat away happily, and suddenly I feel bad for staying away. I know Mum missed me, but this is also good for

Alyssa. She doesn't have any family of her own anymore, and I shouldn't be keeping mine away.

Dominic comes in through the back door and walks straight up to Alyssa. He hugs her from behind and I tense. I ball my fists when he presses a kiss to her hair, and she doesn't so much as step away or look even remotely annoyed. He reaches around her and grabs a piece of apple pie.

"Delicious," he murmurs, his eyes on her. She blushes, and I grit my teeth. He's blatantly flirting with her and she's going along with it. Fucking hell... why did I expect better from her? This must be her dream come true. Of course she won't think of me, or consider my feelings.

Fuck this shit. I run a hand through my hair and walk away. I open my bedroom door with so much force that it bangs against the wall, and I merely look at it in annoyance as I sit down on my bed. What am I supposed to do?

I inhale deeply and run a hand through my hair, staring at the hallway from my bed. I can't believe I'm so affected by this. Just as I decide to go demand an explanation from Alyssa, she and Dominic walk past my bedroom, their hands entwined. He pulls her into his bedroom and closes the door behind them. I tense and stare at the closed door. What the fuck are they doing?

I shake my head and sigh. I'm done with this shit. I'm done pining after someone that doesn't even respect me or our marriage. I rise to my feet and close my bedroom door. I don't want to be staring at the hallway all afternoon, wondering what they're getting up to, or how long she's going to stay in there. I fucking adore Alyssa, but I deserve better than this.

I rest my head against my bedroom door and inhale deeply. I'm done. For real this time.

I try my best to quiet my mind by working my ass off, and I end up falling asleep from pure exhaustion.

It feels like I've only been sleeping for a few minutes when I feel someone touches me. I wake up, startled, and immediately turn over. The last time someone sneaked into my bed in this house, I ended up having Lucy between my legs. I shudder at the thought of it and tighten my grip on my intruder, exhaling in relief when I realise it's Alyssa.

"Alyssa," I whisper, relieved. "It's you." I let go of her and turn back over, lying on my back.

"Who else would it be?" she asks, her tone tense.

"No one," I reply quickly. Even if it was ages ago and not at all my fault, I don't want her to know about Lucy. "I was just surprised. I was fast asleep. What brings you here?"

"I — I couldn't sleep."

"So you thought you'd get into my bed? You could've just shaken me awake, you know."

"Ah, yeah."

I turn to my side to face her and she scoots closer to me. I can smell my brother's cologne on her and scoot back, maintaining some distance between us. I don't even want to think about how she got his scent all over her. My heart fucking breaks, but I still can't send her away.

"You must be enjoying this visit back home. Would you like to come back every weekend?" I ask, half worried she'll actually say yes. For two months we spent every weekend in my apartment, yet just a single day with my brother undid everything we built together.

Alyssa suddenly sits up, looking distraught. "Why do you move away from me? Am I that repulsive to you? You seemed fine kissing me yesterday, so what happened? Do you regret it?"

"Repulsive? What kind of bullshit is that? No, of course not. It's just... being here is weird. Besides, I saw you walk into Dominic's bedroom earlier. You spent hours in there with him."

I'm hoping she'll give me an explanation now. I'm hoping she'll deny my insinuation. Instead, she just pushes against my chest, but she barely moves me. She tries to shove me again, and I grab her hands, keeping them against my chest.

"What's going on?" I ask, annoyed. Why the hell is she mad at me when I'm the one who should be angry?

"You... you just infuriate me," she snaps.

I look at her with raised brows. "I infuriate *you*? You're the one that spent hours with my brother while ignoring me, but *I* infuriate *you?*"

Alyssa suddenly tackles me, and I fall flat on my back. She lowers her lips to mine, and I freeze, confused as hell. She grazes my scalp with her nails and tangles her legs with mine I kiss her back, grabbing her hair and pulling tightly, pouring all of my anger into our kiss.

Alyssa's hands roam over my body hungrily and she slips her fingers down my boxer shorts before I even have a chance to stop her. She gasps against my lips when her fingers curl around my dick. I moan into her mouth loudly when she starts to move her hand up and down.

"Baby, you drive me insane," I whisper. I tug on her nightgown and she lets go of me temporarily to take it off. I'm not sure what's gotten into her, but so long as it's *me* she wants, then I'll take it.

"You too," she whispers. I look into her eyes, trying to make sure she knows what she's asking for, and tug off my pyjama bottoms, leaving my boxers on.

Alyssa glares at me and pushes them down. "These too," she snaps. I chuckle and press a quick kiss to her lips before shrugging out of them.

I lie back on top of her, naked for the first time, and she moans in delight. My lips find hers and I kiss her deeply, grinding my hips against hers. We're only separated by her underwear now, and I'm tempted to push them aside. Every time I slide up against her, I push into her the tiniest bit, as much as the fabric allows, and it drives her insane. She's panting and bucking against me, and I've never seen her so frantic. I'm pretty sure I can make her come just like this.

She groans in frustration when I move down to tease her nipples with my tongue. She lifts her hips in a silent bid for more, but I merely chuckle against her skin. The first time I'm having sex with my wife isn't going to be in my childhood bedroom, where we'll both need to be quiet. Hell no. When I finally fuck her, I want her screaming my name.

She moans loudly when I trail a finger over her underwear. "Fucking hell, baby. Your pussy is soaking wet." I push her underwear aside and slip a finger deep into her. She's fucking tight.

"Oh *fuck*, yes... Daniel."

She buries her face in my neck and places her lips against my ear as I pull my finger back out and over her clit. Her entire body tenses as I tease her. I lift myself up on one arm to look at her and as I touch her, enjoying the expressions on her face.

"So fucking wet for me, Alyssa. I could slip right into you, baby."

"I'm always wet for you, Daniel," she says, and my dick is straight up and starts to throb. I need to be inside her so badly. I wish we were at home, for god's sake.

I kiss her roughly while her hands find my dick. I twitch in her hands as she teases me, her grip tight.

"Baby, you've got me ready to come for you like a horny teenager. You gotta ease off with those hands of yours," I plead.

She grins up at me and shakes her head. I look at her through narrowed eyes and push two fingers into her while stroking my thumb over her clit. Her lips fall open and she moans loudly as I push her towards an orgasm. She's so fucking beautiful.

"Daniel, no. Oh God. I can't take it, please. Dan... *Fuck*."

She lets go of me and wraps her arms around my neck, holding on for dear life.

"Please, Dan. Please, baby. *Please*," she whimpers.

I increase the pace and give her what she's asking for — I don't pull my fingers away until the last ripple passes through her body and then I kiss her gently.

"Wow," she whispers, and I grin against her lips.

"Wow indeed," I agree. She's fucking spectacular. Her body is so fucking responsive. I'll never get enough of her.

Alyssa hugs me tightly and brushes her lips over my ear. "My turn," she whispers.

I chuckle and shake my head. "No. Now we sleep, beautiful."

There's no way I can even remotely be gentle with her right now. If she touches me, I'll fucking lose it. I want to do things right. We'd better be going home tomorrow, because I'm done waiting. I'm done wondering.

Thirty-Seven

I startle awake when my bedroom door opens and tense. Alyssa is curled up against me, her chest pressed against my back. The sound of my mother walking in must have woken her up too, because she scoots down a little, hiding herself better. I pull the blankets tight and clamp them underneath my arm, creating a little tent behind me that should hide Alyssa pretty well, so long as my mum doesn't get too close.

"You're still asleep, darling?" Mum asks. Alyssa tenses against me, and I'm suddenly just as tense. I'm naked, and Alyssa is only wearing her panties. I glance around the room and sigh in relief when I don't see any of our clothes on the floor. Mine must be tangled in the sheets somewhere, while Alyssa's must be on her side of the bed.

"How come you're sleeping in? Usually you'd be up by now, in the kitchen. I was looking forward to your breakfast, you know. It was so nice to have you back in the house for a couple of weeks. No one takes care of me like you do."

I glance at Mum, unsure how to send her away without looking suspicious. I'm a grown man, but getting caught in bed by my mother is still a hard pass. "Uh... Mum... I'm just tired. I thought I might sleep in longer. Why don't we have a chat later?"

She ignores me and sits down on the chair by the door instead. I sigh. If she's sitting down, then I'm in for a talk of some sort, and nothing I say will get her to leave. Alyssa's hand wraps around my waist and I'm worried Mum will catch her movements.

"I guess Alyssa and Dominic are still asleep. I thought for sure things would've changed between you and Alyssa with you two being by yourselves in that apartment of yours, especially since you two haven't been coming back here much. But she and Dominic seem closer than ever. The way he hugged her yesterday and then dragged her off to his room surprised me. You weren't there and I didn't know what to say either."

I tense, and Alyssa's grip on me tightens. She slips her arm over my chest and squeezes herself against me tightly, crushing her breasts against my back.

"I used to think they were just friends, but now I'm wondering if I was just blind to what was happening between them. Daniel, if I'd known I'd never have let you get married to Alyssa. I would've made that nasty grandma of hers an offer she couldn't refuse and buy back the shares."

Alyssa presses a silent kiss against my skin and pushes her forehead against my back, but her attempt to reassure me doesn't set me at ease at all. Even my mother can see that the way she acts with Dominic isn't appropriate.

"You should start seeing someone, Dan. I've let you be and let you sow your wild oats, but you aren't getting any younger."

Alyssa freezes, and so do I. Surely she doesn't think the odds of Alyssa and me working out are *that* low?

"Mum, I'm only thirty-two. Chill," I murmur, trying my best to reassure her. I can see where she's coming from, though. She's right. The way Alyssa and Dominic act... it's clear I'm standing between them.

Mum huffs. "Yeah, but it'd probably take you a year to find a good girl, then another year or two of dating before you finally get engaged. Then another year while we plan the wedding. By the time I'm finally holding my grandchild, five or six years will have passed."

I laugh and shake my head. "There we go. So that's your real objective. You just want a grandchild. Why don't you just go adopt one?"

She crosses her arms over each other and glares at me. "I want a grandchild that looks like you. You'll have to make me one, and I'm running out of patience. You and Alyssa won't work out. You've been married for months and you're still sleeping in separate bedrooms. You didn't even speak to each other all day yesterday, and I checked. She was with Dominic all day while you hid in your room. You two don't even seem to be friends. I would've loved to have her as my daughter-in-law, but your marriage is clearly just a paper marriage. It shouldn't stop you from seeing someone. I'm sure if you find the right person, she'll understand the situation. Or otherwise you just buy out Alyssa's grandma and divorce her. Lord knows we can afford it."

Alyssa tightens her grip on me and I wonder how she'd feel about me seeing someone else. I genuinely can't tell anymore. We've been married for close to a year and we don't even share a bedroom. It's not even about the sex. Intimacy is just lacking between us. I wonder if I'm forcing something to be there... that just *isn't.*

"Mum, I don't know. I'm still married. It would feel too much like cheating to me. I'd rather not," I say carefully. I'm not entirely sure how to get out of this, because I can't refute her words either.

"Well, you have no choice. I invited Olivia and her mother over for lunch today. They should be here in an hour or so. Do you remember her? She's always been crazy about you. Besides, she's a university professor and she's really pretty. Very sweet and polite too. I think you'll like her."

I stare at her in disbelief. What the fuck? She knows I'm

married and invited someone over without even asking me? "Seriously, Mum? With Alyssa here? What are you thinking?" I ask, snapping at her.

Mum tuts and rolls her eyes. "She won't care. I doubt she'll even notice that I'm trying to matchmake you. It's just lunch, isn't it? Not like we've never done that before. It'll also relieve your brother's guilt. Maybe Alyssa's too."

My heart sinks. Is she seriously telling me to step aside so those two can be together? "So, what? You're trying to push me towards someone else so Dominic can covet my *wife* without feeling guilty about it?" I ask, my tone harsh.

Mum sighs. "Nothing like that, and you know it. Those two aren't right for each other. Maybe they need to get it out of their systems or something. It doesn't matter. It's not like you and Alyssa are actually together. She's only your wife on paper, Daniel. Besides, I'm sure you'll really like Olivia. Just give it a chance, sweetheart. Please. Just do it for me. I'm tired of worrying about you."

She looks so worried and heartbroken that I can't help but give in. Besides, Mum is right. Alyssa might feel possessive, but she doesn't *love* me. There's a big difference, and I need to start remembering that.

Alyssa pinches me angrily, and I yelp. Mum looks at me in alarm, and I look up at her, panicked.

"Are you okay?" she asks, confused.

"Uh, yeah. Just cramp," I stammer.

Mum rises and walks up to the door, looking back. "Wear something nice, okay? Maybe a nice button-up? What do girls these days like? Maybe a t-shirt, actually. Just don't come out wearing your pyjamas like you have been doing."

She closes the door behind her and I exhale in relief just as Alyssa pushes the covers off, her eyes blazing with anger. She glares at me and grits her teeth as she sits up, not caring that she's mostly naked. My eyes fall to her breasts and I harden instantly. She's so fucking gorgeous.

Alyssa gets out of bed and storms into my walk-in wardrobe, giving me one hell of a view of her ass. Fucking hell.

She walks back to my bed with two of my ties in her hands, and I lean back against my headboard, curious as to what she's even up to.

Her eyes are flashing as she pulls the sheets off me. I'm naked, and her eyes drop to my dick. I hide a grin when she looks startled, and just a little fearful, and put my arms behind my head. I lie back relaxed, curious, and turned on as hell. Alyssa climbs back onto the bed and straddles me. I stare at her with wide eyes and she grins at me as she leans over. She grabs my wrists and ties them together before tying them to my bed. I try to tug my hands loose, but she's got me tied up good. She smiles in satisfaction and I bite back a smile.

"What are you doing?" I whisper, my voice husky. Alyssa glares at me and my eyes fall to her breasts. She's so fucking gorgeous. I need to touch her. I try to tug my wrists loose again, but there's no way I'm going anywhere unless she releases me.

"Punishing you," she says. She lies down on top of me and buries her hand in my hair, pulling on it hard enough to make me tilt my head. Once she's got me how she wants me, she leans in and places her lips against my neck, right below my ear, and sucks on my skin harshly.

I moan and turn to give her better access. "Fuck, Alyssa," I whisper, quickly losing my sanity. I move my hips against hers until I've got her right where I want her, squirming until I'm sliding against her. Her underwear prevents me from slipping inside, but I can still drive her crazy.

Alyssa tightens her grip on my hair and turns my head to place her lips against the other side. She bites down bang in the middle of my neck and sucks harshly, marking me as hers. I moan, and she covers my lips with her hand. I press a soft kiss to her palm and thrust harder, losing control. I need to be inside her.

She lowers her lips to my collarbone, and I groan. "No," I whisper pleadingly. She's moved down a little, but it means I can no longer grind against her. I tug on my restraints and throw my leg around hers to try to move her back up again, but she won't budge. She laughs and takes her time giving me a kiss mark on my collarbone, and then my chest before moving to my abs. I'm breathing hard and watching her with heated eyes as she presses her lips against my V muscles, making me there too.

Alyssa grins up at me as she follows the trail of hair on my lower abs down and down with her lips, pressing soft kisses against my skin. I lie as still as I can, my entire body tense. Her lips are so close to my dick... fucking hell. She grabs my throbbing cock and wraps her hands around the base.

"Baby, you'd better let go of my dick *now*," I murmur.

She smiles up at me. "Or what?" she asks, lowering her lips to the very tip. I moan and bite down on my lip.

"What if I don't want to let go of your... dick," she whispers, nearly stumbling over the word. I gulp and stare at her with wide eyes as she slowly takes the tip into her mouth. My eyes fall closed and I moan loudly when she swirls her tongue.

"Alyssa, baby. Please," I moan. "Oh fuck, Lyss."

She bobs her head up and down, taking me in deeper each time. I pull on my ties, but I'm well and truly stuck.

"Baby, you gotta stop. I'm gonna come. Lyss, I — I can't..."

I try to pull my hips away, but she takes me in deeper. I moan louder and my pleas get more and more desperate.

"Please, my love. Alyssa... I can't hold it..."

I buck my hips and push deeper into her, coming deep in her throat. Alyssa pulls away, coughing. She wipes her lips and then smiles at me smugly.

"Baby..." I whisper. "I don't think you quite understand the definition of punishment."

She bursts out laughing and shakes her head. "Don't you provoke me. I'm tempted to leave you tied here naked so you'll miss that damn date you should never have agreed to in the first place. If this wasn't your mother's house and if I didn't love her so much I would've really done it."

She leans over me and loosens my restraints just enough for me to get out of them, while still giving her enough time to escape. She throws one of my t-shirts over her head and glances back at me in satisfaction before walking out.

Thirty-Eight

Fucking hell... What the fuck was that? The way Alyssa just sucked me off was insane. She's never wanted me like that before. All of that just because my mother's words angered her?

I get up, feeling better than I ever have before. That mouth of hers... it was better than I expected. I walk into the bathroom with a huge grin on my face and freeze when I look into the mirror. Alyssa marked me all over. I've got kiss marks down my neck and my chest. Fucking hell.

I've never let a woman mark me before, and I fucking love it. I love this possessive side of her.

I grin as I walk into the shower. I fucking knew it. I knew Alyssa would be a freak in bed. She's fucking amazing. I can't walk out of here with visible kiss marks on my neck, though. Mum would be mortified. I can't do that to her.

I sigh and reluctantly stick a plaster right below my ear before getting into a button-up that covers the rest of the marks she left on me. I can't remember the last time I was in such a good mood. I wish I could show off her possessiveness. I want Dominic to see. I want it to be clear that she's mine.

I'm in a fantastic mood as I walk to the garden where Mum

will be hosting lunch. I can see she went all-out with name cards and everything. Olivia and her mother are already there, and they both rise to greet me.

Olivia smiles shyly and I smile back at her. I sit down and eye the name cards. Mum put Alyssa and me on either side of the table, as far from each other as possible. It's obvious what she's done. She's got Dominic sitting opposite me and Olivia next to me, while Alyssa is next to Olivia, where I won't even be able to see her well. What was she thinking, pairing Olivia and me up so blatantly? This makes me uncomfortable as fuck.

Alyssa joins us at the table and takes one look at the seating arrangements before gritting her teeth. She grabs Mum's name card and switches it with her own, so she ends up sitting across from me. She sits down with a tight smile on her face and remains silent when Mum walks up to us. Mum frowns when she realises the seating arrangements have been changed and then sits down as though nothing happened. How would Alyssa have explained her new seat of choice?

"Gosh, Olivia. You look prettier every time I see you. Isn't she pretty, Daniel?" Mum says. I glance at Olivia and smile tightly before nodding at my mother. I can't insult a guest in our own home, but Mum is really putting me on the spot here.

Alyssa looks pissed off, and oddly enough, my heart fucking soars. This has gotta be the first time she's showing me any kind of real emotions. She orders a double gin and tonic, and I frown. She rarely drinks spirits.

"It's so lovely to see you again, Alyssa," Olivia says. "I was so sorry to hear about your father."

Alyssa nods politely. "Thank you, Olivia. It's lovely to see you too," she says, smiling. The staff put down Alyssa's drink and Olivia frowns. "Oh, Alyssa. You shouldn't! You're still underage, aren't you?" she says, sounding genuinely concerned, and I cringe. Sometimes it's easy to forget how young Alyssa is.

"I'm twenty-two," she murmurs, and Olivia chuckles.

"Wow, you've grown up," Olivia says. She glances at me and

smiles. "Do you remember being twenty-two, Daniel? Fresh out of university. God, those were the good old days."

I feel awkward as fuck. I hate these little reminders of Alyssa's age. I'm a good ten years older than her, but she's so mature it's easy to forget.

"So you'll be starting your career soon, huh? That must be exciting."

Alyssa smiles. "Yeah, I'm working for DM Consultancy," she says, a tinge of pride ringing through her voice.

"Oh, Alyssa. Don't you think it'll be better to get a real job rather than relying on nepotism? Your father's company will always be there, but it's so important to work for an actual boss first. Someone who doesn't care about your surname. I worked for my dad's company for a while, and it was so easy compared to working for the university. Take it from me, sweetie. It'll really build character to work elsewhere. I have plenty of connections if you struggle to find a job."

She glances at me and smiles. "Or Daniel can help you find something. I'm sure you'd help your little's brother's friend, right?"

Olivia places her hand on my arm and grins up at me, while Alyssa tenses. "He's always been so supportive. He's actually the one who introduced me to the professor I currently work for. I still had to go through the whole interview process, but it was nice to have someone to talk to beforehand."

Alyssa blanches, and I hate seeing that look on her face. She looks so defeated. "I'll keep that in mind, thank you, Olivia," she says.

What the fuck is she thanking Olivia for? "Actually, Alyssa has a *real job*," I say, my tone harsh. "She works harder than any of my other staff members and has been with DM since she was eighteen, often working sixteen-hour days to get all her work done in addition to attending university. In four years she's worked her way up to becoming a managing consultant. Are you insinuating that my company is guilty of nepotism when all we're doing is nurturing talent? That we hire and promote unfairly?"

Olivia stares at me open-mouthed and shakes her head. Mum shoots me a warning look and clears her throat. "Of course not. That's not what you meant, right Olivia? She's just looking out for Alyssa. She doesn't know much about DM, after all. Maybe you should show her around."

Olivia nods and smiles up at my mother in relief. "Yes, I'm sorry if that came out wrong, Alyssa. I meant well. I would love to see DM. Maybe I can bring you some lunch sometime, Daniel?"

Mum nods happily, just as I'm about to decline. "Oh, that'd be wonderful. How about sometime next week? I'll give you the phone number for Daniel's secretary so you can set up a lunch date."

At least she isn't going around giving *my* phone number away. I watch as Alyssa takes a sip of her second G&T. She looks stunning today. She's wearing a summer dress that looks beautiful on her, and all I want to do is get it off her. My mind keeps replaying the way she toyed with me this morning. I can't wait until I get her alone again.

I can barely focus on what Olivia is saying at all and end nodding and smiling at her mindlessly. Olivia giggles and I glance at her. "We got so drunk, do you remember?" she says. It takes me a little while to remember what she's even talking about. I only barely remember half the events my mother drags me to.

"*We* didn't get drunk. *You* got drunk. I had to carry you home," I say, laughing. I must've only been sixteen and Olivia had probably never even drank before then. It's so long ago that the memory almost escaped me. Fucking hell... It's sixteen years ago. Alyssa was only six years old then. What the fuck.

"It's been so long since we've had a chance to catch up. I'm so happy to see you today. We should really do dinner sometime soon. How about that new Italian place?" she says.

I glance at Alyssa, wondering what she's thinking. All I need is the smallest sign from her. Just a bit of jealousy or just something to show me she cares. Instead, all she does is ignore me. It's like she isn't even listening to our conversation. If she wasn't in such a bad mood, I'd think she doesn't care at all, but now I'm sure she just hides it well.

"Maybe," I murmur, not committing to anything with Olivia. I don't want to be rude, but there's no way I'm gonna go out with her.

"So, Alyssa," Olivia's mother says. "You've grown up to be a beautiful, hardworking young woman. Are you dating anyone?"

I freeze and look up at her. She smiles tightly, but she doesn't say that's she's single. I'll take that.

"You might remember my son, Oliver. He's only a couple of years older than you are. He's twenty-five. Perhaps you and he could go for drinks sometime? He's only just moved back to London. It'd be nice for him to date a little. He's become such a hermit these days."

What? Over my dead body. I sit up in my seat, and just as I'm about to speak up, Alyssa shakes her head.

"Actually, Dana... I'm sorry, but I'm seeing someone right now," she says, and I exhale in relief. Fuck Oliver. There's no way he's getting near my girl.

Alyssa is sipping her fourth G&T by the time dessert comes around, and she's obviously buzzing. She's far more relaxed, and even her bad mood seems to have diminished.

I'm ready to get this lunch over with and drag Alyssa to my room so we can finish what she started this morning, but my mother smiles at Olivia brightly, and I just know we're far from done.

"You did bring your swimsuit, didn't you?" she says. Then she turns and looks at me pleadingly. "I told her you'd take her for a swim since the weather is so lovely out. We can all sit by the pool and sip some cocktails. Wouldn't that be wonderful?"

Wonderful, my ass.

Thirty-Nine

"I'm not feeling all that well. I think I'll sit this one out and go take a nap," Alyssa murmurs, and she genuinely doesn't look okay. She looks tired, and I guess... hurt? Fuck.

Dominic shakes his head and grabs her hand. "Nope, you're coming," he says. He pulls her away from the rest of the group and the two of them fall behind. I glance back to find that he's thrown his arm around her, their heads close to each other. My heart twists painfully just seeing them together like that. His confession is still fresh in my mind, so it must be in Alyssa's too. The two of them stop, and he cups her cheek. I tense and Olivia looks up at me.

"Everything okay?" she asks. I nod and sigh.

"Yeah, all good," I murmur. Dominic and Alyssa disappear into the house together, and the thought of the two of them alone makes me anxious. I know she promised me fidelity, but will that promise hold up when she's faced with the guy she's loved for years? I can't help but worry.

I'm nervous and antsy as I sit down by the pool with Olivia, Dana and my mother. Ten minutes. That's all I can take. I glance at my watch in annoyance. I'll give my mother ten minutes since she went ahead and made a commitment on my behalf. But that's all I'm willing to give her. If Alyssa doesn't get back within ten minutes, I'm going after her.

"Are you sure you're okay?" Olivia asks. She takes off her dress and angles her body for me as she lies down on one of the lounge chairs, but all I can think is how her body has nothing on Alyssa's.

"Yeah. Don't have swim shorts, though. I think I'll head out soon. I've got a headache coming on too."

The ten minutes are almost up when Alyssa and Dominic finally rejoin us. I jump up when I see them approach and glare at them. "Where were you two?" I shout.

Dominic glances at me in amusement. "Went to change, bro," he says. "Do you like the bikini I picked for Alyssa?"

Alyssa looks at him through narrowed eyes as Dominic takes her hand, twirling her around. My eyes drop to her breasts and I grit my teeth. What the fuck does he mean he picked it for her? A thousand different scenarios drift through my mind, each worse than the last. I shake my head and pull myself together. They were only gone for ten minutes. Nothing could've happened.

Her body looks phenomenal in this little red bikini of hers. Fucking hell. It looks like it's just a bit too small on her, and it showcases her body perfectly. The small bottoms make her waist look tiny, and I can't wait for her to turn so I can take a good look at that ass.

Dominic hands me a spare pair of swim shorts, and Mum walks up to us, excited. "Oh, fantastic. See, problem solved, Daniel."

I shake my head. "I *really* don't think that'll be a good idea, mum," I say, looking at her sternly. I went through all this effort to save her from the embarrassment she'll face when our guests see the kiss marks on my body, but at this point I'm past caring. I want Dominic to see what Alyssa did to me. Hell, I want Olivia to see.

Alyssa laughs mockingly and brushes past me, looking infuriated. I grab her wrist and pull her back. She stumbles and braces herself against my chest. All I need is one word. I just need her to say I'm hers. To tell me she doesn't care about Dominic seeing the marks she left on my body. All I need is a sign to tell me she wants me as much as I want her. Instead, she stares at me provocatively. I let go of her and glance at her body angrily. She looks way too fucking good in the bikini my fucking brother picked for her.

I lean in and whisper into her ear. "You asked for this, Alyssa. I have no problems showing your lover boy all the marks you so happily left on my body. Let's see if he's still so keen on picking you bathing suits when he sees what you did to me this morning."

She laughs humourlessly and rises to her tiptoes. She grabs my shirt and yanks me closer. "Don't pretend to be the good guy here, Daniel. You just don't want Olivia to see the kiss marks. You went as far as putting a plaster on to make sure she didn't see them. Don't want to ruin your chances, do you? I wonder if she'll still go for dinner with you when she finds out my lips have been all over your body..."

She lets go of my shirt roughly and pushes past my astonished mother. "What did she say to you?" Mum asks me curiously as Alyssa lies down on one of the empty lounge chairs.

I storm into the boathouse, fucking furious. I spent all afternoon watching *her.* Yet she's angry? I'm not the one that let someone else pick out a fucking bathing suit.

I change into my swim shorts but keep my shirt on, still undecided. I walk back feeling slightly calmer and drop my trousers to the lounge chair beside Alyssa's. I glare at Dominic and make up my mind. She's mine, and he'd better fucking get the message. I slowly unbutton my shirt until it falls open.

I can't help but grin smugly as I shrug my shirt off, letting it drop to the floor nonchalantly. Everyone stares at me with wide eyes, and Olivia pales while Dominic looks away. Even Alyssa looks shocked, as though she didn't remember just how much damage she did. I have a good dozen kiss marks all over my body, all the way from my neck to the waistband of my swim shorts. It's obvious what went down.

Mum clears her throat and looks shocked, her eyes automatically moving to Alyssa before returning to me. Realisation dawns and for a second, she looks a little contrite. Mum purses her lips and tries her best to hide her amusement. "Cramp, my ass," she murmurs, and I bite down on my lip in shame. So she's figured out Alyssa was in bed with me this morning, huh?

Alyssa hides her crimson cheeks with her hair, and I grin. She asked for it, and she got it. Dominic now knows what she did to me, and Olivia knows I'm off-limits.

I walk up to the pool and smile at Olivia. "You wanted to swim, right, Liv?"

She stares at me and blinks a couple of times before nodding uncomfortably. "I — you... uh, your chest, Dan."

I look down at the countless marks on my skin and smile to myself. "Oh, that... yeah. To be honest, I didn't expect to walk around half-naked today or I would've told my girlfriend to behave. She wasn't pleased with a decision I made recently. We had a disagreement and worked through it... *vigorously*."

I smile and shrug, pleased with myself. It's strange to call my wife my girlfriend, but I love it. I don't care what title we use, so long as it's clear that she's mine.

"I didn't know you had a girlfriend, Daniel," Dana says, sounding just as disappointed as Olivia. I grin at her and then glance at Dominic.

"I do."

Forty

I'm seething all the way home. All I can think about is Dominic telling me he picked out Alyssa's bikini. I've been wanting to question her about it all afternoon, but we haven't had a single second together between entertaining guests and packing up to go back home.

Alyssa glances at me worriedly as we step into the lift to our apartment and her eyes widen when I drop our luggage to the floor the second we walk in. I lift her into my arms, one hand underneath her knees and one wrapped around her. She yelps and tenses when I kick my bedroom door open. I place her on my bed gently and help her take off her flip-flops before kicking off my own and lying down next to her. I roll so I'm on top of her and glare at her.

"What's wrong?" she asks, her voice quivering.

"Nice bathing suit you had on today. Dominic picked it out for you?" I say, my voice harsh.

"Oh, that," she murmurs nervously.

"Hmm, *that*," I repeat. I glance at the red strap that's peeking out from underneath her sundress, my eyes darkening. I grab the hem of her dress roughly and lift it up. "Off," I order. Alyssa's eyes widen and she raises her arms obediently. I throw her dress on the floor and stare down at her body.

"I've gotta say, this bikini top does cup your perfect tits beautifully."

I grab a handful of her breast and squeeze, eliciting a small whimper from her. I glare down at her top and put my hands on the cups before pulling it apart. It tears like it's nothing and Alyssa gasps as her breasts spring free. I throw her ripped bikini top on the floor, never wanting to see the damn thing again, and then I lean in. I place my lips over her nipple and Alyssa moans and arches her back. I chuckle against her skin and move to her neck, sucking harshly, marking her the way she marked me.

Alyssa's eyes fall closed and she moans, the sound going straight to my dick. I pull back and look at the mark I made in satisfaction before doing the same to her collarbone, her chest and her stomach. I want her body as marked as mine is.

I pause when I reach her bikini bottoms, my anger climbing all over again. I look up at Alyssa and glare at her. "I saw you. I saw the way you hugged him. I saw the way he stroked your hair and held your hand. The way he pulled you away and towards the house. Did you let him into your bedroom? Did he go through your outfits to pick out the one he liked best?"

Just the idea of it pisses me off. I trail my nose against the inside of her thigh before sucking down and leaving another mark. She trembles underneath me and I glance up at her, grinning wickedly before ripping apart her bikini bottoms.

I smile as I kiss her stomach, and down until I've got her trembling with need. I look up at her and then drag my tongue down her slit, making her moan loudly. I moan at the same time she does. "I knew you'd be fucking delicious," I whisper. Alyssa bites down on her lip as I torture her with both my tongue and my fingers, and I've got her ready to come in minutes.

"I don't want him even thinking about you," I snap. "You're mine, Alyssa, and I'm done playing games. I'm done stepping aside and trying to do the right thing. You're *mine*."

I don't even care who she loves. Not anymore. She's mine. I push a finger against her g-spot while I swirl my tongue around her clit, keeping her right at the edge. I want her desperate for me.

"Ohh, *fuck*. Dan. Please..."

"Say it, Alyssa."

"I — what?" she whispers, her eyes glazed over. I won't get what I want from her unless I give her what *she* wants first. Alyssa shatters on my lips, wave after wave of pleasure coursing through her body. She's still trying to catch her breath when I gently lift her into bed and pull the covers against both of us.

I roll on top of her and hold myself up on my arms. She's naked while I'm still fully dressed. We'll need to do something about that soon.

"Tell me you're mine, Alyssa. Officially from now on. No more games. No more blurred lines. No more flirting with other people and making each other jealous. No more guessing and no more miscommunication. I want you, heart and soul. Tell me you want that too."

Alyssa pulls me to her and kisses me gently. "Only if you promise me, there'll be no more pulling back and hiding your thoughts and emotions, no more unwarranted jealousy and definitely no more separate bedrooms," she whispers.

I exhale in relief and drop my forehead to hers. "I promise, Alyssa. I promise."

I glance at my walk-in wardrobe and grin. "I'd better make some space for you, huh?"

Alyssa giggles and throws her arms around me. I nuzzle her neck and pull back to kiss her. She pulls away all of a sudden and I frown. "What is it, baby?" I whisper.

"I... do you... it kind of seems like, I don't know. Do you not want to sleep with me?" she murmurs, her words tumbling out in a rush. She blushes and looks away, embarrassed.

My eyes widen in disbelief. "What?" I say, shocked. "What the fuck?"

I grab her hand and shove it down my shorts, making her feel how much I want her. I've been rock hard since we walked into our place.

"Alyssa, you could merely glance at me and I'll want you. Hug me, and I'll be hard. I *always* want you, baby. What could possibly make you think I don't?"

Alyssa hesitates and I brush her hair out of her face gently. "Communication, right baby?" I remind her.

"It's just that you never seem to want to go all the way with me. You'll kiss me and then just go to bed... or you know... you'll touch me and then you won't let me touch you in return and just go to sleep. It makes me think you might not really want me."

I groan. "Alyssa, I've been trying to treat you respectfully. I didn't want to rush into anything with you. You're not some one-night-stand or a girl I know I'll dump in a few weeks. You're my *wife*. I wanted to do right by you."

I pull a hand through my hair in frustration and shake my head. Fucking hell. "Damn, Alyssa. I'm *dying* to sink my cock deep inside you. Fuck, you were so wet just now, all I could think about was how you're going to feel wrapped around my dick. I'm throbbing at the mere thought of it. I need you so desperately, baby... But you're not just a quick fuck. I want it all with you. I want to make out with you and play with you without any expectations. Just pleasuring you brings me enough satisfaction."

She bites down on her lip and throws her arms around me, hugging me tightly. "Okay," she whispers. "You've done it. You've done right by me. Don't make me wait much longer, Daniel. A few more days and I'll jump you myself."

I smile at her and kiss her tenderly. It's cute how she thinks I could possibly last more than a few more days.

Forty-One

I wake up alone and sit up, instantly searching for Alyssa. I breathe a sigh of relief when I hear the shower running and smile as I get up. I walk to the shower quietly and lean against the door. Alyssa notices me immediately and she smiles shyly, making my heart skip a beat. She bites down on her lip, the glass steamed up from the heat of the water, and this moment couldn't have been more perfect.

I undress and walk into the shower, and Alyssa takes a step away, her back hitting the wall. She looks at me, her eyes heavy with expectation and lust. "Morning, baby," I whisper, leaning in. She kisses me, her cheeks flushed.

"Morning," she whispers. Alyssa seems nervous and it's so fucking cute. She looks up at me in regret and drapes her hands around my shoulders. "I need to get ready," she murmurs, and I nod. I want her pressed up against the wall. Soon. I don't think I can wait much longer.

She kisses me one more time before walking out, and I rush through my shower, missing her already. She looks up in surprise when I walk into the wardrobe just minutes later. Her eyes are on my body, while mine are on her. She looks hot standing here in nothing but her underwear. She bites down on her lip yet again, and I decide I've had enough. I walk up to her and bury my hand in her hair, kissing her roughly. She moans against my lips and melts against me. Her hands find their way to my hair, and she scrapes her nails over my scalp.

"Alyssa," I whisper. I lift her onto her dresser and step between her legs, deepening the kiss. I'm rock hard, and I want nothing more than to take her back to bed. "I can't believe I have to go to Deveraux Inc. I miss you already."

Alyssa giggles and looks at me with so much affection that my heart starts to race. She pushes against my chest and I lift her off the dresser. "Come on," she says, giggling. "We need to get ready."

She grabs my hand and pulls me towards my suits, and I follow reluctantly. "Shouldn't you want to *un*dress me?" I ask, whining. Alyssa laughs and shakes her head as she browses through my clothes.

"Here," she says, handing me a navy coloured suit. "Wear this."

I grin at her and do as she says. I never thought I'd be the kind of guy that wears what his wife tells him to, but I fucking love it. Alyssa's eyes are heated as she watches me dress and I bite back a smile. Looks like my wife has a thing for suits, huh?

She grabs a tie and loops it around my neck, tying it for me carefully. I wrap my hands around her waist and pull her flush against me, my lips crashing down on hers. She rises to her tiptoes and kisses me back hungrily. Finally... it took us a while to get here, but this is exactly what I've always wanted.

I sigh and kiss her one more time. "I wish we could go to work together," I murmur, and Alyssa nods. She rises to her tiptoes and presses another quick kiss to my lips. "Soon, babe. But today you gotta go to that meeting. You're gonna be late."

I walk away reluctantly, already counting down the hours until I get to see her again. I can barely focus during the meeting. All I can think about is Alyssa. I can't get enough of her. I'm pretty sure I'll go crazy if I don't have her back in my arms soon.

"Daniel," my mother snaps. I look up at her dazedly and she

shakes her head. I look around the room to find the meeting has already ended, and I didn't even realise.

"I assume things are going well between you and Alyssa, since you look so love struck?"

I smile at her, feeling a little awkward. No matter how old I get, it's still strange to talk to my mother about a woman. "Yes," I say simply.

She frowns at me and crosses her arms. "You're still on track to take over from me, right? I'm not sure how much longer I can do this for, and your father would turn in his grave if we elected an external CEO."

I nod at her, but I'm not sure Alyssa is ready yet. I don't even tell her what I expect of her, because I worry the pressure will be too much for her. I don't want to push her too quickly.

"Very well," Mum says, walking me out. I sigh in relief when I'm finally back in my car. Just a few more minutes until I'm back at DM. Mum wasn't wrong. I'm behaving like a love-struck fool, but I'm enjoying every second of it.

I pick up a mocha for Alyssa and reluctantly buy coffees for the rest of the staff too, so it's not so obvious that I'm playing favourites. She looks up at me when I walk into the office, her entire face lighting up. I wink at her and put her mocha down in front of her before handing out coffees to the rest. She takes a sip and sighs in delight, her eyes finding mine. Mocha's always make her day, but for whatever reason she rarely has them.

When I run out of excuses to linger, I walk into my office reluctantly. I manage to focus on work for a grand total of ten minutes before finding an excuse to call Alyssa in. I lean out of my office and shout her name, trying my best to sound stern.

Alyssa frowns and jumps up, looking worried. She joins me in my office and stands by my desk. "What's wrong?" she asks.

I grin at her and lift her onto my desk with ease before parting her legs and standing between them. I cup her head gently and lower my lips to hers. "God, I missed you," I whisper. My hands trail down her legs as I kiss her until I reach the lace of the panties she's wearing. I've been wanting to trail my fingers over them since I saw her wearing them this morning. I push them aside and moan against her lips. "So wet for me already, baby."

I pull away from her and sit down on my chair. Alyssa tries to close her legs, but I shake my head and keep them open. "Do you remember that time you sat down on my desk and caged me in with your legs? We were arguing and I was being cold to you."

The smiles on her face drops, and she glares at me. "Yeah. You told me you wanted to see other people," she snaps.

She tries to jump off my desk, but I hold her in place. "Easy, baby. Let me finish," I say. "I thought you were the most beautiful thing I'd ever seen. And when you sat down on my desk, your stunning legs on either side of my thighs and those damn red lace panties right in front of me... All I wanted was to bury my face between your legs."

I grin and lean in to kiss the inside of her thigh. "So let me overwrite that bad memory, my love," I whisper, right before I push her underwear aside and find her clit with my tongue. I make her come right there on my desk, my name on her lips. She covers her mouth with her hand and tries her best to keep her moans quiet as she shatters, and it's gotta be the most beautiful thing I've ever seen.

"I'll never get enough of watching you come for me, Alyssa."

She blushes and jumps off my desk, unsteady. I grab her waist and help her balance until her legs finally decide to work again, and I can't help but feel smug.

"You — you..." she says, still trembling and panting. "Did you actually need something?" she asks.

I shake my head at her, and she looks at me through narrowed eyes. "No playing around at work," she warns me, before storming out.

I laugh and shake my head. "We'll see about that," I whisper. I grin to myself as I open up the internal chat software. It takes me a second to find her, because I keep forgetting that she uses her mother's maiden name as her surname in the system.

. . .

Daniel Devereaux: *but I like playing with you, Wifey. There are so many things I've been fantasising about doing to you. Surely you won't begrudge a man such a small request?*

Alyssa Carter: *Have you lost your mind? This is the work intranet! It's on my screen! What if someone walks past me?*

Daniel Devereaux: *I'll fire them. Do you know how long I've wanted to bend you over my desk and fuck you? Baby, I want you kneeling down between my legs underneath my desk. I want you sitting on top of your desk with your legs spread wide... You can't just kill my dreams, my love.*

Alyssa Carter: *You can't just fire someone, Dan. There are these things called labour laws. You'd better get to work. Stop making me wet and desperate for you.*

Daniel Devereaux: *Wet and desperate, huh? How do you expect me to work now? All I can think about is your tight, hot pussy. I'm taking you tonight, Alyssa. I can't wait any longer.*

I can't fucking wait. It's been long enough. I'm making her mine tonight. Heart, body and soul.

Forty-Two

I'm cranky and exhausted when I finally walk into my apartment. All I've been able to think about today is what I told Alyssa, but work has kept me away. I glance at my watch and sigh. I wouldn't be surprised if she's already asleep.

I walk in quietly and freeze when she rises from the sofa, wearing some sort of sexy silk dress. "Wow," I whisper, dropping my briefcase on the floor. Alyssa blushes and I grin as I walk up to her. She looks seductive as fuck, and I can't believe she got all dressed up for me. I breathe a sigh of relief; she wants me as much as I want her.

As soon as I'm close enough, I pull her into me and lower my lips to hers. Alyssa moans and tugs on my tie, loosening it before pulling it off entirely. I take it from her and throw it on the floor, a smile on my lips. "You can't be trusted with ties," I whisper, and she looks away shyly.

I kiss her roughly and she gives it back to me just as hard. I can't get enough of her, my hands roaming all over my body. "This... is this for me?" I whisper, my fingers trailing over the silk that's covering her skin.

Alyssa glances down at her dress and nods. "Who else could it be for?" she whispers, tugging on my suit jacket. I shrug out of it and Alyssa pushes me against the wall. I look down at her, my heart racing, as she slowly unbuttons my shirt.

"I need you," she whispers. "Those messages you sent me today… did you mean it?"

I tug a strand of hair behind her ear and cup her cheek. "About wanting you? Yes, I meant every word."

Alyssa smiles. "Good," she says as she pushes my shirt off my shoulders. I shrug out of it and lift her into my arms. She wraps her legs around my waist and I kiss her as I walk to our bedroom.

I place her down on the bed and she rises to her knees to undo my belt and zipper. I grin down at her and help her get it off. Before long, I'm standing in front of her in nothing but my boxer shorts.

I get into bed and roll on top of her, cupping her face gently as I run my thumb over her lips. "Alyssa, I can't believe you're really lying here with me," I whisper. "You're so fucking beautiful."

I lean in and kiss her gently, tenderly, pouring all my feelings into it. Her eyes shutter closed and she wraps her arms around my neck. I pull away and kiss her forehead, and then her cheeks, her nose, and finally her lips. Alyssa moans as my tongue brushes against her lips.

She tugs on my boxer shorts and I smile before finally giving in and taking them off. I play with the hem of her nightgown and push it up. "You're breathtaking in this, but I want you naked."

Alyssa nods and lifts her hips to help me take it off. It falls to the floor as my fingers close around her panties. I pull them off and drop them on top of her discarded nightgown.

"I've waited far longer to have you than you can imagine," I whisper. I tangle my hands into her hair, my lips hovering over hers.

Alyssa cups my head and pulls me closer, pressing her lips against mine. I sigh and kiss her tenderly. She spreads her legs and shifts underneath me, so I'm pressing against her.

She deepens the kiss and I tangle her tongue with mine as I

slowly move my hips up and down, sliding against her wet heat. I align myself to push into her, but hold back. Instead, I keep teasing her, sliding against all the right places every time I move.

"You're so wet," I whisper. I pull back a little and lift myself onto my forearms so I can look down at her. "So beautiful, Alyssa. I can't get enough of you."

I kiss her again, gently and slowly, taking my time. My heart is filled with love when I pull away. I've never wanted anyone this way before.

"I want you, Alyssa."

She nods and tilts her hips so I'm sliding into her slightly deeper. My lips fall open and I moan. It's taking everything not to push in all the way. I tense and drop my forehead to hers. "Fucking hell, Alyssa," I whisper, pulling away.

"No," she whimpers. "I need you, Daniel. Please. I can't wait anymore."

I kiss her and tangle one hand in hers while cupping her cheek with the other. "Are you sure you want this, baby?" I ask.

Alyssa rolls her hips up and my eyes fall closed, a soft whimper escaping my lips. "Yes, Daniel. I want you," she whimpers.

I fumble around looking for a condom, but she grabs my hand. "When's the last time you got tested?" she asks, her voice quivering.

My heart sinks. Surely she isn't worried about that? "I've never fucked anyone without a condom, Lyss. Not even once. I had my annual check-up a couple of weeks before we got married. I'm clean. I... I didn't know you were worried about it. I'm sorry, I should've told you."

Alyssa blushes and shakes her head. "I wasn't worried, Dan. It's just... I'm on the pill," she whispers. "I've been on it for years to regulate my periods."

I look at her with wide eyes, my heart racing. "I — you... are you saying you want me bare?" I ask. I've never fucked anyone without a condom before, but if it's Alyssa, I'd want nothing more than that.

She bites down on her lip and looks away shyly. "Yeah," she whispers, looking away.

I grin and lean in for a kiss. "Look at me, baby," I whisper. She tilts her head and looks at me with the same desire and affection I'm feeling. I look into her eyes as I push into her. "You're so tight, baby. Damn. Is this okay?" I whisper, worried. She so wet, but fuck, she's so tight that I'm half worried I won't even fit.

She nods and scrapes her nails over my back. I push in deeper, slower, before pulling back out and thrusting in all the way, fast and hard.

Alyssa cries out in pain while I cry out in pleasure, and I freeze. "Shit, are you okay, Lyss?" I ask. She nods as a tear escapes her eyes, and I panic. "Fuck, baby. What's wrong?"

She shakes her head and pulls me closer. "It's nothing. It just hurt more than I expected," she murmurs. "It's nothing, Dan. Just kiss me for a little while, just a few minutes. Let me get used to your size."

Her muscles contract around my dick and I moan, my forehead dropping against hers. Fucking hell. "I could come just like this," I whisper, and Alyssa giggles as she wraps her arms around me.

I lean in and cup her face with my free hand. "I… did I hurt you? You're definitely wet enough, I don't understand. Should I pull out?" I ask, my voice soft.

Alyssa shakes her head and caresses my face, trailing a path from my forehead down my nose and lips with the tip of her finger.

"Dan, it's okay. The first time is meant to hurt. It'll be okay soon enough," she whispers, and my heart fucking stops. It's her first time? What the fuck? How the fuck did I not know that? I should've been so much more careful with her. *Fuck*. I move to pull out of her, but she tangles her legs with mine and keeps me in place.

"Please," she whispers, her voice breaking and her eyes filling with tears. "I promise I'll be okay soon, please don't stop." She sniffs as a tear runs down her cheek and my heart fucking breaks. "Next time will be better, I promise. I'm sorry," she says, trembling underneath me.

I inhale deeply and wipe her tears away with my thumb and kiss her tenderly, taking my sweet time with her. More tears fall down her cheeks and my heart shatters.

"Alyssa, my love, don't cry. Please... You're breaking my heart, baby."

I kiss every tear away and cup her face gently. Alyssa looks up at me, distressed. "I just... I just wanted it to be perfect. I've wanted this for so long, and I — now I... I ruined it."

I lean in and kiss her, over and over again until she relaxes underneath me and her tears subside. "I'm still rock hard. I'm still inside you. How is anything ruined, beautiful? We haven't even started yet, and this is already the best sex I've ever had. You feel amazing, Lyss. So wet for me, so tight. This is absolutely perfect, my gorgeous wife. So much better than I ever could've dreamed."

I pull back slightly and push back in, moving little by little, showing her I'm definitely still hard. Alyssa squirms underneath me and I kiss her as I make love to her as slow as I possibly can.

"Daniel," she whispers, and I pull my lips away from hers to look at her. "You don't need to hold back," she says, looking worried.

"Baby, I've been ready to burst from the moment I sank into you. I'm not holding back, I'm just trying my best to make sure your first time lasts more than a couple of thrusts, but *fuck*. I've wanted you for so long and so badly..."

Alyssa laughs, and somehow that makes her pussy feel even better. She pulls me towards her and kisses me deeply. I moan against her lips as I pick up the pace. I lean back a little and look into her eyes before thrusting hard.

"Alyssa, my love... I can't... I'm gonna come, baby." She nods and tilts her hips up to meet my thrusts. "Yes... Fuck yes, Alyssa," I moan, coming harder than I ever have before. I close my eyes and collapse on top of her, my heart racing and my ears buzzing.

"Sorry, I must be heavy," I whisper. I hate that the sex wasn't good for her. Fucking hell. I've never been with a virgin before. I have no idea what I should've done. I don't know how to make things better for her. After a couple of minutes, I slip out of her and press a quick kiss to her lips.

"Stay here, babe," I murmur as I get up to grab her a washcloth. There's a small amount of blood on my dick and I stare at it in disbelief before rinsing it off. How could I not have known?

I walk back to Alyssa, and she gasps in horror when I lift the sheets. She clutches the blankets and tries her best to cover herself again. I kneel beside her and brush her hair behind her ear. "Let me, my love. It would mean the world to me if you'd let me take care of you now."

Alyssa nods and releases her death grip on the covers. I tug it away gently and spread her knees, trying my best not to flinch. Her thighs are coated with blood and sperm, and it looks like I really fucking hurt her. I feel awful as I clean her up.

"Daniel, it's embarrassing," she whispers.

I shake my head and smile up at her. "It's not, Lyss. It's fucking beautiful," I say, meaning every word. To have had one of her firsts is fucking amazing.

"Come on, baby," I whisper as I lift her into my arms. "I'm running you a bath. That'll make you feel better for sure."

Forty-Three

I stare at the search results on my phone and inhale deeply. According to Google, I should give Alyssa's body some time to recover. Looks like we'll have to wait at least a week. I'll need to try to make sure things don't escalate between us. How I'm gonna do that, I don't know.

I put my phone away when Alyssa walks into my office. I rise to my feet and hug her tightly. Alyssa steps onto her tiptoes and kisses me.

"How're you feeling?" I whisper.

Her cheeks turn crimson, and I can't help but smile. "Fine, just a bit sore."

I drop my forehead to hers and sigh. "I'm sorry, Lyss. I didn't know. I wish you'd told me you were a virgin. I would've gone easier on you. Maybe stretching you out first would've helped," I say, recalling the results of my google search. Apparently it would've been much easier on her if I'd just stretched her out with my fingers first. I can't believe I fucked up with her. I wanted things to be perfect, but instead I've left her with a less than ideal memory of her first time.

"It was fine," she murmurs, and my mood drops. Fine? I can't remember a single woman that's ever described sex with me as *fine*.

I pull away from her and shake my head. "Maybe we shouldn't have," I murmur. Why was she even holding onto her virginity? I bite down on my lip and look into her eyes. "Why did you wait to lose your virginity? Were you saving it?"

I see the brief flash of panic in her eyes and my heart sinks. Of course she was. There's only one guy she's be doing that for. Fucking hell. I always knew, but this fucking tears me apart.

"I wasn't saving it, per se. I just... it just never happened."

"Hmm, I see.". I don't even want to think of her reasons why. She held out for him for years, huh? Fucking bullshit. I take a step away from her, my anger rising. Why the fuck did it need to be Dominic?

"You'll be sore for a while," I murmur. I doubt she'll want to have sex anytime soon, anyway. I doubt it was even remotely good for her.

"It's fine. I'll be fine. I'm okay. I'm sure it'll be better next time."

I clench my jaw. That bad, huh? Fucking hell. Alyssa takes a step closer to me and wraps her arms around me. She kisses me, and I kiss her back, properly this time. A small moan escapes her lips and I harden against her stomach. She slides her hand down my chest until she's cupping me, and I take a step back. I'll go crazy if she touches me like that, knowing I can't have her without hurting her again. "Ah, we're at the office, Lyss," I murmur.

She nods and clears her throat awkwardly. "Uh, yeah," she whispers. She hands me the document she wanted me to sign, things suddenly awkward between us. She smiles at me as she walks out and I sigh.

Alyssa ends up working late, and by the time I see her again I'm sprawled out on the sofa, documents surrounding me. She rushes into our bedroom to shower and change, and when she walks back into the living room my heart skips a beat. She's wearing a nightgown that I haven't seen before, and she's stunning.

"Hey, Lyss," I murmur, my eyes moving back and forth between her face and her breasts. I clear the space next to me and hand her a takeout box. "Got some Chinese on the way home."

I try my best to focus on my paperwork, but I can't help but glance at her. I can't focus on shit when she's sitting next to me, looking like that. The worst thing is I can't even have her. I know she's still sore, so this is fucking torture.

She puts on a movie and settles against me comfortably as she eats and I work. I manage to get a small amount done until about halfway through the movie, when Alyssa pulls my documents out of my hands before climbing onto my lap. I harden underneath her immediately. "Hey, I was working," I whisper, trying my best to sound annoyed and failing miserably.

"Hmm, I know," she says. "But I feel neglected. Give me ten minutes of your time and I'll let you get back to work."

I laugh and stretch out my legs, shifting us both into a more comfortable position. To think Alyssa and I got this comfortable with each other. I love this. I spoon her, and she sighs in delight when I start to kiss her neck, trailing a path from her ear to her shoulder and back. Alyssa turns around and buries her hand in my hair, pulling my lips to hers. She hooks her leg around me to get me where she wants me and I moan against her lips. I roll on top of her and grind against her..

"Daniel," she moans. I push myself up to look at her, and Alyssa blushes. She looks stunning like this, her hair messed up and her skin flushed.

"This thing you're wearing... it's torture," I whisper. I lean in and suck on her nipple through the lace covering it, and Alyssa arches her back as she moans. I smile and move to her other breast, and she bucks her hips against mine. I love driving her wild. She slides her palm down my abs and I freeze when she grabs my dick. She's still sore from yesterday, so there's no way we can take this further.

"Your ten minutes are up," I murmur, sitting up.

Alyssa stares at me in disbelief. "You're kidding, right?"

I shake my head and stand up to move away. I need to google if it's okay to touch her with my fingers, at least.

"Dan... you can't leave me like this," she whispers, and I glance back at her heatedly.

"Lyss, I'm sorry. I've got a video call with Liam Evans in a couple of minutes," I say, but I fucking wish I didn't.

I walk to my home office and dial in, instantly irritated when I see Liam's dumb face on my screen. I still remember him asking out Alyssa, and he's going on my shit list for the rest of our lives. Alyssa walks in a few minutes into the meeting and I glance up in surprise. She lifts her finger to her lips and walks towards me in complete silence.

"Everything okay, bud?" Liam asks.

I glance back at my screen and nod. "Ah, yes. My girlfriend just walked in. I apologise."

Liam frowns. "I didn't even know you had a girlfriend. Can't believe someone finally managed to lock you down. Who's the lucky girl?"

Alyssa sinks to her knees in front of my desk and crawls underneath it. She places her hands on my thighs and I look down at her and then back at my screen, panicked. What the hell is she doing?

"Uh, we're keeping it quiet for now. We haven't been official for long," I tell Liam. I need to talk to Alyssa about this. I'd love for everyone to know, but she did make secrecy a rule.

She unbuttons my suit pants and tugs my boxers out of the way. I'm already half hard just having her this close. I see her lick her lips from my peripheral vision and I shake my head, my eyes wide. I try to grab her hands to stop her, but she lowers her lips to my dick and sucks down on me. I moan and try to cover it up with a cough.

"No wonder you haven't been seen with anyone in months. I'm surprised the press hasn't caught you with your girlfriend yet," Liam muses. "Can't wait to meet her. The girl who tamed Daniel Devereaux."

Yeah, I doubt that. I bet he's going to be really fucking disappointed when he finds out that Alyssa is *mine.* Alyssa takes me deeper into her mouth and bobs her head up and down. Liam asks me something about Luxe's project management, and I can barely focus on what he's saying.

I thread my hand through her hair subconsciously and push my hips up, urging her to go faster and harder. She drives me fucking nuts. When I realise what I'm doing, I pull my hands away and bury my face in my palms. She makes me lose my damn mind.

"You okay, Daniel? You don't look so well," Liam says.

"Yep, fine. Just uh... just a headache," I say, sounding breathless.

Liam is silent for a while before he starts laughing. "Fucking hell, your girlfriend is still there, isn't she? What a girl. You fucking lucky asshole."

I shake my head frantically. This prick doesn't need to know what happens between Alyssa and me behind closed doors. I want this part of her all to myself. "No! She's uh... she's in the living room," I say, rambling.

"How do you know?" Liam asks. "She just walked into your office and then allegedly back out, so how do you know where she went?" he asks, laughing heartily.

I gulp and Liam laughs even harder. "Anyway, I'm happy with the answers you've provided. Let's do lunch sometime next week? I want to meet this girlfriend of yours."

I nod, wanting him off the call as soon as possible. "Uh, yeah, sure. Thanks for your time."

As soon as the call ends, I moan loudly and pull my hips away, trembling as I cover Alyssa's neck and chest.

"Fucking hell, Alyssa. You're going to fucking kill me, baby."

I push my chair away and then pull her onto my lap, panting.

I grab a couple of tissues from my desk and clean her up before hugging her tightly. "Fuck," I whisper, and Alyssa giggles.

I can't believe I won't get to sleep with her again for another week. I'll fucking lose it.

Forty-Four

I'm annoyed as we walk into my mother's house on Friday night. I forgot Alyssa promised her we'd come back for the weekend, and I'm so fucking gutted. It's finally been a week since we first had sex, and I really want to show her how good things can be between us. I'm terrified she'll think sex just sucks.

I carry her luggage to her room like I usually do and freeze. Should we be sharing a room here too? Since she insisted on secrecy, she might not want Mum and Dominic to know that we're official now. I walk to her door, hoping she'll glare at me and order me to take her luggage to my room instead, but instead she just smiles at me. I sigh and walk into my own bedroom, feeling oddly crestfallen.

I unpack and walk into the living to find Alyssa and Dominic sitting next to each other. He's poking her arm and it fucking irritates me. I don't want him anywhere near her. I sit down in my usual seat and cross my arms.

"Dude, what did you do to her? She's been sulking ever since she walked in," Dominic says.

Alyssa glares and pokes him, and I'm literally two seconds away from pulling her away from him. Alyssa rises and sits down next to me.

Mum laughs as she glances at the TV. "The Notebook? Good choice," she says.

Alyssa scoots closer until our sides are touching. All I can think about as she watches the movie is that she'd been saving her virginity for Dominic. It's my brother she's always loved. I wonder how she feels now, sitting here opposite him. She gets up halfway through the movie, an anguished expression on her face, and she walks away. I stare after her, feeling like she's suddenly so far away. Every time we come here, it's like she's an entirely different person. Like she isn't mine.

I spend all night expecting her to sneak into my bedroom like she has been doing, but she doesn't. I find out why the next morning, when I walk into the living room to find her on the sofa, tangled together with Dominic, both of them fast asleep. My stomach twists painfully and I kick against the sofa, waking them both up.

"Ugh," Dominic mutters as he stretches, both of them disoriented and sleepy. She spent the fucking night with Dominic. Fucking hell. Why the hell did I expect better from her? She's always shown me it's him she wants, yet I ignore the signs over and over again.

Alyssa stretches and her eyes find mine. She freezes and pinches Dominic, waking him up. He yelps and sits up when he sees me, both of them looking guilty. Fuck. I don't even know how to feel. I'm a fucking idiot. I look at the two of them and smile mockingly. Alyssa is wearing one of her sexy nightgowns — the ones I thought she only ever wore for me. Guess I wasn't as special as I thought.

"Breakfast is ready," I tell them, walking away. I can't stand to look at the two of them for even a second longer. I sit down in my usual seat and hide behind my newspaper, my mind whirling. I glance up briefly when Alyssa and Dominic walk in. They eat in silence and I stare at my newspaper. I've never felt like I don't want to be around Alyssa. No matter what she does, I always want her there. Today though... today I want space.

"Uh, about just now... Dominic and I were just watching movies last night and fell asleep on the sofa," she murmurs, her voice tinged with guilt. Watching a movie dressed like that? Who does she think she's fooling?

"It's fine. I don't care," I say, snapping.

Alyssa stares at me. "You don't *care*?" she repeats slowly.

I sigh and put my newspaper down. I'm not in the mood to play these dumb games with her. "What is it, Alyssa?"

Dominic stands up and smiles at her. "Uh, Lyss. I thought maybe we could go swimming today? Let's lounge by the pool. What do you think?"

Alyssa looks at him and smiles, her explanation forgotten. "Hmm, yeah, sure," she says.

I shake my head and pick up my newspaper as they both walk out. What the fuck am I doing?

Alyssa walks back in minutes later wearing a pink bikini that definitely doesn't fit her properly. Her entire body is on display, and I clench my jaw. First she watches a movie with Dominic in her nightgown, and now this? I'll be damned if I let this happen.

"You wanna come swimming with us?" she asks. I wrap my hands around her waist without thinking and bite down on my lip as my eyes drop to her chest.

"The weather is great, and we don't have a pool in our apartment. Might as well make use of the one here. Who knows how long we'll be able to enjoy this weather."

I look up at her, barely able to contain my anger, and nod. "Hmm, I think I will."

Alyssa grins and walks away, giving me a spectacular view of her ass. There's no way I'm leaving her alone, dressed like that. I walk to my bedroom and change into swim shorts, walking to the pool minutes later.

I freeze when I reach them, my heart twisting painfully. Dominic has her lifted into his arms, and she's looking up at him. He laughs and she glares at him. He grins mischievously and bends down as though he's about to drop her. Alyssa tightens her grip on him, pushing herself flush against him, and I grit my teeth. "Don't you dare!" she shouts, just as she drops her into the water.

Alyssa finally notices me as she catches her breath and I stare at the two of them, arms crossed. Dominic and she both turn towards me as I enter the pool. I swim towards them leisurely, trying my best to keep my anger in check.

"Struggling to get onto the float, Lyss?" I ask. She nods wordlessly and I bend down to lift her into my arms. I place her down on the unicorn float and turn away. I swim laps in hopes of getting my emotions in check, but unfortunately for me, Dominic follows me.

"It's not what you think," he says. "I know that looked wrong, and this morning too. She's my best friend, Dan. That won't ever change. I know she's happy with you and I'm not trying to stir any trouble. She just seemed a bit down, so we watched movies together last night."

I glare at him and stand, my arms crossed. "I don't need your explanation, Dominic. My wife is a grown woman, fully capable of making her own choices. She chose to spend last night on the sofa with you, half dressed. She let you touch her just now."

Dominic nods. "Yes, okay, fair enough. But we've always done that, haven't we? Just a year ago you wouldn't have thought twice about us doing that. I understand things are different now, but neither Alyssa nor I really consciously thought about it. She told me she was insecure about her relationship, you know? Seemed like things were going well between you, but she says you've been distant all week, and now you're in different bedrooms again? I just wanted to cheer her up. It's nothing more than that, I swear. I know she's yours, even if she doesn't fully realise it herself. I see the way she looks at you, man. I know I don't stand a chance, and I'm not even gonna try. I just want you both to be happy."

She said she felt insecure? What the hell? We swim back to Alyssa and much to my surprise, Dominic ruthlessly pulls Alyssa off her float. I'm as startled as she is. "You asshole," she shouts. She pushes at him with all her might, intent on throwing him off, but he holds onto the float for dear life.

I throw my hands around her waist and pull her flush against me, her back to my chest. She struggles and kicks the float in an attempt to dislodge Dominic, and I laugh.

"It's fine, Lyss. Just let him have it for a while. Why don't we go soak in the jacuzzi for a bit?" I murmur into her ear. She melts against me and nods. She glares at Dominic one more time before following me to the jacuzzi next to the pool.

Alyssa sighs in delight as we sink into the heat. Her eyes fall closed and she leans back in her seat, her back pressed against one of the jets.

"You look like you're enjoying that."

She glances at me and nods. "I am," I tell him. "The jets are amazing. It's like getting a tiny massage."

I hold my hand out for her, and she grabs it instinctively. I pull her out of her seat and onto my lap, and she yelps, making me laugh. I grab her ass and position her so she's nestled on my lap comfortably.

"You — what are you doing?"

I nuzzle her neck and sigh. "I'm sorry," I whisper. "I didn't stop to think about how my behaviour would affect you, and I broke one of the promises I made you. I didn't communicate well at all. I didn't realise I was making you feel insecure. It took my brother talking to me before I realised what I did to you. I'm sorry, baby."

She stiffens in my arms and looks at me, her insecurity clearly reflected in her eyes now. "I wasn't trying to be distant, sweetheart. I was worried. I was scared I'd hurt you again. I know having sex wasn't even remotely enjoyable for you, and I didn't want to put you through it again. I stopped you every time because I didn't want you to do anything out of obligation."

I stand up and turn her around before pulling her back to me as I sit down. She falls onto my chest, straddling me. I pull her close and lean back into my seat.

"I always want you, Alyssa. Always. But I never want to put you in a position where you're doing something just because you think I might want or expect it."

I cup her cheek gently and pull her face close to mine. She relaxes against me when my lips find hers and kisses me back. My hands roam over her body before finally settling on her ass, and I lean forward a little to shift her right on top of my erection. I moan against her lips and grip her tighter. Her body feels amazing against mine. I could literally push into her so easily.

I slip one of my fingers underneath her bikini bottoms and right into her. She moans and pulls her lips away, gasping for air. I grin as I play with her, the two of us obscured by the jacuzzi's bubbles. We're so wrapped up in each other that we forget we aren't alone.

Dominic pulls us back into the present by throwing a bucket of water over our heads.

"Hmm, well... I guess we had that one coming," I murmur.

Forty-Five

Alyssa seems so frustrated as she storms into her room that she doesn't even realise I'm right behind her. "Ugh!" she shouts as she undresses and walks into the shower.

I grin as I push my swim shorts off and join her. "What's got you so frustrated, baby?"

She whirls around and looks at me with wide eyes. She looks at my body hungrily and I walk up to her. She takes a step back, and her back hits the wall. I grin and lower my lips to hers. "Now where were we?" I whisper, right before kissing her.

My body slams against hers and I moan when she kisses me back. I lift her into my arms and push her against the wall as she wraps her legs around me. "Fuck. I missed your body. You have no idea how hard it was for me to stay away from you. I'm fucking craving you so badly."

I bury a hand in her hair and tug on it to expose her neck. A shiver runs down her body as I bite and kiss her neck. She tilts her hips, subconsciously trying to get me to slide into her, and I pull away to look at her.

"Babe," I whisper.

Alyssa looks devastated and sniffs. She clearly took me pulling away from her as a rejection and pushes against my chest. "Just put me down," she snaps.

I shake my head. "No," I murmur as I turn the shower off. I walk out with her in my arms, both of us dripping wet. I sit her down on her bed carefully and walk back to grab a towel. I wrap it around her carefully as I sink down in front of her, drying her off carefully.

"I can do it myself," she mutters as she tries to grab the towel from me. I shake my head as she yanks it out of my hands and scowl at her.

"Looks like you're going to be difficult. Very well," I say as I stand up and walk to her wardrobe. I walk back to her with one of her scarfs in hand and grin. I'm hard and naked, and I don't miss the desire in her eyes. I lift her into my arms and reposition her so she's lying flat on her back and then I grab her wrists, tying them together before she has a chance to object.

"Daniel, release me," she says, sounding tired.

"I seem to recall you doing the same thing to me with one of my ties. Payback's a bitch, huh, Lyss?"

I smile at her and yank her towel away, letting it fall to the floor. I lean in to kiss her, but she turns her head away, and my smile falters. I inhale deeply and kiss her neck instead. I keep kissing her neck until she's out of breath and needy. When I move back to her lips, she kisses me eagerly. I chuckle and deepen the kiss until I've got her moaning.

I keep my lips on hers as my hand slides down her body. My finger slips into her easily and I freeze. "*Fuck*," I groan. "So fucking wet."

I slip another finger into her and she arches her back to get me to push in deeper. I chuckle and pull away, reaching underneath her pillow for the lube I put there earlier.

"Dan, what's that?"

I smile at her awkwardly as I fidget with the bottle. I've never actually had to use lube before, so this is pretty damn awkward for me. "It's... uh... it's lube."

Alyssa stares at me in confusion and shakes her head. "Dan, I don't think we need that," she says quietly.

I shake my head and swallow hard. "I googled it. I think it hurt so much because maybe you weren't wet enough."

She smiles and tugs on her restraints. "Baby, could you please undo this?" she asks.

I hesitate and then nod, undoing the ties. She wraps her arms around me and pulls me in for a kiss. "What exactly did you google?"

I hide my heated cheeks in her neck and sigh. "I just googled why sex might hurt, and what we could potentially do to make it better for you. Maybe you just weren't turned on enough, or maybe you weren't wet enough. For some people it hurts the first handful of times, but it seems like lube might help."

"I see," she whispers. "Dan... it didn't hurt that much last time. Only at the start, and then it got better. I was just uncomfortable because of your size. I wasn't in pain. I just kind of felt overly stretched out. Honey, the lube isn't going to make a difference. There's no way I could possibly get wetter or more turned on."

I push myself up to look at her and she cups my cheeks, bringing my lips to hers. I kiss her deeply and gently, and it's not until she rakes her nails over my scalp that I deepen the kiss. My hands roam over her body and I tease her nipples before sliding them down. I slip two fingers into her with ease, and her entire body jerks when I slide against her g-spot. I smile against her lips and kiss her harder when I slip another finger into her, stretching her out and keeping her stimulated. The last thing I want to do is hurt her again. By the time I sink into her, I want her well and truly ready for me.

"Baby, I want you," she whimpers.

I pause and look at her before shaking my head. "No," I whisper, though it kills me to say it. "Let me make you come first."

Alyssa grins up at me and presses a lingering kiss to my lips. "Hmm, Google tell you to do that?"

I regret telling her that already. I push against her g-spot harder in retaliation and she almost loses it. She moves her body out of my reach and grabs my dick to line it up to her.

"I need you *now*, Daniel. Won't you fuck me? Won't you slide into your soaking wet wife?"

My lips fall open in shock, and then I grin before pushing into her ever so slightly. I stop when the tip is in and glance over at the bottle of lube. I don't think I've ever had a wetter pussy, but I'm still worried I'll hurt her.

Alyssa chuckles and pulls me closer, kissing me roughly. She tilts her hips up and takes me in deeper. I moan and thrust the remaining bit into her, unrestrained and out of control. I pause immediately and look up at her in worry. Why can't I ever stay in control when it comes to her?

"Shit, Lyss. I'm sorry. I did it again. *Fuck*. Did it hurt? Are you okay?"

She shuts me up by kissing me, and I relax on top of her. "I'm fine," she whispers, and I frown.

"Fine?" I repeat. I fucking hate that word. I don't want her to be *fine* when I'm deep inside her.

My thoughts must be written all over my face, because Alyssa laughs and shakes her head. "I'm *perfect*, baby. Please, Daniel. Will you give it to me or not?"

I exhale in relief and pull back out almost all the way before pushing into her fully. Alyssa moans loudly and bites down on her lip to silence herself, and I grin. "Fuck," I groan.

I smile and fuck her slowly as my lips find hers. I kiss her as the two of us lose ourselves in each other. "Dan, it's so fucking good. Don't stop," she whispers.

I chuckle and bite down on her lower lip. I pull out of her and she whimpers. The sound is music to my ears. I grab her legs and push them over my shoulders before sinking back into her, and she moans in delight.

"Hmm, seems like those yoga classes of yours were worth it

after all," I murmur, hitting her g-spot with every thrust. "Is this okay, Lyss? Does it hurt? Is it too deep?"

She shakes her head, almost incapable of forming a response, and I smile as I fuck her harder.

"Daniel... I — I can't hold it," she groans. I increase the pace and come seconds after she does. I grin at her and take her into my arms, hugging her tightly.

"You stayed away because you were scared of hurting me?" she asks. I tighten my grip on her and nod tersely.

"Baby, why didn't you just talk to me? If you'd told me, then I wouldn't have started to overthink everything. I thought the sex was so bad that you didn't want to sleep with me again."

I pull away and look at her in disbelief. "What the fuck, Alyssa. How could you possibly think that? Fuck. Do you know how bad I felt knowing that the worst sex you've ever had is the *best* sex *I've* ever had?"

She pulls me back to her and kisses me. "Hmm, well, I didn't know sex could be this good. You know, we're spending a couple of days in Singapore next week. How about you show me what I've been missing out on?"

I feel an overwhelming sense of desire. We never got to go on a honeymoon... looks like we've got some catching up to do. I'm going to make sure this trip is one she'll always remember.

Forty-Six

I'm tired and annoyed by the time we walk into our hotel in Singapore. Alyssa has been behaving weirdly in the last couple of hours, and I can't tell what the deal is. She's trying so hard to keep our relationship from Kate, I have to wonder if she's somehow embarrassed of me. I guess I'm a lot older than her, even though most days I barely feel like an adult myself. Is that what's holding her back?

Kate stares at us awkwardly as she checks us in. It's obvious something is up. She walks towards us and clears her throat. "Um, this is yours, Alyssa," she says, handing her a room card. I forgot Kate booked us two different rooms. This entire trip was booked before Alyssa and I got together. Alyssa stares down at the card, and part of me hopes she'll ask to cancel her room, but a larger part of me knows she won't.

"Is everything okay?"

She blinks and nods at Kate. "Yes. Of course."

I sigh as we make our way to our rooms. I'm in no mood to convince her to stay with me. I feel like I'm always chasing her, and I'm tired of it. Every once in a while I want her to *choose me*.

Alyssa hesitates as we reach our floor, but eventually she walks to her own room. I stare after her and shake my head. Every time I think we've come far, she shows me I'm mistaken.

I'm absentminded as I enter my suite and walk straight to the bathroom. I'm exhausted, and tomorrow is going to be filled with meetings. I'm startled when my doorbell rings mid-shower, and I walk out, annoyed.

I open the door to find Alyssa standing in front of me. I breathe a sigh of relief as I open the door wider. I take her suitcase from her and carry it in, putting it down beside my own.

"I'm sorry," she murmurs. "I was being stupid. I wasn't thinking at all. I lasted about three seconds before I realised I can't spend a whole night without you."

I lean in and kiss her. "Thank god, because I was about ten minutes away from cancelling my room and joining you in yours."

Alyssa looks around the suite and smiles in delight. "You're crazy. You should've just thrown me over your shoulder and shown me this suite. Not a chance I'd want to stay in my room then."

This girl. I laugh and shake my head. "Hmm. I was going to tell you something's wrong with my room and they're fully booked, so I have to stay with you."

She grins up at me. "You really thought that one through, huh?"

I look away, a smile on my lips. Alyssa pushes away from me and walks into the bedroom to unpack her suitcase. I'm just about to follow her into the shower when the damn doorbell rings again.

I open the door, a scowl on my face, only to find Kate standing in front of it, a surprised expression on her face.

"I'm sorry," she says. "I thought we agreed to have dinner at six? Would you like me to come back later? I can call room service?"

She glances at the robe I'm wearing with a frown and then looks away. I shake my head and let her in.

"No, not at all. Please, come in. Give me five minutes to get dressed, and I'll be right with you."

I sigh as I walk to the bedroom. I selfishly wish Kate wasn't staying in the same hotel as us. We'll have to have dinner with her every night, which means I'm missing out on some date time with Alyssa.

"You okay?" Kate asks when I finally join her on the balcony where she's had room service lay out dinner.

I nod and smile at her. "More than fine."

Kate and I both look up when Alyssa walks in. Both women look surprised, and I wonder how long it'll take Kate to figure out that Alyssa was in my room all along. There's no way we'll be able to enjoy this holiday if we keep trying to hide our relationship.

"Hey, come sit," I murmur, patting the seat next to mine. I push a plate towards her as she sits down. "I got the wagyu and the sea bass. Couldn't choose between them, so I thought we'd share."

Alyssa nods and takes a bite while I pour her a glass of wine. Kate stares at us suspiciously, but I ignore her gaze.

"Feel better now?" I ask. Alyssa nods and narrows her eyes at me. How does she see through me so easily? Does she know I'm not going to try to hide our relationship?

"Yeah, much better," she says, before looking at Kate. "Was the flight okay for you?" she asks.

Kate nods but looks confused as she glances at the two of us. She knows we're married, but she also thinks that despite that, we aren't together. Alyssa and I treat each other so politely when we're at work that our current relaxedness must surprise her.

I place a hand on Alyssa's thigh, and she bites down on her lip. She throws me a knowing look and steals a bite of food from my plate.

"Is your room to your liking, Alyssa?" Kate asks.

"Well, to be honest, I like this one more," Alyssa says, glancing at me with a mischievous look in her eyes. "Why don't you let me have this room?"

I blink at her in surprise and grin. Maybe I was wrong. Maybe she isn't ashamed of me at all. She isn't trying to keep our relationship hidden like I thought she was.

"Hmm, it's yours," I murmur, shrugging. I lift my fork to my lips, but Alyssa grabs my hand and closes her lips around my fork, stealing my food. My heart skips a beat. I can't remember a single time when Alyssa has so blatantly and publicly flirted with me.

"You want it?" I ask, pushing my plate to her.

Alyssa shakes her head. "Just wanted a bite."

I lean back and put my arm around the back of her seat. "By the way, if you wanted to book any tours for our holiday afterwards, just let Kate know," I murmur, grinning at her.

"Hmm, you're going to make it impossible, aren't you? Are you gonna be like this throughout the entire trip?" she asks, and I pretend I don't know what she's talking about. Had she really frozen me out then I wouldn't behave the way I am, but it's clear she wants Kate to know too.

Kate smiles at us. "Oh, yes! I'm looking forward to spending some free time here. That was a really good idea, Daniel. You're the absolute best," she gushes. "What should we do?" she asks, looking excited.

Alyssa's smile drops and I bite back a grin. She crosses her arms over her chest and glares up at me, and I can't help but find her cute. So she wants to spend some alone time with me, huh?

I throw my arm around her and lean in, pressing a kiss to her cheek, startling both her and Kate. "I'm sorry, Kate. I promised my girl some alone time."

Kate looks at me in surprise and then smiles. "You two finally got together, huh? Good for you," she says, her eyes twinkling.

Thankfully, Kate doesn't linger around after dinner, giving us some privacy. I breathe a sigh of relief when the door closes behind her and turn to face Alyssa.

"Finally alone," I whisper. She giggles and walks into my arms. "I was convinced you were trying to keep our relationship a secret," I admit.

Alyssa inhales deeply and looks away guiltily. "I was. I don't know. I wasn't sure. I thought maybe you wouldn't want anyone to know."

I press a kiss to her head and shake my head. "Me too. You're the one that insisted on secrecy when we got married, so I didn't want to pressure you into going public before you were ready."

Alyssa rises to her tiptoes and kisses me. "Well, it's just Kate for now. Small steps," she whispers, and I sigh in disappointment. I want to shout from the rooftops that she's mine, but I'll take what I can get.

She giggles as I lift her into my arms and into the bedroom. "We never did get to go on a honeymoon," I tell her as I lay her down on the bed.

Alyssa looks at me through lowered lashes and smiles. I doubt we're going to get much sleep tonight.

Forty-Seven

I'm about ten seconds away from knocking Sasuke's teeth out. I don't care he's the new CEO that we're meant to win over. If he keeps looking at Alyssa like that, he and his company can go to hell.

"You're truly as beautiful as my father claimed you were," he says, smiling at Alyssa for the millionth time. She doesn't even notice that he's flirting with her. Nah, my wife is completely obvious. But I'm not.

Mr. Takuya smiles at his son and nods, and I tighten my hand on my glass. "Alyssa is very clever and very beautiful. You should date a girl like her. All you do is work, work, work. You should give me a grandchild to play with now that I'm retired."

Babies? If Alyssa ever has any, they'll be mine. He'd better stop eyeing her like that. There's no way she's ever becoming his daughter-in-law.

"Hmm, there aren't many women like my Alyssa," I say, my voice hard. I wrap my arm around Alyssa's shoulder as a clear warning, and smile at Sasuke humourlessly. I reckon I can knock him out with one well-aimed punch. Let's see if he dares look at my wife's chest again after that.

Mr. Takuya looks at Alyssa and then back at me, and I tighten my grip on her. He pours me a glass of sake and pushes it towards me. "You've done well, son," he says, laughing. Mr. Takuya being here means we probably won't get anything signed and done, anyway. He prefers to socialise and drink first and do business after. I feel like we're wasting precious time that Alyssa and I could be spending together, and it irritates the hell out of me. I take the glass he poured me politely and empty it.

Mr. Takuya surprises us both when he eventually nods at Alyssa with a serious look in his eyes. "I read your proposal, Alyssa. I was very impressed. You inherited your father's mind. If you work on the project personally, then Sasuke and I will sign the contract."

She smiles and I see the brief amount of shock in her eyes. It still baffles her when someone recognises her brilliance, and I can't for the life of me understand why. "I'm honoured you think so highly of me, Mr. Takuya. My father would be proud to hear your words. I'll be sure to work on your campaign myself. I'll make sure to live up to your expectations."

He nods, and it's done. I know he'll sign the contract if he's given his word. Sasuke doesn't look annoyed at all when his father makes a decision that should be his. Instead, he looks somewhat contrite, as though he knows it's the right call and he's glad he didn't have to make it himself. His father claps him on the back and all of us share another shot of sake to seal the deal.

I'm frustrated as hell by the time we stumble back into our hotel room. I've had to drink far more sake than I wanted to, and I'm still pissed off about the way Sasuke flirted with Alyssa all night. I should've made it clear that she's mine from the start.

I grab her as soon as the door closes behind us and push her against the door. I kiss her roughly before pulling away, and she looks up at me with wide eyes. "I need to put a ring on you, Wifey," I murmur. "A tiny little collar for your finger. I'm sick and tired of men hanging around you, coveting what is *mine*."

My lips trail over her neck before returning to her lips and she inhales sharply. "A wedding ring?" she asks, her voice shaky.

I was thinking of an engagement ring to start off with, but I like her thinking. "Yeah," I whisper, capturing her lips all over again.

I want her in my bed. I want her entire body marked. But instead, I pull away and bury my hand in her hair. "We still have some time. It's only 10pm. Is there anything you'd still like to do?"

Alyssa's eyes light up, and I smile at her. We haven't gotten a chance to see anything yet, and I know she's dying to explore Singapore. "The thing I wanted to do most was to see the light show at the Gardens by the Bay, but I think we're too late now. We might've already missed it," she says, her smile dropping.

I chuckle and grab my phone as I stroke her cheek. "Baby, if there's something you want, then I'll make it happen. Let me make a call. You go get changed."

I shake my head and call one of my friends that owes me a favour. He's going to fucking love that I ended up cashing it in for something so simple, but whatever. What my wife wants, my wife gets.

An hour later Alyssa and I are standing in the middle of a closed park, no one else around us. We sit back and watch the light show that they've put on just for us. I wrap my arm around Alyssa and hug her tightly. "So, is it everything you thought it would be?"

She shakes her head and kisses my cheek. "Better. It's even better."

I kiss her and the two of us spend our evening just like that. Wrapped up in each other as though the rest of the world doesn't even exist.

Forty-Eight

I hold Alyssa's hand as we roam the streets, and I can't wipe the smile off my face. We never used to hold hands in public back at home, but I've come to realise that I love it. I love having her close. I love the way her hand fits into mine. I entwine our fingers and pull her along as we explore Haji Lane.

We sit down at one of the outdoor tables and I pull out my phone, taking what's gotta be the hundredth photo of us together. We're like two tourists that are travelling outside of their own country for the first time. Alyssa poses with the laksa she just ordered, and I laugh as I take a photo. I snap another few of her taking a bite of the noodles and she snatches my phone away to get me to stop.

"I love this place. We should just move here," she murmurs.

I smile at her, wishing things could be so simple. "Hmm, I wish. What would happen to Devereaux Inc. and DM if we just moved?"

She sighs and nods. "Hmm, I know. I was just kidding. I'm just having such a great time here. I definitely want to come back."

I'm inclined to agree. This is the first place we've ever travelled to together. It'll be amazing to return someday. "We can look into buying some property here if you want?"

Alyssa nods, and my heart skips a beat. "Might actually be a good idea," she says. I struggle to hide my satisfied smile. If we bought a place here, then that'd be the first property we own together. I love the idea of that. The apartment we currently live in is just mine. Alyssa hasn't even really redecorated it or anything, and more and more I find myself wanting a place that is *ours*, and not just mine.

I hold her hand as we continue to stroll down the countless alleys until we end up on a big road again. I glance at a large jewellery store and drag Alyssa towards it.

"Let's go have a look," I murmur. The security guard at the front lets us in immediately and I pull Alyssa towards the ring section. I was dead serious when I told her I wanted to put a ring on her, and I can't get it off my mind now.

"I know we never did rings, but if our marriage was different... If you'd been proposed to with a ring, what would you have liked?"

Alyssa's smile drops, replaced by wistfulness. I see the longing in her eyes, for everything we never had. I never proposed to her and we never planned our wedding together. There's so much we missed out on. She didn't even get to go wedding dress shopping. I'm pretty sure that's a thing.

"This," she says, pointing at a ring. She doesn't even think twice about it, and it's clear that she's always imagined what she'd have one day. I want to make sure she'll still have it.

I nod and ask the clerk to take it out for me. He smiles and informs me that it's a three carat cushion cut ring with a pave band, whatever the hell that means.

"Oh, no, I don't want to try it," Alyssa says. She looks annoyed all of a sudden, and I can't make sense of it. I know she wants the ring, so why won't she try it?

"Hmm, we're here anyway. We might as well."

Alyssa shakes her head and turns to walk out of the store, a stormy expression on her face. I stare after her and glance at the clerk.

"Put this on hold for me," I say, putting my credit card down. "My secretary will come to collect it later, and she'll give you the sizing information too."

I run after Alyssa, confused. "Hey, what's wrong, babe?" I ask, throwing my arm around her shoulder.

She rises to her tiptoes and presses a kiss to my cheek. "It's nothing, honey. Come on. Let's go to the hotel. I can't wait to spend the afternoon in the pool. It's been on my bucket list *forever.*"

I know it's not nothing, and I can't help but worry. Is she reminded of everything she could've had if not for her father's will? I can't help but wonder if it's Dominic she's thinking of. I know she's a romantic. I wouldn't be surprised if she'd mentally planned out their entire relationship. I wonder if reality is a disappointment compared to what her fantasies were like.

I try my best to cheer her up the rest of the evening, but she's absentminded. Even in bed, though it's clear that she wants me, it's like she isn't really here with me. Things have been so perfect lately. What the hell went wrong?

Forty-Nine

I stare at the presentation one of my employees is giving and nod along absentmindedly, my mind on Alyssa. I hate being back at work. Alyssa and I were in our own little bubble in Singapore, and it was perfect. It was just us. No work. No distractions. No Dominic. Just us and endless fantastic weather. Now that we're back, we don't even get to see much of each other anymore. I spend most of my time in client meetings or at Devereaux Inc. and she spends most of her time at DM. I sigh and open the chat window on my laptop.

Daniel Devereaux: *I can't stop thinking about you. It's only been a few hours since we've been apart and I miss you already.*

Alyssa Carter: *Aren't you in a client meeting?*

Daniel Devereaux: *I am in the meeting, but I can't focus on it at all. I need you... alone... in my office.*

. . .

Alyssa Carter: *I fucking wish. I miss you too, baby. Too much work to do, though. I have a literal pile of documents on my desk and 300 emails to get to. I'm not even exaggerating.*

I know she's dead serious, because my own inbox is even worse. It's fucking ridiculous that everyone acts like they can't function without Alyssa and me here. I'm grumpy as fuck by the time I walk back into DM, and Alyssa doesn't look much better. Looks like she's loving being back as much as I do.

"Lyss, a word please," I say, my tone biting. She frowns and follows me into my office. I slam the door closed behind her and then slam her body against it, my lips crashing down on hers. I kiss her with impatience and desperation, and she kisses me back just as eagerly. I pull away from her only long enough to carry her to my desk. I shove a bunch of shit off it without thinking twice and put her down. Alyssa yanks on my zipper as I shove her underwear out of the way and slide a finger into her. I grin when I realise my wife is wet as fuck.

"Now," she pants. "Need you now."

I groan and sink deep inside her in one single thrust. She closes her eyes and leans back, but I'm having none of that. I grab her hand and push it between us, urging her to touch herself as I fuck her. She moans and kisses me, the two of us moving frantically. I fucking love that she wants me just as bad.

"Alyssa, *fuck*. I fucking adore every single piece of you."

I thrust into her hard and fast, and her eyes glaze over. I love it when she looks like that. Like she can't even think straight. It doesn't take us long to lose control, and Alyssa giggles against my lips as we both try to catch our breath. I do my best to straighten out her hair and she helps me zip up while I fix her clothes.

"I thought you needed a word," she murmurs.

I laugh and kiss her. "Hmm. The word I needed was *now*. *Please* would've worked just as well, though."

She glares at me and shakes her head. "I have to get back to work. No more of this. We're at work, you know."

I sigh. "Does it matter? Who cares if people know about us? I mean, yeah, we probably shouldn't get caught having sex in my office... But you know."

She frowns and shakes her head, and my heart sinks. "Hmm, I'm not sure. I don't even tell people at work my actual name. I can't really imagine sharing my relationship with colleagues. I think work and private life should be kept separate as much as possible."

What she's saying is she still wants to keep our relationship a secret. What for? Does she think we won't last? Or is she just having some fun while our marriage lasts?

The hours fly by, and I try my best to stay away from her. It takes all of me to keep things professional between us. I've gotten so used to holding her hand and touching her randomly whilst in Singapore, that it feels unnatural to stay away now.

"Hmm, this," I murmur, pointing at something on her screen. I lean over her chair subconsciously, my face close to hers. "Those numbers don't add up."

Alyssa turns and her lips graze my cheek, the two of us closer than either of us expected. I want to lean in and press my lips against hers. It'd be so easy. I smile at her and Alyssa blushes. She moves away from me a little, flustered.

"Boss, maybe I can help you instead. Alyssa is quite busy," Jake says. He looks tense as his gaze shifts between Alyssa and me. He obviously thinks he's looking out for her, and it pisses me off. What the fuck does he think I'm doing? Did it look like Alyssa didn't *want* me close? I hate that I can't tell him she's mine. I grit my teeth and straighten.

"It's quite all right. I'll do it myself, Jake," Alyssa says, smiling at the asshole. I walk away from her, pissed off. Ignoring her is easy for the rest of the day. What other choice do I have? I'll look like I'm harassing my fucking employee otherwise.

I walk out with a document in hand, only to pause in the

doorway. The entire floor is empty, and it looks like Alyssa and I are the only ones left at work. I glance at my watch, surprised to find that it's so late already.

"Hmm. Now that we're alone, I guess I can finally touch you," I say, snapping at her. "Or can't I sit too close to you while we're at the office? Can I smile at you? Is that okay, or is that also not allowed?"

She sighs and rises as I walk to her desk. She takes the document from me and shakes her head. "It's not like that, Dan," she whispers. Except it is.

"Isn't it?" I ask, fuming. I grab her hand and pull her close before changing my mind and turning her around so her back is facing me. I push against her shoulders and she stumbles, bracing herself on the desk closest to her. I part her legs with my knee and push down on her lower back to keep her down while I grab her hair and yank it back. A small moan escapes her lips and I chuckle.

I trace a finger down the back of her thighs and yank her skirt up, exposing her ass. "Hmm, what a fucking view," I whisper. I raise my hand and spank her, the sound of my hand hitting her ass reverberating through the office. Alyssa clenches her thighs together and I grin. I knew this would turn her on. I slap her ass again, on the other side this time, and she moans loudly. I chuckle and push down her underwear, leaving it hanging mid-thigh. I'm not even remotely surprised to find her so wet that even her thighs are soaked. I push a finger into her and she moans, sounding so fucking turned on and needy.

"So needy, Alyssa. So wet. You want me, baby?"

She groans. "Yes. *Yes*."

I pull away from her to open my zipper. It only takes me a couple of seconds to slide into her and Alyssa moans in relief, as though I kept her waiting too long. I slam into her all the way, taking her roughly.

"You could have my hands on you all the time if you'd just agree to go public with our relationship," I say through gritted teeth.

I fuck her so hard that some of the shit on the desk falls off, but I couldn't care less. My fingers find her clit and she rides my hand eagerly.

"You want to come for me, Lyss? If you tell me we can go public, I'll make you come like this every day."

She moans and trashes against my fingers. "You already do anyway," she whispers.

I increase the pace and pull out almost entirely before slamming into her so hard that the desk moves.

"Say it. Say you'll be mine. I want to shout to the world that you're my girl. Tell me you want the same."

I feel her pulse around me, and I know she's about to come. I get impatient when she doesn't reply, and slap her ass, hard. She comes as soon as my hand lands on her ass, her muscles gripping me tightly. She comes hard and just two thrusts later, so do I.

I collapse on top of her, both of us sweaty. I push her hair out of the way and kiss her neck softly. "Please, baby," I whisper. "I want everyone to know that you're mine."

Alyssa giggles. "I'm yours, honey. Tell the whole world if you must, but that won't change the fact that I'm *already* yours. Heart and soul, Daniel."

Heart and soul huh?

Fifty

The lift doors close behind us and I push Alyssa against the wall, kissing the lipstick right off her lips. I've been giddy all morning. It took forever for us to agree to be together publicly. I'm happy just holding her hand or kissing her in public. Alyssa smiles and bites down on my lower lip. "We're at work, baby. We need to keep up some sort of professional image," she says, right before deepening the kiss.

She's breathless by the time she pulls away, and I grin to myself as we reach the top floor. If I didn't have my hands full with documents and the coffee she insisted on buying, I'd be holding her hand instead.

We walk into the office together and Alyssa freezes suddenly. I pause beside her and stare at Alyssa's colleagues, Luke, Linda and Jake.

Luke suddenly jumps into action and walks towards me, his hand curled into a fist. I frown and put Alyssa's coffee on one of the desks seconds before he tries to swing a punch. I grab his wrist and twist it behind him, making him yelp in pain. What the fuck is this puny little shit trying to do? He cries out and Alyssa jumps away from the two of us, both of us confused as hell.

Linda grabs Alyssa's hand and stands in front of her as she

grabs her phone with trembling hands. "I — you better stay away from Alyssa. I'm going to call the police," she tells me, her voice shaking.

Alyssa and I stare at each other in confusion. I let go of Luke and hold my hands up in surrender. "Can someone please tell me what's going on here?" I ask, frowning. Jake walks up to me and pushes against my chest, but the little fucker doesn't even move me. Alyssa rushes to get between us, but Luke grabs her before she can reach me. He wraps his arms around her protectively, as though he's shielding her from *me*. What the fuck? Alyssa pushes him away and stares at her colleagues.

"Okay, what the fuck is going on here?" she says, her voice high pitched.

Linda looks at her with tears in her eyes. "We know, Alyssa. We know what he did to you. I'm sorry we didn't realise sooner."

Alyssa and I both stare at her, neither one of us sure what she's talking about. Linda bursts into tears and Alyssa jumps in panic. "I didn't know," Linda sobs. "I should've been there for you."

Alyssa grabs her shoulders gently and pats her hair. "Sweetie, you need to explain to me what exactly you're talking about.".

Linda sniffs and nods. "This morning all my things were rearranged. The cleaners usually leave everything in the same spot, so I thought maybe someone stole something. I called security and used my credentials as an executive office member to access the security feed for our floor. And that's when I saw... I saw what he did to you."

Linda points at her computer screen, and I freeze. She's got last night's video footage on her screen, and the video is paused at the exact moment I slap her ass. It's on full display and her skirt is pooled around her waist. Alyssa looks at it wide-eyed and jumps to close the window. She closes her eyes and buries her hands in her face, looking distraught as hell.

Fuck. I did this. In the video, it looked like I was so fucking rough with her. Fucking hell... did I hurt her? God, I hope not. I never should've acted the way I did. I shouldn't have treated her the way I did. I fucking got us caught on camera. Because of my fucking possessiveness the team saw my wife half naked.

Alyssa walks towards me. "Are you okay?" she asks me, and I stare at her, completely lost. Even in this fucked up situation, it's me she's putting first. She takes in my expression and sighs before turning back to Linda. "Did you actually watch that video? Because I was enjoying the hell out of that."

Linda looks startled, and a hint of unease enters her eyes. "I — you don't have to stand up for him. We all have your back, Alyssa."

Fucking hell. What have I done? Alyssa sighs and stares up at the ceiling. "Linda... Daniel and I are *dating*. What you saw on the security feed was entirely consensual. Hell, if that video had sound you'd *know* I enjoyed the hell out of it."

Linda looks startled as understanding slowly begins to dawn on her, but Alyssa pays her no mind. She walks towards me and pulls me in for a kiss. I stand there, frozen, but she kisses me nonetheless. "Don't you think for a second that I didn't want that as much as you did," she whispers. Logically I know she wanted it, but looking back at it, it does look fucking awful.

I sigh and gently brush the hair out of her face. "I forgot about the cameras, baby. I never should've exposed you like that. I never should've let anyone see your body like that."

Alyssa rises to her tiptoes to press a kiss to my cheek before turning back to her colleagues. "Get back to work, you absolute morons," she snaps.

Everyone stares at us with wide eyes before they finally get back to work. Just as Linda walks back to her desk, I call her into my office. My eyes meet Alyssa's, and I smile at her reassuringly before following a trembling Linda through the door.

I walk up to my desk and sit down as she fidgets in front of me, unable to look at me. "Thank you," I tell her, startling her. "Thank you for looking out for Alyssa, and for having the courage to step up. Let's be real, I'm the CEO, and I'm a Devereaux. I can make you disappear before the day is over, yet you still decided to do the right thing. I'm impressed, Linda. I always knew you were a hard worker, but you're loyal to a fault too. We need more people like you. Not just at DM, but in the world. I'm sorry to have shocked you, though. Feel free to take the day off, fully paid, of course."

She stares at me and nods in disbelief. She doesn't say a word and just turns to walk out. I wonder how long it'll be before she can look me in the eye again. I chuckle as the door closes behind her, and the rest of the morning passes by painfully slow. It's awkward as hell, and I bet it's even worse for Alyssa. At least I get to avoid those idiots by staying in my office, but Alyssa doesn't have that luxury.

I've only just started work when my phone buzzes endlessly. I stare at it and open the article half a dozen people have forwarded to me. Photos of Alyssa and me in Singapore are all over the tabloids. Some of them are close ups of us making out in the pool, while others are just us holding hands as we walk through the streets.

Hold your heart, ladies. Daniel Devereaux might soon be off the market entirely! It seems that Alyssa Moriani has stolen the Casanova's heart. Not only is Alyssa the late Charles Moriani's only daughter, she is also DM Consultancy's largest shareholder and a bona fide heiress. It makes us wonder who wears the pants in that relationship... Our sources tell us that Alyssa and Daniel have known each other all their lives and have worked together for at least the last four years.

After some digging, we found out that the two have been living together in Daniel Devereaux's luxurious penthouse. It's no wonder that our favourite heartthrob hasn't been seen in public in months now. We can totally imagine what the two lovebirds have been getting up to in their home. To our knowledge, this is the first time Daniel Devereaux has lived with a woman. By our calculations, the two have been keeping their relationship under wraps for months now. It's unclear when they started dating, but our source confirmed the two visited a prestigious jewellery store whilst on their romantic getaway. Is that wedding bells we hear?

I can't lie, I'm pretty pleased with the article, but how the fuck did they manage to tail us without us noticing? I click through the articles to find some of them contain in-depth background information about Alyssa while others are just speculation. I'm used to this shit, but she isn't. Fucking hell... most people at the company don't even know she's Charles's daughter. She's not going to like everyone being informed this way. I check my latest messages and freeze. Seems like the building is surrounded by paparazzi.

I walk out of my office to find her staring at her screen in shock. I throw my arms around her protectively and she hugs me tightly. "I'm sorry," I whisper. "We can sue, if you want."

Alyssa shakes her head. "It'd be too complicated, and it'll only fuel their interest more. I'll deal with it."

I kiss her cheek gently, neither one of us realising that we're shocking our team more than the articles could. I lean over and open the countless messages she's received on the intranet. Most of them are tinged with hurt and betrayal over her hiding her identity rather than hiding her relationship with me. I know it was never her intention or even her idea to hide her surname, though. That was all Charles.

"They're just surprised, honey," I murmur. "Take a moment to decide how you'd like to reply, but keep in mind that you don't owe anyone an explanation. What your name is shouldn't matter, and for so long it hasn't."

She nods and I tuck a strand of her hair behind her ear gently. "There's one more thing, babe. The lobby is swarming with paparazzi. We can either face them now, or we can take the heli to our apartment. I think the latter might be best for today. It'll give us some time to decide how to respond to this."

She smiles and kisses me. "I agree, but there's no real need to think about it. Just get your spokesperson to draft a statement confirming our relationship and asking for privacy. I don't think we need to do more than that."

I look at her in wonder and grin smugly. "You're fine with it then?"

Alyssa glances at Linda's desk and chuckles. "Hmm, shout it to the whole world, baby. I'm yours."

Fifty-One

"Saw the photos of you and Alyssa in the papers," Mum says. She pauses in front of my desk at Deveraux Inc. and I sigh. She doesn't look pleased, and I can't blame her. In the last couple of days, the press has fucking hounded us. They've delved into Alyssa's background and our relationship, and some of the shit they've come up with is really fucked up. I've been likened to a paedophile and I've been accused of abusing my authority, since Alyssa and I work together. Alyssa, on the other hand, has had to deal with unexpected scorn from colleagues that suddenly no longer believe she earned her current position. Now that everyone knows she's Charles's daughter, they seem to have forgotten that she worked far harder than they ever did. It's been a total shit show for both of us, but at the same time, I'm happy it's all out in the open. Everyone knows she's mine now.

"Deal with it," she tells me, as though I'm not trying my best already. Which part of *free press* does she not understand? I nod at her and suppress a sigh.

"What about Devereaux Inc? Are you ready to take on my position? You've spent years at DM and I'm getting older, Daniel."

I nod and try my best to smile. I know my mother needs me,

but the idea of leaving DM breaks my heart. I love working there, and I love working with Alyssa. I always knew there'd be an end to it, but still.

"Yes, Mother. I'm calling for a board meeting to appoint Alyssa as my co-CEO. I'll stay a little while longer to onboard her, and then I'll join Devereaux Inc. fully as CEO." My mother sighs in relief, and I instantly feel bad. I never meant to rely on her as much as I have. In the last couple of weeks I've started to take over from her while increasing Alyssa's responsibilities, but I should've done it sooner. When did my Mum start to look her age? I can tell she's tired, and I should've put her first. Charles would've understood, and so would Alyssa.

Mum straightens and walks to the door. "One more thing," she says. "This thing with Alyssa... I hope it's not too serious. The papers are right, Daniel. She's young. All she's ever done with her life is work her ass off and study. She's never even dated, and I doubt I've ever seen her in love. A marriage like yours... it's doomed to fail. Enjoy it while it lasts, but you'll need to let her go soon. You'll need to give her a chance to live her own life. You're letting her use you as a crutch, but she'll need to stand on her own two feet someday."

Mum closes the door behind her, and I sigh. I wonder if she's right. I've thought the same thing, but lately it's easier and easier to ignore unwanted thoughts. I always thought I'd one day let go of her, but now that the time is here, I'm not sure I can.

I feel unsettled as I make my way to DM. Alyssa looks up when I walk into the office and she grins at me, making my heart skip a beat. "Hey, Lyss," I murmur, pressing a kiss to her lips. She leans into me eagerly and I chuckle against her lips. I love this. I love being able to kiss her in public. I love calling her mine. How much longer *will* she be mine, though? When I give her the good news later, her father's last wishes will officially be fulfilled. "Come into my office for a bit. I need to speak to you."

She nods and follows me. I close the door behind us and she grabs me, pulling me closer for another kiss, a proper one this time. I kiss her back and lift her into my arms to place her on my desk.

"I *actually* needed to talk to you this time, you know," I murmur, my lips already finding hers again. I pull back reluctantly, and Alyssa hooks her legs around my hips to keep me close. "I'm going to call a board meeting, Lyss. You've done so well over the last couple of months. You've proven you can take on the role of CEO and I've spoken to all the board members, and they agree. The board meeting is just a formality at this point. I'm so, so proud of how far you've come in so little time."

She stares up at me in disbelief. I know she knew it was coming, but I bet it's still hard for her to believe it's really happening. "Wow," she whispers. "Are you sure? I don't know if I'm ready."

I laugh and kiss her again, my lips lingering on hers. "Baby, you've already been doing the job for weeks now. How could you not be ready? You even landed more clients this year than I did."

She bites down on her lip and nods, lost in thought. The expression on her face tells me she's thinking of her dad, and I sigh, wishing he could be here to see her fulfilling her goals. "He'd have been so proud of you, you know. He always told me you'd do it in no time at all. That you'd be a better CEO than either he or I ever could be. He never had a single doubt that you could do it. I wish he were here to see you fulfil the dream the two of you shared."

Alyssa's eyes fill with tears, and she buries her face in my neck. I hug her tightly and gently rub her back as she tries her best to hold back her tears.

I bury my hand in her hair and tilt her face up before kissing her forehead gently. Alyssa tilts her head up and I capture her lips, kissing her softly and sweetly. I rest my forehead against hers and close my eyes. "I've missed you," I murmur.

Alyssa sighs and presses her lips against mine. "I missed you too."

We've both been coming home completely exhausted every

night. It feels like ages since we've had a chance to spend a couple of hours in bed together. I kiss her again, more urgently this time.

"Baby," I whisper, a pleading look in my eyes. Alyssa chuckles and nods, and I grin as I slowly unbutton her blouse. She's not quite as patient and makes quick work of my shirt, pushing it off my shoulders. She places her lips against my chest and sucks harshly, leaving a kiss mark. I groan and return the favour, leaving a mark on her breast. I love marring her skin like this — marking her as mine. I push her skirt up while she opens my zipper and I grin when I find her already soaking wet. "Always so eager for my cock, baby," I whisper. She couldn't get more perfect if she tried. She blushes and guides me inside . I sink into her slowly, inch by delicious inch. She leans back on my desk and tightens her legs around me, taking me in deeper.

"More, Daniel. *Please*."

I laugh and give her what she wants. "Fucking hell, baby. I won't last long if you want it like that."

Alyssa moans loudly, and I kiss her to keep her quiet. Her fingers find their way between her legs and before long she's contracting around me. I moan and increase the pace, erupting inside her.

I hold her tightly as the two of us try to catch our breath. Neither Alyssa nor I have said anything about it, but I know it's on her mind too. The second the board approves her appointment as CEO, there will be no need for us to remain married.

Fifty-Two

"Are you guys ready?" I ask, glancing around the office. Everything is in place to surprise Alyssa. The board voted almost unanimously on her appointment, like I knew they would. She's been doing my job for months before I even asked them to consider giving her my title, so she had plenty of time to prove herself, and she's outperformed even my own expectations.

We're all quiet as Alyssa walks into the office, fumbling with the light button. I don't doubt that she's confused why the office is empty and dark at nine am. She turns the lights on and we all jump up, shouting, "Surprise!"

Alyssa jumps and stares at us in shock before smiling. Jake, Luke and Linda stand next to me in the middle of the office and the entire ceiling is covered in balloons. She grins and tries her best to hide her emotions, but she's transparent to me. I walk up to her and sweep her into my arms, twirling her around in a tight hug. She giggles and kisses me as I put her down gently. "Congratulations, baby," I whisper.

The rest joins us excitedly. Linda is clapping and jumping up and down with a wide smile on her face. The official announcement was made early this morning, but she still seems to be in disbelief.

"Thank you," she whispers, glancing around us. Everyone hugs her one by one and I hand her a wrapped box. She frowns as she unpacks it and grins when she realises what it is. She runs her fingers over the nameplate in her hands, her eyes twinkling with joy. It says Alyssa Moriani, CEO. She smiles at me, looking both overjoyed and emotional, and I press a kiss to her forehead. I pull her into my office and take the nameplate from her, placing it on her dad's old desk that I had moved back in here last night.

"I'd like to take credit for the gift, but your dad actually had it made years ago. He knew you'd need it one day and he was as impatient as you were for you to get here."

Besides, had it been me, I'd have made sure it said Alyssa Devereaux instead. She stares at the nameplate with tears in her eyes. "He had this made for me?"

I nod and wrap my arms around her. Alyssa inhales shakily and tries her best to smile. She probably knows her dad wouldn't want her to cry today of all days.

Linda walks into my office with a bottle of champagne in her hands and Alyssa takes a step away from me. She smiles at them and shakes her head. "It's only nine am, guys," she says.

I shrug and pop the cork. "It's five pm somewhere, baby," I tell her, grinning. I hand her a glass of champagne and we all toast.

"To our new CEO," I say. Alyssa giggles and clinks her glass against the others. She keeps looking at her dad's desk, and I wonder what it'd be like if he were here today. I guess Alyssa and I wouldn't be married, but at least she'd get to share today with Charles. I miss him. I wonder what he was thinking when he pushed us together.

Alyssa walks up to me and rises to her tiptoes to kiss my cheek. "This is amazing. I can't believe you arranged all of this for me." She sighs as she pulls away. "Unfortunately, we've gotta get back to work, though."

I nod and kiss her, my lips lingering on hers. I glance back at her before walking out, feeling conflicted. Rather than driving back to Devereaux Inc., I end up driving to the cemetery. I stop by the flower shop at the front and grab a bouquet before walking to Charles's grave. I pause in front of it and stare at the headstone, feeling lost as hell.

"Hey, old man," I murmur. I place the flowers by his headstone and sigh. "I'm sorry it took me so long to come see you. It was hard, you know? It's like I was in denial and visiting you here would make it all real. I guess it does. I still can't believe you're gone, and I can't believe the will you left behind either. I know you meant well, but how could you? How could you force the two of us together, when you knew how Alyssa felt about Dominic? Didn't you realise I'd always live in his shadow, and she'd always feel like she gave up this potentially epic love for me? I just can't understand. What was the goal here, Charles?"

I sigh and sit down on the floor. I run a hand through my hair and shake my head. "Did you know I love her? That I've always loved her? I guess you did. You must have. If you were aware of my feelings, then there's no way you didn't know about hers. Either way, it doesn't matter anymore. She fulfilled the terms of your will today. I bet you're happy up there, or wherever you might be. You must be celebrating in your own way, huh?"

I stare down at my hands. "She and I are doomed. She thinks she loves me. I can see it in her eyes. But how could she? How could it be love when she never chose to be with me? When she never would have? It's almost like Stockholm Syndrome, you know? It might take years, but one day she'll wake up and she'll wonder what she could have had. Who she would've been with had she been given a choice, and what her life might have looked like. I don't understand why you'd put us in this situation."

My phone rings and I rise to my feet and dust off my suit trousers. "Hello?"

"Daniel, it's Vincent. I was informed that Alyssa and you have officially fulfilled the terms of Charles's will. I spoke to Alyssa earlier today and informed her that her father's shares are unconditionally hers. You two are free to get a divorce now. I've had a copy of the papers prepared since the start, so I'll send those over to you."

I inhale sharply and glance at Charles's tombstone. He must've had this all prepared from the start. "I see. What did my wife say when you told her about the papers?"

Vincent hesitates before answering. "Nothing much. I'm not sure it even registered what I was talking about in the middle of her celebrations."

I nod absentmindedly and instruct Vincent to deliver the papers to my apartment. Part of me wants to rip the papers up with Alyssa, but another part of me wonders... if she were given a choice, would she still be with me?

Fifty-Three

I stare at the divorce papers in my hands and inhale deeply. It took Vincent a little over twenty-four hours to have these delivered. Just last night I filled the house with roses and candles to celebrate Alyssa's new job title. Right now, though, it all feels like a sham.

Staring at these papers reminds me of how we got here in the first place. I'm reminded of her drunken confession and the way she looked at Dominic on the day she married me. Of the times I've seen them act all close despite our marriage. Had this marriage not been forced upon her, would she ever have chosen me?

I think back to the media's response when they found out about Alyssa and me. Some of the articles were truly scathing, likening me to a sexual predator of some sort. Sometimes I feel like one too. She was a virgin when she married me, for God's sake. I took away so many life events that she had every right to. She should've dated someone, fallen in love, and gotten engaged before getting married. I still want her to have all that, and I want her to have it all with me. I want it to be by choice, though. And I need to be okay with it if it's not me she chooses.

I grab a pen from the inner pocket of my suit jacket and sign the papers with trembling hands. I drop them to the table before walking to the bedroom that Alyssa and I share. I'm barely present as I pack myself a bag. I walk back into the living room and walk straight to the lift, dropping the bag next to it.

I lean back against the wall, second guessing myself, when my eyes fall to the bottle of Macallan I bought Charles. I grab it and walk to the table in the living room. I grab the divorce papers and carry them to the armchair in the corner. I'm so tempted to set them on fire. To pretend we never received them. I doubt she'd even bring it up. She seems happy with me, but I'll never know if that happiness is real.

I owe Alyssa this. I've taken so much from her and it's enough now. It's time I give her her life back. I drink my whiskey as I watch the sun go down, the room slowing falling into darkness. I drop the divorce papers to the floor and take another big swig of my drink. I need to set her free. I love her more than life itself, and I can't in good conscience keep her trapped in a marriage she didn't choose.

The lift dings and my eyes fall closed. She's home. Tonight is probably the last night she'll be coming home to me. Alyssa fumbles with the light switches and I squint when she turns them on.

"Daniel?"

She walks up to me and drops her hand to my shoulder. I can't even bear to look at her. I know that the second I do, I'll rip those papers apart. I'll destroy them and keep her shackled to me. Alyssa leans down to tidy up the papers on the floor and freezes mid-reach. "Divorce papers?" she whispers, her voice trembling. She looks up at me and I stare out the window. All it'll take is one pleading look from her. One look, and I'll forget about doing the right thing. Alyssa sinks to the floor with the papers in her hands and I steel myself before turning to look at her.

"You signed them," she whispers.

I force myself to smile. "Hmm, I signed. Our time is up. You reached your goal of becoming CEO. Your father's shares are yours, and my stake in DM is secure now."

I sigh and look away, my heart breaking. She's going to want to fight for us, because she isn't a quitter. It'll destroy me to push her away, but I have to. I know what she's like, and she won't try to move on if there's no clean break between us. I need to give her at least a few months. A few months to recover, to date, to fall in love. I can't bear to witness any of that, but I must. Because if I walk away and in a few months she's still single? Then I'm making her mine. For real this time.

"It's been fun playing house with you, but enough is enough. I guess the sex wasn't bad and I'll definitely miss your sweet pussy, but there are plenty of fish in the sea. You're too young to be married. Hell, you were a fucking virgin. I definitely didn't think I'd be married now either."

She clenches the papers in her hands. "Playing house? That's what our marriage was to you? You're telling me the sex *wasn't bad*? I thought you didn't mind me being a virgin. I never once heard you complain about it."

How could I? Sex with her has always been the best I've ever had, but she has nothing to compare me to. How could *she* know if it was good or not?

"Alyssa, of course we were playing house. You and I were never together because we wanted to be. We were forced together. If your dad hadn't written that will, then you and I never would've gotten married. Hell, we never would've even gotten together. I'm ten years older than you. You've never even really dated."

She looks at me with such a lost expression that my heart fucking shatters. "So what were we doing last year if we weren't dating?"

I turn towards her and suppress my emotions. "We were making do."

Alyssa lowers her head, but I don't miss the single tear that falls down her cheek. I'm tempted to reach for her, but I can't.

"So when you asked me to make our relationship official, you were just making do? If you knew you wanted to divorce me, then why did you insist on being with me? Why did you tell me we'd be faithful to each other and why did you publicise our relationship? If all you wanted was sex, then why didn't you just agree when I suggested that we both keep our separate lives? It makes no sense, Daniel. Please tell me you're joking. Please tell me this is all just a misunderstanding."

I rise to my feet and walk away from her. I can't stand to see her like this. She rushes after me and grabs my arm, but I shrug out of her hold. "Fine. I did want to see what might happen between us. I did want to fuck you, and I didn't want anyone else to have what was mine. We got that out of our systems, and it's time to move on now, Alyssa. I guess we *were* dating, so let's break up. We're done."

She grabs my shirt and shakes me, as though she's trying to make me see reason. "Don't do this to us. What we have is something other people can only dream of. Aren't you happy with me?"

Her voice breaks, and it tugs at my heartstrings. I turn around and bury my hands in her hair, lowering my forehead to hers. She grabs me and pulls me closer. She kisses me, and I try my best to resist her, but I end up giving in and kiss her back hungrily. I tighten my grip on her hair and push her against the nearest wall, her tongue tangling with mine. She unbuttons my shirt while I push her skirt up, our lips never leaving each other. As her hands find my zipper, my hands find her breasts. I rip her blouse open, sending the buttons flying, and I groan when she grabs hold of me. I pull back long enough to lift her up and push her back against the wall. She squirms in my hold and I smile against her lips when she positions herself so I can slip into her easily. I look into her eyes as I sink into her.

"Oh god, Daniel," she whispers, and I inhale deeply, my heart twisting. I kiss her as I thrust into her roughly, wanting all of her.

"This is the last time, Alyssa. This is the last time I'm fucking you."

She bites down on my lips harshly. "No."

I pull out almost all the way and then thrust into her hard. "Yes," I say through gritted teeth.

Alyssa pulls on my hair and drags her lips to mine, kissing me before moving onto my neck. "No," she says, sucking down on my skin hard enough to bruise me. "You're mine."

I moan and change the angle so I'm pushing against her g-spot and she barely holds on.

"I'm not letting you go," she tells me, her voice husky.

I kiss her and fuck her so hard I know she's going to be deliciously sore for days. She'll think of me every time she moves, even though I won't be here.

"I'm not giving you a choice."

Alyssa closes her eyes and I can tell she's trying to hold on, but she won't be able to.

"Baby, please," she whispers. I smile and slow down the pace, keeping her at the edge. "No," she whimpers. "*Please.*"

I chuckle and fuck her slowly. I love everything about her. I love how hungry she is for my cock and I love how she looks at me. I love how responsive she is and how she feels. I want this for the rest of my life.

Alyssa scratches my back with her nails, making her annoyance clear, and I grin.

"I need you. Now, baby."

I bite down on my lip and nod, thrusting into her hard, my eyes never leaving hers. She shatters around me and seconds later, I do too. The two of us collapse onto the floor, still connected. I shift so my back is against the wall and she remains in my lap, her hands on my chest.

"How can you call this making do?" she whispers, her voice breaking. I look into her eyes, my heart crumbling.

"Is it her? Is it the girl you said you'd propose to when we divorced? Is that why you're leaving me?"

This again. I wonder if she'll ever realise that this girl she's so jealous of is *her*. I wonder if this is what she needs. An excuse. A way to make herself feel better for letting me go. For moving on with her life and going after the things she's always wanted.

"Yes," I say. "I don't know when and I don't know how, but I'm irrevocably in love with her. She occupies my every thought and all I want to do is make her happy."

She trembles in my hold and stares at me in disbelief, her eyes filling with tears. I can't take this. She pushes away from me and turns her back to me.

"Did you cheat on me, Daniel?" she asks, her voice hollow.

I hesitate before answering her. How she could even dream of me doing such a thing is beyond me. "No, Alyssa," I whisper.

I stand up and straighten my clothes. Alyssa grabs her blouse and throws it on, but the broken buttons don't allow her to cover much of herself. She clutches it together and inhales deeply.

"Who is she?"

I look at her and take a deep breath. "It doesn't matter, Alyssa. You and I are done. You have no right to pry into my private affairs going forward."

She looks at me through narrowed eyes and crosses her arms over each other. "I haven't signed the divorce papers, Daniel. I have every right. I won't let you do this to us. I'm not signing. You might think you're in love with someone else, but you're wrong. I'll prove it to you."

I wish. I hope I'm wrong. I hope she'll fight for us and she'll choose me. But before she does that, I hope she'll take some time for herself. Some time to truly reflect on what she wants and what we had. Chances are pretty high she'll realise I was just the easy option.

I run a hand through my hair and sigh. "You will. You'll sign the papers eventually. I'm leaving, Alyssa. I want you out of my house by the end of the day tomorrow. If you refuse I'll just find somewhere else to live."

I'm only half dressed as I walk towards the lift and grab the bag I put there earlier. I don't look back as I walk out and leave my heart in her hands.

Fifty-Four

I look up in surprise when Olivia walks into my office. She called me the moment she found out about Alyssa and me separating. Turns out my mother didn't hesitate to let her know. It hasn't even been a week. I've been honest with her and I told her that nothing would ever happen between us, but she merely smiled and rolled her eyes. "Not everyone wants to get into your pants," she said, shoving my arm. "I just want to be here for you, that's all. I promise."

And she has been there for me. True to her word, she hasn't even remotely hit on me. Not even once. I don't even think she likes me that way. Thinking back to that day my Mum forced me to have lunch with her, it does seem like she was forced to have lunch with *me* as much as I was.

"Trouble," she says, holding up a newspaper. I frown and she drops it to my desk. She points out the tabloid bit and I grit my teeth when I see dozens of photos of Olivia and me. What's wrong with these people? Don't they have anything better to do?

Trouble in paradise?

It's been some time since Daniel Devereaux has been spotted with his girlfriend, Alyssa Moriani. Instead, he's been seen hanging out with his childhood friend, Olivia Diaz, on numerous occasions. This isn't the first time the two have been spotted together and over the years we have wondered whether something was going on between them, but they've always denied it. This time both parties declined to comment. That on its own is telling. Will we soon get a statement from Daniel Devereaux confirming his new relationship?

We've done some digging and found countless photos of Olivia and Daniel throughout the years. Though we feel bad for Alyssa Moriani, who has also declined to comment, we must admit that Olivia and Daniel look incredibly cute together.

"Alyssa will have seen this. You know that, right?"

Just the mention of her name still hurts me. The first few days she called me every single day. I ended up having to block her number just to get her to stop. I should've known she wouldn't get over me in a flash, but I doubt it'll take very long either.

"I know. What's worse is she'll be receiving my resignation today too."

Olivia sighs and walks to my settee. She unpacks the lunch she brought me and waves me over. "You need to fix this," she tells me. "I don't know what dumb game you're playing, but you're an idiot. You'll never find a girl better than her. She's the youngest CEO I've ever heard of, you know? She's incredible."

I look away and smile wryly. "She's far more than that. The problem was never whether she was good enough for me. Quite the opposite, really."

I take the food she's offering and take a bite, though I can't taste shit. I always thought this whole heartbreak thing was bullshit. Turns out it's not. I can't sleep, I don't eat, and when I do, I can't taste anything. I think of her all the time and end up looking at old photos of us. It's ridiculous.

I glance over at Olivia. I can barely get a bite down, but she's having no such issues. She's shoving so much food down her face that her lipstick is smudged all over, and I can't help but chuckle.

The door to my office opens and I frown as I turn my head to look at it, only to find Alyssa standing by the doorway, a shocked expression on her face. Her eyes move from me to Olivia, and then zero in on her lips before moving to my messy desk. I see the hurt and betrayal in her eyes, and every fibre of my being begs me to rectify her misunderstanding. Instead, I steel myself and pretend to be unaffected.

It's been a week since I last saw her, and she looks even more stunning than she did in my memories. Granted, her eyes are as red and puffy as mine, and the bags underneath our eyes are identical too, but she's still the most beautiful thing I've ever seen.

"Can I have a word, please?" she says, her voice calm and strong.

Olivia jumps up and smiles at me tightly. "I'll go," she murmurs as Alyssa sits down opposite me.

I shake my head and pull her back down. She tenses and I know she's about to bolt, so I wrap my arm around her tightly. If Olivia leaves, I'll be alone with Alyssa, and that absolutely can't happen. I can't be alone with her. I won't be able to resist my desire to mess up that neat knot in her hair. I'll kiss her until her lips are swollen and I'll lift her onto my desk and fuck her silly. Yeah, Olivia definitely can't leave. "Stay," I tell her.

Alyssa looks at my arm around Olivia's shoulder and grits her teeth. She looks down and inhales deeply before speaking. "I received your resignation today. I won't accept it."

I chuckle. "The board already accepted it, so I don't care what you think of it. It's done."

Alyssa looks up at me, and I have to look away. "I would like you to reconsider," she says. "I'm not ready to handle the company by myself. I can't do this without you."

I'm so fucking tempted to give in. To do whatever she asks of me. "Then you'd better look into hiring another external CEO. I won't come back," I say instead.

Olivia fidgets in her seat, clearly feeling awkward, and I grab her hand, scared that she might actually run off.

Alyssa clenches her teeth and grabs another stack of documents from her bag. "Very well," she murmurs. She hands me a copy of the photos the press published of Olivia and me this morning, and places a copy of our fidelity contract and a share transfer agreement on top.

"This needs to stop. I won't sign the divorce agreement, Daniel. Unless you want to lose your three hundred million shareholding, I suggest you keep it in your pants. I won't hesitate to sue you. You've done most of the work for me. All I need to do at this point is to show these photos to a judge. I'll let it go if you stop now."

I stare at her and then back down at the documents, thoroughly impressed. Fucking hell, she's really pulling out the big guns, huh? Clever girl. Had I been anyone else, she would've been able to tie me back to her successfully with that contract. Three hundred million isn't nothing. It's a good thing I always intended to give the shares to her anyway, or she'd really be doing some damage.

I reach for the pen in my inside pocket and proceed to sign the share transfer agreement without hesitation. I never wanted these shares. They were always hers, and one way or another, I would've given them to her anyway.

I glance at the documents with a bittersweet smile before handing them to her. This is the last tie between us; the last tie that binds us together. Now it's out of the way, it'll truly be a clean break.

"What does this mean?" she asks, her voice trembling. "Did you..."

I hear the words she doesn't say. Did I already cheat on her? Never. For a second, I want to make her believe I did. I want her to give up on me, but I can't. I can't stand the devastation in her eyes.

"No," I say, losing my composure. "No, I haven't... but I want to," I lie. "So I might as well just sign now and settle, rather than having to go through court proceedings."

She looks from me to Olivia, her heartbreak clear. She nods as she puts away the documents. She looks so lost, so defeated, and I hate that I put that expression on her face. I stare at the door after Alyssa leaves and sigh.

"You two are *married*?" Olivia asks, shocked. I glance at her and nod before looking away.

"I'll tell you all about Alyssa and me," I say. "But I'll need a drink or two."

Fifty-Five

I stare down at the documents on my desk in disbelief. Five weeks. All it took was a measly five weeks for her to sign. I don't know what I expected. Isn't this exactly what I wanted? I've avoided her as best as I could and I've given her all the space she needs to move on, so why am I so surprised she actually has?

I reach for the letter clipped on top of the documents and unfold it carefully.

Dear Daniel,

I'm sorry for withholding my signature when you've made it so clear where you and I stand. You were right. We did have an agreement and our time was indeed up. I'm thankful that you chose to honour my father's last wish and I realise that that was the only reason you married me. I guess along the way the lines started to blur for me. It was selfish of me to hold on to you longer than your obligation required. Especially since you told me from the very start that there's someone else you've got your heart set on.

. . .

I'm beyond grateful that you were beside me during the toughest time I've ever had to face. All I wish for is your happiness, and I know these documents are the first step to achieving that. I hope that over time you and I can find a way to be in each other's lives again. Perhaps we can even be friends one day. Until then, I'll give you all the space you need.

All my love,

Alyssa

I don't even know what to think of this. Did she sign only because she thought it's what I want? Or is that just what she's telling herself? Fucking hell, I don't know. I can't see right from wrong anymore. This is it now. She's officially no longer mine.

I wonder what she'll do now. I'm hoping she won't date. I'm praying she won't go after Dominic. But I'll need to learn to be okay with it if she does. I put her through all of this because I wanted her to have the freedom to make her own choices.

Sure, I did it for selfish reasons too. I didn't want to spend the rest of our lives feelings like I'm second best. I didn't want to wonder if she's still pining after my brother, or if she occasionally thinks of what it'd be like to be with him instead. I didn't want to live in his shadow, and I didn't want to be the guy she settled for.

But that doesn't mean I don't want *her*. I do. I want her body, heart and soul. And I want her to want me too.

Two months. I don't think I'll last longer than two months. If two months from now she's single and hasn't tried to pursue Dominic, then I'm going after her. I'm going to give her everything we missed out on the first time. I'm going to woo her. I'll take her for candlelit dinners and I'll date her, before proposing to her the way she always deserved.

Two months. I pray she'll still be single by then.

Fifty-Six

I notice her the second she walks in. I notice the guy she's with too. Fucking Liam Evans. He cups her cheek and looks into her eyes. I can't tell what he's saying to her, but I do know I want to knock his teeth out. Why the fuck is Alyssa attending a charity function at the Devereaux mansion with that asshole? She must've known I'd be here too. Does she not care at all?

Liam slides his hand down her arm until he's holding her hand, and I watch as the two of them walk towards us, their hands entwined.

It's only been a week since she signed the damn papers, and she's with Liam already? I bark out a humourless laugh and shake my head. And I thought she'd still be single in two months. I was so worried about my brother that I failed to account for all the other assholes around her. Fuck.

My mother, Dominic and I are standing beside each other, in a receiving line of sorts. We do this goddamn auction every year, and usually I don't mind it so much, but this year? This year I fucking hate it. This was supposed to be the first public event Alyssa and I would attend as a couple. But instead she's here with Liam fucking Evans.

Mum smiles when she sees Alyssa and hugs her tightly. I bite back a pleased smile when she ignores Liam. "I'm so glad you made it, honey," Mum says.

Alyssa smiles at her and moves on to hug Dominic, who also ignores Liam. My brother isn't one to show solidarity, so I can't help but wonder if he's annoyed to see her with him. He hugs her tightly and smiles at her. "You look good, Lyss. Beautiful," Dominic says, a wide grin on his face.

She freezes when she's finally standing in front of me. She doesn't hug me. She doesn't even lean into me. But I don't miss the way her eyes roam over my body. She's always loved me in a tux, and I see today is no exception. I look at her and then at Liam before looking back at her with raised brows. I clench my jaw and stare her down.

Alyssa clears her throat and tries her best to smile at me. "I — It's good to see you, Daniel. You look good," she murmurs.

"Hmm, what is this?" I ask, glancing at Liam. "Is this a *date*?"

Liam wraps his hand around Alyssa's waist and pulls her in closer, intimately. I'm about three seconds from punching him in the face. How fucking dare he touch her.

"Thanks for having us," Liam says. I scoff and shake my head, trying my best to rein in my temper. I should've known this would happen when I let her go. I still remember him asking her out shortly after we got married. I can't believe she'd do this. I was so convinced she loved me. I was so convinced that all she needed was a bit of time and space to realise she'd never want to be with anyone else, even if she suddenly had the freedom to.

Liam grabs her hand and pulls her to the dance floor, and all I can do is watch. I watch as he wraps his hands around her waist and she wraps hers around his neck. I watch as he pulls her closer and dances with the woman that was once mine. Alyssa leans in closer and rests her head on his chest, destroying my fucking heart in the process.

I don't snap out of it until Olivia walks up to me, elbowing me hard. "Are you really going to stand here and let him steal your girl?" she asks, her eyes flashing with rage. I look away. If this is what she wants, then who am I to take it away from her all over again? I walked away from her for a reason. I wanted to give her a chance to pursue her own happiness, so that's what I'll do. I'll stand aside, and I'll watch her go after what her heart desires. I'll do it, even if it kills me.

Olivia grabs my arm and pulls me to the dance floor. "I don't want to dance," I tell her.

She stomps on my toe and glares at me. "Shut up. Just dance. You're so convinced she doesn't want you, and you're so stupid, Daniel. So, so stupid. So what if she's trying to find a rebound or something? That doesn't mean anything. I guarantee seeing us dance together will make her jealous. How could it not after all those articles about us? And you know why people get jealous, Daniel? It's because they care."

I sigh and do as she says. It's easier that way. I know Olivia is recovering from a bad break-up, and I guess she feels better when she thinks she's fixing Alyssa and me. But there's nothing left to fix.

"Told you," she says, tipping her head towards Alyssa and Liam. I glance over to find her standing still on the dance floor. She pushes away from Liam and shakes her head before rushing out of the room. I don't hesitate to follow her.

She enters the mansion and I'm only a few steps behind her, but she's so distraught that she doesn't even notice me. She walks into the library and I pause in the hallway, torn. I don't even know if I should follow her or not. I'm so mad she's with Liam, and I'm not sure I can keep from showing my emotions. But I also need to know she's okay. I hate it when she's hurting.

I walk in to find her kneeling on the floor, spaced out and shivering. I walk past her and light the fire in the corner. I sink down to the rug on the floor and shrug out of my suit jacket before patting the space beside me. "Come here," I say.

Alyssa rises to her feet silently and drops beside me. She raises her hands to the fireplace to warm herself, and I'm filled with conflicting emotions. I'm angry, but I'm happy to see her. I'm jealous as fuck that she's with Liam, yet I want her to be happy. I'm a selfish fucking asshole.

"What are you doing here?" I ask. "Your boyfriend couldn't keep you entertained?"

She looks down at her knees and ignores my question. "I'm sorry for intruding," she says. "Would you like me to leave?"

I chuckle darkly. How the fuck does she manage to piss me off even further? I turn towards her and have her flat on her back in a second. I lean over her and pin her down with my weight, every vein in my body filled with rage. I bury my hand in her hair and tilt her face towards mine.

"Liam fucking Evans, huh? I thought you were madly in love with Dominic, so where the fuck did this guy come from?"

Alyssa blinks at me and tries to turn her head away, but I'm not having it. I tighten my grip on her hair and I see that familiar flash of lust in her eyes. Only my girl can get turned on when I'm this mad at her. She glares at me, but she's already breathing hard and her eyes keep dropping to my lips.

"I don't see how that's any of your business, Daniel," she says. She's trying to sound stern, but she sounds husky and breathless instead.

I laugh and lower my face until my lips are hovering above hers. "Is he the reason you signed the divorce papers after refusing so adamantly?" She looks at me but remains silent. "Answer me," I demand.

She smiles and pushes against my shoulder. "You'd better let go of me. I'm sure Olivia is waiting for you."

My hand slips out of her hair to cup the back of her neck, and I lower my lips to hers until I'm almost touching her. "So are you dating him?" I whisper. My lips brush against hers on the last word and Alyssa's eyes shutter closed.

"Does it matter?" she asks.

I bite down on her lower lip and she tilts her head in a silent bid for more. I smile against her lips and then kiss her roughly. She kisses me back just as fiercely. I moan when her tongue tangles with mine and push her dress up. She lifts her hips to make it easier for me and tugs on my bowtie.

"I've been wanting to rip this damn thing off ever since I saw you wearing it," she whispers.

I chuckle and kiss her as my fingers find their way between her legs. I gasp when I realise she isn't wearing underwear. For a split second I wonder if it's for Liam, and my arousal is instantly gone.

"I can't wear anything underneath a dress this tight," she whispers, as though she can read my mind. I smile at her and Alyssa pulls me back to her, kissing me passionately. I slip two fingers into her and she moans loudly. I shut her up with a kiss and she fumbles with my suit trousers, trying to get them off. Her eyes shutter closed when she feels how hard I am.

"Look at me," I snap. She blinks, startled, and looks into my eyes. I want her to see who she's with. I want her to see *me*. "So fucking wet for me, Alyssa. Such a wet fucking pussy."

She's trembling with need and bites down on her lip when I align myself right where she wants me. I pause there and grin at her, knowing full well she hates it when I do this. My girl has always been impatient.

She fumbles with my shirt and pushes it open when she's got the buttons undone. Rather than waiting for me to give her what she wants, she lifts her hips and turns us over. I fall to my back in surprise and she climbs on top of me before I have a chance to react. I grin and yank on the zipper of her dress. My eyes widen when her dress pools around her waist, exposing her amazing breasts.

"Such fucking amazing tits. No bra, huh?"

I fondle her roughly and she moans before positioning herself on top of me. She lowers herself fully, taking me in deeply, and I moan. She sits back, fully stretched out and filled. She only gives me a second before she starts to move, and I almost blow my load right there and then. She moves her hips up and down frantically, desperately. I grab her shoulders and pull her on top of me, so her upper body is flush with mine. She can't take me in as deeply like this, but I know my dick hits all the right spots.

Alyssa lowers her lips to my neck and sucks down, marking me in a clearly visible spot. Her possessiveness turns me on even more. Alyssa increases the pace and I meet her every movement, both of us frantic. Alyssa leans down and sucks down on my collarbone, leaving another mark, and I groan in delight.

She sits back up and rotates her hips just slightly every time she comes down on me. Before long she's the one that's panting and barely holding on. I know I'm hitting both her g-spot and her clit at this angle, and I know she won't be able to take it. I grin and continue to thrust into her.

"I can't... I can't hold on," she moans.

I look at her in satisfaction and smile. "Then don't, baby. Come for me, Lyss."

Her muscles contract hard and her entire body trembles as wave after wave crashes through her. Just as she begins to catch her breath, I turn us over and continue to fuck her.

"One more, Lyss," I whisper. She's so turned on I know I can make her come again. I angle my hips and thrust into her slowly, teasing her. Within minutes, she shatters around me again. "Hmm, what a good girl. What a good pussy. Always so wet for me."

I pick up the pace and fuck her hard, and within seconds I come too. I collapse on top of her, and she grins up at me lazily.

"You were so hard for me, Daniel. Did you miss this wet pussy?" she murmurs, throwing my earlier words back at me. I grin at her language and kiss her. It's a wet and sloppy kiss, and I fucking love it.

"Where did you learn that language, huh?"

Her eyes flash and she looks away. "Hmm, well... Let's just say I finally understand why you said the sex between us *wasn't bad*."

My stomach fucking drops and I freeze while still inside her. What the fuck? She slept with someone else? Who?

"You fucked Liam?" I ask. I can feel the colour drain from my face. "Well, fair enough," I say, my heart breaking. "To answer your question... I did miss your pussy, but it was better in my memories. I've had better since you," I lie, wanting to hurt her as much as she's hurt me. I grab her hands and push them above her head, trapping her with my weight.

"Since me?" Alyssa repeats numbly. "You *slept* with her?" she asks, her voice breaking. Her eyes fill with tears and she tries to get her wrists loose with all her strength, but there's no way I'm letting her go. Not now. "How long did you wait after you bought your way out of the fidelity contract? Did you do her the same day? Did you even wait at all? Were you sleeping with her before you left me?"

She sniffs and tries to get her hands loose again, endless tears streaming down her face. Her heartbreak is obvious, and it's also obvious she lied to me. There's no way she could be this hurt if she's slept with someone else herself.

"Get off me, you asshole. I fucking hate you," she yells.

I smile at her and gently kiss away her tears. This girl... I almost believed her. She pushes against me as a sob escapes her lips and I pull out of her. I roll onto my side and keep her in my arms. Alyssa pushes me away and sits up, wiping at her tears angrily. She tries to inhale deeply but just ends up choking on her sobs, and it breaks my heart. She yanks her dress up to try and cover herself, and she stands up, but I pull her back down. My own eyes fill with tears seeing her like this. I don't ever want her crying over me. Especially not over a petty lie. I pull her down to the floor and roll on top of her, caging her in.

"I lied. *I lied*, Alyssa. I never slept with her. I swear. Of course I didn't. Please, baby. I'm begging you... Please stop crying. You're tearing me apart, Lyss. Please."

I cup her cheeks and wipe away her tears, my forehead dropping to hers. "You didn't?" she asks, hopeful.

I shake my head. In our frenzy neither one of us got fully undressed, and I wipe away her tears with my sleeve. "No. I didn't. I just lashed out because for a second I believed your little lie."

I smile at her and she pushes against my chest weakly. This time I let her go. I follow her with my eyes as she escapes from the room, her clothes and hair a mess. Even if she manages to fix it, one look at her will tell any man that she's just been thoroughly ravished. Liam will know.

I might have let her go to allow her to pursue her own happiness, but I'd be a fool if I stepped back entirely. Fuck this shit. I won't stand here and let him take my girl. I'll fight for her, and I'll make her fall for me all over again, out of her own volition this time.

Fifty-Seven

I walk back into the auction hall to find Liam looking at Alyssa, crestfallen. I grin to myself. He raises his hand to touch her hair thoughtfully, and it's obvious he knows what just went down. He glances past Alyssa and I meet his angry gaze head on. I didn't bother dressing properly. My collars are loose enough to showcase the kiss mark Alyssa left on me, my bowtie is lying around my neck loosely, and my hair is still a mess from how she pulled at it. I'm pretty sure I even have lipstick stains on my neck and collar. The only place I wiped it off was my lips.

Liam stares down at the floor and I walk past them, feeling smug as hell. I walk up to Olivia and she bursts out laughing when she sees me. "It's safe to assume that went well then, isn't it?"

I shrug and turn to look at Alyssa. Her eyes meet mine, and she turns to look away, flustered. Fuck Liam. I know I should've stayed away tonight, but I couldn't. If she cared for him at all she would've stayed with him. She wouldn't have walked away to find some peace and quiet, and she wouldn't have let me touch her. Hell, she wouldn't have enjoyed it as much as she did.

"Yeah, I guess it went well."

Mum walks onto the stage and we all walk to take our seats as the auction commences. Some of our guests are here to buy presents for others while contributing to charity, others are here to bid for the same items they've put up for auction as a way to contribute and donate at the same time, without losing a precious item. Alyssa has done the latter every year, and every year I've wanted to be the one to buy back her item. I never could, though. That type of behaviour is reserved for suitors and partners, and I was never either.

I sit back as Olivia bids on the ancient vase that she donated, and I feel Alyssa's eyes on the back of my head. I bet she's wondering why I am not the one bidding, because she's like that, my girl. She's clueless. I just fucked her silly, but I bet she still thinks I'm interested in Olivia.

Eventually Alyssa's mother's necklace goes up for auction. I look back at her to find her raising her hand, but Liam grabs it and brings it to his lips. He kisses the back of her hand while he raises his own hand. This fucker. Even after the way she walked back into this room, he still won't let her go, huh?

"One million," he calls. I clench my jaw and look back at them, my eyes lingering on their joined hands, still pressed against Liam's lips.

I turn back to the front and raise my hand. "One point five million," I say, my voice loud and clear. The room falls silent as most people glance between Alyssa and me. Our names have been on everyone's lips tonight, and I'm outright fuelling the rumours now. But I don't care.

"Two million," Liam says. I glance back at them to find him cupping her cheek. The way he looks into her eyes pisses me off. Liam drops his forehead to hers and I grit my teeth.

"Three million," I shout, angry as hell.

"Three point five million," Liam says, his eyes never leaving Alyssa's. This fucker. He presses a kiss to her forehead and I only just manage to stay seated when all I want to do is yank him away from her.

"Four million!"

Mum shoots me an amused look and proclaims the necklace sold when Liam remains quiet. She hasn't said much about Alyssa and me. I know she thinks I made the right choice, though. She didn't deal well with the scathing articles the press wrote about me.

What Mum and Alyssa don't know is that the story doesn't end here. Fuck that. I'm rewriting this shit. I'm rewriting it all, so Alyssa will have everything her heart desires. And I… I'll have *her*.

Fifty-Eight

I walk into the courtroom with a bittersweet feeling. It's been weeks since I last saw Alyssa at the auction. I've tried my best to stay away from her because I know I'll end up sabotaging whatever relationship she tries to pursue the second I see her. I can't stand the idea of her not being mine, but I need to see this through. Just one more tie remaining between us, and that'll be gone by the end of today too.

I rise when she walks in and her eyes find mine immediately. I see hope and desperation in her gaze. I see the silent plea. I try my best to smile at her politely and sit back down. Just pretending not to notice her heartbreak kills me, but it gives me hope too. I've purposely avoided every mention of her for weeks now, not wanting to know if she truly did move on. But the look in her eyes just now? That tells me she isn't over me. That she still wants me, and part of her is still hoping I'll call off the divorce.

Both of us remain silent as the judge reviews our case, and I inhale deeply before signing the papers. I feel her eyes on me when it's her turn to sign, and she hesitates. I bite down on my lip and exhale in relief when she signs the papers, finalising our divorce. It's done. She and I are officially single. Neither one of us tied together by duty or responsibility.

I look at her and smile, filled with hope for the future. I offer her my hand, and she takes it without realising, her body still so attuned to mine.

"How about we get a drink?" I ask.

Her eyes flash with pain and anger, and she grits her teeth.

"*What*? You want to get champagne and toast to finally getting rid of me?" she snaps. She pushes past me but I catch up to her and wrap my arms around her waist from behind, closing the distance until my body is flush against hers. How long has it been since I've held her? Fucking hell... I've missed her.

"Come on, Lyss. Just one drink, okay?"

She leans back against me and sighs, and I doubt she even realises. I'm worried she'll say no. I know she's angry and I know I may well have my work cut out for me.

"Yeah, okay," she murmurs, sounding defeated. I offer her my arm as we leave the courtroom, and she glances at me with such a bittersweet smile that my heart skips a beat. I know exactly how she feels. It's strange to be together after everything we've been through. After all those weeks of not seeing or speaking to each other.

I take Alyssa to the same hotel I took her to on our first date, back when she was upset that Dominic invited Lucy to go with them for ice cream. I was already in love with her, but she only had eyes for my brother. I wonder if anything happened between them. I wonder if she finally pursued him the way she always wanted to. I'd like to think I'd never get over it if she did, but truthfully... there isn't much she could do that I won't take.

The rooftop bar is mostly empty, but we sit down in a secluded spot nonetheless. Alyssa grabs her purse and takes out her own Devereaux Black Card. She places it on the table and slides it towards me. "This is yours. I'm no longer entitled to have it. I'm no longer a Devereaux, after all," she murmurs.

I look at her, wondering whether I'll be able to win her back for real this time. No excuses, no hiding behind Charles's will. Just me and her. I wonder if she'll want me.

"Did you ever really consider yourself to be a Devereaux?"

She looks startled by my question and doesn't respond. I smile and bite down on my lip. "Hmm, I guess you did. I recall you once ordering me to call HR and explain to them that *Mrs. Devereaux*, my own wife, was harassing me."

Just the memory of it has me rock hard. The way she caged me in with her legs... fucking hell. Alyssa blushes and looks away.

"Keep it," I say, sliding the card back to her. "You're still family."

She frowns at my words and looks up at me. "Family? You see me as family?" she asks, her tone sharp. I have a feeling that she'll find fault with everything I say today, but that's okay. I know I've hurt her by signing those papers, and I deserve this.

"I meant that you're a family friend. You should keep the card. Who knows when you might need it. It'll guarantee you access to anything that I have access to. It's a duplicate of my own card. You should be able to enter any Devereaux building with it, including our summer houses and the office."

Most people would die to have one of these cards, yet my girl just gets angry because I let her keep hers. I sigh and shake my head.

"Family friend, huh? Did you give Olivia one of these cards?" she asks, her voice harsh.

I smile and shake my head again. "No. You're the only person outside of the family to have one. You'll always be the only one, Alyssa."

She picks the card up and stares at it. I know she's contemplating giving it back. Hell... she's probably contemplating throwing it in my face. I smile when she puts it back in her bag. Guess she's not planning on cutting *all* ties with me.

One of the waiters walks up with a bottle of champagne and Alyssa frowns. "I thought champagne was only for celebrations. What exactly is it you're celebrating?" she asks, angry.

I can't help but grin at her. I fucking love seeing her so mad.

My worst fear was her not caring and truly moving on. "A new beginning. Here's to us," I say.

I wait patiently for her to clink her glass against mine, and for a second, I'm sure she won't. I love seeing her being so true to her emotions. I thought she might put up an act and pretend like she doesn't miss me, but instead she's visibly angry and I adore her even more for it. She taps her glass against mine with a scowl on her face and empties it in one go. I chuckle as she puts her empty glass down.

"We were here when we'd just gotten married, do you remember?"

She nods and looks around the restaurant. So much has changed since then. She and I were close as coworkers and family friends, but not as the husband and wife we were.

"I remember. We'd only been married for a day then."

I nod. "Hmm, you told me then that you'd always been in love with Dominic. He told you he feels the same not too long ago, right? Now that you're finally free, you can follow your heart."

I feel a flash of fear as the words leave my lips. I worry that I'm misreading her, and she does still have feelings for him.

Alyssa laughs mirthlessly. "Did you know back then? Could you see what I couldn't? Did you know I was merely comfortable with him and perhaps a bit infatuated…? Did you know it wasn't love?"

I *didn't* know. I'm still not sure those words are true. I look away and take a sip of my champagne. "Are you sure you aren't in love with him? There's no marriage and no fidelity contract tying you to anyone else now. You and I haven't been together in months now, except for that one time at the auction… You should follow your heart, Alyssa."

I hope she does follow her heart, and I hope it'll lead her back to me. But if it doesn't, then I'll still try my best to be happy for her. That's all I want for her.

"Hmm, I'm sure it wasn't love. I doubt that he's in love with me as well. He'll realise that it was merely infatuation when he truly falls for someone. I doubt Dominic knows what love is."

I nod, pleased with her answer. "So what's happening with Liam Evans, then? You brought him to the auction and he's clearly very fond of you."

She glares at me, and I bite back a grin. If she'd still been in love with Dominic I'd have found a way to deal with that. After all, he had her heart long before I did. But Liam? He can go to hell.

"That might have led somewhere if I didn't disappear with my ex, only to come back looking thoroughly ravished. I actually felt quite bad. He's a great guy, but I'm not ready to be in a new relationship. Maybe in a few years. Who knows?"

She shakes her head and tries her best to smile, but it doesn't reach her eyes. "When we were last here, you told me there's a girl you couldn't get off your mind, but you weren't sure if it was love. But by the time you signed the divorce papers, you told me you were irrevocably in love with her."

Fucking hell. What's with her memory? One slip of the tongue, that's all it was. A little white lie. Hell, it wasn't even a lie. Not really.

"It seems like you fell for her while we were married. Was it Olivia or was it someone else? Someone who works at Devereaux Inc. maybe? You did spend most of your time leading up to our divorce there."

I bite down on my lip and look away. She'll never let this go. I kinda want to find out what expression she'll show me when she finds out that girl is *her*.

"It's not Olivia," I tell her. "Liv and I are just friends. Nothing more. We've never been more and we never will be."

She nods. "Someone at Devereaux Inc. then. Will you tell me who it is?"

I sigh and run a hand through my hair. "You'll find out soon enough," I murmur. If everything goes to plan she'll find out sooner than later anyway.

"So you're dating her, then?"

She looks so hurt, I instantly want to deny it, but I gotta admit I love her jealousy. I always wondered if she has any real feelings for me and this proves it. It's been months since I ended things with her and she's had every chance to be with whoever she wants, yet she's sitting here with me, acting jealous.

"It's complicated."

Alyssa nods and empties her recently refilled glass. "I'm sorry I stood in the way of your happiness for so long, Daniel. I know firsthand how good of a partner and husband you will be. Whoever she is, she's a lucky girl. I genuinely wish you happiness and love, because you really do deserve it," she says. She hesitates before continuing and inhales deeply. "But I don't think I can be part of your life going forward. I don't think we should be friends, and I don't think we should stay in touch either. Maybe in a few years, but not now. I hope things work out for you, Daniel. I hope she gives you what I couldn't. I hope she makes you happy... but I don't want to be around to see it. I can't."

She stands up and walks away, but that's okay. She'll end up coming back to me. I'll pursue her until she does.

Fifty-Nine

I grit my teeth as I sit down on my mother's sofa. "You said she'd be here," I say to Dominic, angry as fuck. Alyssa has suddenly become fucking Houdini. The second she finds out I'm going to be somewhere she bails. She won't take my calls and she's blocked me on social media. This is *not* how I saw things going. How the hell am I supposed to win her over when she avoids me like the plague?

"I don't know, man. She doesn't want to see you. What do you want me to do? You divorced her. Why the hell are you bothering her anyway?"

I grit my teeth and grab his phone from the table. I hand it to him with a scowl on my face. "Because I'm trying to woo her. I'm planning on pursuing her, dating her, proposing and marrying her — in that order."

Dominic looks at me in shock. "You w-what?"

I run a hand through my hair in annoyance and sigh. "Do you really think we were gonna last when we both knew we got married without a choice? When *my wife* thought she was in love with *my brother*?"

Dominic blinks at me in disbelief and takes his phone from me. "Are you serious? Are you really going after her?"

I look at him through narrowed eyes and cross my arms. "Why? Did you think you stood a chance? Were you happy I finally got out of your way?"

He shakes his head vehemently. "No. Of course not. You're my brother, and all I've ever wanted for Alyssa is to be happy. I could never make her as happy as she was with you. Does she know? Does she know that you want her back?"

I shake my head. "No. I don't want to pressure her in any way. I want things to happen naturally this time. I don't want her to feel like she *has* to try because *I am*. I just want to pursue her like I would if we didn't have so much standing between us. If we didn't have so much history. I want to give her everything she missed out on because of me and I want to be the one to give it to her."

Dominic stares at me and chuckles. "That's why you kept your distance from her for so long? To give her a chance to get over you? You're a crazy bastard, you know that? What would you have done if she'd really dated me? What if she'd starting dating Liam?"

My heart sinks at the thought of it. "If it isn't me she wants, then I need to learn to be okay with that. That's the reason I let her go, isn't it? Because she was never with me by choice. She has every right to choose someone else, and I'd understand. I'd wish her well and I'd walk away. I still will if she decides she doesn't want to be with me. But I have to try. I have to know."

Dominic shakes his head. "You really love her, huh?"

"With all my heart."

He unlocks his phone and I watch as he calls Alyssa, putting her on speaker. Just hearing her voice again makes my heart race. I've missed her.

Dominic glances at me and nods. "Just come over for dinner. You've been avoiding us for weeks now. You're breaking my mum's heart, you know?" he says.

Alyssa sighs. "I know… I don't mean to. It's just been difficult. Do you think Daniel will be there?"

Dominic glances at me, and I glare at him. "Nah, doubt it. He rarely comes home these days. He's usually at his apartment or at work. Don't worry about it. Just come over and have dinner with me and Mum. Stay the night if you want. We could watch movies? It's a Saturday, so don't tell me you have to work."

"I guess dinner wouldn't hurt," Alyssa says, and I breathe a sigh of relief. Dominic cheers and fist bumps me, and Alyssa chuckles at his excitement. He walks off while still on the phone with her, and I'm tempted to follow him so I can hear more of her voice. I don't, though. Instead, I walk out to move my car. The second Alyssa sees it, she'll bolt, and I can't have that. I hide in my bedroom until she gets here and change my clothes, putting on an outfit I know she loves on me — jeans and a tight black tee. I spray myself with the cologne she bought me too. Every time I wore it she'd be all over me and I'm hoping she still will be. I skip dinner purposely and work through it, knowing full well she'll leave after dinner if I show up.

By the time I walk back into the living room, she and Dominic are cuddled up on the sofa, a chick flick on and the lights off. Friends with Benefits, I believe. I lean back against the wall behind the sofa, unsure what to do or say.

"Do you think we'd fall in love with each other if we slept together?" Alyssa asks, and I tense. What the fuck?

Dominic sits up and lets go of her. "I'm not sure. I think we already established that it would destroy our friendship. Besides, your heart belongs to someone else."

Alyssa nods and leans back against the pillows. "I guess so. A rebound with someone I actually know and like isn't the worst idea though."

Over my dead body. I know she hasn't slept with Liam, and it's clear she hasn't slept with anyone else since me. I'm going to make sure it stays that way.

"Can you actually see yourself sleeping with me?" Dominic asks, smirking. I can just about see her side profile and she scrunches her face in disgust.

Dominic bursts out laughing and shakes his head. "I guess that's a no," he says.

Alyssa shakes her head too, and I exhale in relief. "Yeah, no," she says.

Dominic glances behind him and notices me standing against the wall, our eyes meeting. He turns back to Alyssa before she notices and he grins. "Maybe you should just bang Liam. I know he wasn't too pleased with how things played out at the auction, but I'm sure he'd forgive you. Even if you told him clearly that it's just sex, he'd probably go for it."

This little asshole. I'm going to fucking kill him. "Yeah, maybe," Alyssa says. "Daniel told me the sex between us *wasn't bad*. Ever since he said that to me, I've wondered if I'm really bad at it. I'm embarrassed and insecure. I wonder if it was ever okay for him at all, or if he just humoured me. I'm so inexperienced. I guess sleeping with Liam isn't a bad idea. If nothing else, it might improve my skills. Maybe I should call him."

I grit my teeth and straighten. "Hmm... Is that so?" I say, my voice loud and clear.

Alyssa tenses and turns around, shocked. Her eyes meet mine and she looks thrown. She gazes at my body and the longing in her eyes is obvious.

She looks from me to Dominic suspiciously and rises from her seat. "I uh... I should go, actually. I have plans tomorrow that I totally forgot about," she says, blatantly lying.

Dominic pulls her back down and shakes his head. "You said you'd stay over. Leave early in the morning if you must, but you're staying. Don't even dream of breaking your promise."

She rolls her eyes and pulls her arm away from him. "Fine," she says, snapping at him. "But I'm going to bed."

She storms past me and I'm so tempted to follow her. I want her pinned against the wall with her lips on mine. I want to hear her say she'll never want anyone but me.

Sixty

I change into my pyjamas bottoms and keep my chest bare the way I know Alyssa loves. I'm still fuming at the thought of her with Liam. How could she even dream of it? Fuck that shit. I wait patiently until I hear her shower turn off, and then I give her an additional twenty minutes before walking into her bedroom.

I close her door behind me and walk up to her bed. She sits up in surprise; the sheets falling to her waist, revealing a t-shirt that's most definitely not hers. She's so fucking stunning. The idea of Liam seeing her like this kills me. There's no way that's happening.

"Y-you... what are you doing here?" she stammers.

I sit down on her bed silently, trying my best to keep my anger in check. Her eyes roam over my pecs and abs, and the appreciation in them sets me at ease. My eyes drop to the t-shirt she must have stolen from me, and I smile. It looks far better on her than it does on me. I wonder if she wore it because she misses me.

"Overheard your little chat with Dominic. Sounds like you're looking for a rebound? That's no reason to sleep with someone, Alyssa. You shouldn't fall in bed with someone if there's no mutual affection."

Alyssa laughs. "Is that what you had with all the women that came before me? Mutual affection? If that's the case, then there's plenty of affection between Liam and me."

This girl. Always pushing my damn buttons. "You know what I meant. You shouldn't sleep with someone unless you love them."

Alyssa rolls her eyes. "Are you serious? Are you telling me you loved all the women you've fucked? You either fall in and out of love frequently, or you're confusing lust for love. Either way, you're being a hypocrite."

I groan and pull a hand through my hair. "Lust, huh? You *want* Liam?"

"Well, he's handsome, that's for sure," she says, and she might as well have stabbed me in the heart. "I doubt he'd ever tell me the sex wasn't good if I slept with him. I have a feeling he'll never make me doubt my own sensuality. Besides, even if I do suck at sex, the only way I'll improve is by practising."

I look down and sigh. "I didn't mean it that way. When I said that, I had no idea it would impact you so much. Hell, it isn't even true. Every time I've slept with you has been the best sex I've ever had."

Alyssa scoffs and looks away. "The only man I've ever slept with told me the sex *wasn't bad*. What did you think that would do to me? I mean, it's fine. I'm glad you were honest with me. You don't need to take it back now, and you don't need to try to make me feel better. It's fine."

I don't regret many things in life, but I regret saying that to her. I went too far in my attempt to push her away. "It's clearly not fine. Very well. If you want to improve your skills, I can teach you. There's no need to sleep with anyone else. You and I are already familiar with each other, so it stands to reason that I'm the most logical candidate to help you with this endeavour."

Alyssa stares at me angrily, and I know she's about to snap at me. "God, don't sound too excited to sleep with me. Damn. Forget it. I doubt I'll struggle to find someone that actually wants me. I doubt Liam would tell me he'd be *a logical candidate to help me with this endeavour.*"

I grit my teeth and glare at her. Fucking Liam. I don't even want her to say his name. I rip away the blankets and spread her legs with my knees. I lie down on top of her and press my erection against her. Even when she infuriates me, she still turns me on.

"You think I don't want you? Alyssa, does this *feel* like I don't want you?"

Her body responds automatically, and she subconsciously rolls her hips against mine. I moan and bite down on my lip. A single touch from her and I'm already losing it. Her hands find their way to my chest, her palms moving up and down my skin. She pushes against me weakly, but there's no way I'm letting her go.

"Aren't you seeing that girl you're oh so in love with? How can you even think of sleeping with me when it's her you love? Didn't you just say that I shouldn't sleep with someone I don't love? So why are you doing it?"

I groan in frustration. Fucking hell. This again. "She and I aren't together. It's complicated. You're the last person I slept with, Alyssa. There's been no one else."

My fingers find their way between her legs and she spreads them wider to give me better access. I doubt she even realises she's doing it. I push her underwear aside and slip a finger inside her, finding her soaking wet already. She moans loudly and I chuckle. "Such a good girl," I whisper. It only takes me a few minutes to get her to the brink of her orgasm, but I can tell she's fighting it. She won't win this fight. I know her body inside out.

"Didn't you say you'd teach me?" she says angrily.

I pull away from her and grin. Fine. If she wants to play, we can play. I undress and she gasps when my dick comes into view. I'm rock hard and throbbing. I'm dying to be inside her. I pull her up and take her clothes off in a rush. Just seeing her lying here with me, her bare skin against mine, *fuck.*

"What do you want to learn, Lyss?"

She licks her lips and looks down. "Teach me how to suck you off good."

My cock twitches just from hearing her say that. I swallow hard before scooting over to the headboard. I lean back and beckon her closer, instructing her to sit between my legs. She grabs my dick eagerly and bites down on her lip as she pumps her hand up and down. I grab her hands and position them so she's holding me at the base.

"Now try to take it in. Don't go all the way. Just have some fun first. Use your tongue and move however you like. It's important that you're enjoying this."

She nods and follows my instructions, swirling her tongue around the tip with every move. There's no way I'm going to last long.

"Good, baby. That's so fucking good."

She pulls away and looks up at me with flushed cheeks. "I want to learn how to take you in deeper, Daniel. Can we try something?"

I nod, curious. She's acting all shy and embarrassed, so whatever she wants to try is bound to be good.

"Stand in front of the bed like this," she whispers, pulling me up. She positions me where she wants me and my eyes widen when I realise what she wants. She lies down on the bed so her head is over the edge and tips her head back. I guide my cock between her eager lips, slowly and steadily. I stop when I hit the back of her throat and Alyssa breathes in deeply. I lean over her to play with her breasts, giving her as much time as she needs to adjust. Alyssa shifts her head a little and I slowly start to move my hips, thrusting into her mouth.

"Fucking hell, baby. This is incredible," I moan. I didn't think she could get any more perfect. Turns out she could. I don't last long at all and pull out just in time, spraying cum all over her breasts.

"Where the fuck did you learn to do that?" I ask, breathing

hard. I grab my underwear and use it to wipe away the mess I made on her skin before getting into bed with her.

"Google," she says, giggling. "Remember when you googled how to make sex more comfortable for me after we slept with each other for the first time?"

My cheeks heat up, and I cuddle her, hiding my face in her hair. I've missed her so fucking much, it's unreal.

"Where did things go so wrong for us?" she asks, her voice breaking.

I roll on top of her and look into her eyes. "You and I started off with an expiration date, Lyss. We always knew that our marriage was going to end. Besides, we were forced into our marriage. There's no way we could've survived that. We would've always wondered who we might have married had we been given the choice. We always would've wondered if there's something else out there for us. Something better, maybe."

Alyssa's eyes fill with tears and she blinks them away furiously. "I never once thought that, Daniel. You were it for me. I would've happily stayed married to you."

I drop my forehead to hers and sigh. "Maybe that's true. Maybe it isn't. You went on a date with Liam, didn't you? You never would've had that chance if we'd remained married."

She throws her arms around me and hugs me tightly. "I understand," she whispers. "I don't wish to tie you to me when it's someone else you want to be with. I get it."

I chuckle and lower my lips to hers. I kiss her gently and softly. I can't help but harden against her again. I've never been able to kiss her without getting hard.

"It's not just an end, baby. It's also a new beginning. You now have the choice to do whatever you want... to be with whoever you want."

I kiss her again, passionately this time. I don't pull away until she's breathless and squirming against me. "Lyss, I want you," I whisper, aligning myself with her. Alyssa looks at me with eyes filled with equal parts love and lust, and she nods. She gasps when

I push into her and I sigh in delight. It's been so long since I've been inside her. She feels even better than I remember.

"Baby, I need you rough and hard," I tell her. Alyssa nods and I rise to my knees, lifting her up by her hips. I thrust into her hard and deep, just the way she likes it. With every thrust I stroke her g-spot, keeping her right at the edge, teasing her.

"Daniel, I need you. *Please*. Stop teasing me, baby," she says, calling me out.

I grin and increase the pace, still pulling out almost entirely before slamming back into her. "Yes," she moans. "Fuck yes, Dan. I fucking love the way you do me."

I give her what she wants and she shatters around me. "God yes... I love you, Daniel," she says, high on lust. I doubt she even realises what she said, but the mere words make me come inside her, *hard*.

I take a deep breath and drop my forehead against hers. I kiss her roughly, pouring all my emotions into our kiss. I'm going to make her tell me she loves me outside of bed, when she isn't high on lust. "So how are you going to repay me for these lessons?" I whisper against her lips.

"What?"

I chuckle. "Let's take the yacht out tomorrow. You can repay me by accompanying me. If you're lucky, I'll assist you with another lesson tomorrow."

I don't wait for her to reply. Instead I get comfortable in her bed and close my eyes, my arms wrapped around her.

Sixty-One

I stare at Alyssa as the wind blows through her hair. I'm so fucking in love with her and I'm pretty sure she loves me too, but she's wary. I beckon her closer and pull her towards me. I let her take the wheel and stand behind her, caging her in. She leans back against my chest and I drop my chin to the top of her head.

"I love this," she murmurs. I lean in and press a kiss to her cheek. "I may need to buy one of these for myself," she says.

"Why would you? We've already got one. We've got a bigger one too. We should take Mum and Nic out on the big one next time."

She looks up at me, startled, and I ignore her expression. She doesn't know it yet, but she's spending the rest of her life with me. She doesn't need to buy a yacht. Everything I own is hers.

I kill the engine and lead her to the lounge deck. She laughs when I grab a bottle of champagne and two glasses. I tilt my head to the small built-in fridge and she walks up to it, smiling when she sees a bowl with strawberries.

She joins me on the lounge bed and takes a glass from me. My eyes roam over her body heatedly. She's so stunning in the bikini she's wearing. I don't know what's worse. Having her naked, or seeing her like this. Both are torture. Alyssa glances at my swim shorts and blushes when she realises how hard I am. She raises her glass to mine and I smirk as I clink it to hers.

"To us," I say, as I always do.

Alyssa looks at me with an expression I can't quite decipher. She looks so... sweet. "To us," she whispers.

I grab a strawberry and hold it over her lips. She takes a bite and a drop of juice runs down her chin. I chuckle and lean in, licking it clean before brushing my tongue over her lips. She opens up for me eagerly and clenches her thighs as I kiss her.

I pull away from her with a lot of effort and take a sip of my champagne. This is meant to be a date. The last thing I want is for her to think I just want her body. I sigh and grab a strawberry, biting down on it.

Alyssa leans in to steal the other half from me, her tongue brushing over my lips before she pulls back. She chews slowly and smiles at me. "Delicious," she whispers, and I gulp. I chuckle nervously and run a hand through my hair. She's making this so fucking hard. I can't go ten seconds without wanting her.

I close my eyes and lean back, soaking in the sun. Alyssa startles me when she straddles me, pressing up against me. She grabs the bowl of strawberries and grabs one, holding it up for me. I stare at her through lust filled eyes and open my lips. She feeds me and I bite down, halving it. She pops the other half in her mouth and I bite down on my lip.

My hands move from her hips to her waist and back again. Eventually they settle on her ass and I grab on tightly. I'm throbbing underneath her. I'm so fucking turned on. Alyssa tangles her hands into my hair and pulls me against her, forcing me to sit up. I kiss her desperately, moaning against her lips. My hands find their way to the strings of her bikini top and I pull at them. I'm about to push them out of the way when my smartwatch starts buzzing. I groan as I glance at it, retying Alyssa's top.

"There's a bit of trouble, baby. Looks like there're paparazzi near. Our security team just notified me of a potential media team trailing us. They're handling it now, but we'd better keep our clothes on until we get the all clear."

Alyssa looks dismayed and moves to get off me, but I grin and pull her back. "I said we should keep our clothes on, my love. I didn't say you should move."

I hug her tightly and cup her head, angling her so her lips are on mine again. I take my time kissing her, driving her wild. Alyssa groans when my watch buzzes again, and I glance at it, sighing in relief.

"All clear," I whisper, tugging at her top. It comes loose and I inhale sharply when her breasts come into view. I lean in and graze her nipple with my teeth, making her moan in delight.

"Am I lucky?" she whispers, and it takes me a few seconds to figure out what she's talking about. Last night I told her she'd get more lessons if she was lucky.

"I think the lucky one is me, baby."

Her hands slip into my swim shorts and I moan when she grabs me. I tug on the strings that keep her bikini bottoms together and Alyssa lifts her hips so I can remove them. She sighs in delight and aligns herself with me, sinking down on me without warning. I moan as her wet heat captures me and drop my forehead against hers. "Fucking hell, baby. Didn't even give me a warning there. I was planning on playing with you first."

Alyssa shakes her head as she moves her hips up and down frantically. "No. Can't wait. I need you now."

I'm already fucking ready to burst. She rides me like there's no tomorrow and I bite down on my lip. "Can't hold it like this, Lyss. You gotta go easy on me, baby."

I bury my hands in her hair and tug on it while wrapping my other hand around her waist. Alyssa leans in and kisses me, slowing down the pace slightly. She looks at me all smug and satisfied, like she knows how hard I'm trying to hold on. She moves her hips in circles and I tighten my grip on her. "Fuck, Alyssa. My love, when you move like that..."

She rides me harder and I can't hold on. I jerk my hips up as my eyes shutter closed. I come harder than I ever have before, and I'm so annoyed with myself for being unable to last. Alyssa stays on top of me, the two of us still connected, and she pulls my head towards her. She kisses me gently and smiles against my lips.

I turn us over so she's lying in my arms and I stroke her arm gently, Alyssa stares up at the cloudless sky and grins. I lean in and kiss her hair over and over again. "Hey, since I helped you practise the whole sex thing, don't you owe me another date?"

Alyssa turns to face me. "A date, huh? Is that what this is?"

I chuckle and press a quick kiss to her lips. "Of course it is. A boat trip, champagne, strawberries and mind blowing sex... for me at least. How is it not a date?"

Alyssa giggles and kisses me, her lips lingering on mine. "I guess so. But then again, we divorced a couple of months ago. Does it even make sense for us to date? And what about that girl you're in love with? You're sleeping with me when you divorced me to be with her. How does that make any sense at all?"

I groan and put my arm over my face. "Fucking hell, baby. You have one hell of a memory, don't you? I only brought up this girl you keep reminding me of twice. Twice, babe. Once when I told you I couldn't get her off my mind when we'd just gotten married, and then again when I signed the divorce papers. Why is it you speak about her more than I do? I wish I'd never told you anything at all. Seriously, are you going to keep reminding me of this when we're grey and old?"

"Grey and old?" she snaps. "If you wanted to grow old with me, you never should've divorced me in the first place. Why the hell do you want to date me now when you dumped me a few months ago?"

I roll on top of her and pin her down. I grab her wrists and push them above her head, locking her in. "You're right. We're divorced now. We can date whoever the hell we want. There's no stipulation that says we can't date *each other*. If that's what we want, then why can't we?"

She squirms underneath me and I lower my body on top of

hers, locking her in further with my weight. "Forget about that girl, Alyssa. There's no one but you. You're all I can see. You'll always be my one and only."

Alyssa looks away, annoyed. "If that were the case, you never would've divorced me, Daniel. Let me guess, you pursued her and she rejected you? So now you've come running back to me. I don't want to be second best, Daniel. I want to be with someone who puts me first. Someone who will always put me first."

I sigh and drop my forehead to hers. "Alyssa, baby. What am I going to do with you? I wonder if you'll forgive me when you finally figure it out..."

I kiss her forehead and then pull away to look at her. "It's just a date, Lyss. It won't hurt to have some fun together, right?"

I lower my lips to hers and kiss her passionately and roughly. She kisses me back, but when I pull away, she shakes her head.

"No," she whispers. "All we'll have is today. When the day ends, we're through."

Sixty-Two

I glance at the tabloid in my hands with excitement. These papz sure are good at what they do. Alyssa and I made it to the front cover. In the photo, she's in my lap on the yacht, her lips on mine. The photo is grainy, but it's obvious who we are. I love it. I was worried about them capturing her naked, but I have no issues with the two of us getting caught kissing in our swimwear. The more people know about us, the better. I've given her months to follow her heart. It's my turn to follow mine now. I put the tabloid away carefully. I'll need to cut this photo out for my personal collection. We look cute as fuck.

My phone buzzes and I pick it up to find a text from Kate, my old secretary. I open the message and grin at the picture she sent me. It's a photo of Alyssa's office door, the tabloid front cover stuck on it. I burst out laughing and text her back, thanking her.

Alyssa says she won't date me, huh? Let's see how long she'll last. I grab the documents I prepared and rise to my feet. It only takes me a couple of minutes to reach DM and I grin as I take the lift up.

I pause in front of her door and knock, only mildly disappointed that she's clearly ripped the photo off her door. I walk in, and her eyes widen. I look around the room and I smile. She's redecorated, and it looks stunning. I walk up to her desk and sit down in front of her.

She stares at me before snapping out of it. "What are you doing here?" she asks.

I grin and slide a folder towards her. "I want to hire DM to implement the project I told you about a while back. I want to tighten Devereaux Inc's internal controls."

Alyssa shakes her head immediately. "No."

"It's a multi-million pound project, Lyss. Are you sure you can afford to say no? I know you have the resources and the knowledge to pull this off."

She grits her teeth in annoyance because she knows I'm right. Despite that, she shakes her head. I cross my arms and stare her down. "Saying no to this project would mean destroying shareholder value. Is that something you should be doing as the CEO? You're not one to let emotions cloud your judgement."

She sighs and crosses her arms, mirroring my stance. "I personally own the majority of the shares. I'm fine with a little bit of value being destroyed."

I look down. Clever girl. It's a good thing I came prepared. "Hmm, I wonder if the board will feel the same way. I spoke to Christian the other day, and he seemed to think the project was a great idea and told me to run it by you."

She glares at me when she realises I've already discussed this with the board. Her hands are tied. She won't get away with declining. They'd just question her leadership if she did.

Alyssa grits her teeth and takes a look at the documents I handed her. It's a highly valuable project that, quite frankly, she's lucky to get so easily.

"Very well. It looks good. I'll have a team look over it and get back to you."

I grin and point out a specific clause I put in there. She frowns and glares at me when she reads it. "Why would you need the CEO of a company to work with you directly?" she asks angrily.

I shrug. "It's an expensive project. I need you to oversee it personally. Gotta make sure I'm getting my money's worth."

Alyssa closes her eyes and I know she's really close to throwing me out. She grits her teeth as she grabs a pen and signs the papers. "Asshole," she mutters under her breath, and I grin. That's at least a few weeks of us spending time together. Let's see how she avoids me now.

I'm impatient as I wait for Alyssa to arrive. My stipulations ensure that she has to check in personally at least once a week, but twice now she's managed to come in when I was in a meeting. I'm pretty sure my new secretary is in on this, and I'm not pleased.

I smile when I see her, my eyes lighting up. "Hey, you're here," I murmur. I place my hand on her lower back and lead her into my office.

"Lyss?"

She's stares into space absentmindedly as she takes a seat, and I wonder what's she's thinking so hard about. "I apologise. My mind wandered," she says, smiling. She pushes a document towards me. "This is our schedule. The five consultants I brought with me will be stationed here permanently from this week onwards. You should be familiar with all of them. You're welcome to reach out to me should you have any questions."

I bite down on my lip worriedly. She's being distant and I hate it. What changed in the last two weeks?

"I'll go check up on the team and ensure everything is in place. I'll ensure that there are no delays and that the quality of the work will be as high as you're accustomed to."

She rises and turns to walk out, but I grab her by the wrist and stop her. She turns to face me, a torn expression on her face.

"Let me go," she whispers.

I shake my head and pull her towards me, my free hand finding its way around her waist.

"No."

I lean in and bend my head towards her, my lips hovering over hers. Alyssa sighs and her eyes flutter closed. "We can't keep doing this, Daniel. You and I… we're done. We need to try to move on. You've got to let me go."

My lips come crashing down on hers and I kiss her like she's the air I need to breathe. She kisses me back just as desperately. My hands roam over her body and she moans. I deepen the kiss and lift her into my arms. Her legs automatically find their way around my hips and I carry her to my desk.

"Never," I whisper against her lips. "I will never let you go again, Alyssa."

I kiss her as my hands roam over her body and she moans when I stroke the inside of her thigh. She can never deny me. Her body betrays her as soon as I touch her.

I slip a finger inside her and rub my thumb over her clit. A small moan escapes her lips and I grin. Alyssa's hands fumble with my trousers, her movements eager and impatient. She smiles when she realises I'm rock hard. I push her underwear aside and she guides me into her. I look into her eyes as I enter her, slowly and steadily. I stretch her out deliciously and she's panting by the time I'm deep inside her. I kiss her as I thrust in and out, my hands on her hips.

"We shouldn't be doing this," she whispers, but her muscles contract around me every time I move, betraying how much she loves this. I moan and fuck her harder. She knows it drives me insane when she tightens around me like that.

"Alyssa, baby… you better hear me when I say this," I groan, thrusting into her harder. "I won't ever let you go. I made that mistake once, and I'll never do it again. I'm going to pursue you until you give in and agree to be mine again."

I pull her closer and pull her legs over my shoulders, fucking her even deeper. "You're mine, Alyssa. You hear me, baby?"

I fuck her hard, hitting all the right places. She looks up at me pleadingly and I know she's close. I grin at her. "You want it, baby? You wanna come for me?" Alyssa nods, a frenzied expression on her face. "Tell me you'll go on a date with me and I'll give you what you want."

I slow down the pace and she groans in despair. "No!" she whispers. "I'll go, Dan. I'll go on a date with you," she says, her voice pleading.

I smile and give it to her. Her muscles clench around me, and I come seconds after she does.

"Good girl," I whisper, pulling her in for another kiss. "I'll pick you up tonight."

Sixty-Three

I'm nervous as I pull up at Alyssa's house. I haven't been nervous before a date since I was a teenager. I'm excited to see her and eager to wow her. I ring the doorbell instead of pressing my palm to the biometric scanner and wait patiently.

Alyssa takes my breath away when she walks out wearing a figure-hugging red dress that looks stunning on her. "Hey," I whisper.

I offer her my arm and walk her to my car. Alyssa smiles up at me but she looks insecure, awkward. I'm tense as I get behind the wheel. Why do things feel so... weird?

"You never told me where we're going."

I glance at her and smile as I tip my head to the compartment in my car. "Check in there," I tell her. She reaches inside and gasps when she sees the tickets for Swan Lake.

"The ballet," she whispers. "I *love* the ballet. How did you know I've been wanting to see Swan Lake?"

I smile to myself. "I kinda figured. Besides, this is what we did on our very first date. I took you to see The Nutcracker, remember?"

She looks at me in surprise. "Wow. That was what, four, five years ago?"

I nod and look away. Back then I was already falling for her, but she only had eyes for my brother.

"But that wasn't a date, was it?"

I glance at her, a bittersweet smile on my face. "Wasn't it?"

I sigh and focus on the road, my heart twisting painfully. It wasn't long after I took her to the ballet that she confessed her undying love to Dominic. I've seen her heart break over him and I've seen her pick up the pieces. Even now, I can't be sure she's truly over him — that no part of her still loves him. I'm glad we separated for a while. If nothing else, I know she isn't secretly dying to make a move on him. I've given her a fair chance to do that, and she hasn't.

I wonder if one day she'll love me the way she loved Dominic. I still remember how lost she was after he told her he didn't feel the same way. How much of her spirit she lost. As far as I know, she wasn't like that when I ended things between us. Is it sick that I wanted her to? That I wanted her to hurt over me the way she did over him? That I wanted her to care just as much? Back then she couldn't even format documents properly, she was so absent-minded. But after we ended things, she closed one deal after the other. I want her with my heart and soul, but I can't help but wonder if she'll ever want me the same.

We arrive at the London Colosseum and Alyssa grins. "I didn't know you liked the ballet, you know."

I shake my head and grab her hand. "I don't. Matter of fact, I hate it. The feet creep me the fuck out. But *you* love it, and that's all that matters."

Alyssa pauses and tugs on my hand. I turn to face her with a frown on my face. "But... if you hate it, then why did you take me all those years ago?"

I sigh and gently push her hair behind her ear. "I told you, baby. I took you because *you* love it, and you'd been wanting to go. You'd been talking about The Nutcracker for weeks, but neither your dad nor Dominic would take you. So I did."

She stares up at me in confusion and I smile at her. I lean in and press a kiss to her cheek. "Come on," I whisper, pulling her along. Unlike last time, she keeps my hand in hers. And unlike last time, she's focused on me instead of on the performance. She keeps glancing at me, a thousand questions reflected in her eyes.

I turn to look at her, losing myself in her eyes. "You're not watching the performance," she whispers.

I nod. "I'd rather watch you, like I did all those years ago. Like I've done for years."

Alyssa blinks and leans in, pressing a feather-light kiss to my lips, and my eyes shutter closed. I love this girl. I always have. Dare I hope that someday she'll feel the same?

Alyssa and I are both quiet as we make our way back to the car. "What did you think of the ballet?" she asks me.

I look into her eyes and smile. "Captivating," I murmur, referring to her and not the damn ballet.

Alyssa blushes and looks away. "Thank you," she whispers. "Thank you for taking me then, and taking me today, when you don't even like the ballet. Thank you for noticing that I wanted to go so badly back then, and thank you for everything you've done for me over the years. I didn't even realise it, you know? But thinking back, you're in all my most precious memories."

I smile at her and grab her hand. "You don't ever need to thank me, baby. Everything I do for you, I do because I want to. I always have."

She smiles at me and looks at me in a way I've never seen before. I can't quite decipher it, but I decide I enjoy it anyway.

I drive her home reluctantly. I don't want tonight to end, but I don't want to rush things with her either.

"Stop here," she says suddenly. I frown and look around the deserted dirt road that leads up to her property. I do as she says and park the car on the side of the road.

Alyssa smiles and undoes her seatbelt. She grins at me before climbing into my lap, startling me. She lowers her lips to mine and kisses me, softly at first, and then roughly.

"Fine," she murmurs against my lips. "I won't *say* thank you. I'll show you instead."

She pulls back and looks into my eyes as she undoes my shirt buttons. I stare at her, my heart racing. What is she doing?

She undoes my belt and shoves my clothes out of the way, grabbing onto my dick. She grins as her hands wrap around it and I inhale sharply when she uses her other hand to push aside her underwear, sinking down on top of me.

I moan loudly and drop my forehead to hers. "Fucking hell, Alyssa."

She smiles and kisses me, moving just a little, enough to drive me crazy. She pulls back to look into my eyes and I wrap my arms around her waist. She rides me slowly, her eyes never leaving mine. I've never felt this intense connection with her before. I thought what we had was special, but this? This is insane.

I capture her lips with mine and kiss her as she rides me. No, scratch that. My girl fucking makes love to me, and I love every second of it.

"Alyssa," I whisper. "My love, I can't hold it. Not when you ride my cock like this."

She smiles and leans in to kiss me. "Then don't," she whispers against my lips. "I want you to lose control, Dan. I want you going crazy about me. I want all of you."

My eyes flutter closed as she increases the pace, milking me. "Baby, I've always been crazy about you."

She grins in satisfaction when I come deep inside her, and I smile against her lips. "Baby, if this is how you're going to thank me every time we go to the ballet, then I'd better invest in an annual pass. That's a thing, right?"

She bursts out laughing and shakes her head. "Annual, huh? So you're planning on taking me to the ballet again someday?"

I nod. "Of course. You'll go out with me again, won't you?"

Alyssa nods, and my heart flutters. This. This is what I wanted. Dating her and winning her heart, one step at a time. There's nothing I want more.

Sixty-Four

I'm nervous as I prep dinner. Alyssa and I have been dating for a couple of months now, but tonight is the first night she's coming over to my apartment since she moved out. The last time she was here, we were still married. We've gone on numerous dates and we've ended up sleeping with each other almost every time. A few times in my car, often in hotels owned by Devereaux Inc. and a couple of times at her place. For some reason we never came back here, though. I guess we might've been avoiding it subconsciously, since it's where we spent our entire marriage.

I hear the lift ding and walk over to find her standing in the hallway, frozen. "Hey, you're here. I thought I heard the lift. Why are you just standing there? Come in."

Alyssa snaps out of it and walks in, but I can tell she's assailed by memories. I walk back into the kitchen with her by my side and she hops onto the kitchen counter, like she used to. I grin at her and spread her legs to stand in between them before pulling her face towards mine. I kiss her thoroughly before stepping away to get back to cooking. I wanted to have dinner finished by the time she got here, but I ended up taking forever just lighting all the candles and shit.

Alyssa grabs the glass of wine I poured her and hops off the counter, opting to walk around the house instead. She shrieks all of a sudden and I run up to her, worried. She stares at the living room wall in shock and my cheeks heat up.

"Dan, why do you have paparazzi photos of us on the wall?"

I glance over at them and grin. In many of them, we're caught in compromising positions. There's one where we were making out on the yacht. She's in my lap and we're all over each other. They're far from appropriate. There are other photos of us in Singapore or other trips away, and some where we were on other dates in restaurants. There are even a few of us just walking hand in hand or smiling at each other. I love them.

"Well, we rarely take photos together. And to be honest, these guys don't actually do a bad job. They're annoying as hell, but the pictures are kind of cute."

"Cute?" she repeats numbly. I nod and stare down at the floor. I probably should've taken them down before she got here, but I completely forgot about.

Alyssa shakes her head, and I grab her hand to lead her to the dining table. It doesn't take me long to serve her dinner.

"Do you need some help?" she asks, and I shake my head, refilling her wine glass instead. Tonight I just want to spoil her.

"I made you the stir-fry you used to love when we lived together," I murmur. Alyssa smiles and takes a bite, a small moan escaping her lips. Fucking hell. She's the only woman that can turn me on while eating fucking stir fry. "It's still the best," she whispers in delight.

I smile at her and shake my head. "I was thinking we could maybe watch a movie afterwards?"

It's exactly what we used to do when we were still married, and I guess I kinda want to remind her of how good things could be again, if we start to live together again. I want to ask her to move back in with me, as my girlfriend this time.

"Yeah, I'd love to."

I grin and give her two options. "Harry Potter and the Prisoner of Azkaban... or the Order of the Phoenix?"

She looks at me with wide eyes. "Aw damn. Trick question. I love both. Obviously, we must watch both."

I laugh and shake my head. I knew she'd say that. "Let's see if we get through half of one first," I mumble. Alyssa blushes and looks away. She knows as well as I do we can't stay away from each other for that long. Those movies are long as fuck.

I spoon her on the sofa and try my best to focus on the movie, but her exposed neck keeps distracting me. It's practically begging for kisses, so I give in. I kiss her neck lazily. We're only twenty minutes into the movie when my hand finds its way underneath her blouse.

"Baby," I whisper. "How about we watch the movie tomorrow?"

She giggles and nods at me. I lift her into my arms and carry her to the bedroom. I put her down on the bed carefully and lie down next to her. I kiss her softly, but Alyssa deepens the kiss impatiently. She moans and pulls on my shirt, eager to get it off. I laugh and pull it over my head. She ogles me and I fucking love it.

Just as I'm about to lean in and kiss her, she freezes. She narrows her eyes and stares at my pillow before reaching out. I gasp and try to stop her, but before I can move she pulls the red lace from underneath it.

"Women's underwear?" she says, shocked. She sits up and stares at me in disbelief. "You took someone home recently? To *our* apartment? In *our* bed?"

I shake my head and hold my hands up. "Babe," I whisper.

"I thought we were exclusive. I mean, we haven't specifically said it, but surely there was an implicit agreement that we were?"

"Babe..."

"How could you do this to me, Daniel? How could you break my heart over and over again? I'm done with this. I'm done with you. I'm done putting my heart on the line only for you to let me down time and time again."

"Babe," I whisper yet again, my voice tinged with exasperation.

"Who the hell is it? Is it that girl again? The one you're in love with?"

"Alyssa!" I snap. I grab the underwear from where she threw it and hold it up for her to see. She's panicking without even looking at them. "Honey, these are *yours*. They're yours."

She glances at them and then back at me. Her cheeks turn crimson as she realises that I'm right.

"I — you — what the hell are they doing in your bed?" she shouts, angry and embarrassed.

I chuckle and run a hand through my hair. I can't tell which one of us is more embarrassed right now.

"I — uh... well... you left them here."

Alyssa frowns. "Okay, but even so, why are they in your *bed*?"

I look away and clear my throat uncomfortably. Okay, so I totally jacked off with them. "I... uh... I just missed you. I forgot I put them there. I didn't really intend to get caught like this. I mean, I don't know. I don't really have an excuse."

Alyssa smiles and looks back down at the red lace. She bursts out laughing and holds them up. "Dan, what exactly were you doing with these?"

My cheeks are so hot that my entire face is probably crimson. "Seriously, though. You gotta stop being like this, Lyss. There's no one but you. You keep bringing up another girl when the only one in my life is you. It breaks my heart that you don't trust me. We've been together for so long and you know what my schedule is like. Where the hell am I supposed to find time to cheat on you? I spend every free second I've got with you. I'm yours. There's no one else."

Alyssa looks away. She looks insecure, even though things have been so perfect between us.

"I don't know, Dan. You divorced me. You *left* me. Things were going well between us and I genuinely thought we were happy, but then you just up and left. You signed the divorce papers and asked me to move out of the place I'd started to consider my own. You blocked my phone number and avoided me for weeks. You even went so far as to sign over your shares to me so you could be free of the contractual obligation of fidelity you had towards me..."

She inhales deeply and looks into my eyes. "I might be the only person in your life right now, but how long will that last? How long until you walk out again? How long until you go back to ignoring me? You ask me to trust you, but you keep breaking that trust. You might not have cheated on me, but you *have* taken away the security I used to have with you. You were all I had, Dan. And you left me. You left me saying you were in love with someone else. I spent our entire marriage falling deeply and irrevocably in love with you. But while I was falling for you, you were busy falling for someone else. How long will it be until you break my heart again?"

I grab her hands and rise to my knees to face her. I press our joint hands to my heart and look into her eyes. "Alyssa, I wasn't thinking clearly when I did what I did. It's no excuse, but I genuinely thought I was doing the right thing for both of us. I never should have ignored you the way I did, but baby, it's the only way I could stay away from you. I swear to you, Lyss... I will never ever leave you again. I'm only human, baby. I made a mistake. It was a grave mistake, but I'll happily spend the rest of my life making it up to you. Fucking hell, Alyssa. I'm so fucking in love with you. You're probably the only person around us that doesn't realise it. There's no one but you, Alyssa. I swear it."

She looks at me as though she doesn't believe me. I've waited months to tell her I love her, wanting to make sure that I show her with my actions first.

"Daniel, if your version of love entails letting down your partner and abandoning them when they need you most, then I don't want it. I'm sorry, but I genuinely think we should break up. We should've just left things be when we got divorced. I don't know what I was thinking."

I tighten my grip on her hand and shake my head. "Lyss, no. Don't do this to us," I whisper. "I know I made mistakes, Alyssa. Fuck, I know. But I love you. I love you so fucking much. I'd do anything to make it up to you. I'd do anything to regain your trust. I just need you to give me a chance. An honest chance. Just one, Lyss."

I drop my forehead to hers just as a tear escapes her eyes. She sniffs and shakes her head. "I can't, Daniel. I'll just destroy myself in the process if I do."

I fucked up. I never even realised she felt this insecure. And all this because she's jealous of *herself*. How the fuck did I get myself into this mess? How did all my good intentions result in *this*?

I throw my arms around her and hug her tightly. I bury my face in her neck and inhale deeply, unsteadily. "Baby, if you truly decide you don't want to be with me, I'll respect your wishes. But before you decide, give me a chance to tell you my side of the story. Meet me tomorrow evening at our restaurant. I'll explain to you why I did the things I did, and if despite all that you don't think you could ever trust me again... then I'll let you go, Lyss. Just give me that one last chance. Just hear me out tomorrow, that's all I ask."

Sixty-Five

I'm anxious as I wait for Alyssa in the restaurant I've come to consider ours. Part of me is worried she won't even show up. I've spent all morning preparing everything, ensuring it's perfect, but she might never even see it.

I stare at the countless candles and roses that have transformed the space. It's exactly the kind of thing she'd like. A familiar place, a stunning view, candles and roses.

I breathe a sigh of relief when I see her walk in. I straighten and tug at my bowtie. I wore a tux for her tonight, and the way her eyes roam over me tells me she loves it. She pauses in front of me, speechless. I take her hand and smile at her.

"I told you I'd tell you my side of the story today. Will you let me?" I ask, my voice trembling. I don't think I've ever been this nervous before. Alyssa bites down on her lip and nods. I take a step closer to her and brush her hair out of her face.

"Where do I even start? I guess the story starts a couple of years ago. I came back to resume working for DM Consultancy after taking a break to do my MBA, in part because I owed your father so much, and in part because I wanted to fulfil my father's wish of succeeding him. Both our dads always wanted the company to fall into our hands, and I wanted to honour that wish. The day I got back to work was also your first day at the office. You started your internship and well… you'd changed so much in the two years I hadn't seen you. I was seriously awed. You were always beautiful, but seeing you then and there… Maybe it's because I hadn't seen you in so long, I saw you in a new light. But god, you were so beautiful. So beautiful, but so freaking young. So out of reach."

I look away nervously. I've never admitted this to anyone. She was so young back then. Even to me, it feels kinda wrong.

"You weren't just beautiful. You were so smart and so hard-working. You wowed me every single day, and I lost a bit more of my heart to you every single day. But you were too young. You hadn't even started university then. I knew there was so much of your life you still needed to live, and I didn't want to take away any of those experiences from you. Besides, you didn't see me that way at all. I tried so hard to forget about you. I tried to move on and deny my feelings, but it was all to no avail. You'd smile at me and I'd be lost all over again. I'd find excuses to see you all the time. When you were too busy to work from the office, I'd find a way to work late with your dad at his home office, just so I could have dinner with you."

I glance at her briefly and then look back down. I'm surprisingly embarrassed. I never thought I'd tell her how I've been pining over her, but it just feels right to tell her the truth.

"I'm ten years older than you, so I knew I'd probably never stand a chance, and I was fine with that. I never intended to act on my feelings, and I kept telling myself that one day I'd get over it. But then something happened. The way you looked at Dominic started to change. You were falling for him right before my eyes. You'd smile at him in a way you didn't used to, and it tore me apart. Do you remember the night you got drunk and confessed your feelings for him? I overheard it all. You two were so drunk and I was about to check up on you when I heard you. God,

Alyssa. My heart fucking broke. The idea of you becoming my little brother's girlfriend. Of you two being *together*. Fuck. I could barely cope with my jealousy every time you'd act chummy with him while you treated me with cold politeness. But seeing you in his arms? I don't think I could've survived that. When I heard your confession… I knew I'd truly never stand a chance. I knew I needed to give up, and for a while I managed it. For a while I convinced myself I wasn't in love with you. But then tragedy struck."

I inhale deeply and raise our joint hands to my chest. I suddenly feel insecure, telling her all this. I'm taken back to that time when I was so sure I'd never be with her.

"You lost your dad and his will gave me a chance to be with you. I knew I could've contested it or I could've just bought you back your shares. He knew how I felt about you, and I guess this was his way of pushing us together. He'd told me to ask you out for dinner so many times, and I always refused. I was always scared of disturbing the status quo, and you'd never given me any indication that you even saw me as a man at all. I guess his will was his way of giving us his blessing. Even so, I never should've forcefully tied you to me the way I did. But I just wanted to be selfish. Just once, I wanted to call you mine. I knew it was a mistake when you walked down the aisle with Dominic. The way you two looked at each other… I felt fucking awful for breaking your heart. For taking away your chance at happiness. I knew right there and then I couldn't keep you tied to me."

Alyssa lifts our joined hands to her lips and kisses the back of my hand, like I just did to her. I see the regret in her eyes and I smile at her reassuringly.

"The first couple of weeks of our marriage were rough on me. It was so obvious that you were in love with Dominic. It hurt to know you were my wife, and it wasn't me you wanted. I knew I had to let you go someday. I was surprised when things slowly changed between us once we moved into the apartment. I could see the attraction in your eyes every time I walked around the house half-naked, and I guess I might've done it more often than I really should have. I just... I was just so excited to see you responding to me at all. But every time I thought we were getting somewhere, Dominic seemed to intervene. Every time I thought you might feel the same way, you'd show me it's still him you put first. Over time, we fell in love, but I just wasn't sure if any of it was real. I was certain you wouldn't have been with me if not for your father's will. It wouldn't have been me you'd choose, and I couldn't keep you tied to me when I knew I wasn't your first choice. It broke me to do it, but I had to let you go. I was so convinced that all you felt for me was lust. I mean... I was your first, Lyss. You hadn't had a chance to date and you didn't even get to be with the person you and I both thought you loved. I figured you'd get over me quickly and things would return to how they were meant to be."

I hesitate and wipe away the tears that have fallen down her cheeks. She looks startled, as though she didn't even realise that she'd started crying.

"But things didn't get better. You didn't get over me. I thought you would've gotten with Dominic soon after I ended things with you, but you didn't. I thought maybe you just needed some time... but then you showed up with fucking Liam Evans. I lost it. I couldn't stomach the idea of you being with him, so I ruined your chance of moving on. I felt horrible about it afterwards, but I just couldn't stand it."

I run a hand through my hair and look away, a moment of pure devastation coursing through me. After I ended things with her, I couldn't even stand to look at another woman, but she managed to go on a date just fine.

"I don't understand," she whispers. "If you knew... If you knew I couldn't get over you, why did you still come to court to sign the papers?"

I cup her cheek and inhale deeply. "I didn't ever want you to feel like you were forced into our marriage. I kind of figured that if you and I were meant to be, we'd come together naturally all over again. I wanted a chance to pursue you honestly; the right way. I wanted you to have a choice, and I wanted you to *choose* me."

I drop down on one knee and pull the ring box out of my pocket. Alyssa's eyes go wide and she slaps her hand over her lips.

"I've loved you for years, Alyssa. I know I've made mistakes and I know I'm a fool sometimes. I don't communicate my feelings very well and I've hurt you so many times needlessly, but I never meant to. I've always loved you and I've always wanted what's best for you. Please, Alyssa. Let me make my wrongs right. I'll spend each day of the rest of my life trying to make you happier than you were the day before. Please, will you make me the happiest man in the world and marry me?"

Alyssa bursts into tears and nods. "Yes, Daniel. *Yes*. A thousand times yes."

I slide the ring onto her finger and rise to wrap my arms around her. She kisses me and giggles against my lips. We're so wrapped up in each other that it takes her some time to even look at the ring. When she finally does, she gasps.

"I — this... Daniel..."

I chuckle and kiss her again. "Hmm, it's the ring you picked out in Singapore. I bought it the same day. I always hoped I'd be proposing to you someday... and if I did, I wanted you to have the ring of your dreams."

I drop my forehead to hers and smile wickedly. "Hey babe, guess what? You owe me a new Aston Martin."

Alyssa bursts out laughing and I kiss the hell out of my soon-to-be wife. In the end, we found our way back to each other. I glance up at the sky and tighten my arms around Alyssa as I send a silent thanks up to Charles. He was right, like always. Alyssa and I were meant to be.

"I'm going to spend the rest of my life making you happy," I vow to her, and Alyssa smiles at me.

"And I'll make you even happier," she promises, and I know

she will. She's the one for me. Hell, I'm pretty sure she was *made* for me.

The End

Don't want the story to end? Download an exclusive extra chapter of Alyssa & Daniel's Wedding on my website

Also by Catharina Maura

Forever After All: A Marriage Of Convenience Novel

Desperate and out of options, Elena Rousseau walks into a gentlemen's club, ready to sell her body in a last attempt to save her mother's life.

She didn't expect Alexander Kennedy to be there, and she certainly didn't expect him to propose a marriage of convenience instead.

Marrying Alexander means knowingly becoming a tool in his revenge plan. But what choice does she have?

Better the devil you know than the one you don't.

Until You: A Brother's Best Friend Romance

Left without a job and evicted from the house she so carefully turned into a home, Aria is offered two choices: move back in with her brother... or take the job her brother's best friend offers her.

Their lives weren't meant to collide — but everything changes when Grayson realizes that Aria is the mysterious woman behind a wildly popular vigilante platform.

She's the woman he's been falling for online, the one whose coding skills outdo his, the one he's been trying to track down.

It's her. And she's off-limits.

The Stolen Moments Trilogy: A Best Friend's Brother Romance

What if the one person you can't have is the one person you can't resist?

It was hate at first sight for Emilia and Carter. Neither can remember how their feud started, but that doesn't stop them from pulling some crazy pranks on each other.

Until one night. One kiss is all it takes.

The lines between love and hate blur, and things are forever changed.

They know they can never cross that line, though...

Carter is Emilia's best friend's brother, after all.

Printed in Great Britain
by Amazon